THE LYING-DOWN ROOM

Anna Jaquiery is of French-Malaysian descent and grew up in Europe and Asia. She has worked as a journalist in several countries, starting out as a freelance reporter in Russia. She is currently based in Melbourne with her husband and two sons. *The Lying-Down Room* is her debut novel – and the first in a series to feature Chief Inspector Serge Morel. The second, *Death in the Rainy Season*, is out now.

Follow Anna on Twitter @AnnaJaquiery

ANNA JAQUIERY

THE LYING-DOWN ROOM

PAN BOOKS

First published 2014 by Mantle

This paperback edition published 2015 by Pan Books
an imprint of Pan Macmillan, a division of Macmillan Publishers Limited
Pan Macmillan, 20 New Wharf Road, London N1 9RR
Basingstoke and Oxford
Associated companies throughout the world
www.panmacmillan.com

ISBN 978-1-4472-4443-1

A CIP catalogue record for this book is available from the British Library.

Typeset by Ellipsis Digital Limited, Glasgow
Printed and bound by CPI Group (UK) Ltd, Croydon, CR0 4YY

Visit **www.panmacmillan.com** to read more about all our books
and to buy them. You will also find features, author interviews and
news of any author events, and you can sign up for e-newsletters
so that you're always first to hear about our new releases.

For Selwyn

'What? Is man just God's mistake?
Or is God just man's mistake?'

*Nietzsche: The Anti-Christ, Ecce Homo,
Twilight of the Idols. And Other Writings*

'I will incline my ear to a riddle:
and unfold the mystery to the sounds of the harp.'

The Liturgical Psalter

PROLOGUE

For a long time, he watches the people in the queue. It's remarkable how patient these tourists are. It's 38 degrees Celsius and there's a bedraggled air about the line leading into the Pop Art exhibition here at the Centre Georges Pompidou. Yet they seem happy enough to wait. In the meantime, they're making friends and swapping tips. *Last night we had a steak-frites at the Assiette au Boeuf, have you heard of it? Best steak-frites I've ever had and the Béarnaise was heaven. I know a small place off the Place du Marais, you'd never guess it was there, it was just us and the locals. Forget about the Champs-Elysées, no one in their right mind goes there any more except the nouveaux-riches.* Everyone likes to think they've made a discovery when it's generally the case they're the last to find out.

A shuffle of feet and the column lumbers half a step forward. It amazes him that so many will go out of their way to see this, will line up in a heatwave for the opportunity to gaze at a giant tube of toothpaste or a reproduction of a tin of tomato soup. If this is art then he obviously knows nothing about it. Art, he believes, should have an illuminating effect, should permeate the soul.

He has a headache and he's dizzy from standing in the stifling heat for so long and from the buzz of conversation coming from the queue. It's a wonder no one's fainted or had a heart attack, or just walked away. A quick look at his watch tells him he's been here twenty minutes already. How much longer should he wait? His coffee's cold but he sips at it till the grainy residue at the bottom of his Styrofoam cup spills onto his tongue. A bead of sweat rolls down his eyelid and he blinks.

He's never liked the industrial style of the Pompidou Centre with its utility pipes and exposed ducts on the outside of the building. To him it's like a carcass, the worthless remains of a structure that never quite came to life. It stands there with its innards exposed, stripped of all mystery. Down on the square the jugglers and mime artists and musicians are competing for attention. A woman is singing 'La Vie en Rose' and playing the accordion and he thinks about the tourists who will take this moment home as though it's genuine and says something about this city.

But at least the visitors are courteous. Paris is nearly civilized in August, with the Parisians gone. The tourists are harmless, with their shiny new sneakers and eager faces, taking snapshots of everything. Every other month of the year he has to contend with his hard-nosed, pushy compatriots here. It takes a great deal out of him to ignore them and focus on the exhibitions – this year there have been such treasures, particularly at the Louvre and Orsay.

His headache is under control still, but there's the dizziness and he thinks he had better eat soon, before nausea sets in. Something light, maybe a *salade de chèvre*. At the Café des Halles they make the goat-cheese salad just the way he likes it. He should go there now, before it gets too crowded.

He looks at his watch one more time, just to confirm that it's time to give up and leave, but then he sees the boy out of the corner of his eye, heading towards him with his left foot trailing slightly. If you didn't know, you'd mistake his lopsided gait for an adolescent's exaggerated nonchalance. He wears his backpack over one shoulder and his grey cap turned back to front. His clothes hang too loosely on him. He is trying hard to look cool, and at the same time holding back a smile.

To the man, the boy seems breakable, like his skinny, loose-jointed limbs might easily snap.

When he reaches him, his face shiny with sweat, the boy raises both hands in the air, as if to say his lateness is not his fault but due to circumstances beyond his control. As usual, he seems oblivious to the fact that there are other people around and the world contains a great deal more than just the two of them. He tugs at the man's sleeve and rubs his stomach. *I'm starving*. Maybe it has something to do with his age: the boy is always famished.

The man nods. 'Come on. Let's get some lunch.' He takes one last look at the queue which has just inched forward again, and turns towards the escalator. He throws his coffee cup into a bin.

He watches the boy step down the escalator, in his over-sized clothing. It's almost as though he is absent, beneath his clothes. It's almost as if he doesn't exist.

ONE

Commandant Serge Morel finished his coffee and tossed the cup into a bin before crossing the street and entering the nineteenth-century stone building on Rue de l'Eglise. He looked at his watch: 9.16 a.m. He'd driven straight here after getting the call, without stopping at home.

He looked at the sky. Another muggy and uncomfortable day to look forward to. He could have done with a cold shower and a change of clothes.

In the red-carpeted lobby he debated whether to take the lift but one look at the tiny old-fashioned cage with its iron gate was enough to change his mind. Besides, his doctor would probably tell him that taking the stairs was a smart option. What had the GP said? A man in his forties is at risk of, well, just about everything.

He walked up to the fourth floor and waved his badge at the police officer standing outside the door of the dead woman's apartment. The man stepped aside and Morel found himself in a living room so cluttered it looked like a furniture auction house before the bidding starts. As he entered the room he felt the tension crackle in the air like high-voltage power lines in damp weather. A buzzing of anxiety beneath the calm and measured movements of the experienced people gathered in the apartment, most of whom he knew. The tension was always there. The first stage of the investigation was its most crucial: no one wanted to make a mistake or miss anything.

Considering the lack of space it was a wonder so many people were able to move around at all without climbing over each other. Morel counted eight in this room alone. One of them was his boss, Commissaire Olivier Perrin. The minute he spotted Morel he hurried up to him on short, bandy legs.

'What took you so long? Don't you live just down the road?'

Morel looked at Perrin and marvelled for the hundredth time at how closely his boss resembled a bulldog. The same muscular build and permanent scowl. The same hanging jowls.

'I came as soon as I got the call,' he said. No point going into details.

Still, he wished he'd arrived sooner. He felt like the latecomer at a party. Two of Morel's team members, Jean Char and Marco Lancel, wearing protective gear on their heads, hands and feet, were talking to one of the technicians. There were only two men Morel didn't recognize. Probably the local, Neuilly boys who had initially been called in. In the hallway two women waited on chairs to be interviewed. One of them was sobbing, wiping at her eyes with her sleeve.

'Where have you been? Are you ready to take a look at the body?' Lila Markov, the youngest member of Morel's team, was standing next to him with her hands on her hips.

'In a minute.' He took a quick look at Lila. Dressed in jeans, a V-necked white T-shirt and black Doc Martens, she had that look of intense concentration on her face which he knew well. Her hair was tied into a ponytail and she looked strong and fit. There was nothing soft and yielding about Lila Markov.

The police photographer emerged from what Morel guessed was the victim's bedroom.

'Morel,' he said by way of greeting. 'I've got all the shots I need for now. But when you're ready I'd like to get the rest of her body. Didn't want to pull the sheet back till you'd seen her.'

'I'll be right there,' Morel said.

As he surveyed the living room one last time, Lila waited patiently. She was used to the way he did things.

Every available surface was covered in ornaments. One was a bronze owl. Morel gazed at it, momentarily distracted by its glistening feathers. The bronzework was delicate, the feathers detailed with great precision.

His eyes shifted across all the other knick-knacks on display. So much clutter spoke of an empty life. The room looked out on to a street lined with chestnut trees that looked care-worn from the relentless heat of these past weeks. In the apartment too it was beginning to feel uncomfortably warm. Morel crossed over to the window and slid the balcony door open. He took several deep breaths before sliding it shut again. In the background the woman's sobs went on, quiet and insistent.

'That's the cleaning lady,' Lila said. 'She found the body. The victim's name is Isabelle Dufour.'

Morel nodded. 'Anything else you want to tell me before I take a look?' he asked.

'I'd rather not spoil the surprise.'

It took Morel several seconds to understand what he was looking at.

The old woman's face was grotesque. The closed lids caked in blue eye shadow. Her lipstick overlapped the shape of her lips, making them look like they'd been surgically enhanced.

Her cheeks wore bright circles of pink and the foundation across her face was thickly applied, spread unevenly across the wrinkly, parchment-like skin.

To top it all off, she wore a wig. The hair down to her shoulders, curly and bright red.

Morel was reminded of a couple of the regular 'girls' on Place Blanche who had long since passed the age of retirement but seemed to think that with extra layers of make-up they might still score. And it was true there were men who would make do with such ghoulishness.

The make-up was in stark contrast to everything else. The dead woman wore a virginal cream-coloured nightgown tied at the neck with a bow. She lay on a plumped-up pillow with perfectly white sheets stretched tightly over her thin body.

Leaving aside the face painting, if it had been a wake Isabelle Dufour couldn't have been better prepared.

Morel looked at her and felt the familiar sense of unease that always accompanied this initial violation of a victim's private world. The first thing the dead gave up was their intimacy.

'Not what you'd call a typical crime scene, is it?' Lila said.

One of the two police officers who'd called in the murder came into the room. Morel turned to him. He guessed that the man was in his early thirties. His black hair was cropped military-style and his eyes were the molten colour of maple syrup.

'Akil Abdelkader,' the man said and Morel nodded. There seemed little point in shaking hands when they were both wearing gloves.

'What alerted you?' Morel asked.

'It didn't feel right. First the make-up on her face – that lady who cleans for her, the one who found her like this,

said she never wore any make-up – and then the sheets,'
Abdelkader said, pointing to the bed. 'They are too tight.
No one can go to sleep like that, right? Even to tuck yourself in that tightly isn't possible. Especially with your arms
underneath the covers. So I started thinking, someone put
her here like this, someone not quite right in the head maybe.
Was I wrong to call it in?'

Morel pulled the sheet back. Both the victim's arms lay
straight down her sides. In her right hand, she held a wooden
cross, with four blue stones embedded one at the end of each
arm. There were no visible signs of injury. But the scene was
all wrong. The woman's ramrod posture, the make-up, the
fact that someone – who? – had tucked her in that way.
Abdelkader had made a good call.

'You did the right thing,' Morel told him, and he saw the
other man visibly relax.

The photographer had returned to the room and moved
in to take more shots. While he clicked away, Morel looked
at Madame Dufour's hands and face for anything that might
reveal something about how she'd died.

Next he checked the bedside table. It held a lamp, a novel
and a stack of religious pamphlets. At first glance they looked
like the sort of thing you found in your mail box or people
handed out to you on the street. There were three of them,
all identical. Nothing in the drawer except a pair of reading
glasses and a packet of tissues.

Morel pulled the sheet back over the victim. Even someone
with more experience than Abdelkader might have been forgiven for thinking she had died of natural causes. Wearing
too much make-up, admittedly. But still. Morel made a mental
note to remember the officer's name.

*

'So? Any ideas? I'm hoping the answer is yes. The last thing we need is to give the press another excuse to bang on about soaring crime rates. They're supposed to be going down, remember? If this government is telling the public that we're getting tougher on crime, then we'd damned well better be getting tougher. And getting results.'

Morel waited. There was no point in responding, he'd heard it all from Perrin before. The pressure he was under because of the results culture brought in by Sarkozy.

'Numbers. That's all that matters to them,' he said now, for the hundredth time.

He sighed meaningfully and looked at Morel. 'So what have we got here?'

'We'll need to wait for the results of the autopsy before we jump to conclusions,' Morel said mildly. Perrin eyed him with suspicion.

'I need to know *today*,' he said, articulating the last word as though Morel might have trouble understanding it. 'I need to know what happened to her and what leads we've got. I'll expect to hear from you before I head home tonight, and I'm leaving early to get changed for dinner.'

'I understand,' Morel said.

Perrin stared at Morel as if he didn't know what to make of him. He started to say something else but just then he caught sight of the deputy public prosecutor entering the room and, without another word or even a look in Morel's direction, he sidled up to the woman with his arms outstretched, all smiles.

Morel had been dozing happily in Solange's arms when the call had come through at 8.34. Knowing he was running late but telling himself he deserved a break. Over the past six months Morel's team had closed more cases than any other team at the Criminal Brigade. Even Perrin had been forced to acknowledge their performance.

'The cleaning lady has been working for our victim for sixteen years,' Lila explained. 'She let herself in with her own set of keys. Looked for her employer and thought that maybe she was sleeping in, though she was an early riser. Then realized something was wrong. She ran out and alerted the concierge.'

Morel listened and looked over at the two women sitting in the hallway. The thin-lipped concierge and the cleaning lady made an unlikely pair. He had a feeling, looking at the former with her beady blue eyes and tight curls, that she would not typically show such warmth to the stout woman who sat by her side wearing a headscarf and clutching a shopping bag. But clearly this was an event that superseded any perceived issues of class and sophistication.

The two Neuilly *flics* had done a good job sending nosy neighbours away, Morel thought. Aside from a change of menu at their local bistro, this was probably the biggest thing that had happened to most of the tenants in years.

'That Abdelkader was the one who decided to escalate this,' Lila said.

'Yes, smart guy,' Morel said.

'Speaking of which . . .'

Abdelkader was making his way over to them.

'There is something you need to know,' he said.

'What's that?' Morel said.

'The victim. It turns out one of my colleagues took a call from her a week ago. She wanted to make a complaint.'

'About what?'

'About two guys who had knocked on her door. Evangelists. Jehovah's Witnesses or something, I can't remember.'

Morel thought of the pamphlets on Dufour's side table. 'What was the big deal?'

'She was freaking out because they had come into the building and all the way to her front door. Normally the concierge keeps a close eye on who comes and goes.'

'What happened to the complaint?'

'We got her to come in and took her testimony. That was about it. We never followed up on it.'

He looked unhappy.

'Well, that sounds right,' Morel said. 'There wasn't anything else you could have done. What's bugging you?'

'Nothing. Just that one minute two guys turn up at her door and she seems really freaked out. And the next she's been killed in this weird way.' He shook his head. 'I've seen a few dead people since I took this job but nothing like this.'

'It's certainly an unusual crime scene. I'll give you that,' Morel said. 'We'll have to see what the forensic pathologist has to say.'

'Let me know if I can help.'

Morel noted the restraint in the other policeman's tone. Abdelkader looked like a man who kept his emotions to himself but Morel guessed how much he wanted to be a part of the investigation. His hunger was evident.

Morel hadn't been that different himself, back then. And he was impressed by the younger man's professionalism.

'Don't worry. I will.'

After sending Jean and Marco to interview the other tenants in the building, Morel took Lila with him and instructed one of the two women who had been sitting in the hallway for the past half hour to follow him to the ground floor.

'Sorry to keep you waiting. Would you mind coming downstairs with us? We'll use your living room, if that isn't too much trouble,' Morel told the concierge.

'Not at all,' she said, clearly flustered. 'If you could just give me a tiny minute to make sure the place isn't a complete mess.'

Once they reached the ground floor, she trotted ahead of them to her apartment while they followed at a slower pace. Through the half-open door they heard a bout of furious whispering before she reappeared.

'Please come in.'

The room they found themselves in was fussy and feminine. Morel guessed that the concierge, who'd introduced herself as Rose Jardin, was solely responsible for the interior decoration. It certainly seemed to have little to do with the man who sat as well he could on the pale leather sofa, between two rows of symmetrically arranged heart-shaped cushions. He wore a pair of blue overalls over a short-sleeved shirt and hardly looked away from the TV screen when they entered the room.

'Georges,' she hissed at him and turned to Morel with an apologetic smile. 'My husband has been working on the pipes all morning. We've had some plumbing issues. Sorry. Would you care to sit down?'

'Thank you. Commandant Serge Morel.' He extended a hand to Rose's husband.

Reluctantly, the man turned the television off and turned to the two officers. 'Georges Jardin. So she's dead, is she? Madame Dufour?'

'I'm afraid so.'

'Murdered.'

'We're investigating what happened,' Morel said while Lila fidgeted on the sofa, trying to make a space where she could sit comfortably. In the end she picked up two of the cushions and shoved them aside. Morel noticed how the concierge flinched. He saw that Lila had noticed too.

'We hope you won't mind if we ask a few questions.'

'Not at all.'

'Though I'm not sure how we can help,' the husband said.

'*You* might not be much help,' the concierge said. Then, turning to Morel, 'Georges wouldn't notice if someone took an axe to me right in front of his nose. But happily, I'm more observant. No one gets past me in this building.'

'Did Isabelle Dufour have many visitors?'

'No. The only people I ever saw were her son Jacques – and even that very rarely – and her daughter-in-law and grandchildren. Mostly her daughter-in-law came with just the younger of her two children.'

'Anyone else?'

'No.'

'How often did her son visit?'

'In the eight years I've been here I've probably seen him four times. That's how rarely he comes. The last time was just last week, in fact. He stayed for about an hour. He probably had lunch with his mother. It was around midday.'

'Did he visit with his wife and children?'

Rose shook her head.

'No. Always alone. The wife came separately. About once a month, I saw her and the little boy. They usually spend some time in the afternoons.'

'What about the cleaning lady? How often does she come?'

'Maria? She cleans at Madame Dufour's three times a week. Tuesdays, Wednesdays and Fridays. Always comes in at 8 a.m. and leaves at 12 p.m.'

'We've been told there might have been a couple of people, a man and a boy, distributing religious pamphlets.'

'I've never seen anyone like that.'

'Yet Isabelle Dufour filed a complaint with the police about them.'

'When?'

'A week or so ago.'

Rose looked put out.

'Well, I never saw anyone like that.' She looked at Morel. 'I wish she had mentioned it. After all, I am responsible for this building.'

'Yes, well, I'm sure she didn't want to trouble you.'

The entire time Rose's husband hadn't said a word. Now Morel turned to him.

'Monsieur Jardin, did you ever see any visitors that fit that description?'

'No.' He hesitated and looked at his wife. 'But we aren't *always* aware of who comes and goes. There are times when Rose and I are having our lunch. And often we like to take a quick nap in the afternoons.' He blushed then, and Morel forced himself not to smile.

But he couldn't resist looking at Rose Jardin. Her face had turned bright red and she was staring carefully at the ground.

'Well, thank you for all your help,' Morel said, standing up. 'Now if you don't mind I'll call Maria in. If there is a room where we could speak to her . . .'

'Of course,' Rose Jardin said. 'You can use this room. My husband and I will leave you to it.' She still wouldn't meet Morel's eye.

Morel stepped out of the flat and gave Jean a call. 'Can you get the cleaning lady to come down now?' he asked.

Morel and Lila waited for Maria in the lobby.

'I bet Georges is in for a telling-off,' Morel said.

'I don't know about that. I think she'll be too busy re-arranging the cushions,' Lila said. 'Did you see her face when

I moved a couple of them? I wonder if she uses a ruler or if she relies on instinct?'

The interview with the cleaning lady revealed very little.

'It was horrible, to see her like that,' Maria said. She was clearly distressed about Dufour's death.

'Any idea who could have done this?' he asked.

She shivered. 'I have no idea. A monster! It must be someone who is crazy.'

'What sort of employer was Madame Dufour?' he asked.

'Very good.' Maria shook her head. 'I have a son, Alfonso, and Madame Dufour always remembers his birthday. She always gives him something special.' She seemed to realize she was using the wrong tense and paused, unsure of what to say next.

'She was thoughtful,' Lila prompted her. 'Sounds like she was fond of you.'

'I was fond of her, too,' Maria said, and she started crying all over again. 'She helped us with the plane tickets when we went home to Portugal every summer. This year we went back for four weeks. I brought her a gift.'

'Did anyone visit her?' Lila asked.

Maria wiped the tears from her face. 'Her daughter-in-law and grandson. Once or twice I saw Madame Dufour's son.'

'Anyone else?'

'No. She sometimes met a friend for lunch but they never came here.'

Morel showed Maria the pamphlets he'd placed in a sealed bag.

'Do you know anything about these?'

Maria shook her head. 'No. They have been lying on Madame Dufour's bedside table for a little while, maybe the past week or so. I don't move anything, except to clean underneath, of course.'

'Was she a religious woman?'

'I don't think so. But we never talked about it.'

'How would you describe her, generally?'

Maria thought. 'I think she was a nice lady who was quite lonely. She was usually alone.'

'Did that make her unhappy?'

Maria looked at them with troubled eyes. 'I don't know. She was a very quiet person. We talked mostly about practical things. What cleaning products she needed, whether we should think about replacing the shower curtain, that sort of thing.'

'But you worked for her for sixteen years,' Lila said. 'Surely you had some idea of the sort of person she was?'

Maria shook her head. 'I don't know what sort of person she was. We weren't friends. I cleaned her house and she was kind to me. But she wasn't looking for someone to talk to.'

It was well past 2 p.m. when Morel and the three members of his team left the apartment and headed back to Quai des Orfèvres. They stopped on the way for takeaway sandwiches and coffees.

While he and Jean waited in the car for Marco and Lila to return with the food, Morel thought about Isabelle Dufour's painted face and the clothes she'd been dressed in. A strange, ritualistic murder. There was no doubt that someone had taken their time with her. There had been nothing impulsive about it.

He wondered what sort of person they were looking for.

Two

Morel balanced his weight carefully on the swivel chair and turned to face his visitor. Six months he'd been waiting for a new seat. This one concertinaed and slumped without warning, leaving him at times with his knees up to his chest. Looking at his visitor, Morel hoped the chair would behave itself, just this once.

Through the open window directly behind him, he could hear the morning traffic in the distance, commuters making their sluggish way along the quays. Drivers slammed their horns to let off steam.

It was already warm. He wished he'd worn a short-sleeved shirt. He wished he could have a cigarette, but Perrin had caught him once puffing away and blowing the smoke out his window. All of a sudden Morel was fifteen again, trying to hide his humiliation while his father delivered a lecture on the debilitating effect of nicotine on the brain.

He would rather not give Perrin another opportunity to dress him down. Still, he would have killed for a smoke. The day had not started well. His father had thrown a tantrum at the breakfast table after finding butter in the strawberry jam. Morel had ended up shouting, then apologizing. *I'm a forty-four-year-old man, fighting with my father about the way I like to do things*, he thought.

'Commandant?'

Morel suddenly realized he'd turned away from his visitor and was gazing without seeing at the pattern of leaves against a cobalt sky and the outline of a boat carrying sightseers along the Seine. Another world to the one he'd walked into this morning. Arriving at the inner courtyard of the Judicial Police Headquarters at eight he'd found a team from narcotics pulling a car apart following a tip-off from one of their informants about a sizeable heroin stash.

Morel turned to his visitor and managed to look contrite. 'I'm sorry.'

The woman sitting across from him couldn't have been much more than five feet tall but she radiated an intensity that Morel found unsettling. She was the third and last of the women whose testimonies Morel's team were hearing. Three women who, like Dufour, had called their local police stations to complain of two visitors handing out religious material.

'Doesn't that seem strange to you?' Morel had asked Lila. 'All four of them, reporting something so innocuous?'

'Unless our evangelists visited others. For whatever reason, these four found it unsettling enough to call. Others might have had the knock on their door but didn't think anything of it.'

She had a point. Still, Morel couldn't figure out why these women had bothered to complain at all, except for the fact that they were elderly and perhaps easily scared.

His visitor certainly didn't look like the fearful type. But he remembered Isabelle Dufour's body lying prone under the sheets. He was not giving this woman the attention she deserved, he realized.

'So where were we?' he said, feeling abashed.

The old lady shifted in her chair. Her eyes darted across the room as though the walls were made of rubber. She was humming the tune again. He was sure he knew it, but it evaded him no matter how often she did this. How long exactly had the two of them been at it? He didn't dare look at his watch, not with her sharp eyes observing him.

That tune. What was it exactly? Morel's father would know. Of course he would. At the thought of his father, Morel's mind began to wander again. He forced himself to focus. Maybe if it wasn't so hot, he told himself. It didn't help that the windows opened only so far and that there was no ventilation. No air-con unit, no fan.

He tugged at his collar. This Wednesday heralded the first heatwave of the year. Belatedly, considering it was the fourth week of August. Half the city's indigenous population had long since left town, heading south for the congested beaches or for holidays in the country. Morel would have liked to be among them. Right now he'd be grateful for a square foot of sand on the beach in Antibes, to sit among the lobster-coloured people and gaze at the sea.

'Like this, you see,' his visitor said, and she started up again. Morel found himself straining forward again, as though the problem were to do with volume rather than her inability to carry a tune.

'An English piece, perhaps? I seem to remember—'

The old woman shook her head vigorously. She seemed offended.

'English! Never trust the English,' she said. Her voice rang like a rusty old bicycle bell.

He ignored the comment, much as he'd ignored her comments at the start of their encounter. He had been making small talk to put her at ease and telling her how much Paris had changed since he was a child, to which she'd replied that it was all due to the Arabs. It was they, Morel learned, who had introduced cockroaches to the capital due to their lack of hygiene. Morel could have told her that French history was riddled with unhygienic practices – all authentically local. For centuries this had been a country awash with lice, bedbugs, fleas. But he held his tongue.

'Anyway, it wasn't just the tune, it was something about his face,' she continued. Morel leaned closer so that the chair tilted dangerously.

'What about it?' he asked.

'Oh, he had all the airs and graces,' the woman said. 'But.'

You could tell she liked to choose how she told a story. She wouldn't be rushed.

'But,' she continued, pausing for effect – 'what sort of well-mannered man comes knocking on a stranger's door at eight o'clock on a Sunday morning, handing out business cards? Calling me sister and telling me Jesus is coming. Sister!' she repeated, with a disgusted air. 'I told him, I'm not your sister. I'm old enough to be your mother, though, and if the poor woman is still alive I hope to God she doesn't know how her son is disgracing himself, intruding on people in their homes.'

Now Elisabeth Guillou was waving a pamphlet at him. It was the same one Morel had found in Isabelle Dufour's bedroom.

'Can you describe them to me? The ones who knocked on your door and gave you that pamphlet?' he asked.

His visitor sighed, as though it pained her to have to explain herself.

'The man was quite ordinary. Pleasant enough, though he didn't fool me for a second. He was dragging a boy around with him, no doubt to prevent doors being slammed in his face. The boy was mute. Literally. A shameful character,' she said.

She glared at Morel, but there was a hint of pleasure in

the old prune's eyes. Something merry and unkind. She leaned forward.

'You know, I was raised as a Christian. We used to recite the Lord's Prayer twice a day, before breakfast and after dinner. My father would watch me and my sister to make sure we were saying the words, not just pretending. I always knew, well before I could read and write, that it was a load of rubbish.'

She laughed as though something excessively droll had just occurred to her.

'You know, it delights me to think of all those people living their lives with the conviction they'll be going somewhere special for eternity once they die. And where are they now? Decomposing, gone, buried underground, reduced to ashes. Just think! How wonderful, how utterly priceless!'

Morel laughed with her. It could do no harm, and might in fact jog her memory further. 'Is there anything else, Madame Guillou?'

She began whistling again, loudly, startling him. Her thin lips clenched into a tune, a better rendition this time, which Morel found overwhelmingly familiar once he got over his initial surprise. He rolled his chair forward. Thankfully, it didn't collapse.

'That's it?'

'Yes, that's the tune.'

'The one the man was humming? Who came to your house?'

'Yes, it is. Do you recognize it?'

'Indeed, Madame, indeed I do.'

They looked at each other, beaming.

'Well, you've been an immense help, Madame Guillou. I thank you, once again, for taking the trouble to come in.'

'Are you a believer, Commandant?' she asked. She was

standing up, adjusting the strap of her handbag on her shoulder and holding on tight, as though she expected some-one to snatch it from her.

'Of sorts, Madame, of sorts. But not the peddling kind, if you know what I mean.'

Not so certain now, she hesitated. 'Yes, yes. Will that be all?'

'Yes indeed. And I thank you for taking the time to come in. You've been a great help.'

'My pleasure.' All briskness and efficiency now. 'Nice to meet you too.' She looked him up and down, as though she might say something more. But then thought better of it.

He walked her to the top of the stairs, thinking to accom-pany her to the ground floor, but she waved him away as though guessing his intention.

'I'm perfectly capable of seeing myself out,' she said.

They shook hands as though they'd just conducted a suc-cessful business transaction.

'Goodbye, then.'

Morel returned to his desk, triumphant. Who would have thought he would recognize the tune? That it would in fact turn out to be one he had grown up with? One his father listened to so often that to Morel it became synonymous with long Sunday afternoons, when, as a child, he waited for something, anything, to happen to relieve the tedium? As he sat down and swivelled the chair to face his computer, he hummed the melody. 'In Paradisum', from Fauré's *Requiem*. In the end, the old lady had rendered it perfectly.

The morning wore on, sticky and warm. Nothing was resolved. The heat seemed to get on people's nerves, in and outside the building. Phones were ringing off the hook. In the sixteenth, a man clobbered his wife with a 300-euro lamp she'd just brought home from a boutique on Avenue Molière. Thirty-five years of marriage, and now this lamp he hated, which he took as a personal affront. A homeless man had thrown himself in the Seine naked, to cool down, he said. No one cared to pull him out of the water and so he floated on his back for half an hour, singing, until the police arrived.

The room Morel shared with his team was dingy, but large enough to accommodate three desks. Morel's desk was separated from the other two by a Song-era Chinese folding screen, a wedding gift from his paternal grandfather ten years ago. Morel's marriage to Eva had lasted less than two years but he still treasured the screen. He'd moved it to the Quai des Orfèvres the day he was promoted to the position of team leader. His father had thrown a fit.

'Have you gone mad? Do you know what this thing is worth?'

'Well, no one's likely to steal it at headquarters, are they?'

This priceless object had the advantage of providing Morel with some much-needed privacy. People thought twice before disturbing him when he was in his lair out of sight.

'Real coffee. I hope you're grateful.' Jean was standing before him, holding a takeaway cup.

'Thanks,' Morel said. 'How's it going?'

To Morel's regret, the older detective was tied up with a warehouse burglary and homicide that had occurred over the weekend. He wouldn't have much spare time, though Jean was trying his best to be two people at once.

'It looks pretty straightforward. We've got footage showing the guys coming in and leaving shortly after our victim arrived for work. They look like they're in a real rush. We shouldn't have too much trouble with this one,' Jean said.

'Good. Hopefully we can close it fast. I'd like you on this new case,' Morel said.

Jean nodded. 'Did the Guillou woman come in?'

'Yes.'

'And?'

'She told the same story as Marie Latour and Irina Volkoff, the two you spoke to,' Morel said.

'Have you heard back from Martin? About the body, I mean,' Jean said.

Morel took a sip of his coffee. 'Not yet. Lila and Marco are at the morgue, they should have some news when they get back.'

Jean sat down and glanced at the line of origami figures on the desk before him. A paper crow was at the head of a marching avian column that included a pelican and a flamingo. Morel had been busy.

'Where's Vincent?' Jean asked.

'I haven't heard from him yet,' Morel said.

The two men exchanged a look. With Vincent's wife dying of breast cancer, no one wanted to comment on his frequent absences from work.

'You're going to have to talk to him,' Jean said eventually. 'I know he has to spend a lot of time at home and in the hospital right now but we need that extra pair of hands. So if he's not going to be fully active anytime soon then we need to get someone in. At least temporarily.'

Morel nodded. 'I'll have that conversation eventually,' he said. 'But I don't want to worry him with it right now. I don't want him thinking he's being pushed aside. He's got enough—'

Before he could finish his sentence, he heard Marco and Lila come in.

Morel stood up. 'Let's hear whether there's any news,' he said.

*

'So what has the great Richard Martin got to say?' Morel asked. He sat on the edge of Lila's desk, looking at the two younger officers in his team.

Lila frowned. Morel knew she would be foul-tempered for at least the next hour. Richard Martin had that effect on women.

'Did Martin behave himself?'

'What do you think?' Lila said while Marco pulled a face at Morel, a warning not to pursue the subject further.

Morel had known the forensic pathologist for seven years now. The two had stepped into their current roles around the same time. He knew that Martin was as driven as he was and that, like him, he'd worked hard to get to where he was now. But the resemblance ended there. While Morel kept his private life under wraps, Martin had become notorious for his ability to make women squirm. Two of his female colleagues had tried and failed to make sexual harassment cases against him. Another had simply resigned. The fact that Martin was considered by many to be the best in his field had kept him in his position, so far at least.

'According to our eminently sleazy pathologist,' Lila began, 'Isabelle Dufour died sometime between five and six in the morning. She was drowned. Martin couldn't find any signs of a struggle. She was a frail old woman so perhaps she didn't get an opportunity to fight her opponent. He could easily have held her underwater till she ran out of breath.'

The room was silent, while everyone considered this.

'How does he know she drowned?'

'The size and shape of the lungs,' Lila said. 'And crepitus.'

Morel had seen it before. The lungs inflated like water wings; crepitus, evidenced by the crackling sound the lungs made when you squeezed them. It wasn't conclusive but along with the circumstantial evidence it painted a pretty convincing picture. Dufour's hair, as well as the bath surface, hadn't been completely dry.

'If she drowned accidentally, that means someone else took the time to doll her up and tuck her in,' Lila said.

'Any signs of sexual assault?'

'None.'

Morel glanced at Marco. He was looking at the floor and Morel found himself growing irritable, as he often did with the young policeman.

'Anything else, Marco?' he said.

'Not really.'

'Not really or no?'

'No,' Marco said. Morel saw him blush and wondered, not for the first time, whether the young man really had it in him to work murder cases. He wasn't assertive enough. You couldn't work a crime case the way he did, by being timid and hesitant.

Maybe it wasn't entirely Marco's fault. He was a decent person, eager and good-natured. He just didn't fit in to this team and would be better off in another department.

'Let's move on,' Morel said. 'But first, I need to catch up with our illustrious chief. Let's reconvene when I get back.'

THREE

'I didn't hear from you yesterday,' Perrin said. He didn't offer his subordinate a seat, which suited Morel well as it meant the meeting would be brief.

'Sorry. I thought I'd wait until I had something to tell you. How was the dinner party?' Morel, who was significantly taller than Perrin, towered over the small man sitting before him. He saw Perrin register this, saw the look of regret on his face as he realized he should have told Morel to sit down. Too late now.

'Don't try small talk with me, Morel,' Perrin said, giving him a dark look. 'Small talk is not your forte. So tell me. What have you got?'

Morel looked at his boss. No matter how hard he tried to look suave, Perrin never quite managed to pull it off. Today he had put gel in his hair to shape it into a slick side parting which gave his skull a flattened look. He'd trimmed his beard and cut himself shaving. A bloodied piece of tissue, clearly forgotten, had dropped from his cheek and landed in the wiry hair around his jaw. His tie and shirt were expensive but his skin was grey and he looked like he was in pain, though he tried his best to hide it. Must have been a late night, Morel thought. He guessed that Perrin was nursing a stiff hangover.

'We've spoken to three women – Elisabeth Guillou, Marie Latour and Irina Volkoff. All three reported the evangelists' visit, said they wanted to lodge a complaint for harassment. Going by their description, it sounds like these are the same guys who knocked on Isabelle Dufour's door days before she died. A man and a boy. These women have something in common with Dufour. They're widowed and live by themselves, which may explain why they found the experience unsettling enough to call us in. Our main focus is to bring this pair in, so we can talk to them.'

Perrin scratched at his beard absently, and the piece of tissue fell from it like an injured bird from its nest. He looked at it, puzzled at first, then angry when he realized it had been on his face the entire time.

'OK, so bring them in. The sooner the better. And if we've got a solid description let's get it out there. I think a press conference might be in order.' Morel could see Perrin's face brighten at the thought of a media briefing. Unconsciously, his hand drifted over his shiny hair and his face took on a grave and pompous expression Morel had seen him use before, whenever there were cameras nearby.

'That may be premature,' Morel said. 'I think we can track them down without that. If we call a briefing, there's a risk that if they've got something to hide, they'll go underground.'

Perrin looked put out. 'Do it, then,' he said. 'But if you don't find them fast, we'll do the briefing. Every minute counts. There's no time for hesitation.'

'Yes, sir,' Morel said, and turned to leave before Perrin could come up with another platitude.

After his meeting with Perrin, Morel returned to the others. By then it was 11.40 and the office was like a sauna. The weather forecast had announced a high of 42 degrees. It felt like more. Morel looked at his team. None of them looked particularly fresh or motivated.

'Come on,' he said. 'Let's see a bit of enthusiasm.' A collective sigh like a deflating balloon greeted his comments. 'Before we start, Vincent hasn't showed up yet. We haven't heard from him but I'm guessing he won't be in today.'

No one said anything. Vincent was hardly a presence in the office these days. When he did turn up he was a ghostly version of himself.

'So where were we?' Morel said. He pulled his chair up and looked expectantly at the three sweaty officers.

'Marco, what about the neighbours? What have they got to say?'

'Not a whole lot,' Marco said.

'Did you talk to everyone?'

'Every living thing,' Lila answered.

She told Morel how they'd canvassed the neighbourhood where Isabelle Dufour lived. They'd talked to people in the neighbouring residential building, and at the newsagent's and cafe across the street.

'The general gist is that no one knows anything about any unusual visits to Dufour's flat,' Lila said. 'No one heard anything that night. The only neighbour who lives on Dufour's floor is eighty-nine years old. At 8 p.m. he watched the news with his earphones on because he's deaf and needs the sound right up. Then he took a sleeping pill and went to bed. Other than that, a couple of the neighbours have seen Dufour's son, once or twice, as well as her daughter-in-law and the kids.'

'So that ties in with what the concierge told us.' Morel turned to Marco. 'Anyone in the building had a couple of bible-bashers knocking on their door?'

'Nope. And the concierge insists she sees everyone who enters and leaves the building.'

'Yes, well, we know that isn't the case. Anything else?'
Marco looked at his feet. 'Nothing.'

'Can you be a bit more specific than that?' Morel said, trying not to let his irritation show.

'Well, the guy who owns the newsagent's opens up early – around six – and he says he doesn't remember seeing anyone enter or leave the building. But then he wasn't paying any particular attention. No one in the building saw any strangers walking in or out. But few of them would have been up and about that early.'

'OK. And anything from the cafe? Anyone see anything out of the ordinary early that morning?'

'No. No one had anything interesting to contribute,' Marco said.

A bit like you, Morel thought, and turned back to Lila, who was chewing her nails.

'What do we know about Isabelle Dufour?'

Lila unfolded her legs and opened her notebook. Morel noticed she wore black leather trousers. Leather trousers, in this heat. He nearly admired her for that. Her hair, usually worn straight down her back, was tied up in a knot. Strands of hair clung to her neck. She looked miserable. Morel knew how she felt.

'Isabelle Dufour. Eighty years old,' Lila said, turning the pages of her pad.

Morel knew she didn't need her notes, her memory was prodigious. He knew a few things about Lila Markov. She had an IQ of 174 and did not suffer fools gladly. She could be short-tempered. Very. As far as Morel could tell, she hadn't made many friends in the department since she'd joined his team. Maybe her cleverness made people uncomfortable. Or maybe they just didn't like her manners.

'Go on.'

'Her neighbours say she went out every day for lunch, like clockwork, at a place around the corner. Usual place, standard menu. She always ordered the same thing and she ate on her own. Her son Jacques lives with his wife and two children in Neuilly, just two blocks away,' she said.

Morel had reached Jacques Dufour on his mobile phone the previous day to inform him of his mother's death. He'd been in London with his wife and younger child. He was due back today, Morel remembered.

He turned to Jean, who was sharpening a pencil with intense concentration. Jean was two years from retirement. He was fifty-eight but looked about ten years older. His life revolved around his job, a fifteen-year-old son resulting from a four-month relationship with the lead singer of a band he'd played guitar in, and a passion for heavy metal – the sort of bands that now drew titters from people too young to remember when they were considered daring. The only sick day Jean had ever taken, as far as Morel knew, was after a Deep Purple concert when someone had thrown an empty bottle of beer his way and knocked him out.

'Jean. Your two widows. Give us a run-down.'

Jean flicked through the pages of his notebook and read out loud.

'Marie Latour. Born in 1928 in Chamonix. Moved to Paris when she married her late husband Hector Latour. She's been living alone since his death. She has a son and a daughter, who live in Paris. She sees them once a month or so.'

'What else?' Morel said.

'Latour says she's never set foot in a church. She was upset when the man and the boy showed up on her doorstep. She'd never seen them before. The man insisted on giving her a couple of pamphlets. Wouldn't leave until she agreed to take them.'

Morel nodded. 'Go on.'

'Irina Volkoff. Russian-born. Seventy-six years old. Quite a looker, actually.'

'A bit past the expiry date, no?' Lila said.

Marco laughed.

'All right, get on with it,' Morel said.

'Her husband Sergey died shortly after the two of them arrived in France with their son. She was only twenty-four when Sergey died and she never remarried. The son lives on a houseboat, not far from here as it turns out. Growing up in Soviet Russia, she didn't get much in the way of religious education, as you can imagine, and she's not interested in starting now. She says her two visitors – a man and a boy who was mute – made her uncomfortable enough to call us, but she couldn't explain why. Just said she doesn't like people knocking on her door.'

One of the pamphlets, the one received by Elisabeth Guillou, lay on Morel's desk. He fetched it and returned to the chair at Lila and Marco's desk.

'Let me give you a quick summary of what Madame Guillou had to say this morning. It'll sound familiar.' He briefed his team, then held up the pamphlet. 'This was at Guillou's house. It's the same one that was found at Isabelle Dufour's apartment, and the same one Marie Latour and Irina Volkoff felt obliged to take, to get rid of their unwanted visitors.

'One thing that bothers me is that Isabelle Dufour lived in Neuilly but the three others all lived in the outer suburbs and nowhere near each other. The fact that they live so far apart suggests they might have been singled out,' Morel went on.

'I thought of that too,' Jean said.

Morel sat up in his chair. 'By the way, how did she know about the boy?'

'What?'

'Volkoff. How did she know the boy was mute? Just because he didn't speak?'

Jean flicked through his notes.

'Her visitor,' he said. 'The man told her.'

'Right.'

So they had had a personal exchange, Morel thought. The man had engaged with the woman, talked about the boy accompanying him. To gain sympathy?

'Did she say anything else? About the boy?'

'She said he wouldn't look at her. Oh and another thing. She thought he might be Russian.'

'How?'

'She said he looked Russian. Whatever that means. And the only time he looked at her was when she spoke a few words of Russian. He looked like he knew what she was saying.'

'And the man? Did she say anything else about him?'

'That he was well dressed.'

Morel thought about it. A seemingly innocuous visit, the sort of thing people were subjected to all the time. A knock on the door and something to sell. A newspaper subscription, a new gas or electricity supply, a new religion. The promise of something better. So what was it about this pair that had upset these women? Morel considered Madame Guillou again. Describing her visitors to Morel, he had seen, for just an instant, the fear in her eyes. Yet nothing in her account had stood out.

Morel fidgeted in his chair. He was hungry.

'All right. I want to talk to the neighbours where Elisabeth Guillou, Marie Latour and Irina Volkoff live. I know it's going to be time-consuming,' he added, seeing the expression on Marco's face – 'but we need to find out whether they have had the same people turn up on their doorsteps. If it was just those three women, then we'll know they were targeted. Jean, any chance you'll have some spare time to help us out?'

'Sure.'

'Thanks. Can you find out whether any fingerprints turned up on the pamphlets at Dufour's house. Maybe we'll get lucky. It's worth a try in any case.'

Jean grabbed the keys to his motorbike and stood up. 'I've got to go. But I'll call the lab on my way out and I'll be free this afternoon to help interview neighbours.'

'Before you go, can you leave the transcripts of your interviews with the two widows on my desk? I want to run them against Guillou's deposition. Maybe something will stand out. Let's see if between the three of them they've given us enough to go on in terms of our guys' physical descriptions.'

Jean nodded and left the room.

'Marco, I want you to meet up with Jean this afternoon. We need those checks with the neighbours done by the end of the day.'

Marco nodded. Morel turned to Lila.

'Lila, I need you here, to write up the statements from the interviews – the tenants, the concierge and the cleaning lady. I want those before we interview Dufour's son. Also, can you give him a call and say we'd like to drop by tomorrow morning. And I want to know where the pamphlet comes from,' he said. 'Is it a self-publishing effort? If not, what's the organization behind it? There's no web address here, no number. I suggest we start making a list of religious groups. Forget the Catholic ones, just focus on the Protestants, the evangelicals. It's a bit of a hopeless task, I know,' he said.

'Like looking for a needle in a haystack,' Lila muttered.

Morel ignored Lila's comment and stood up. His Ermenegildo Zegna shirt clung to his back.

'All right, you two,' he said. 'Let's see if we can make some headway.'

Morel stepped out on to Rue de la Cité to get something to eat. He queued outside a popular *boulangerie* for a ham and cheese baguette and walked down to the river. He needed to stretch his legs in order to think clearly.

With Vincent gone, and Jean stretched, he was going to have to bring in reinforcements. It was ridiculous to carry on with just Marco and Lila. However good Lila was, she was just one person. And he still wasn't convinced that Marco was up to the task.

Along the embankment, couples strolled or sat enlaced on benches, caught up in themselves. A Bateau-Mouche chugged along the Seine, the deck crammed with tourists, turning their faces towards the sun or taking pictures. Such innocent pleasures. Morel envied them. When was the last time he'd taken a break? Was it February, or March maybe? With a woman he'd been introduced to at a party two weeks earlier. They'd driven past Orléans into the Loire region and stayed in a B&B near Chambord. They'd found themselves in a room with a four-poster bed, thick carpets and a fireplace. You couldn't have asked for a more romantic setting, but by the second day they'd run out of things to say to each other and driven back, cutting their vacation short by two nights.

Unsurprisingly, he hadn't heard from her since.

Hundreds of people milled around Notre-Dame. It didn't stop the pigeons from flocking to the square, waiting for the scraps they knew would come their way. Morel moved away from the birds to eat. Once he'd finished his sandwich, he took a piece of paper from his pocket, a square pale blue sheet, and spent a leisurely four and a half minutes folding it into the shape of a crane. As a base, he used his hardback biography of the origamist Eric Joisel, which he carried with him everywhere.

He'd seen Joisel's work up close, in 2005 at an exhibition of fifty eminent origamists from around the world. The French artist's work had made the biggest impression. It was like nothing Morel had ever seen. He had gone twice and the second time he'd run into Joisel himself. Chatted with him for several minutes with a goofy grin on his face like some awestruck teenage fan.

While he worked at the bird, he listened to the chatter around him, fragments of a dozen different languages floating across the sultry afternoon air.

Once he'd finished the crane, he briefly entertained himself by guessing where people were from. The busty woman in the tight white jeans and Versace T-shirt was Russian, the man with the gold signet ring and hair spilling from his shirt front, gesticulating with his hands while talking on the phone, was Lebanese. He looked remarkably like a man Morel's younger sister Adèle had dated, one of a string of seductive and unreliable men in her life. There was no mistaking the Americans, in their sensible gear. Their voices carried above everyone else's.

It was time to go back. Morel stood up and brushed any remaining crumbs off his suit. He took one last look at the river and at the light reflecting off the windows of the graceful stone buildings on the opposite embankment. Paris was always beautiful but in the summer the city always seemed dusty and tired to him. Not so much eternal as middle-aged and beginning to show its age.

Still. Though he complained about the place, it was in his bones. He had lived here since the age of seventeen. Sometimes it appeared to him in his dreams, like one of his paper structures. An origami city, infinitely complex and delicate in its undertaking.

Morel took another look at the crane and frowned. It was sloppy work. He crushed it into a tight ball and threw it into a nearby bin along with his sandwich wrapping.

Back in the office, Morel retreated behind his Chinese screen and opened the folder Jean had left on his desk. It contained the transcripts of his interviews with Marie Latour and Irina Volkoff. Alongside these he placed his notes from his morning meeting with Elisabeth Guillou.

The description of the man was almost identical across the three sets of notes. He was described as being of average height and slim build, with cropped, light brown hair and brown eyes. Clean-shaven and well-dressed. He was polite and spoke like an educated man.

Morel saw that the description of the boy was not so straightforward. He was generally described as being tall and thin, with longish black hair that obscured his eyes. All three women agreed he was dressed as a typical teenager, with oversized jeans and a cap.

From then on, the descriptions diverged significantly. Marie Latour said the boy had a limp while Irina Volkoff said he had no trouble walking at all. Latour said the boy seemed ill at ease while Elisabeth Guillou, for one, had been troubled by his arrogance. Volkoff had called him handsome while Latour and Guillou both said he looked unhealthy. According to Latour, the boy was barely fourteen, while Volkoff thought he must be around eighteen, an adult.

Morel typed out as detailed a description as he could, using the transcripts, and printed out a copy. He walked over to where Lila and Marco were sitting.

Drawing nearer, Morel saw that Lila had pulled together a list of at least a dozen religious organizations. A couple of names appeared at the end of the list. One of these surprised him. He should have thought of his old friend.

'Don't even think of giving me anything else to do,' she told him. 'I've got my hands full.'

'What have you come up with?' he asked.

'Some of the main organizations including the Association of Protestant Churches. I've also dug up the names of a couple of experts. Maybe there's a short cut there, someone might be able to direct us so that we're not wasting our time trawling through hundreds of listings.'

'That all sounds good.'

He turned to Marco. 'Before you meet up with Jean, can you take this description back with you to Dufour's building and run it by the concierge and the tenants. Get hold of the cleaning woman too. I just want to make absolutely sure they haven't seen these two guys lurking around there. Maybe if we give them some specifics they'll remember something.'

'OK, I'm on it,' Marco said.

'Run it by the newsagent's and the cafe as well. Don't come back and tell me that you got nothing.'

'I'll do my best, boss.'

Morel nodded. 'OK. And Lila, don't worry about calling this guy,' he said, pointing to the name he'd recognized on her list. 'I'll do it myself.'

'I'm glad to hear it,' she said.

For the rest of the day, Morel made a reasonable effort at tackling the paperwork piled high on his desk. He ran through the notes on a sexual assault case which Jean and Vincent had worked on and that was going to court in the next week, and on the warehouse burglary.

It was nearly four when he finally pushed his other work aside and returned to the Dufour case. He spread the crime-scene photos before him. Then he stood up and crossed over to Lila's desk again. She sat with her headphones on, staring at the screen. He had to touch her shoulder to get her attention. She took her headphones off and turned to face him.

'I'm just going over the crime-scene photos. I'd like you to take a look as well.'

Though the police photographer had been there, nothing beat Lila's powers of recollection. No one else on his team had that. Perfect recall.

'What sort of person are we looking for?' he said. It wasn't really a question but Lila answered anyway.

'No idea,' she said. 'Except that he's a freak.'

'Well that narrows it down.'

'You know what I mean. The whole business of giving her a bath, actually washing her hair or making her wash it, before drowning her. Then laying her out like that—'

'I know. It seems oddly personal, doesn't it? Almost loving . . .'

'Funny way of showing affection, don't you think?'

Morel looked at her, deep in thought.

'By the way,' she said, 'I called Dufour's son.'

'And?'

'He'll be home if we come early tomorrow, before 8.30. They've just come back from London. He has an important meeting here, apparently, and then he's off again. To Geneva. I reminded him that his mother had died and asked whether he might not be just a tad interested in the circumstances of her death.'

Morel could imagine what the exchange had been like.

'What did he say to that?'

'He said he's only away for forty-eight hours. And that

the trip couldn't be postponed,' Lila said. 'Either way, he didn't sound overwhelmed with grief.'

'People have funny ways of expressing their grief,' Morel said absently.

'Or maybe he's an arsehole who is too busy with his big-shot career to care much whether his mother is dead.'

'Let's just wait and see, and try to be courteous when we meet him, shall we?'

'Whatever you say.'

The sun was still high in the sky when Morel decided to call it a day and go home. He grabbed his car keys and his wallet and shut the window behind his desk.

Walking across the bridge, Morel found his body ached with tension. He took deep breaths and tried to focus his thoughts on something other than the painted face and inert body of an old woman, lying stiff in her bed under crisp, laundered sheets, as though she'd already been laid out for burial.

Through the soles of his shoes he could feel the heat of the day begin to loosen its hold on the concrete footpath. But still there was no let-up in the evening's temperature, not a whiff of air or even a passing breeze to send a brief and welcome chill up his spine, through his sweat-stained shirt. He reached the street where his car was parked, hoping the traffic wouldn't be too bad on the way home. He needed a drink.

As he unlocked the door, his phone began to ring. It was Richard Martin.

'Morel?'

'Martin. How are you?' Morel said.

'As well as can be expected,' the pathologist said cheerfully. 'I enjoyed your detectives' visit this morning. Lila Markov is looking as magnificent as ever.'

'Surely you're not calling just to tell me that,' Morel said, dropping his bag in the passenger seat and climbing into the car.

'No. There's something I thought you might want to know. I examined Isabelle Dufour again this afternoon. You know I like to take another look at the body before we hand it over to the family. In case I've missed anything.'

'Go on.'

'I found bruises on her upper arms. There are clear finger patterns on both sides. There's no doubt about it. Someone gripped both her arms hard. It looks to me like she was held down for several minutes at least, I'd say, for the marks to be so apparent.'

'They weren't there before?'

'You know that's not uncommon with bruises,' Martin said. 'Sometimes they don't show up till a day or so later, well after death.'

Morel had learned this from previous cases he'd worked on, but it still amazed him. The body releasing clues long after the heart has stopped beating.

'I've got to go,' Martin said. 'But I wanted to let you know.'

After he'd hung up, Morel closed his eyes and leaned his head back against the seat. For a while, he didn't move.

Slowly, he sat up again, opened his eyes and started the car. He rolled his window down to let in some air.

Isabelle Dufour had been killed. By someone who'd lingered, who'd prepared her with more care than the most attentive of undertakers. Was it meant as some sort of macabre joke? Or was it in fact, in some deranged way, an act of love? Were they dealing with someone who was unbalanced or someone meticulously rational?

Morel had no idea. But as he began nudging his way out

of the narrow space he'd carved out for his Volvo, negotiating his exit inch by inch, he felt a familiar tingling down his spine that always came with the beginning of a new murder investigation.

FOUR

It took him forty-five minutes to drive home. A truck had run a man over at Place de l'Etoile. Now it blocked Avenue de la Grande Armée, one of twelve arteries leading off the roundabout and the one Morel needed to take to get home. The victim was pinned beneath one of the truck's wheels. Stuck in his stationary car, Morel found he was close enough to make out the man's features. His face seemed devoid of expression. Maybe he was unconscious. Morel hoped so, for his sake. He debated briefly whether to get out, but there were already a couple of police officers on the scene. In the distance he could hear the wail of a siren, drawing nearer.

What had the man been thinking, crossing the busy roundabout? Maybe he had decided his time had come. Morel could think of more convenient, tidier ways to go. If it were him, he knew he would not want to make a public display of himself.

As he waited in his car for the traffic to inch forward, he saw the ambulance stop near the entrance to the roundabout with its flashing blue lights and the letters *SAMU de Paris* written across the front. A man and a woman got out and jogged to where the victim lay. They started working on the body. The usual gaping crowd of onlookers waited at a distance to see the outcome.

'Need any back-up?' Morel called out, thrusting his badge

through the car window. The officer closest to him, in his twenties, looked like he might be about to throw up.

'Thanks, but more people won't make a difference. We're good,' he said, his pale face telling a different story.

Morel nodded. The car ahead of him moved, and he followed, indicating towards his exit.

He thought of the pathologist's call as he drove with the window rolled down, breathing in the pungent blend of diesel and dust that tainted the distinctive scent of the horse chestnuts along the boulevard. The residential buildings around here were stately and the streets quieter than the bustling lanes of the Châtelet, the Latin Quarter and its surroundings, the heart of Paris where he spent his days. At the end of a working day he tended to welcome the contrast, though tonight as he drove past a popular bistro where couples leaned towards each other over drinks he found himself drawn to the bustle and cosiness inside, wishing he were a part of it. Waiting at a traffic light on Avenue de Neuilly, he looked up at a high-ceilinged apartment where shadows moved against the glow of a lamp, and tried to imagine what went on behind the stone building's well-preserved walls.

It was getting dark by the time he parked outside his childhood home. He let himself into the house. The lights were off downstairs but up in his father's room he could see the flicker of the television set.

He didn't go up immediately. Instead he sat on the sofa and took his shirt off. The air felt cool against his back. He took a deep breath and waited for the past hours to recede.

Morel's living quarters, on the ground floor, were private. Several years ago, his father had hired an architect to see whether he could come up with a solution that he and his son could live with. The place had become too big for the two of them. All that space reminded them of the woman whose death had robbed them both of their closest ally.

The architect had done a good job. Now Morel accessed his quarters through a door in the living room. There were only two sets of keys, one for Morel and the other for Augustine, the cleaning lady. Morel had a bedroom and a large study which could double up as a small living room if anyone visited, as well as a bathroom.

His father occupied the whole top floor, which included a living room, a bedroom and a bathroom. Hardly anyone used the shared downstairs living room any more, and the dining room stood empty too. Morel senior was too much of a recluse these days to entertain and his son tended to work late.

This way they managed to keep out of each other's way, though the kitchen was still communal. The two men had their meals at the counter on a set of Ikea stools Morel had bought when he realized how formal and stilted meals at the dining table had become with just the two of them.

Morel threw his clothes into the laundry basket in his bathroom and fetched a clean T-shirt and a pair of shorts. Then, with a sigh, he crossed the silent living room, climbed the stairs to his father's bedroom and knocked on the door.

'Come in.'

The old man lay propped up by a stack of pillows. He still had an abundant head of hair though it had turned completely white shortly after his sixtieth birthday, in the days following his retirement. He was tall and wiry, with deep blue eyes and a prominent nose set in a narrow face. Except for his height, Morel looked nothing like him.

He looked up from his book and took his glasses off. The news was on, the sound muted.

'You just got back?'

'Yes.'

'Another long day, then.'

'I'm afraid so.'

'Have you had dinner?'

'Yes,' Morel lied.

He could see his father didn't believe him, but he was too tired to make something up.

'What are you reading?' he asked, still standing in the doorway.

'It's not something you'd be very interested in, I think.'

'Tell me anyway.'

'*The Monk and the Philosopher*. It's a conversation between the French Buddhist monk Matthieu Ricard and his father Jean-François Revel.'

'Sounds interesting,' said Morel, who had never heard of either man. He tried to remember the last book he'd read.

'It's a fascinating exchange, between a father with a rational, scientific mind and a son he hoped would build on his budding scientific career but instead chose a completely different path. He became a Buddhist monk.'

'Disappointing for the father, I expect.'

'It isn't as simple as all that. You should read it.'

'Maybe I will,' Morel said.

His father smiled, as though at some private thought, and put his glasses back on.

'I'll let you get on with it then. Goodnight,' Morel said.

'Goodnight.'

Morel went downstairs to the kitchen, where he found the remains of a roast chicken and a ratatouille. Today was one of Augustine's visiting days. She would have cooked for the two of them once she'd finished the housework. It always shamed Morel to think of the old woman having to prepare food for him and his father. But she had known him since he was a child and insisted that she wanted to, particularly now that her children were all grown.

'What else am I going to do?' she said. 'Sit at home and watch TV?'

While he waited for his ratatouille to warm in the microwave, he tried calling his elder sister Maly's mobile number. It rang six times before going to voicemail. He left a message asking her to call back.

He hadn't heard from her in weeks. It was unlike her.

In his room he placed a glass of wine on the bedside table and propped himself up with pillows before sitting up to eat and watch the news. The newsreader was saying the world's population had now reached seven billion.

Seven billion. It was best not to think about it.

His father had turned the volume up on his TV. Morel knew it would continue now, long after he turned the lights off. His father seemed to get by on four or five hours' sleep.

Philippe had been a diplomat. Morel still clearly remembered the day he'd found out that his son was joining the police force. He hadn't even bothered to conceal his disappointment.

'Well, it's up to you of course,' he'd said. The two of them had gone out for lunch. Neither of them had spoken much and Morel had ended up drinking two-thirds of a bottle of wine. During the drive home, a violent argument had flared up, and both had said things they later regretted, things that were impossible to unsay.

Now he felt something like what he'd felt then. A wave of anger so intense that it seemed to drain him of energy. Then, just as quickly as it had flared, it died.

He'd been a rookie still when his mother died. Fresh from the Ecole Nationale Supérieure des Officiers de Police, painfully and proudly aware of his father's disappointment. He'd always looked to his mother for affirmation. His father wasn't talking to him, not since he'd decided not to pursue a career in mathematics even after completing his degree. Morel's mother, who'd arrived in the French capital from Cambodia as a seventeen-year-old music prodigy, knew something about her son's state of mind. Her own father, a minister in Sihanouk's government, had sent her to Paris to study music at the conservatory. She never finished her studies, choosing instead to follow an ambitious young man who'd joined the civil service to his first posting in Beijing, the day after her nineteenth birthday.

The courtyard was filled with shadows. As Morel watched, he saw the neighbour's lights go out. His eyelids were getting heavy but he was on edge, thinking about his father – and of Isabelle Dufour.

In the family living room, among his father's CDs, he found Fauré's *Requiem*, as he had known he would. Back in his room, he put headphones on so that his father wouldn't hear him and sat in the blue armchair by the window, with all the lights off except for his bedside lamp.

'In Paradisum', the tune that Elisabeth Guillou had hummed and whistled so vigorously for him, was the work's seventh and final movement. He listened for a while but found he could not bear it for long. It reminded him of weekends when, as a child, he struggled to fill the emptiness around him. Each hour seemed like it would never end. He re-enacted war games with his toy soldiers on the stairs while just steps away behind closed doors his father played music loudly in the living room, lost in his own private world. His mother and sisters remained upstairs. There was always noise and laughter there. Morel could have joined them but something drew him to the closed door and the presence of the solitary man behind it.

He turned off the CD player and tried to read for a while but ended up watching TV instead. An American cop show where investigators collected evidence in the most improbable ways. Morel found it mildly entertaining for a while, until the absurdity of it all irritated him. Why were these shows so moronic? He poured himself another glass of wine and watched the late news. There was nothing fresh since the earlier broadcast, and nothing about Isabelle Dufour, but then he hadn't expected anything. One old woman's death was hardly news.

Close to midnight, Morel dialled Solange's number. It was far too late to call her but some perverse reflex made him wait until the moment he knew for certain his call would be disruptive.

Neither she nor her husband bothered to answer. He let the phone ring twenty, twenty-five times before hanging up.

He undressed and brushed his teeth, and got under the covers. He was exhausted but too wound up to sleep. As he lay there on his back, he thought about Isabelle Dufour, lying in her tidy bed, her fingers folded around a crucifix.

He thought about the man and the boy going around knocking on doors, seeking out the vulnerable. Could they be responsible for Isabelle Dufour's death somehow? It seemed an unlikely supposition. Where was the motive?

But if not those two, then who? And why had they taken so much care with the body? She had looked so peaceful, lying there. Like she was asleep. It was hard to picture what had gone on before, the violence that had preceded her death. Morel thought about what Martin had said, about the bruises on Dufour's arms. Had she tried to fight back? Or had she given up at once, knowing she was no match for her aggressor?

He got up again and made his bed, tucking the sheets in

tight at each end. Then, slowly and carefully, he slid under the covers. One side was not as tidy as the other now. He reached one arm out and tried to pull the sheet tighter at that end.

He lay still with his eyes closed, picturing the apartment where Dufour had died. Among her many belongings there had been a sense of neglect. The cleaning woman had come three times a week to sweep and collect the dust, to freshen the place up, but you couldn't breathe life into things that were unloved.

What was it Maria had said? That Isabelle Dufour had lived an introverted life. Had she lost interest in the outside world as she grew older or had she always been this way? Morel pictured his father, sitting up in bed upstairs.

Morel pulled a pillow from beneath his head and rolled over to his side. He longed for a cigarette.

His bedside lamp was still on, casting shadows on the ceiling. For a long time he lay awake with his eyes wide open.

FIVE

'So you're still driving that tractor,' Lila said, looking at his car parked next to the police vehicle they were taking to visit Jacques Dufour at his Neuilly home.

Morel ignored her comment. The cherry red Volvo, a 1962 PV544 model, was close to his heart. Never mind that it was a subject of great hilarity to his colleagues, who thought it a middle-aged car. After all, he and his car were only four years apart in age.

Jean and Marco had spent the previous afternoon talking to everyone in the vicinity of Guillou's, Latour's and Volkoff's homes. Before meeting up with Jean, Marco had also gone back to Dufour's building. It seemed that no one recognized the description of the two evangelists.

'How is that possible?' Lila said. 'It's like they don't exist, except in these women's imaginations.'

'We can only assume that there's a reason why the evangelists picked these women. Did they think they needed saving? They turn up on their doorstep and preach to them. Make them feel uncomfortable,' Morel said.

'But why?'

'Let's imagine a scenario where they had something to do with Isabelle Dufour's death,' Morel said, ignoring her question. 'They visit her, stand on her doorstep for a while delivering their spiel on religion, then come back a week later to kill her.'

'Maybe they knew her personally? Maybe she had something they wanted?' Lila said.

'There's no evidence anything was taken,' Morel said.

'So she said or did something that threatened them?'

They were both silent for a while, trying to make sense of this.

'Remember the concierge in Dufour's building didn't always have her eye on the ball,' Lila said. 'Someone else might have visited Dufour without her noticing.'

'True,' Morel said. 'But we also know that the evangelists didn't visit anyone else in the building. So it was her specifically they were looking for. They also went straight to Guillou, Latour and Volkoff. None of their neighbours. That means we need to find them. Right now they are the only strong lead we have.'

Lila began rolling a cigarette. Morel tried to ignore the sharp smell of tobacco, which immediately made him think of the gratification of taking a long, satisfying draw. Lila's fingers moved deftly over the paper, rolling it into a perfect, tight cylinder. A quick flick of the tongue and she was done.

'Did Jean call the lab yesterday?' Lila asked.

'Yes. No fingerprints on the pamphlets at the Dufour apartment, except hers.'

Lila raised the cigarette to her lips before remembering that she couldn't light it yet. She kept it between her fingers, in her lap.

'What's the link between the four women?' she said. 'All four of them, if we include Dufour, live well away from each other,' Lila said.

'Maybe they were acquainted through a shared hobby or interest. Or they frequented the same place. A place where for some reason these two guys marked them. Without being noticed themselves, apparently. None of the widows remember seeing them before they turned up at their door.'

'So maybe the theatre or opera. Or a swimming-pool?'

'They live too far apart to go to the same pool. So it has to be something else.'

'They do have a few things in common, don't they? They are all widows. And they all seem to spend very little time with their kids. At least that's the impression I got, reading through the transcripts,' Lila said. 'Also, they may live in different areas, but the places these women live in are quite similar, when you think about it. Latour lives in Maisons-Laffitte, Guillou in Saint-Germain-en-Laye and Volkoff in Versailles. Not exactly working-class areas,' Lila concluded. 'You'd have to be pretty well off to afford a house in any of them.'

'What about Dufour? She lives in Neuilly, that's an inner-city suburb. All the others live further out of the city. So Dufour's different.'

'Still wealthy, though. Those apartments, in her building? What would they be worth? A million euros? More maybe?'

Lila pulled a lighter from her pocket.

'Don't even think of lighting that before we get there and you're out of the car,' Morel said.

She gave him a malevolent look. 'I meant to ask: how are those patches working for you?'

'I'm not using patches any more.'

'Ah, that explains it.'

They parked outside a house that was so large Morel checked the mailbox to see whether there was more than one occupant. There wasn't. He was about to press the intercom button but then the gates opened. Morel looked up to see a camera pointing at them.

'Well, that's handy,' he murmured.

'His and hers,' Lila said, nodding towards the dark blue Jaguar and silver Peugeot convertible parked in the open double garage.

As they walked to the house they could hear a child wailing, and then the sound of a door slamming inside. Lila lit her cigarette and inhaled deeply.

'Sounds like the family's enjoying some quality time,' she said.

The front door opened and a woman stood before them. She smiled, though she was evidently distraught. The black eyeliner around her eyes was smudged and the tip of her nose red as though she'd been crying. She was in her forties and even in this state it was clear she was striking, the sort of woman who would still turn heads in the street.

'If this is a bad time,' Morel began, but the woman waved her hand to usher them in.

'Sorry about the mess,' she said.

Morel and Lila stepped into a living room that was spotless. The wailing child could still be heard somewhere in the upper floors.

'You must be Anne Dufour,' Morel said.

'Yes. And this is my husband, Jacques,' she said, and from the sofa a man got up and extended his hand. He was a good-looking man in his fifties, a good ten years older than his wife, Morel guessed, and not as striking. Still, they made an attractive couple. Morel could imagine they would be popular at dinner parties.

'I am sorry for your loss,' Morel said, looking at Jacques Dufour as he said it. 'It must have been a shock.'

'My mother and I were not close,' he said. Seeing Morel's expression, he added, 'but yes, it was a shock. She was getting on but in good health.'

'I know you said you think it's a suspicious death,' Jacques Dufour continued. 'I really don't understand how that can be. Who could possibly have wanted to kill her?'

A woman in a maid's uniform walked in with a tray and set it on the table.

'Coffee?' Anne Dufour asked. Without waiting for an answer she poured two cups, for Lila and Morel. Morel picked his up and looked around the room. He thought about Isabelle Dufour and remembered something that Lila had noticed straight away at the dead woman's flat. There hadn't been a single photograph. It seemed odd, for an elderly woman with children and grandchildren.

'At this stage we really don't know. But it's what we're trying to find out. Did you know who her friends were, the people in her life?' Morel said.

Jacques Dufour stirred a teaspoon of sugar into his coffee. 'She had a few old friends but they're all the same age as her. Hardly the sort to go around murdering people.'

'I'd be grateful if you could pass on any names and phone numbers of friends your mother had. Anyone else you've noticed in her life? Any new faces lately?'

'I'll give you any information I have, but like I said, we weren't close. If there was anyone else in her life, anyone she met recently, I wouldn't know, I'm afraid.'

'How often did you and your mother see each other?' Morel asked.

'She came for dinner once a month.'

'And I understand you rarely visited her.'

'Yes, well, I'm a busy man. It was easier for her to come over here.'

Easier for you, Morel thought.

'So the last time you saw her would have been—'

'Two weeks ago. She was here for dinner.'

'Have you spoken to her at all during the past fortnight?'

Jacques Dufour thought for a moment and shook his head. 'She didn't like the phone much. Often she didn't bother answering it. It was maddening. That's old age for you.'

'Sounds quite healthy to me,' Lila said. 'All of us are much too dependent on our phones and gadgets these days, don't you think?' She smiled sweetly.

'I can't afford not to answer my phone,' Jacques Dufour said. 'People depend on me.'

'That must be hard. That burden of responsibility,' Lila said.

'Do you have any brothers or sisters, Monsieur Dufour?' Morel asked. He gave Lila a look. She'd seen it before. It meant shut up and behave.

'Two sisters and a brother.'

'And did they spend much time with your mother?'

Jacques Dufour shrugged his shoulders. 'My sisters both live in America. They couldn't wait to get out of here. They know as well as I do that France is still caught up in the Middle Ages. While the world turns, we're being left behind with our antiquated socialist ideals. We're so caught up in the past, so busy venerating our ancestors that we're completely unprepared for what lies ahead. The future is elsewhere. I should have followed my sisters but things turned out otherwise.'

He gave Morel a bitter look.

A well-rehearsed little speech, Morel thought. He imagined it had been delivered many times and was well received among the Dufours' wealthy friends.

'And your brother? Does he live overseas too?'

'He lives in Marseille. He owns a fishing business. Takes people out on fishing expeditions, that sort of thing. He rarely comes up to Paris.'

'I see.' Morel pretended to write something in his notebook but he was thinking about Isabelle Dufour. A woman with four children, who had lived and loved and raised a family, yet ended up dying on her own, surrounded by indifference.

'I've contacted my siblings,' Dufour said. 'To tell them about our mother. They'll fly back for the funeral, of course.' He looked at his watch. 'Was there anything else?'

'At this point, probably not,' Morel said. He stood up. 'We'll be in touch once we know more.'

Anne Dufour had remained on the edge of the sofa, quiet, smiling vacantly, but now she suddenly spoke up.

'Jacques wasn't always here when his mother came for dinner. But she came regardless of that. And I visited her with the children. Our youngest loved his grandmother.'

'I understand you have two children?'

'That's right.'

'Look,' Jacques Dufour said, standing up. 'I need to leave now if I'm going to catch my flight.'

'How long are you away for, Monsieur Dufour?' Morel asked.

'Two nights.'

'I see.'

'Talk to my wife, she has all the time in the world to answer your questions. The most she's got on is a manicure or a date with her personal trainer, isn't that right, dear?'

His words hung in the air while Morel and Lila glanced at each other and at Anne Dufour, whose face looked like it might crack from the tightness of her smile. Jacques Dufour gave his wife a perfunctory kiss and strode out the door with a wave. They heard the sound of the car engine and tyres on gravel as he pulled out of the driveway.

Upstairs, the sound of the crying child had stopped. There

was instead the sound of a vacuum-cleaner being moved across the floor. Anne Dufour looked at her hands.

'How old are the children?' Morel asked.

She looked up and her eyes flitted over his face, as though struggling to remember what he was doing here.

'The youngest is five. The older boy is fourteen. He's at boarding school.' She shrugged her shoulders and smiled. 'Jacques isn't his father.'

'Madame Dufour,' Morel said. 'Would you sit down and tell us about your mother-in-law. The sort of woman she was. Whether she had many friends, whether she went out much, whether she was religious at all.'

Anne Dufour continued to smile. Morel realized he was smiling too, the same insincere widening of the lips. He stopped.

'I don't know if she had any friends,' she said finally. 'I only know she got very little from her family.'

'Were there any problems?' Morel asked.

Anne Dufour looked at Morel properly then. 'Problems? I suppose it depends what you define as a problem. I mean, these things are relative, aren't they?'

'When did you see or speak to her last, Madame Dufour?' Morel asked.

The reply came without hesitation. 'It was two days before she died.'

Anne Dufour smiled. This time the smile was both sad and genuine.

'She told me on the phone that she was happy, that she hadn't felt so good in years. She sounded cheerful, optimistic.'

'Any idea why that was?' Lila asked.

Anne Morel wiped a tear from her face.

'I didn't ask,' she said.

SIX

He knows the neighbourhood well. He comes here each Saturday when the boys are playing soccer, sits on the sidelines with the other dads and mums. Pretends he is here with his kid too. Cheers, but not too loudly. Wouldn't want anyone to get too friendly, to start asking, which one is yours? It happened to him once before and he pointed his chin towards the playing field, keeping his arms crossed against his chest. He thought he saw the woman look at him a little more carefully than she should after that.

It freaked him out. Not that he's doing anything wrong, it's just an innocent game he likes to play. He sits there and makes himself believe he is a father watching his son kick a ball on a football pitch. Him and César. Only César isn't there, he doesn't take him to the soccer grounds and he knows what people would think if they realized he was on his own.

Now he turns up at a different field, at the other end of the city. Here the parents seem less concerned with chatting. No one's bringing back coffees for everyone or walking expensive dogs on leashes around the pitch. There are no long-legged, smooth-complexioned girls standing on the field looking bored while the fathers try their best to look as if they don't see the unattainable future in their daughters' sleek limbs.

He is not interested in the girls but they are fascinating, in a way. To be so certain that you own the future, that the world will flatter and reward you. Looking at these girls, it seems to him that attitude is all you need. The rest just follows. Someone should have told him that back then.

César too is slender. He has the same refined looks that can't be bought. He could be one of them if it weren't for the weakness in his leg. And then there is his muteness. He cannot speak, has no means to defend himself or tell people his story.

Armand doesn't know the full story but he has lain awake at night trying to block the images. The cold, bleak building where he first met César. Rows of tightly packed beds. The still, malnourished bodies of small children. Lying on their backs or curled up for days on end because no one has the time or the heart to pick them up. And the smell! The first time he'd walked into the room, he'd gagged.

Armand knows what it's like to have a broken heart, but he cannot begin to imagine what César has borne. There is a point at which numbness overtakes pain, which is where César is at, he thinks. How else can you live?

Sometimes he thinks about what will happen to César if he dies. César is not his real name, but he thought it a kindness to give it to him. What better way to wipe out the past and get a fresh start than to take an emperor's name? They had picked it together, that first year of their new life together.

'César,' Armand had said. 'Emperor of the Romans.' The boy had smiled then, for the first time.

God is on their side, Armand thinks. So many people think this means something big and obvious, but it doesn't. Armand sees it as a constellation of stars that brightens a corner of your life, the way a torch will form a tidy circle of light in the dark.

SEVEN

After they'd interviewed the Dufours, Morel dropped Lila back at the office to brief the rest of the team.

'Where are you off to?' she asked.

'Going to see a friend of mine who might be able to help us with the pamphlet,' Morel said.

He had intended to drive straight to Nanterre but instead Morel took a detour by Neuilly, thinking he might drop in at home and check on his father. He'd left early to avoid having breakfast with him, but he felt uneasy. His father was becoming more solitary, withdrawing further into his books. He wondered whether the old man was all right.

It was a broody, restless sort of day. On Avenue de Neuilly, a woman who looked a lot like Solange stepped out of a caterer's carrying a large box tied with a ribbon. A traffic warden was walking the streets, avoiding eye contact. It looked like it might rain. Morel hoped it would, just to clear the air.

He parked outside his house and got out. Just then his phone rang. It was Adèle, asking whether they could meet up.

'When?'

'Now, if you can.'

'Now is a bit difficult.' It amazed him, the way his sisters believed he could drop everything whenever they wanted to see him. He wondered what it was about this time. Not a week went by without one or the other calling about something they thought was essential for him to know. Except that lately Maly hadn't been calling at all.

'Then when? It's important.'

He named a cafe near the Pont-Neuf Métro station, and told her to meet him there at one.

After he hung up, he let himself into the house. In the hallway he ran into Augustine. She greeted him with a kiss on both cheeks.

'Is my father here?' Morel asked.

She shook her head. 'He went out half an hour ago.'

'How did he look?'

'Same as always. Like a gentleman.'

Morel smiled. Augustine searched his face.

'Is something the matter?'

He reached out and touched her arm.

'No, nothing at all. I'd better go, I have a meeting.'

At Nanterre University it took him a while to find the building he was looking for. The place was like a rabbit warren. When he finally found the right door, he knocked. Before Morel knew it, he was wrapped in a hug that left him momentarily deprived of oxygen.

Morel stood back and looked at his old university buddy. He was as big and unkempt as ever. His hair was longer and he wore a beard now, making him look even more like a playful and vigorous Old English Sheepdog.

'Well, well,' the man said, 'this is quite a treat.'

He patted Morel on the back and invited him to sit down. Morel looked around him. The office was tiny and chaotic. He wondered how his friend managed to manoeuvre his way around the place without upsetting the many books and piles of paper. It would require some delicate footwork. That was hard to picture.

'There's public education for you,' Chesnay said, reading his mind. 'Everything done on the cheap.' He raised a meaty forefinger. 'Shitty digs, shitty classrooms. What does that equal? Grumpy lecturers doing a half-arsed job. Everyone has a right to an education though, just as long as they don't expect a decent one as well.'

His voice was deep and sonorous. Morel imagined he would have no trouble holding his students' attention.

'How have you been, Paul?' He asked. The two had been on the same mathematics course at university before both realizing they wanted to do something different. Morel hadn't contacted his friend in years.

'Busy and thriving.' Chesnay gave Morel a keen look filled with the curiosity Morel had always loved him for, and sat back with his hands folded on his stomach. 'So tell me,' he said, 'how a humble professor of theology such as myself can be of assistance to an eminent commandant of the *brigade criminelle*.'

Morel pulled the pamphlet from his pocket and placed it on the desk before him. 'I'd like to know what you think of this.'

Chesnay peered at the pamphlet before putting on a pair of tortoiseshell glasses.

'My sight isn't quite what it used to be,' he said.

'I bet the girls love the glasses, though.'

'Yes, I finally look like an academic,' Chesnay said.

He spent the next few minutes reading through the brochure in silence. Morel looked around the room. Despite being tiny it was comfortable. It was a place that would make you forget the outside world. Morel couldn't remember if Chesnay was married.

'Any idea what sort of church would put out something like that?' he asked finally.

'It's a hodge-podge of things, isn't it?' Chesnay said slowly. 'A bit of this, a bit of that. At times, the language is reminiscent of the sort of evangelical material you might expect, say, a Baptist church to circulate. For example, where it says: *Are you born again? Have you accepted the shed blood of Christ as the atonement for your sins?* But then there's this' – he pointed to an illustration – 'which is very Russian and one of the leading symbols of the Orthodox Church.'

'What is it?'

'A copy of Andrey Rublev's Old Testament Trinity. It depicts the three angels visiting Abraham.'

'I'm afraid I've never heard of Rublev,' Morel said.

'Andrey Rublev is perhaps Russia's most famous iconographer. Late fourteenth–early fifteenth century. The Moscow Patriarchate made a big deal about him in the 1980s – all part of the Gorbachev-led revival, perestroika and glasnost etc. When all was forgiven and God was no longer considered a pariah.'

'Russia?' Morel thought about Irina Volkoff. She had said she thought the boy at her door was Russian.

'Yes. After the collapse of the USSR, and without the safety net afforded by the Soviet state in areas like housing, health and education, people found themselves struggling, particularly the older generation. Many Russians started looking for something to fill the void left by the fall of communism. Religion was the obvious answer, but the Russian Orthodox Church, as you may already know, was discredited during Soviet times; people believed the Church was in cahoots with the Soviet regime, which of course it was. So many Russians turned to other religions.'

'What kind?'

Paul Chesnay rested his hands on his stomach and looked at Morel.

'Everything – you name it. Hare Krishnas, Moonies, Mormons. Some have been more successful than others. As it happens, the evangelical churches have done particularly well over there. Nowadays you'll find, for example, that roughly half of all Baptists in Europe are Russian. It is astonishing in a way, when you consider how different these evangelical religions are to the austere formality of the Orthodox Church. Then again, maybe the very reason they have attracted so many people is because their characteristics are so far from the old-school rituals. When Billy Graham visited Moscow in 1992, just a year or so after the break-up of the Soviet Union, he made quite a splash.'

Morel tried to picture the American pastor on his Russian pilgrimage, anointing a congregation of new converts. It had a touch of the surreal, though it could be said that America had always exported its beliefs in some form or another. Politics or religion, it was a fine line that separated the two as far as that country was concerned.

'Is any of that useful to you?' Chesnay asked.

'Everything you've said is interesting and helps, in a sense. In some ways, though, it doesn't make my job any easier,' Morel admitted. 'I can't work out where I should be looking.'

Chesnay took off his glasses and pinched his nose. 'All I can say is that it's unlikely to have come from an established organization. It's not coherent at all. I'd say it's the work of an individual on a personal crusade. Incidentally,' Chesnay continued, 'I notice your guy keeps coming back to the word "crusade". Now there's a word that crops up often among Baptists, particularly your modern-day Southern Baptists. Including the illustrious Billy Graham,' he said, articulating the word *illustrious* with exaggerated emphasis.

'In what sense?' Morel asked.

'Graham called his evangelizing sessions crusades, after the medieval Christian campaigns to conquer Jerusalem. Like I said, these are people who see themselves as crusaders for truth, seeking to redeem a new Holy Land.'

Morel was wondering what any of this had to do with his case. 'So you think my evangelist could be one of these crusaders?'

Chesnay stood up and paced the narrow area behind his desk. He cut a ludicrous figure, like a bear trying to pace inside a phone booth.

'Could be, could be. He's definitely on a mission. Though *what* he's preaching is hard to tell. Going by what's in here –' he tapped the pamphlet with his hand, 'he's pretty confused. And he's not acting on anyone's behalf. Organizations that are trying to draw people in usually have some sort of contact details on their brochures. This one has no number, website or email – nothing.'

'I noticed that too,' Morel said. 'So why distribute something like this at all, if no one can come back to you? What would someone get out of it?'

'Maybe they genuinely believe they are spreading the word of God.'

'Saving souls.'

'Maybe. Or maybe he's trying to save himself.'

EIGHT

Morel got back to Quai des Orfèvres at 12.30 and parked the car. From the office he walked towards the Pont-Neuf, past the bronze equestrian statue of Henry IV, one of France's most popular kings before he was killed by a fanatical Catholic at the age of fifty-six. His popularity had stemmed from the novel fact that he seemed genuinely interested in the welfare of his subjects. Even more untypical at the time was the monarch's religious tolerance. Maybe someone like Henry IV would be better suited as France's ruler in 2010 than Sarkozy, Morel reflected. Tolerance was not high on this government's agenda.

Henry IV was getting a fair bit of media coverage this week following the announcement that a forensic examiner with Poincaré University Hospital in Garches had identified the king's mummified head, thus solving a 400-year-old mystery. The head had vanished in 1793, presumed taken by robbers during an attack on graves at the Royal Basilica.

Leaving Henry IV behind, Morel thought back to his conversation with Paul Chesnay. He thought about Russia and the New Age missionaries who were flocking there. His conversation with Paul had been stimulating, as always, but did it have anything to do with Dufour's death? Morel felt like a man without a compass. He had no idea which direction he needed to take.

Adèle was at a table drinking coffee when he got there. She smiled when he walked in.

'Thanks for agreeing to see me,' she said. Of Morel's two sisters she resembled him the more. They had both inherited their father's height and their mother's dusky looks – her thick black hair and smooth complexion.

Adèle stirred her coffee and crossed her legs. She wore a red strapless dress that fell to just above her ankles. Black sandals and crimson toenails. Hair worn loose around her shoulders. The dress clung to her body, drawing stares.

'What is it? Has something happened?' He caught the waiter's eye and called him over. He ordered a coffee. Tables were set up outside on the cobbled footpath. Morel watched the smokers sitting at the outdoor tables and wished he were among them.

'It's Maly. Karl has asked her to marry him.'

'And?' Morel said. Already he was beginning to wonder why he'd agreed to this meeting in the middle of a busy day. He didn't have time to discuss his sisters' love lives.

'She said yes.'

'Did she now?' He looked at his sister. 'That's great.'

'Is it?'

'I think so. Karl's a nice guy.'

'You don't know a thing about him.'

'Do you?'

'I know he's dull.'

'What has that got to do with you?' Morel said.

'She's not happy. I think she's going through with this because she's getting on and worries that otherwise she'll miss the boat.'

'What boat?'

'The baby boat.'

Morel sighed and looked at his watch. 'I really can't discuss this now. I have to get back to work,' he said.

'Will you talk to her?'

'What do you want me to say?'

'Nothing! Just see how she is.'

'Sure, I'll give her a ring,' Morel said. He didn't tell Adèle that he'd already tried several times and left messages. Maly wasn't returning his calls.

'Thank you.' She seemed to relax, and she looked at him now, while he fished in his pocket for change to pay for their drinks. 'What about you? How's life at home with Dad?'

Morel counted out the coins and left them on the table. 'It's fine. He's a bit difficult at times.'

Adèle snorted. 'A bit! I don't know how you can stand it.'

Morel leaned over and kissed her cheek. 'I have to go.'

'Promise you'll call Maly?' Adèle said.

'I'll do it,' he said.

'When are you going to move out?' she called out as he started to cross the road.

'Soon.' He raised his hand.

Walking back to the office, he thought about Maly. He liked Karl. Maly had always had a weakness for academics. Karl was one of the more presentable ones she'd latched on to. In her younger days Morel had watched them come and go, a few of them insufferable, more interested in posing as writers and thinkers than in actually producing anything. They let their hair grow long and wore scarves all year round, regardless of the weather. In their back pockets they carried poetry paperbacks, making sure the title was clearly visible. On more than one occasion, as a younger man, Morel had sat and argued with Maly's boyfriends over a cheap bottle of wine at her flat. Animated discussions where some pseudo-intellectual with Trotsky-like hair and glasses would try to tell him that art without suffering was meaningless. That communism was the future, even when it became apparent that the communists themselves had stopped believing it.

Pompous narcissists, many of them. Entertaining, though. Morel had enjoyed riling them.

How long had it been since he'd last seen Maly? Six, seven weeks? It niggled at him, the fact that he'd let so much time go by. The two of them had been close since their mother's death. Over the past year they had grown apart. He wasn't sure why.

He thought about Adèle's question. When was he going to move out and get his own place?

It was more than twenty years now since his mother's death. Morel had made the decision then to move back in with his father.

It hadn't been an entirely selfless decision. Walking back across the Pont-Neuf, Morel thought of Mathilde, his first love, whose memory he couldn't seem to shake, even now. He'd lived with her for two years, the happiest time of his life, before throwing it all away. Then he'd lost his mother. Frightened at the extent of his despair, he'd retreated to his childhood home.

He had grown used to his mother's absence, but he still mourned Mathilde, who was living her life without him.

The truth was that, since moving back in with his father he had never seriously contemplated a change. He'd never hankered for his own place.

It struck him as strange now.

As he neared the police headquarters on Quai des Orfèvres, he started to feel anxious. Would he always live with his father? Would he wake up one day and find that they had become two grumpy old men living together, bickering over who had forgotten to turn the lights off before going to bed? His father lost in his books, and Morel seeking some form of resolution to the violence he dealt with each day. It was a bleak prospect, but for now he couldn't see his way out of it.

Back at his desk, Morel went over his interview with Chesnay and studied the pamphlet. He scanned Lila's list of religious organizations again and added a couple of names to it, based on Paul's suggestions. Lila and Marco were out talking to every religious organization that seemed most relevant. Morel made some calls of his own, but drew a blank.

He tried to picture the sort of man who would produce a pamphlet like the one he had before him. A man who seemed to be acting on his own behalf. Chesnay was right. There was no consistency in the message. Morel had the impression that the pamphlet's author was confused.

Maybe it was a sign of the times, Morel thought. Every day he encountered people who had lost their way. Many who were down at heel and many who had only recently fallen on hard times. Often when he worked nights he saw people brought in looking like they had no clue how they'd arrived here. Once when he'd been working late, it had been a middle-aged woman in a Chanel suit. A couple of the regular girls who worked the Place Dauphine had got into a brawl with her for trying to sell her wares on their patch. Bloody and dishevelled, she'd stayed at the station until her husband was tracked down. When he'd come to fetch her Morel had recognized him as the CEO of one of the larger banks. It was getting harder to predict what you might see, who might come staggering through the door, who might be handcuffed because they were a threat to others or to themselves.

Lila and Marco returned empty-handed. None of the people they'd talked to had seen or heard of the two evangelists described by the widows. His officers looked as discouraged as he felt.

'We'll reconvene tomorrow at eight o'clock sharp. Now get out of here,' Morel said.

He spent another hour in the office, going through the Dufour folder for the tenth time and typing up a brief report for Perrin, which he intended to leave on the other man's desk.

It was close to 7 p.m. when he finally turned the lights off and left the building. For a moment he was tempted to cancel dinner and head home, but then the thought of Solange reminded him of what he would miss.

It was time to go if he didn't want to be late. First, he would pick up a nice bottle of wine and some flowers. White, always her favourite.

Morel parked his car in a no-parking spot right outside the entrance to Solange's building and got out. For a moment he stood under the streetlight, feeling like he had left something behind. But he held the flowers in one hand and the bottle in the other. His wallet and car keys were in his pocket. He pushed the doorbell and waited.

Solange had once told Morel there was something old-fashioned about him that made it seem as though he'd landed in the wrong decade. Maybe even the wrong century. It could have been what drew her to him, Morel thought. Her husband Henri was a relic too. A man twice Solange's age, who rarely left the house and struggled to face the world outside his lavish home. Most of the time he was cooped up in his expansive sixteenth-century apartment with its barrel-vaulted stone cellars and elaborate staircase.

The door buzzed and Morel pushed it open. He climbed the stairs to the first floor. The apartment stretched over three floors of the five-storey building.

It was lucky, Morel reflected, that Henri was enormously wealthy, thanks to a family inheritance and a portfolio of properties left to him by his father, including a nice little vineyard in the Saumur region where, according to Solange, Henri had proposed to her.

At the top of the stairs, the door was open and Solange stood waiting for him, wearing a green silk dress he hadn't seen before.

'I'm sorry I'm late,' he said. The dress with its clingy material and low décolletage left little to the imagination. His eyes travelled back to her face. She was flushed and seemed happy to see him.

'You look beautiful, Solange.'

She smiled and opened the door wider to let him in.

'Come in and make yourself comfortable. I'll get Henri.'

He watched her climb the stairs.

'Morel is here,' she called out to her husband.

'Good,' Morel heard Henri say. 'I'll be right there.'

Solange came back down the stairs and walked up to Morel. She touched his shoulder, her face close to his.

'He's on his way,' she said.

Soon Henri de Fontenay came into the room with a broad grin on his face. The two men embraced.

'It's good to see you. Solange got you a drink?'

'I was about to.'

'Let me do it. What will you have, Morel? And you, darling?'

'You choose,' Solange said. Henri's question was rhetorical. He had already picked out and uncorked the wine, and he poured it now, telling Morel he was in for a treat.

'It's a 1982 Château Margaux. I saved it for you,' he said, handing a glass to Morel.

Morel took a sip, letting the liquid roll around his tongue while Henri watched approvingly.

'How's your father?' he asked.

'He seems well.'

'Tell him he should pick up the phone once in a while.'

'You know what he's like.'

'I do. He's becoming a hermit in his old age.'

'He always was. Just had to work, that was the difference.'

Henri laughed. He and Morel's father had gone to school together before going their separate ways, Morel senior pursuing a diplomatic career and Henri taking over the family's real-estate empire, which he managed from the confines of his home. The two had remained close.

Henri had married Solange on his sixty-fourth birthday. She had been twenty-five then. 'They met at the chemist,' Philippe Morel had told his son, with a look of disbelief. 'She was a pharmacist, or maybe not, just an ordinary shop girl. He liked the look of her and instead of just sleeping with her he decided to get married.'

'He's a romantic,' Morel said.

'Bloody stupid, you mean. What can they possibly have in common?'

Yet eight years on Henri and Solange seemed perfectly happy with each other. They had the sort of partnership that some couples seemed to manage, open and affectionate, each leaving the other to pursue their interests and, in Solange's case, occasional affairs.

Since the wedding, Henri and Morel's father had lost touch. Without saying it openly, Henri clearly felt it was because Morel Senior disapproved of his young wife. Morel thought it had more to do with his father's increasing reluctance – or was it inability? – to socialize.

Thinking of his father now, he wondered what the old man would say if he knew about his son's involvement with Henri's wife. It was unthinkable. The funny thing was that Henri knew and accepted Morel's involvement in his wife's life. There was no way of knowing what went on in the old man's head, whether his generosity was altruism or whether he was getting his kicks out of the situation. Knowing his wife enjoyed being screwed by another man. Morel chose not to dwell on it.

They ate at the bench in the kitchen, where the couple liked to have their meals. The dining table was reserved for dinner parties. Solange had prepared a dinner of cold lobster, poached salmon and salad. She ate very little. Most of the time she sipped at her drink, resting one arm on the counter. The dress, like the lobster, was expensive. It allowed him to see her almost as he would if she were naked. With Henri in the room, he tried not to stare at her too blatantly.

Henri didn't give him much time to feel self-conscious. After dinner, they had another glass of wine together, and Henri made coffee. Then he excused himself, saying he would have his coffee in his study. He gave Morel a kiss on the cheek. Not for the first time, Morel felt he was receiving the older man's blessing. In the early days it had confused him, but he accepted it now without any reservation.

'I have some work to do, and an early start tomorrow. I'll leave you two now.' He kissed his wife tenderly, one hand stroking the back of her neck.

Solange and Morel moved together to the sofa. Solange sat opposite him. Neither one of them said a word. For a while they listened to Henri's footsteps above. Her gaze never wavered from his.

'Long day?' she said.

'Very.'

Morel reached over and pulled down the straps of her dress. It fell easily around her waist. She wasn't wearing a bra. He sighed as he sat back and stared at her.

'I've been wanting to do that since I walked through the door.'

She leaned back, letting her hands rest on the sofa and the dress fall further down her hips. He could tell there was nothing else on her, besides the thin silk dress.

'What else?' she said, while he let his eyes travel from her breasts down to the curve of her hips. 'What else have you been wanting to do?'

Later they got dressed and she offered him another drink. His mouth felt dry and he didn't really want another glass of wine but he took it anyway. After sex, Solange seemed to shed one skin in favour of another, more self-assured.

Out on the balcony the air was barely any cooler. Down below there was a shout, and Morel thought there might be trouble. Perhaps a fight had broken out. But then there was laughter. Still, it made him edgy.

Solange touched his arm. The pressure of her hand was proprietorial. She left it there, unmoving. Gradually, his breathing slowed down. He found himself looking out at the night without trying to guess what it might conceal.

NINE

Elisabeth Guillou closed her book and yawned. She looked at her watch. It was still only 8.30. She would usually be ready for bed around 9.30, but it had been a particularly tiring day. Her son had come for lunch with his wife Clare and their two children. The boy had just turned six and was never still; forever looking for an opportunity to do the things he should not. Clare had spent most of the afternoon barking at him while he ignored her with an air of such complete indifference that his grandmother found something to admire in it, though the child's mother clearly did not. Meanwhile Elisabeth Guillou's own son sat there like a sack of potatoes, grinning like a lunatic at some joke only he was privy to. She'd looked at him and wondered when exactly his face had lost its shape and character. It was as inexpressive as a loaf of bread. He and Clare, they were both that way. They both dressed, too, as though appearance no longer mattered.

Elisabeth Guillou yawned again. She wondered what it was about her son's family. She had raised two children herself and could not remember it being as exhausting as they made it out to be. The pair of them looked as though they'd lost their spirit and the children were not much better. Well, the boy was quite lively. He had spent an hour bouncing up and down on the trampoline, so gleeful it had gratified her. Though it wasn't long before she started wondering how her grandson filled his days to get such manic delight from a trampoline. The girl said little and spent her time drawing stick figures with oversized heads. She had a mild form of autism, her father said. Something Syndrome – Elisabeth couldn't remember. Nowadays everything had a name.

She stood up and found herself swaying for a moment. This happened to her when she'd been sitting for a long time, and when she took her glasses off. Her doctor had told her this was quite normal, nothing to do with age, just an adjustment of perspective.

She headed towards the bathroom. It was warm but she didn't like to leave the windows open. Since her husband's death, many years had gone by but still she had not got used to living alone. She did a good job of hiding just how fearful she was. The truth was she only felt safe in her own house, with the windows shut and the door locked. She thought of the inspector whom she had sat with the day before, the handsome one with the dark, thoughtful eyes. She had felt safe with him too.

An attractive and elegant man. Just because she was old didn't mean she couldn't tell a good-looking man when she saw one. Was that why she hadn't been entirely truthful with him? During their meeting, she hadn't given him any indication that she was scared. She hadn't wanted to appear weak.

Foolish old woman, she told herself. Trying to impress a man half her age.

As she walked past the window where the curtains had been left open she sensed rather than saw something. It made her pause and take a few steps back. She put her glasses back on and turned the light off.

After a moment's hesitation, she moved towards the window and looked out at the garden. It was dark but there was a full moon and it lit up the sky like a fluorescent beam. The gardener had recently been to mow the grass. The trees seemed as attentive out there as she was inside, looking for the thing that had caught her attention a moment ago.

There. She hadn't imagined it.

There was someone sitting on the trampoline.

TEN

Morel left Solange at 2 a.m. and drove home. He was probably over the limit but he chanced it anyway. He didn't like to leave his car on the street.

He went straight to bed, but then he woke up at 4.30. He'd dreamed of Mathilde for the first time in months.

He tried to read for a while but found he couldn't focus on the pages. Lila had lent him the book; the first he was reading in maybe a year. He'd liked the start but now he found he couldn't remember the first twenty pages he'd read the day before. He set the book aside and found himself thinking instead about his conversation with Paul. He was quite sure he'd overlooked something that his old friend had said, something important.

At 5 a.m. he gave up trying to sleep and ended up sitting at his desk. He began working on the plan that had started to form in his head, since visiting Isabelle Dufour's apartment.

There were many owl designs out there, quick-and-easy versions that he'd made, but this one was going to be exceptional, if he could just get the mapping right. He thought about Isabelle Dufour's bronze owl and began to draw, sketching each detail with care. The feathered wings and tail; the large, expressive claws; the expression of the face, which he could picture in his mind, but was still trying to figure out how to convey on paper. It couldn't be rushed.

The magic would happen when the design accounted for exactly the right amount of paper to be deployed for each feather, the half blink of an eye, the curve of a claw. Every inch of paper would be used rather than tucked away. That was the elegance Morel strove for. It was the opposite of disorder and wastefulness, which was the natural order of things.

In a design like this, a lot of the paper was hidden, layers that contributed to the final product while remaining invisible. As far as Morel was concerned, the art of origami lay in one's ability to visualize the unseen parts. As he folded, he retained a mental picture of the layers beneath.

He was so engrossed in what he was doing that, when the alarm went off, it took him a while to realize it was morning and time to get ready for work. There was no sound from upstairs but Morel knew his father would come down before him.

Setting his drawings aside, Morel got undressed and stepped into the shower. He turned his mind back to the Dufour case. Here too there were unseen layers that would help form a complete picture, if only he could see them.

ELEVEN

Getting to work turned out to be a nightmare. It took Morel an hour to get across town. What had possessed him to drive? The whole city seemed to be on the march. At Place de la Concorde, he remained stuck in his car for what felt like an eternity. A young man on roller blades zigzagged through the stalled traffic, selling drinks and sandwiches.

Outside the Jardin des Tuileries, protesters waved banners and signs, railing against Sarkozy's plan to kick hundreds of Roma out of the country. It certainly wasn't something to be proud of, Morel thought. His father would no doubt accuse him of being sentimental, but Morel believed in the principles set out in the post-Revolution Declaration of the Rights of Man and of the Citizen. He believed in the ideal that men were born and remained free and equal in their rights. His mother had believed in it too. For her, France had meant a new beginning, away from her war-torn country.

Morel wound his window down and bought a ham sandwich and a bottle of water from the roller-blade boy. He found himself wishing the car had air-conditioning. Maybe he should have it fitted. But something – maybe his ingrained resistance to change – held him back, which was why year after year he never got around to it.

'Face it, you don't like to admit you're living in the twenty-first century,' Lila liked to say.

She had a point.

That morning he had made an effort and sat down with his father for breakfast. They had passed each other sections from the paper and Morel had refrained from taking the bait, as his father commented on what he read. With half the city on strike, there was plenty for him to get riled about.

'Is it another socialist government they want? So we can be as backward as the Russians?' he grumbled.

For an educated man, he talked a lot of rubbish.

Like Sarkozy, Morel Senior believed that getting a job was just a matter of trying harder. Man creates his own misery, we all have the destiny we deserve. It was one way of looking at things.

At least the political commentary was better than the usual sniping about the breakfast table – whether the right kind of cutlery was being used; whether the butter had been taken out early enough to have softened; whether the toast was overdone. Morel sighed. There was no escaping the fact that meals had become difficult. Too much of what was said was trivial and grating, and not enough about the things that mattered.

He scanned the angry faces on the footpath as though he might recognize someone. Most of them were young. A flash of red hair, long and loose, and his heart constricted. Was it her? Mathilde appeared everywhere, but it was unlikely to be her in this crowd.

The traffic crept forward and Morel wedged the Volvo into a narrow opening. Two days earlier thousands of people had taken to the streets to protest against the president's plan to raise the pension age. He wasn't making too many friends these days.

Morel became impatient, pushed his way between two cars, narrowly missing a mirror. One of the drivers whose car he was trying to get past hollered something at him about an old man driving a tank. Morel pretended not to hear.

After remaining stuck in his car for half an hour, while enduring a talk show about the merits of the Dukan Diet – why was he even listening to this drivel? – Morel gave up and parked the car on the wrong side of the river. It took him forty-five minutes to walk the rest of the way, and he arrived at the Quai des Orfèvres drenched in sweat and irritable. When he reached the fourth-floor office, only Lila was in.

She looked up from her desk. She was wearing a white singlet and jeans, and black lace-up shoes. Her dark hair was tied into a long ponytail. Her fringe pushed to the side with a clip. She seemed to find the sight of him amusing.

'Sleep in, did we?' she asked when he walked past her desk.

'You may not have noticed but there's mayhem out there.'

'I know. I walked in.'

'That's nice. Where are the others?'

'Marco's here, he's just at the coffee machine. Jean is reporting to Perrin on the burglary.'

'Any news from Vincent?'

'He called, wants you to call him back.'

'How did he sound?'

Lila paused. 'It's hard to say.'

Marco walked in with a coffee and Morel immediately recognized the smell of the foul brew from the machine in the hallway. Marco raised a hand in greeting.

'I want to take another look at Isabelle Dufour's place,' Morel said. 'I feel like we're missing something. Lila, you and I will go over it together once more.'

'When are we going to do that?'

'How about now?'

'OK.'

'Want me to come with you?' Marco asked.

'No thanks,' Morel said, pretending not to notice Marco's disappointment.

The phone rang and Lila answered. While she dealt with the call, Morel stepped into his lair. It was exactly as he had left it. Everything in its place. Even the cleaning staff that came in to vacuum at night had strict instructions to leave Commandant Morel's territory alone.

He knew there were people within the division who thought him a snob. It wasn't just the antique screen, but also the clothes he wore. Then there was his lack of propensity for after-work drinks and small talk.

Morel wasn't exactly swamped with invitations and his social diary was as lean as a Buddhist monk's. But he wasn't losing any sleep over it.

'I've just got a couple of calls to make and I'm good to go,' Lila called out. 'Five minutes.'

'Fine,' Morel said.

He would have liked to soothe his irritation by adding a humming-bird to his growing paper column, but instead he opened the Dufour folder.

The folder was in his hand when he and Lila stepped into Isabelle Dufour's apartment for the second time. It was midday and, judging by the silence, most of the building's occupants were out for lunch or having a snooze. Morel would have liked to join them. The two hours he'd had the night before hadn't quite done the trick.

'Busy night, then?' Lila had asked, looking him up and down.

Morel slipped on a pair of gloves. 'Something like that.'

Isabelle Dufour's body was at the undertaker's, awaiting burial. But somehow her presence lingered. The silence was filled with the things Morel had learned about her over the past few days. A woman with four children, three of whom lived away from Paris. A son who seemed cold-hearted and self-absorbed, obsessed with his career. Morel was no stranger to obsession and he would pursue an investigation relentlessly until the truth was unearthed. But he did not see himself as central to his work. No one was irreplaceable. Whereas Jacques Dufour was a true narcissist, convinced of his own essential place in the world.

Isabelle Dufour had, at least, developed a bond with her daughter-in-law. It had been obvious, during their interview of the Dufours, that Anne had cared about her husband's mother.

'Want to divide the work up?' Lila said. She stood before him expectantly with her arms crossed. Morel noticed the room's staleness. The muffled sounds of traffic from the street below.

'You take the bedrooms and I'll go through the living and dining area,' he said.

'Yippee. I get the fun stuff.'

Morel watched Lila disappear down the hallway towards the two bedrooms, one of them Isabelle Dufour's and the other a guest room which couldn't have had much use, before turning to the task at hand.

Everything in the main living area was as Morel remembered it. A crocheted blanket lay on one of the two brown sofas. Dufour had probably placed it on her knees or around her shoulders while watching television. A TV magazine. There were no books. A basket on the table held balls of blue and grey wool and several pairs of needles. She had been knitting something, a child's sweater by the looks of it. It was almost finished. Morel wondered whether it was meant for one of her grandchildren.

The furniture was elegant. A console table with light, turned legs. Undoubtedly Louis XVI, Morel decided. It was a period he liked, with its emphasis on straight lines and flat surfaces and refined use of detail. The walnut and rosewood commode with a marble top was undoubtedly of the same period. Morel Senior had an almost identical one in his room. Morel pulled the drawers open. What he found inside the top drawer made him pause. A ladies' gold watch with a broken leather strap and a jumble of bead necklaces. Black-and-white family photos taken during a skiing holiday. A lace handkerchief and a sewing kit. How lifeless one's possessions became after death, Morel thought. In any case there was nothing there that might help progress the investigation.

He closed the drawers and turned back to the room. While the furniture was stylish, all the knick-knacks were a different story. Their only common denominator was an absence of good taste. Porcelain dogs and clowns. A globe with a snowman that produced snow when you shook it. All things that could have been picked up at a jumble sale. Of the four cushions lining the two sofas, no two matched. One had a tapestry cover, the other a crocheted outline of a house. Two depicted animals, one a horse and the other a Dobermann. They were all equally ugly.

He slid the balcony door open and went out. After the silence of the flat, the noise from the traffic below was an assault. The balcony was bare. There were no plants, not even a chair to sit in. Clearly, Isabelle Dufour had not been a gardener. There was a cafe opposite and a newsagent. From her balcony, Dufour would have been able to see anyone coming from across the street.

Why had she opened her door to a stranger? Maybe because she felt safe in her building. She had no reason not to.

Morel went back inside and slid the door shut. He turned to find Lila standing near him. It gave him a start.

'Nothing in the main bedroom.'

Slowly and methodically, they went through the guest room, the kitchen and bathroom, before reconvening in the living room.

It had been a discouraging search, Morel thought. He could see Lila felt the same. It was time to go.

Before leaving, he took one last look around. As his eyes swept the room, the stereo caught his eye, mainly because it was such a dated and clunky model. One with a tape deck and radio included. Nowadays even the cash converters didn't bother with these. Someone, maybe Dufour's son or daughter-in-law, had bought her a cheap CD player as well. Morel wondered why Isabelle Dufour had bothered keeping the old system but then again, she might have found it hard to part with something she'd had for so long.

Without thinking, he went up to the tape deck. He pushed Play. Nothing happened. He tried the CD player.

Sound blasted from the speakers into his ears and he recoiled, immediately turning the volume down. The slow and solemn opening was devastatingly familiar.

'Do you think it was left there intentionally?' Lila said as they headed down in the lift.

'Unless it was left behind because someone forgot to take it back.'

'Or maybe it's just a coincidence,' she said mournfully.

Morel shook his head. This was the second time in two days that he was hearing Fauré's *Requiem*. It could not be accidental.

'Not a coincidence. But the question is, what is it supposed to tell us? What is it for?'

'Beats me.'

'Come on. There's a reason behind it,' Morel said.

'Is the music part of the ritual? Did Dufour have to sit through it before she was drowned?'

'Or while she was drowning. Or being dressed and laid out on her bed,' Morel said.

Lila rubbed her arms and crossed her legs. 'Shit. You know, I can deal with the stabbings and shootings, the normal stuff we see every day.' She caught Morel's eye. 'You know what I mean. But this is different. I told you, we're dealing with a freak.'

'A methodical freak,' Morel said. 'Someone who likes to do things a certain way, tidy and organized. Someone who thinks things through.'

Back in the office, Jean told Morel that Vincent had called again. Morel went straight to his desk and dialled his number. Vincent answered on the first ring.

'It's me,' Morel said. 'Is everything OK?' He realized as soon as he'd said it that it was a stupid thing to say to a man whose wife was dying of cancer.

'I wanted to say I'm sorry I haven't been around. I even forgot to call yesterday . . .'

'Don't be ridiculous, there's nothing more important than what you're doing now. No one expects you to come in when you've got Sylvia to look after. How is she?'

There was a sigh at the end of the line, followed by silence. For a moment, Morel believed he could hear Vincent crying. He felt powerless. This wasn't something he was equipped to deal with.

'Tell me what I can do to help,' he said.

'That's the thing,' Vincent said, his voice unrecognizable. 'There's nothing you or anyone can do. We're alone in this.' He then seemed to make an effort to speak. 'She's running out of time. We're looking at days, maybe a week if we're lucky. They're telling me she should be hospitalized but she really wants to be at home for the little time she's got.'

'Bloody hell, I'm so sorry, Vincent. And the girls?'

'The girls are heartbroken.'

'Look, I'll drop in later, I—'

'Thanks, but please don't,' Vincent said.

Morel waited. Wondering whether he should insist.

'Sure, I understand,' he said finally. 'Just take as much time as you need. You know we'll do anything to make this easier for you.'

After he hung up, Morel looked up to see Jean, Marco and Lila standing there. For a while, no one said anything.

TWELVE

When Lila opened her eyes and saw it was just after 6 a.m., she felt cheated. What was the point of having a day off if you couldn't sleep in? What were you supposed to do at 6 a.m.? Especially if you were waking up alone.

She'd been out late, dancing at a Cuban club where, with the right dose of alcohol and dim lighting, she could convince herself that she moved like a Latin goddess. For close to an hour she'd been trapped in the arms of a sweaty Argentinian who'd flicked his fingers and paced around her with the intensity of a matador facing off a bull. It had been a laugh. She'd come home dripping with sweat, feeling like she'd managed to shake off the disquieting image of Isabelle Dufour's corpse. That hideous make-up and the cheap wig. Coupled with the virginal nightdress and clean white sheets, it added up in Lila's mind to a form of sexual violation as brutal as rape.

She couldn't articulate this clearly. Which was why she hadn't shared her thoughts with Morel or anyone else.

If only she'd brought the quick-footed Argentinian home. Around about now she might be getting a healthy dose of attention. The sort that might help her go back to sleep. Alone, though, there wasn't a hope in hell she would. She was buzzing, feeling like she did sometimes coming out of a club in the early hours of the morning, high from the pumping noise and closeness of bodies, her stomach clamouring for food.

Only it was hours ago she had got home and now she really should be fast asleep. Something had nudged her and woken her up despite her intense tiredness. What was it? Like an urgent reminder in her ear. Something to do with Isabelle Dufour.

She got up to go to the toilet and brush her teeth. In the dead-end street below a Chinese man, one of the workers at the Happy Dumpling restaurant, was dragging a rubbish bin. He seemed to be making a point of going slowly, making sure that everyone in the street would hear it. He unlocked the rear entrance to the restaurant and disappeared inside, taking the bin with him. A skeletal cat followed at a watchful distance and sat on its haunches, waiting for scraps.

'Forget it, pal. You're wasting your time,' Lila said out loud. 'People are having a hard time of it these days. There's no room for charity.'

She thought about getting back in bed but she needed to eat something. She could barely remember what she'd had the night before but she was fairly confident none of it included solids. In the fridge she found a family-sized pot of strawberry yoghurt past its expiry date and she sat at the table with the pot and a spoon. One of two teaspoons in her drawer and a parting gift from the former tenants, a couple of American students who'd moved back to the States. They'd also left three plates, two bowls, two forks and a knife.

There was no coffee left, Lila remembered. Great. Six o'clock on a Saturday morning and no coffee. She turned to the crossword book on the table and tried to pick up where she had left off. But her mind kept drifting. She remembered Anne Dufour's face, closed, alert, as though trying to identify distant sounds.

Morel had told her not to make it personal, as if it was something she could choose. She knew to trust her instinct. Anne Dufour was scared. She had the helpless air of a woman left with no options. Lila wished they could get her on her own. She might open up then.

Jacques Dufour was not a nice man. Lila didn't pick him as a murderer, but she wanted to dig deeper into his life. A man like that was bound to have dirty secrets. Who knows, she thought. I might get lucky. If I could nail him somehow, it might help shift the balance of things in the Dufour household. Maybe Anne Dufour would start smiling again, once in a while.

She could still see his face. Vain. Cruel. Convinced of his own power and superiority. How had he behaved towards his mother, Lila wondered. Had Isabelle Dufour spoilt her son? Was she responsible for the fact he was such an arsehole? Was any mother responsible for the way their children turned out? Lila thought of Isabelle Dufour's apartment and wondered. She remembered every object, every painting and rug in that house, the same way she could list everything she had seen at Jacques Dufour's lavish home.

According to the concierge, he had visited his mother four times in eight years. Lila could picture him, pacing the apartment, looking at his watch and trying not to look bored.

'Jacques Dufour. It's people like you that make the world a shitty place,' she said to herself. She got up and dropped the yoghurt pot into an overflowing rubbish bin and the spoon into the sink. A dirty plate sat in it from two days earlier when she'd warmed up a ready-made lasagne.

She looked at her crossword clue again. In the street below she heard a single plaintive miaow, then another. Soon it became a series of calls, an ongoing lament that made Lila feel like someone was scraping the inside of her skull with sharp claws. She looked at the ceiling. Cobwebs of dust hung from the corners. She needed to vacuum the place sometime.

'I need to get out of here,' she said to the walls. The thing that had nudged her was back, a memory that hovered in the back of her mind. Maybe if she talked to Morel, she would remember. She picked up the phone and tried his mobile number. It rang eight times before going to a recorded message.

'Morel. Pick up the phone. It's important.'

She hung up and swore. Where the hell was he?

She dialled his number again. No answer.

'Shit.' Lila hung up. She took her pyjamas off and pulled on a grey T-shirt and a pair of jeans. She would get coffee first, then go to the pool and swim a few lengths. Think carefully about what she remembered about the Dufours. Maybe it was nothing.

Though that seemed improbable, Lila thought as she jogged down the stairs. Her beating heart told her that she was on to something.

The swimming pool was busier than she'd hoped. While the desk attendant scanned her card, she saw through the glass people swimming two or three to each lane. She'd hoped for a lane to herself, where she could pound the water till exhaustion overcame her. This was the only way she knew how to exercise, by reaching her limit then surpassing it, until there was no feeling left.

Once she had changed into her blue one-piece swimsuit she looked for a lane that was not as busy as the others. She picked one that had just a single swimmer, a man with a powerful back and strong arms whose butterfly stroke came across as a warning for others to keep away.

Perfect, she thought. This was someone unused to having

to share his space. With a bit of luck it would piss him off to have her in his lane and he'd leave.

With the goggles on, everything receded. Feet and wet floors and the smell of chlorine, the shrieks of children and repeated instructions by swimming coaches. Everything except the underwater sound of her breathing and the water's movement where her body flew.

Freestyle, backstroke, breaststroke. And back to freestyle again. Normally she could keep this up indefinitely. But today was different. After twenty-five minutes she stopped to catch her breath. She stood at the end of the lane, waist-deep in the warm water and leaned her elbows on the concrete. Looked at the families coming in with small children, loaded with bags. Coming to the pool seemed like a major expedition. The time it took to get the kids changed and unload bags filled with towels, goggles and toys.

On the seats a boy sat in his swimming trunks, alone. His fringe was too long but he did nothing to push his hair out of his eyes. An old man wearing a white polo shirt and tight white shorts went over to him. Lila could see him speaking intently to the boy, whose face betrayed nothing, not even polite interest. There was something wrong with the whole scene. Lila realized what it was. The old man was leaning far too close, his face inches from the boy's.

Before she knew what she was doing, she'd pulled herself out of the water and hurried, dripping, to where they were.

As she got near the old man looked up. He immediately scurried away.

'Everything OK?' she asked the boy. 'Do you know that man?'

The boy shook his head.

'What did he want?'

The boy was growing uneasy. Time to shove off, Lila, she

thought. Before someone starts wondering what you're doing. She gave the boy a quick smile which she hoped seemed reassuring and walked over to where her towel lay on a chair. She'd swum half the distance she'd normally swim but she wasn't in the mood for it any more.

Once she was dressed, she dialled Morel's number again.

'Pharisce? Remind me what that means?' Morel said.

'It refers to many things. A member of an ancient Jewish sect, for one.'

'Surely it has a capital P?'

'A minute ago you didn't know what the word meant. Now you're assuring me it has a capital P.'

'Look, never mind, just put it down.'

'I'll look for another word, it's all the same to me.'

'Please, just put it down,' Morel said.

His father complied with the air of a man acting under duress. Morel watched his father count his points. He tried to remember whether the old man had always played games like this, with such avidity, as though he were scoring points against the whole world. Then he remembered that the two of them had never done this together before.

'What are you working on these days?'

'Me?'

'Do you see someone else in this room?' his father said.

'I have this one strange case,' Morel said.

'And?'

'A man and a boy, knocking on people's doors and talking to them about God.'

'Doesn't sound like much of a case.'

'We have one victim. Though it isn't clear how she died, and whether these two are involved. There are a number of things that point to a link.'

His father said nothing. Morel wondered how long a game of Scrabble might last.

'You ready to put a word down?' his father said.

Morel put down the word 'tube' and his father laughed. 'Is that it?'

'How about a snack?' Morel said.

'We ate breakfast an hour ago.'

'Coffee, then. Would you like another coffee? I'm having one. You think about your next word and I'll be right back,' Morel said. He needed to get out of the room.

When he came back with his cup, his father pointed to the board.

'I've done my turn. It's yours now. Try to do something a bit better this time.'

Morel looked down at the board, then at his father. 'Very funny.'

'What? What's funny?'

'Your word. FXUTJS. Now why don't you put down a real word?'

There was a pause, a silence that lasted less than ten seconds but seemed to fill the room. When Morel looked up at his father he saw an expression there he'd never seen before. He looked like a man who has come to an intersection and doesn't know which way to turn.

Morel could not look at the old man's face now. Instead, he watched Morel Senior's hand move across the board and pick the letters up, one by one. It seemed to take a very long time.

'Yeah, OK. I was just mucking around. I wanted to give you a fighting chance,' he said.

While Morel struggled with how to respond, the phone rang and he reached for it, grateful for the interruption.

'Morel speaking,' he said, while his father walked out of the room.

'It's me. Lila.'

'Why are you calling this number?'

'I wouldn't have to if you bothered answering your mobile phone.'

'Shit. I left it in the car. Sorry.'

'Yeah well. We need to talk. Can we meet somewhere? I can come to your place if you like.'

'No need,' Morel said quickly. He suggested they catch up over lunch. He gave her the name of a bistro in Neuilly and heard her snort.

'I hope you're paying,' she said, before hanging up.

'I was picturing something fancy but this is OK,' Lila said.

They were sitting in a booth, in an Italian restaurant. The tablecloths were red and white checks and the walls decorated with trellis and fake vine. Andrea Bocelli was belting out that tune that people seemed to like so much. Lila didn't get it. Already the tables were filling up with families, all very presentable, even the children with their neatly combed hair and good manners.

Morel opened a menu. Lila looked him over. He was dressed in jeans and a blue collared shirt. She wondered whether she had ever seen him wearing jeans before. It didn't make any difference. He wore denim the way he wore a suit. His clothes still had that look of having been pressed just moments before he put them on. He was clean-shaven and sharp. Good cheekbones, eyes slightly slanted, reminding her that he was part Asian, though most people never saw it. Dimples when he smiled. Not her type exactly, but she knew plenty of women who would think differently. Looking him over, she realized all of a sudden how she must look. She'd had about three hours' sleep and the T-shirt she wore had a rip at the collar and a stain at the centre where she'd spilt a takeaway coffee earlier.

'I hope I didn't interrupt anything this morning,' Lila said.

Morel thought of his father's confusion over the word he'd put down. The old man had said he didn't want to play any more and retreated to his room. Morel had escaped to his until it was time to meet Lila.

'Not at all.' Morel pretended to skim through the menu but he knew it by heart, having come here so often over the years.

'What do you feel like?' Morel asked.

'I'll have the gnocchi and a Coke.'

'OK.' He gestured to one of the waiters hovering around the tables and placed their order. When the waiter had left, Morel turned to Lila.

'So what is it you want to tell me, that couldn't wait till tomorrow?'

'I was thinking about the Dufours,' she said.

'What about them?' Morel pulled open a packet of bread-sticks and bit into one.

'Something stayed with me. Remember the cross we found in Isabelle Dufour's hands?'

'What about it?'

'It had those stones embedded in each arm of the cross. I remember thinking it was quite pretty, as far as these things go . . . Remember?'

'Yes.'

'Well, Anne Dufour, the daughter-in-law. She was wearing a cross around her neck when we went to interview them the first time. She wasn't flaunting it, in fact it was quite discreet, tucked away beneath her buttoned-up shirt. But when she leaned forward to pour more coffee, I noticed it.'

'Lots of people wear crosses.'

'It was the exact same one. Wooden, with those blue stones. How many of those have you come across?'

Morel leaned forward and Lila moved back slightly, her eyebrows raised.

'What's so special about it?' he asked.

'Well, I did a Google search, to see whether I could find it. And it finally came up.' She pulled a piece of paper from her pocket. It was a colour print-out of the cross, with a brief description under it. Morel looked at it, then at Lila.

'It's an Orthodox cross,' she said triumphantly. 'It's not immediately obvious, with this one. But it definitely is. And it occurred to me that we should visit the Orthodox churches – starting with the Russian Orthodox Church in Rue Daru. Maybe someone there has seen our two guys.'

Morel looked at the print-out. 'Nice work, Lila.'

'And another thing,' she said, looking pleased. 'Remember how Dufour's son was about to head off to Geneva for two nights, when we interviewed him?'

'Yes?'

'Well, he left without a bag. You'd think a man would have an overnight bag at least, if he was going to be away from home for two nights.'

'He could have had it in the car. He might have put it there earlier.'

'I think we should ask his wife, don't you?'

'Yes. I'll be interested to see what she says.'

The food came and they ate in silence. Ten minutes later Lila had cleaned up her gnocchi while Morel's fettuccine lay mostly untouched.

'Coffee?' Morel asked. Lila shook her head.

'I'm too full.'

He called for the bill and paid.

'Thank you,' Lila said.

'You did say it was on me.'

'Well, I knew you'd want to pay, being the perfect gentleman.'

'And you the perfect lady.'

'Ha ha.'

'Come on,' he said. 'Let's walk.'

They headed towards the river. A barge heaped with coal was making its way down the Seine. An elderly woman in a suit was walking a poodle along the pathway. They passed a couple of joggers. The river seemed to mark the divide between past and present. On this side, Neuilly with its elegant architecture; on the other a skyline of office and apartment blocks. Across the water, the Great Arch of La Défense framed a taciturn sky. The design of the Danish architect Johann Otto von Spreckelsen looked more like a cube than the triumphal arch it was meant to be, Morel thought. Either way it didn't add much to the high-rise office district.

'When we go back to the Dufour house we can ask the daughter-in-law about the cross,' Morel said.

'It may be nothing.'

'Or not. This is a woman who supposedly wasn't religious.'

They stood there much longer than necessary, observing the river's turmoil, a deep wedge carved by the passing boat.

'I'd better get going,' Morel said.

'Me too,' Lila said. 'See you on Monday?'

'See you on Monday.'

Morel accompanied her to the Métro station and watched her jog down the stairs. Then he turned around and slowly walked back home.

Thirteen

When Morel arrived at work on Monday morning he found Marie Latour and Irina Volkoff waiting with Jean in the office. Morel was never under-dressed but he was glad he'd remembered today to wear a tie. It was a dark-red Nino Cerruti which Solange had bought for him two years ago, before they'd become lovers. Jean introduced him to the two women.

Morel noticed them give him the once-over. They both smiled. Visibly, he'd passed the test.

The same was perhaps less true of Jean. Morel saw Marie Latour examine Jean's snakeskin boots and the stud in his left ear. She was probably wondering what he was doing out of handcuffs.

'Thank you for coming in,' Morel said. 'We really appreciate it. We can call you a taxi when you've finished here. We'll try not to keep you here any longer than necessary but we're keen to get as clear a portrait as possible of the man who came to your house. And the boy, too.'

'Why?' said Irina Volkoff. 'I thought we'd already done that. Why do you need more?'

'Because we've had other complaints since you provided the testimony,' Morel said, keen not to give away too much. There was no point worrying them when he still had so little to go on.

He called Marco over.

'Is Madame Guillou on her way?' he asked.

'I don't know,' Marco said.

'Well, perhaps we'll proceed without her. I don't want to keep these ladies waiting,' Morel said. He moved closer to Marco, out of earshot. 'Get her on the phone now or find her; either way I want to know where she is,' he said quietly.

He turned back to the two elderly women. They couldn't have been more different. Marie Latour was short and plump, with a round face. Irina Volkoff was the opposite, angular and tall. Watchful and silent where Latour was chatty and eager to please.

Morel turned to Marco. 'Do you want to drive these ladies? I'll be with you shortly.'

'The illustrator is expecting you,' Morel told the two women.

As per custom, the composite sketch would be worked out at the Quai de l'Horloge, where the judicial identity section in charge of all the technical and scientific analyses was located. It was only a hundred metres or so from the Criminal Brigade headquarters. A short stroll, but given the witnesses' age, Morel did not consider asking them to walk.

Two hours later Morel had a sketch in hand that the two women had agreed on. He passed copies on to Lila, Marco and Jean.

'Marco, I want you to go back to the women's neighbourhoods again with this, talk to everyone you and Jean spoke to last time. In case it helps jog someone's memory. Lila, you run the composite by all the organizations we've listed, including the Orthodox ones.'

'I'll go with her,' Jean said. 'I can spare a couple of hours.'

'Thanks. And wherever we can send a scan by email, let's do it. Save some time,' Morel said.

He looked at Marco. 'Did you make contact with Guillou?'

'No. She's not at home.'

'Let's try again in an hour's time. If we don't hear from her I'd like to get someone down there.'

Marco nodded. Morel watched him gather his things and head out, while Jean and Lila drew their chairs together and began looking at a very long list of religious institutions.

Things were picking up slowly. It wasn't what you'd call real progress but at least they now had a clear picture of the person Morel wanted to talk to.

He intended to go over the evidence once more, starting with the photos of the Dufour crime scene, the testimonies by the three widows and the interview with the Dufours.

He looked at his watch. Maybe he'd grab some lunch first.

Instead of getting his sandwich at the usual place he found himself driving across the bridge to a narrow street off the Boulevard Saint-Michel. Just a quick drive, he told himself, knowing he should be back at his desk, focusing on the case.

He slowed down and looked out of his window, scanning the street numbers. He'd known for a long time now that Mathilde lived here and he'd made a point of staying well away from this part of town. He didn't want her to know he had tracked her down. Mathilde, he suspected, would not find this endearing.

He was dreaming of her on a regular basis. He had come to expect it when he went to sleep. He took it as a sign, of what he wasn't sure.

He parked across the street from her building. While he waited, he opened the Dufour folder and started looking at the photos of her apartment. He looked up often to see whether Mathilde had appeared.

After a few minutes he rolled the window down to get some air. He felt bruised from the relentless heat. Maybe after this case was closed he would take a holiday. Away from the crowds, a place where he could wake up to the chirping of birds.

He thought of his father. Should he try to talk to him about what had happened with the Scrabble game? Maybe he had simply been confused. Morel promised himself to raise it if it happened again.

Thinking of his father reminded him that he still hadn't spoken to his sister Maly. He would try calling again and maybe drop by if he couldn't get through. He knew she was home most evenings.

He thought about Isabelle Dufour and about what Paul had told him. Could there possibly be a link between the dead woman and Paul's little lecture on religious revivalism in Russia?

He was so caught up in his thoughts that when Mathilde appeared he wasn't ready. She walked right past his car, without looking his way. He could have reached over and touched her arm. With a galloping heart, he sank further into his seat, cursing his own stupidity. What the hell was he thinking? He pictured what he might look like to her if she happened to see him. A middle-aged creep, stalking a woman he'd dated over twenty years back.

Mathilde crossed the road towards her building. She was holding a Leclerc shopping bag. A child walked by her side, a boy, maybe ten years old. He was nearly as tall as her. Her hair seemed shorter, though it was hard to say because she wore it tied up. She was still the small, slight woman he'd had no trouble lifting in his arms yet couldn't keep up with in a race. She wore a loose white cotton shirt over a light grey skirt that stopped just below the knees, and silver sandals. She had always preferred silver to gold. On her birthday that first year they'd had together he'd given her a Celtic ring. Her arms and legs were still pale. When he'd known her, she'd taken pains to avoid the sun. That hadn't changed, then. She stopped outside the front door and searched her bag.

Mathilde.

In a matter of seconds she was gone, long before he was able to translate the shock of seeing her into feeling. How long had it been since he'd last seen her? Ten, eleven years? They had run into each other at the house of a common friend, both surprised and uncomfortable at finding themselves in the same room. He'd left soon after her arrival.

He waited in the car for some time, for something to happen. When it became apparent that nothing momentous was on the horizon, he started the car and backed out of his spot.

His phone started ringing, halfway out of his parking space, and he answered it. It was Perrin.

'Where the hell are you, Morel?'

'On my way back to the office.'

'Don't bother.'

Even before Perrin said it, Morel knew. 'He's done it again.'

Morel listened to his boss and because he didn't have a pen, he memorized the address Perrin gave him. It would take him a while to get there but this was the middle of the day in August and the protests were over. The traffic would be light.

He thought of the woman who had commanded his attention with her caustic presence, whose fears and prejudices he had understood on some instinctive level though he did not share them, and whose life had just been snuffed away. A wave of sorrow washed over him. He should have known something was wrong when Elisabeth Guillou hadn't shown up in the morning. He should have driven to her house straight away and checked on her. While he'd been busy looking for a stronger link between Dufour's death and the evangelists, the killer had struck again.

'I'm on my way,' he said.

FOURTEEN

Lila's nausea had more to do with Richard Martin's smile than with the carved-up body lying on a slab between them. The pathologist looked like a hungry lion that has just spotted a lone gazelle across an empty plain. It was a good thing she'd brought Marco along. She had a sudden vision of Martin chasing her around the autopsy table and had to stop herself from smiling, lest he think he was making a winning impression on her.

'Well, I think it's safe to say Elisabeth Guillou was killed in the same way as Isabelle Dufour,' Martin said. He licked his lips. Lila looked away. She wished she'd picked something other to wear than the clinging red T-shirt she had on. A paper bag, for example.

'Water in the lungs?' said Marco, who seemed oblivious to what was going on.

Martin gave him an impatient look, the one he reserved for most people except for the more attractive members of the opposite sex.

'If you took the time to read something other than bad crime novels, you'd know that forensic pathology is the art of interpretation, not an exact science.'

He paused, and turned to the body. 'What we've got here is a case of lung expansion, the water-wing phenomenon I've described before, and lung crepitus – just as with Dufour.

Also,' Martin said, looking straight at Lila's cleavage, 'her hair was still wet underneath the wig when you brought her in. The skin on her hands still tender. It doesn't take a genius to figure out she was in the water not long before she died, which would have been somewhere between five and six this morning. That much I can tell you.'

Lila turned to the woman lying on the slab before her. Naked and exposed. The first wide cut from ear to ear across the top of the skull, the skin tugged back to remove the brain. The Y-shaped incision along her thorax, skin and tissue peeled back to allow for the removal of the ribcage and organs.

Still, as far as Lila was concerned, this clinical display of Guillou's open carcass was an improvement on the dolled-up version they'd found when they'd entered the woman's home. The victim's daughter had been the one to find her after letting herself in to the house. She hadn't seen her mother in four months. The shock of seeing her like that had sent her over the edge. They'd had to sedate her.

The corpse had been dressed in a bright red wig, too much make-up and a nightie that looked like it could have come straight out of one of those wholesome American shows that were aired on French television, with dreadfully dubbed soundtracks.

There was little doubt that the two murders were connected.

Marco turned to Lila. 'Anything else we want to ask?'

'There doesn't appear to be any bruising on the arms like the one you described on Isabelle Dufour,' she said, looking Martin straight in the eye.

'You're right. I didn't see anything. I'll let you know if that shows up later today or tomorrow morning.'

'Thanks.'

As they left, Martin managed to move in and say a few words in Lila's ear.

'What did he say?' Marco asked her in the corridor. He watched her move quickly ahead of him and felt a familiar thrill. She could never know how he felt about her. Lila was definitely not in his league.

Without answering, Lila strode ahead and swung the exit doors so hard Marco had to put his hand up to avoid getting hit when they swung back. He hurried after Lila, who was already halfway across the car park.

'Well?' he called out.

'He said he thinks you're cute,' she said without turning around.

The way she said it, Marco thought it best to shut up.

Morel sat at his desk, looking over the photographs taken by the technician at Guillou's place. Her death had affected him in ways that surprised him. Whoever had killed her had robbed her of her life, but also stripped her of all dignity.

He thought about her attacker. He had held her underwater, watching her life ebb away. To what purpose?

And why hadn't Guillou fought back? She was a battler. There had been nothing to show that her hands might have been tied. A toxicology report would soon reveal whether she had been drugged. Right now none of it made sense to Morel. And it bothered him that she may have given up without a fight.

He had let her down, by not taking Dufour's death seriously enough, but there had been so little to tie the two women together. A bunch of pamphlets. Still, he berated himself for being slow on the uptake. He wouldn't make the same mistake again.

The trouble was that he couldn't see the motive. What

was the link between Isabelle Dufour and Elisabeth Guillou? Why had they been killed?

He studied the photograph before him. Elisabeth Guillou's body lay under the covers just as Dufour's had. In her hand she held a plain silver cross. For a minute, standing at her bedside, Morel had felt uneasy, as though she might all of a sudden sit up and berate him for intruding upon an old woman in the privacy of her bedroom. He remembered the way she had examined him in his office, her intense scrutiny. Dead, she seemed smaller than he remembered.

Morel had searched for a sound system and found a CD player in Guillou's living room. In the player he'd found a copy of Fauré's *Requiem*.

Morel spread the other photos on his desk. Lila walked over to him and looked at the display.

'We just got back from the morgue. Martin confirmed what we already know – that Guillou died the same way Dufour did. No signs of bruising yet, though.'

'OK. He wasn't too painful?'

'One of these days I'm going to wipe that smug smile off his face and knock his teeth out.'

'Do you want me to take it up with his office? I will, you know. I can't do anything about the other complaints against him, it's outside my jurisdiction, but if he's harassing you—'

Lila rolled her eyes. 'I can handle Richard Martin,' she said. 'We've got more important things to attend to.'

Together they looked at the photos of Guillou's home. Unlike Dufour's cluttered flat, Guillou's house was a study in minimalism. There was a lot of empty space. The surfaces were bare. No magazines, nothing that pointed to how she might have occupied herself or the things that interested her. The only family photographs on display were on a side table in the living room. The garden was tidy. There was a trampoline, presumably for the grandchildren to play on when they visited.

Morel and Lila had delivered the news to Guillou's son at the accounting firm where he'd worked.

It was the part Morel disliked most about his job. But it could sometimes reveal a great deal about a victim's life. Take Guillou's children. The son's expression had been one of mild regret, while the daughter had become hysterical. No doubt due to the shock of seeing her mother in that state. Morel wondered what her reaction might have been otherwise.

It was important to note these things, but at the same time he was careful not to over-analyse them. People did not always express their sadness in obvious ways.

He thought about Perrin. After calling Morel to tell him that Guillou was dead, he had turned up at her flat minutes after Morel, his face dark with anger.

'How did this happen?' he'd said. 'I thought you were going to find those guys. Now we've got a fucking double homicide on our hands. Jesus Christ! Do you know how this makes me look?' He jabbed a finger at Morel. 'I. Want. Results.' Then he'd stalked out of the flat before Morel could say anything.

Numbers. These days it was all about the statistics. The trouble was that there weren't enough people to get the results they wanted at the top. With thousands of jobs being cut across the police force, everyone was complaining these days of being under-resourced. In some of the outer suburbs, stations were even shutting down at night and over the weekends due to lack of staffing.

Yet another Sarkozy pledge that had been broken. He'd promised in the lead-up to his 2007 election to tackle crime through increased policing. What had happened to that brilliant idea? Police numbers were steadily dwindling, while crime was ramping up.

'Are you still with me?' Morel realized he'd stopped listening. Lila moved into one of the chairs across from Morel's seat and crossed her legs.

'You know, I've been thinking. What if there are others?' she said. 'Other women who haven't bothered to complain to us just because two guys knocked on their door. I mean, why would you?' She looked at Morel. 'I hate to say this, but maybe Perrin is right. We need to go public and see whether anyone else can tell us anything about these guys.'

'If we do that we'll have every woman over the age of fifty panicking,' Morel said. 'And the press will be on our back. We need to be able to focus on the job.'

Lila looked doubtful. 'If you say so.'

Morel rubbed his eyes and gathered the photos to return them to the folder.

'We need to proceed as tactfully as possible,' he said, thinking of Perrin.

Tactfulness was not high on Lila's list of concerns when she rang the bell at the Dufour home. For a start, she would ask Anne why her husband hadn't taken a bag on the overseas trip he'd been about to embark on when Lila and Morel had interviewed him. Her guess was that he hadn't gone quite so far and that, where he'd been, he hadn't needed too many clothes. There must be a girlfriend Anne knew nothing about. Or maybe she did. Maybe she welcomed a break from her odious husband.

While Lila waited for someone to appear, she rehearsed her lines mentally. The door opened.

'Do you mind if I come in?'

Lila could tell by Anne Dufour's face that she did mind, but she couldn't come up with a good reason not to let the policewoman in. She opened the door wider and turned back into the house. Lila followed her, thinking that she must clarify the matter of the wooden cross with the blue stones.

'Can I offer you anything?' Anne Dufour asked her.

'No thanks.'

She looked relieved. She seemed a great deal more composed than the last time they'd met. Her make-up was perfect. There were no traces of black eyeliner and mascara running down her cheeks. She was dressed up too, in a two-piece linen suit and black heels.

'A lunch date?' Lila asked.

The other woman gave a vague smile but didn't answer. 'What can I do for you, then?' she asked. She sat on the sofa and looked up at Lila, who remained standing.

Now Lila could take a closer look at her she saw there were dark shadows under her eyes. She looked thinner than the last time Lila and Morel had visited. On the inside of her wrist there was a mark that looked a lot like a burn. Anne Dufour caught Lila's look and pulled at her sleeve.

'Is your husband home?' Lila asked.

Anne Dufour shook her head. 'He's away.'

'Another business trip?'

'Yes.'

'Does your husband always travel without luggage when he goes away?'

Anne Dufour's expression told Lila all she needed to know. She had a look on her face that said this was something she was used to.

So Jacques Dufour was a cheat. Well, what a surprise, Lila thought.

'How did your mother-in-law's funeral go?' she asked.

Anne Dufour shrugged. 'Well, I guess.' She emitted a strange, mirthless laugh. 'As well as these things can go.'

'How is your husband coping?'

'With what?' When Anne Dufour looked up at her, Lila wondered for the first time whether she was on medication or whether she'd been smoking a joint.

'With his mother's death, Madame Dufour.'

'Oh. That.'

'Have you seen any changes in his behaviour?'

'No.' Anne Dufour looked at Lila as though she'd suddenly woken up. 'Why are you here anyway? I thought you got everything you needed from us last time.'

Lila decided on a direct approach. 'I wanted to make sure you were all right,' she said.

'I didn't know that was part of your duties, as a police officer.'

'It isn't. I also have a couple of questions I'd like to ask.'

'Ask away.'

'Have you heard of someone called Elisabeth Guillou? She may have been a friend or an acquaintance of your mother-in-law's.'

Anne Dufour shook her head. 'No. But I wouldn't know if she was. I never met any of her friends.'

'Can you tell me about the cross we found in her hand?'

Anne Dufour shook her head. 'I don't think so. What kind of cross?'

Lila was running out of patience. 'The same one you were wearing the last time we came to speak to you and your husband,' she said. 'The Orthodox cross.'

The transformation was astonishing. Lila watched as Anne Dufour went pale and started trembling. Her fingers went shakily to her throat and she dropped her voice to a whisper.

'I can't talk about that,' she said.

'What is it you're afraid of?' Lila asked, more gently this time.

'I'm a Christian, you know. Before I married Jacques, I used to attend church every week.' She spoke in a hurried voice, so quietly Lila had to strain to hear. 'Jacques hates the whole idea of it. Which is why I never – but my mother-in-law was interested in these things. She and I spoke of God and she wanted to understand. One day we were out together and we bought the crosses. It didn't even mean much. I mean, neither of us is – was – Orthodox or anything,' she said, becoming confused about which tense to use. 'We just thought they were beautiful and that it would be nice to wear them together.'

Her face was so drained of colour Lila worried she might faint.

'I never wear it, I usually keep it hidden from Jacques. But after Isabelle died I put it on, under my clothes so Jacques wouldn't notice. As a sort of tribute to her, so I could still feel her near. I thought no one would see it, not under my shirt.'

'Where did you buy the crosses, Madame Dufour?'

'Does it matter? It was at an exhibition. In May.'

'Which one?' Lila asked. She wasn't sure why she was even asking, she was more preoccupied with how to lessen Anne Dufour's agitation.

'An exhibition on Holy Russia. At the Louvre.'

'OK.'

Anne Dufour tugged at the buttons on her jacket. Without thinking, Lila placed a hand on the other woman's arm.

'I can help you,' she said in a low voice.

Anne Dufour looked at her carefully. Then, with visible effort, she pulled herself together. She got up from the sofa. She seemed unsteady on her feet.

'I don't believe in self-pity. And besides, there are people with far bigger problems than mine.'

Lila nodded slowly. 'You're right. Still, I believe in the power to change things when they make us unhappy.'

Anne Dufour managed a forced smile.

'That's very uplifting.' She looked at her watch. 'I'm sorry but I have to go now. Was there anything else?'

Lila hesitated. But it was clear she had done all she could. 'No.'

Lila walked to her car. She heard the door close softly behind her. Why did she fancy that it was closed reluctantly, as though the person on the other side secretly yearned to open it wide again?

With her eyes cast downwards, Anne Dufour turned and slowly walked back to the living room.

'Is the nosy bitch gone?' her husband said.

'Yes,' she said.

She stood still and waited for what was to come. Only her galloping pulse betrayed the terror in her heart.

FIFTEEN

The day of his return is mild and sunny.

A rich, earthy smell rises from the muddy ground. On either side of the dirt road, fields of corn extend beneath a rain-washed sky. Long-stemmed sunflowers turn their faces to the light. In the distance, he can see a green tractor lumbering down a track through the fields, like a corpulent bride bearing down the aisle. Otherwise, the road ahead of him is deserted.

Time has always been unhurried here. On the surface, it seems like nothing changes. But if you dig deeper you begin to see the cracks.

Now Armand has been away so long he sees only the tranquil, rural landscape he once knew so well. So much of it is familiar. The buzzing of bees on a sleepy afternoon. An overturned wheelbarrow in the shade of a willow tree. He can almost taste his childhood. The raw texture and smell of milk, brought home at dawn from the farm, straight from the cow's udder. The milk was poured from a bucket, still warm. Bits of hay floating on the surface. As a child he didn't mind the dirt. He'd drink the milk to the last drop regardless of what it contained, and feel it trickle through his bones, making him stronger.

It took him a surprising amount of time to find his way back here. Paris to Rennes was easy enough; you just had to follow the signs. In Rennes he stopped for coffee and a sandwich, which he had on a park bench overlooking a children's play area. There were few people about. A cool wind blew across the square and he wished he'd brought something more substantial than the thin cotton shirt he was wearing.

As a student, he used to drive from Rennes back to his village most weekends. He never thought to look at the map this time. Surely he could still do it with his eyes closed. Only after taking the wrong exit twice did he admit defeat. He stopped at a village very much like the one he was looking for and asked for directions. The young girl he spoke to had no clue but the restaurant owner had a cousin who lived there and gave him detailed instructions. She looked like someone he knew, someone he might have gone to school with.

He didn't say much, just smiled and thanked her. It's funny, when he is with César he can talk to God himself, but without the boy he feels lost.

It is exactly as he remembers it. If anything it is smaller and quieter than it was twenty years ago. There is still a bar, a post office and a church. That pretty much sums it up. You have to travel twenty kilometres to find the nearest supermarket and shops. Last time he checked, five years or so ago when he was curious enough to study the latest census, the head count was 522. From memory, two-thirds of these were sanctimonious old biddies whose curtains twitched every time he walked down the street. They tended to stay put from the day they were born till the day they died. But most of their children would have moved on because there was nothing for them here.

He still remembers the names of several of the women who turned up without fail at church when he was a child.

They talked to his mother but as far as they were concerned children were there to be seen and not heard. Often they talked about him as if he wasn't there.

'He looks placid enough but he can be wily, that child,' his mother said, and they all nodded like crows at a banquet. Dressed in black from head to toe and with beady eyes. Revelling in the scrutiny of others. Armand held his tongue and listened.

When the women were gone, his mother grew scornful. Armand was suddenly her ally, someone she could vent to about the small-mindedness of her neighbours.

'Gossipy witches,' she called them. But then why did she keep inviting these witches back every week, to sit in her living room, drink her tea and eat her biscuits? Why did she put up with their simpering and the way they examined everything, from the frayed cushions on the tapestried sofa to the ugly ornaments his mother collected. Porcelain swans and kittens and turtles, a whole menagerie of prissy pets.

His mother, a devout Catholic, seemed to believe that by baking once a week for these stalwarts of their church she was taking a step closer to heaven. As far as Armand could see, it was more like a step back. These tea parties only soured her.

As a child, until he started school, he'd assumed the world was mainly made up of old people, most of them women without men. He only wondered later where all the men had gone, but as a child he assumed it was the war; the village had a monument to the dead, and there were more names etched into the grey marble than a child could count. Never mind that the war was a thing of the past and could not possibly explain away the widows of today. Later on he knew better, saw the men sitting at the bar not long after breakfast. They were still there at lunchtime, drinking their way into an early grave.

So that left the women. There was the neighbour who sometimes watched over him while his mother ran errands and could barely lift herself out of her chair. She wore thick woollen socks no matter what time of the year it was. At the post office, the woman who weighed letters on a pair of old-fashioned scales looked about a hundred years old. She added up her numbers on an abacus and her mouth was never still as she muttered and chewed over private grievances.

'Don't forget to post the letters on the way back,' his mother would say, when she trusted him to wander off on his own, which was a great deal later than other mothers did. While she searched for the right stamps, the old woman peered at Armand through thick glasses as though trying to read his mind. At the time it was full of thoughts that he would not even have entrusted to the local priest at confession. While he counted his coins, he withstood her scrutiny and tried hard to keep his mind as still and uneventful as a Sunday afternoon.

Now as he walks past the building he sees the post office still there. Through the glass he can't make out who is inside, and he doesn't want to slow down to look.

The bar is open but he doesn't go in. He is not particularly worried about running into people who will recognize him, after all he is nothing like the man who went away, but he's not going out of his way to get noticed either.

He hasn't thought about the house he grew up in. It's not like he's forgotten it but where it sits in his mind is a tight, enclosed space he doesn't visit. What would be the point? The house was sold such a long time ago and it has probably changed hands a few times. Any restless spirits have long since moved on.

Instead he seeks a house he has never been to before, but he knows what to look for. There are people who wear their lives entirely on the outside, while inside is like an empty room with open windows and curtains ruffling in the breeze. The man he is looking for, the one he once loved, is one of these people. He isn't sure why he is here, beyond the fact that César is growing less affectionate and that he, Armand, is lonely and in need of reassurance. That man, that love, once anchored him.

When he finally sees the house, set apart from the others in the street, yet unremarkable, it's as though he is remembering a place he's visited many times before. For a moment he stops, uncertain. He can hear the sounds of laughter, two boys chasing each other across a field, digging for treasure, climbing a tree. One was always more nimble than the other. But it wasn't rare for the nimble one to pretend otherwise, so they would stay together.

A lifetime ago.

He walks around the back first, just to make sure he isn't mistaken. Behind the house is an orchard planted with apple trees and a sprawling, untidy garden. Scattered petals and deep-green patches of moss fill the shady recesses, while in sunlit places the air quivers with the scent of bruised apples and roses ripe for the picking. A slice of paradise. Someone clearly loves this oasis of greenery and doesn't intend to tame it.

It is still and quiet. He can hear his heart thudding against his chest. After he knocks he stands back and listens for signs of life. It takes so long for anyone to come that he's about to give up and turn around when the door opens. He looks at the person standing on the threshold; the two of them mute with embarrassment or surprise, until Armand speaks, with an unfamiliar note of apology in his voice, because he wants to make clear that he has no right to be there, that he is at the other person's mercy.

'It's me,' he says.

Armand and Charles sit across from each other at the dining table. Though he doesn't want it, Armand is now holding his second cup of coffee. It helps him deal with the long silences. The house is just as he pictured it, as is Charles. But Armand hadn't expected to feel quite so raw. Everything comes flooding back, filling his chest like a tidal wave.

He takes deep breaths, focusing on the cup of coffee before him.

'Well, this is a surprise,' Charles says. He is wearing an expensive pair of brown leather loafers, Armand notices. Though the house is a mess, everything about it spells money. Where they are sitting is a large open-plan area, with sliding glass doors overlooking the garden.

'How long are you here for?' Charles asks. What he means is why. Armand keeps his eyes trained on the table littered with junk. Everything is a reminder of the life Charles chose for himself. Crayons, paper, a crossword book.

'Not long.' He hazards a look at Charles's face. The eyes are clear, nothing is concealed. He wonders what Charles sees.

He is asking Charles about his family, his job, his life, but inside his mind is reeling.

You were my soul mate. You meant everything to me once. What happened? Why is it so hard to remember? Revisiting the past is like wading through quicksand.

Charles's answers are perfunctory, a banal résumé of a seemingly ordinary life. He is droning on about management and mortgages and a litany of things Armand knows nothing about.

The more he talks, the worse Armand feels. Gradually, his world turns black. In his mind he is frantically clawing at the darkness, looking for a way back into the light.

'Armand?' To hear Charles saying his name, so close to his ear, gives him a shock.

Charles is leaning over him, with one hand on his shoulder. He is so close Armand can see his pupils, and the brilliant blue of his eyes. He can see the lines carved in his face by the passage of time and the dark blond hairs on his chest, where the first two buttons of his shirt are undone. Charles's smell is so overwhelmingly familiar. A soapy freshness that makes him suddenly want to weep.

He stands up, as though he's received a jolt of electricity. How long was he out for? He tries frantically to remember whether he said or did anything embarrassing.

'Are you OK? You looked like you were about to faint then, I thought you'd passed out, I—'

'I probably should go,' Armand says.

'Finish your coffee.' Charles is looking at Armand now with, what? Regret, hesitation? Or is it guilt? 'Are you still teaching?' he asks.

'Yes.' Armand feels the sweat against his back as he returns to his seat. The panic has eased and his heartbeat is almost steady now.

'Where?'

'In Paris.'

Charles nods.

Armand looks at his watch. He wants to get back to Paris before nightfall if he can. He is not a confident driver by night and besides he is worried about leaving César alone for too long. It's not as though the boy can't look after himself, but his surliness worries Armand lately.

The coffee is weak. He remembers a time when he and

Charles sat up late together to prepare for exams, and drank coffee to stay awake. Armand's mother had approved of Charles.

'You two are such good boys,' she'd say. 'Look at the pair of you, working hard.'

Time to go. Armand stands again and hands his cup over to Charles.

'I have to leave now.'

'Me too,' says Charles. 'I'm picking the kids up from school.'

There is a pained silence as the two stand together at the front door. What are they supposed to do now? Shake hands, like men? Unconsciously, Armand takes a step back. Charles is still a head taller than him.

'Thanks for the coffee.'

'Sure. I'll see you next time,' Charles says.

Next time could be another twenty years, Armand thinks, as the door shuts in his face.

After leaving Charles's house, he walks back the way he came, to the main intersection. Here the bar and the church face each other. Maybe it's the relief of being alone again: all of a sudden he's laughing. It could be the premise for one of those cartoons where the character – Donald Duck or Mickey Mouse, say – is torn between two decisions. On the one hand, an angel is urging them to do the right thing while, on the other, the devil tries to lead them astray.

As far as Armand is concerned neither of the two places is particularly conducive. In any case he should be on his way now if he wants to get back before dark. Still, at the crossing he finds himself hesitating, before turning left, not towards the place where he parked his car but towards the house where Charles grew up.

The house is set apart from the others in the street. It is

still concealed by a stone wall covered in vine. A majestic elm tree towers over the wall. There is no obvious way to get in apart from the front gate but Armand knows better. He manages to crawl through the hole in the garden wall and to find a spot in the bushes. He's been here before.

The garden is empty but a sprinkler has been turned on. He is too far back to get wet. The smell of wet grass and the chugging of the sprinkler soothe him. The day's drive and his encounter with Charles have worn him out. The sprinkler's trajectory, around and around, is like a refrain, repetitive and comforting. Armand starts to yawn. He tries to fight the torpor taking hold of his weary limbs but, against his better judgement and before he knows it, he is asleep.

When he wakes up, it takes him a while to realize where he is. This is the house he ran to as a child, every time he could, and he was always welcome here. Now there are other children in the garden, he can hear them though it's hard to see without being noticed. Then he hears Charles too and realizes these must be his children. Where the sprinkler chugs its way in circles there is a blur of small feet, trampling the wet grass. Shrieks of delight, followed by Charles's own laughter. He thinks of Charles as he saw him earlier in the afternoon, removed, unsmiling, and tears come to his eyes.

He edges forward just enough to see and still remain invisible. The two little boys and a girl grow tired of the sprinkler and disappear into the miniature maze where Armand and Charles once played, pretending to be lost even though there is little danger of that – it is simpler than a child's puzzle. There is still delight in solving the conundrum, and now Charles's children emerge flushed and victorious, as though they've found the answer to a riddle. They tumble across the grass and uproot the flowers when the old lady isn't looking.

The children line up at the kitchen door with their offerings – wilting arrangements of flowers and leaves and twigs. She takes the flowers from them and smiles. He hears Charles's voice, calling for the children to come inside. He hears the sound of a tap being turned on and off. Two white butterflies chase each other across the lawn. He closes his eyes and smells wet grass and lemons. Bumblebees drone, weaving amongst the flowers. The sky is a billowing blue sheet.

The children tumble out again, followed by Charles and then his mother. She is paper-thin now, with a halo of white hair. She wears a pink and blue shawl wrapped around her shoulders. Charles leads her to an old wooden bench placed under the large elm. This bench and this tree have always been there, for as long as Armand remembers. Charles's mother sits there for a while, with her hands resting in her lap, while Charles tilts his head back and soaks in the sun. This is the old Charles, lost to Armand forever. The old lady turns and says something to her son. She seems so content. Armand wonders whether she remembers him at all.

He thinks of César. The boy is so irritable these days, quite unlike his usual self. Maybe it has something to do with puberty. He seems bored or indifferent a lot of the time. Even his posture is changing. He sits and stands with his shoulders slouched and he never quite connects with Armand's eyes.

A memory resurfaces in his mind of César, aged eight. They have been together nearly two years now. The boy's body forms a question mark as they lie curled up together, reading *Asterix and the Laurel Wreath*. With his forefinger the boy traces the outline of words, and Armand reads them. When César appears on the page, the boy makes a gurgling sound which Armand interprets as laughter.

'There's you!' Armand says. The gurgling sound grows

louder. The boy is like a vessel, emptying itself of the debris inside.

These are the only times Armand hears him laugh. When he sees César on the page. The man with the oversized nose and great ambition. Otherwise he is silent. At times he is so withdrawn Armand thinks he will never come out of his shell again.

The problem with time is that it never stands still. Armand wishes he had understood this earlier, he would have held on tight to the things that mattered. This is what he would ask for, if, like in the fairy-tale, he was granted a wish: another chance.

It takes him a while to notice the child crouching in the bushes. Staring right at him. Before the child can utter a sound Armand has turned and is fleeing the way he came, rushing through the opening in the wall so fast he scrapes his arm against the bricks. The pain is searing. Holding on to his arm, he starts running down the road even as he hears the wailing of a child calling for her father.

SIXTEEN

The pastor hurried across the sun-filled courtyard, nodding and smiling to the students he recognized. Many of them smiled back.

Their greetings pleased him. The knowledge that he was well-liked and respected even as he entered his seventh decade was deeply satisfying.

The heat had eased over the past few days. In the courtyard, a family of sparrows sat on the edge of a water fountain, dipping their beaks. The magnificent plane tree which had been left to grow for decades till its branches spread low and wide across the ground gave out plenty of shade.

It was easy to forget where you were. Stepping outside the gate, you found yourself in a different world: Rue du Faubourg Saint-Honoré, where the likes of Hermès, Lancôme and Lanvin stood with their long-established awnings alongside foreign embassies and the Élysée Palace. None of the faculty students were likely to be able to afford so much as a shoelace from any of the luxury boutiques there.

The ground beneath the plane tree and the benches around the courtyard were more crowded than usual with people taking their lunch break. It gave the pastor an inordinate amount of pleasure to see so many choosing to remain here rather than venture outside. It proved what he had always thought, that this place was a haven, an inner sanctum of peace located in the heart of Paris. It was a place where students could form friendships and also reflect without being constantly pulled in different directions.

He felt certain that the faculty's success was largely due to its non-denominational aspect. It was a place of learning, and advertised itself as such.

The pastor entered the building's wing known as La Maison, where a handful of students and researchers were housed. He took the stairs, looking at his watch to check that he still had plenty of time before his next lecture. He saw that he had slightly over an hour.

Those who managed to secure one of the rooms here were privileged. It was a pity more couldn't be accommodated, the pastor thought, climbing the stairs easily. He was still fit, and for that he had his many years of running to thank. He'd taken part in his last marathon seven years ago, one of the oldest participants in the race who'd made it to the finish line. He'd realized then that it would be his last. Another one would surely kill him, and he wasn't ready to go just yet.

The pastor walked down a quiet corridor, looking at the numbers on the doors even though he knew which one he was searching for. The people who lived here tended to be post-graduate theology students and lecturers undertaking research projects. Lodgers were also selected on the basis of need, either because they could not afford to rent a room in the city or because they were a long way from their home country, with no relatives or acquaintances here to help lessen their sense of isolation. Of the fifteen rooms on offer, more than half were occupied by students from eastern European and African nations.

The pastor stopped before a door at the end of a hallway and listened for a while before knocking, at first gently then more firmly. While he waited, he thought about the man and the boy who lived in these rooms. The Frenchman was aloof and uncommunicative but the pastor, who liked to know the lodgers, had managed once to waylay him in the corridor. He knew that the boy was adopted from Russia. Once the man had told him this, he'd seemed to regret saying anything. They'd never spoken since.

When the pastor saw that no one was coming to open the door, he pushed it open, knowing it would be unlocked.

Every tenant had their own key, of course, but this was a community built on trust. So far this system seemed to be working. In all the years the pastor had been teaching here, hundreds of people had come and gone. Yet there had not been a single incident or complaint of theft.

The pastor looked around. There was no one in the main living area. The furniture was basic and the walls were bare but everything looked neat and tidy. The place was sunny and comfortable. He walked down a hallway, knowing the two bedrooms were down that way.

The boy was curled up on a corner of his bed, looking out the open window at the courtyard below. He turned to the pastor with listless eyes.

'I hope I am not disturbing you,' the older man said, looking at him.

The boy shook his head and smiled. He looked ill. The pastor cast his eyes furtively around the room, feeling a little guilty. While he generally made himself available to those who sought him out, he also prided himself on his discretion. Clearly, this time he was not minding his own business. But he justified his behaviour by reminding himself that he hadn't seen either of the two lodgers in over two weeks, which was unusual.

'Is your father here?' he asked. It was strange, to refer to the older man as the boy's father, even though there was probably a twenty-year gap in their ages. Maybe it was because the boy gave the impression of knowing far more than his years. His eyes were filled with a weariness you did not expect or wish to see in an adolescent.

Now he was shaking his head and making a sign as if to say his father had gone away. The pastor wondered whether the boy was able to look after himself.

'Have you eaten?'

The boy didn't answer. He pressed his legs against his chest and rubbed them with his hands, as though trying to warm himself up. The pastor took two steps forward, and held out his hand.

'Come on. It's a beautiful day out there. Let me take you out for lunch.'

After a moment's hesitation, the boy held out his hand.

Morel was on his way to Irina Volkoff's house. He had gone straight from home and rung Marco from the car to say he should meet him there. He had also told him to pack an overnight bag.

He was feeling more than a little irritable. Before calling Marco, he'd spent ten minutes on the phone with the police chief in Versailles. Less than twenty-four hours and already they were moaning about the extra workload. The gist of it was that if Morel wanted continued surveillance at Volkoff's home, he'd have to rely on his own resources.

Straight after that call, Perrin had rung to tell him that the press conference was on.

'Didn't I tell you we should have one? Remember what you said? That a press conference would scare these guys away and make them go into hiding? Well, it seems to me . . .' Morel hadn't heard the rest of his sentence. He'd put the phone down beside him and waited, the distant voice like the buzzing of an angry insect.

He'd been pissed off with Perrin but most of all with himself. The fact that his boss was an arsehole didn't change the fact that two women were dead. Maybe Perrin was right, maybe if Morel had agreed to call a media briefing earlier, Guillou would still be alive.

When he'd finally heard Perrin call his name, his voice becoming louder and more insistent, he'd picked up the phone and held it to his ear.

'I'll be there,' he'd said before hanging up.

Morel set out straight after the phone calls, hoping to avoid the worst of the morning traffic. Versailles at this time of the day could take him well over an hour if he waited too long.

It had rained during the night and for the first time in two weeks the temperature was bearable. Along Avenue de Neuilly, people were walking their dogs. Over the past week, the extreme heat had made both pets and humans too lethargic to venture outdoors.

Morel wondered whether to call Solange and suggest dinner. But he wasn't sure whether he felt like company. He'd decide later.

On the way to Versailles, he ran over his interview of Elisabeth Guillou and tried to think whether he had missed anything important. What had she said? That her visitor, the older of the two, had been well-dressed and polite. The women had all said he was educated and courteous. Morel thought about the significance of Fauré's *Requiem*. Maybe the man's profession had something to do with the arts. Or maybe he was a teacher of some sort.

Morel thought of something else. Keeping his eye on the road, he called Lila.

'I'm sorry to bother you so early.'

'Don't lie. Besides, I've been up for an hour.'

'Doing what?'

'Cleaning.'

Morel wondered what she was doing cleaning so early, but he didn't say anything.

'Listen, can you get Marie Latour to list every event she's been to these past few months? Concerts, theatre, exhibitions. You mentioned that Isabelle Dufour had been to the Holy Russia exhibition at the Louvre. Ask Latour if she went to that one. And can you also check whether there have been any concerts in the past six months featuring Gabriel Fauré's works?'

'It's Fauré with an e, right?'

'You're kidding. Seriously?'

'Yeah, I always enjoy a good laugh at my expense around this time of the morning,' she said before hanging up.

Irina Volkoff's house was hidden from the street by a high stone wall and conifers planted along its side. Morel drove through the gates up a perfectly manicured driveway that circled a marble fountain and a weeping willow. Its drooping branches formed the perfect hideaway for anyone seeking some privacy, Morel thought. The house was an imposing two-storey villa with pale pink walls, a chimney and tall windows on the ground and upper floors.

Morel was so busy admiring the house that he nearly hit a large black and white dog that came bounding out of the bushes, barking and wagging its tail. As he parked the car outside the front door, Irina Volkoff came out of the house. The dog lolloped up the steps and parked its lean, shaggy frame next to its mistress. It was a strange creature, with a head that seemed oddly narrow and out of sync with its tall frame.

'Thank you for coming,' the woman said.

Morel remembered her visit to the station when she'd been asked to help with the composite sketch. As far as he could remember she had been cooperative, if not particularly friendly. But Jean was right: she must have been beautiful in her youth.

'Your colleague is already here,' Irina Volkoff said. Just then Marco's face bobbed up in the hallway behind her. He looked relieved when he saw his boss.

'That's a beautiful dog you have,' Morel said. 'Lucky I saw him in time.'

'He gets excited when he hears a car come down the driveway,' she said.

'What breed is he?'

'He's a Borzoi. Also known as a Russian wolfhound.'

Morel patted the dog's head and followed Volkoff and Marco into the house.

'Do you mind telling me why you are sending your own people in? I had a man from the Versailles station last night. Is it because the threat has become greater that I need someone from the headquarters in Paris?'

'No,' Morel said. 'Our Versailles colleagues have a number of other priorities to attend to. We're just making sure we don't overload them.'

He thought he saw her smile briefly and wondered whether she'd detected the sarcasm in his voice.

'Would you like some tea or coffee?'

'We're fine, thank you,' Morel said.

For the next ten minutes he provided Irina Volkoff with a brief update. He could no longer shield her and he told her now about Elisabeth Guillou's death since Volkoff and Latour had come in to help with the composite sketch. She seemed shocked but not particularly frightened.

'So you think this man will now look for me? Why?'

'Right now I can't tell you much more than what I've told you so far. But until we track the man and the boy down, we want to keep you safe,' Morel said.

'This is all quite unbelievable,' she said. 'How do you know you will find these people? Are you close?'

'We're making good progress,' Morel said vaguely. 'In the meantime, try not to worry. My colleague will stay here for the rest of the day and after that we will make sure there is always a police officer on duty.'

In the end Morel accepted a cup of tea from Irina Volkoff. She poured it from a silver samovar on the side table between them. He was not a tea drinker, and quietly wished she'd offered a strong cup of coffee instead, but he sipped at it anyway, amazed that anyone should find this drink invigorating.

'We will keep you up to date with any new developments. Feel free to ask my colleague here anything.' Morel gestured to Marco, who was fidgeting in his chair.

'Is he going to follow me around the house?' she asked.

'Rest assured, you will have as much privacy as you need. But it's important we keep you safe,' Morel said again.

He looked around him at the high ceiling and drawn curtains, the heavy, uncomfortable chairs. It smelled as though the room hadn't been aired in a while. Where the curtains were slightly parted, light poured in, revealing dust motes in the air. Irina Volkoff blinked and got up to draw the curtains fully.

'Have you spoken with your son lately, Madame Volkoff?'

'Yes, on Sunday,' she said, her eyes gliding over Morel's hands and the half-empty cup. 'More tea?'

'No thank you,' he said. 'It might be a good idea for you to call him.'

'If he hears about this he will get nervous and panicky,' she said. 'He's not a brave man.'

'You told my colleague Jean Char when he spoke with you that you thought the boy was Russian,' he said.

'That's right.'

'Why did you think that?'

'How can I explain? Surely it is the same for you, that you recognize a French person sometimes without being told they are French. I saw it straight away.'

Morel looked pensive. 'How did he seem?'

'Who?' the old lady asked testily.

'The boy. You said his eyes told you that he understood every word. That he realized he was with a fellow Russian. Being spoken to by a compatriot, in his own language if what you say is right. Did that realization seem to give him pleasure or to make him uncomfortable? Do you remember?'

Irina Volkoff was silent for a while, her grey eyes lost in thought.

'I'd say he looked scared,' she said slowly. 'I don't want to say I know for certain. We were not together long, you know. But he certainly did not look happy about it.'

'One more thing,' Morel said. 'Would you mind telling me what events you might have attended over the past six months or so? By events I mean any plays or concerts, for example.'

He wrote down the places she listed. She had been to two concerts featuring Russian composers and a production of Chekhov's *Cherry Orchard*.

'And also an exhibition at the Louvre, titled Holy Russia,' she said.

Morel froze.

'Would you excuse me for a moment? I need to make a phone call,' he said.

He ducked into the hallway and dialled Lila's mobile number. This time he caught her on her way into work.

'Volkoff also attended the Russia exhibition,' he told her.

'So did thousands of other people, no doubt.'

'It's worth pursuing,' Morel said. 'Think about it. The exhibition has a religious theme. It is about Russia, and the boy may be Russian. Maybe there's a reason the widows were marked at this particular event.'

'If that's how it happened.'

After Morel hung up, he stood for a while in the hallway, thinking about what he'd just heard. Could the exhibition be the common link between the widows?

Morel wandered down the hallway. Several icons lined the wall. Morel stopped to look at them more closely. They were beautiful.

'You are done with the phone call?'

He turned and found Irina Volkoff standing before him. He felt like a child being caught shoplifting. Now her eyes wandered over Morel as though making sure he hadn't slipped anything into his pockets.

'I was admiring your icons,' he said by way of explanation.

'They belonged to my mother. She kept them hidden. I only found out about them when we left the country,' she said.

'How did you find that Russian exhibition at the Louvre?'

Irina Volkoff's face lit up. 'It was most memorable. I was so happy to see it.'

Just then Marco appeared behind her. 'Excuse me, Madame Volkoff, would you mind if I helped myself to a glass of water?' he asked.

Irina Volkoff shrugged her shoulders and followed the young detective back down the hallway.

'Don't hesitate to ask my colleague here if there is anything you need,' Morel said when he caught up with Volkoff and Marco in the kitchen.

Before leaving, he turned to Marco and raised his hand in a gesture of farewell.

'I'll be in touch later today. One way or another we'll organize for someone else to take over from you.'

Marco's smile was strained. 'Sure, just let me know how it's going.'

Poor Marco, Morel thought absently. But as he stepped into the sunny driveway he was glad to be escaping the stifling house and its eagle-eyed occupant.

He drove out carefully, watching for the large dog. Switched the radio to his favourite frequency and listened to the Glenn Gould aria from the *Goldberg Variations*. His mother had struggled with Gould: she admired his genius while at the same time finding his eccentricities irritating. She felt they were put-on, part of his public persona.

There was nothing put on about the piece of music he was listening to now, Morel reflected as he headed back towards the station. The sun was high in the sky and Gould was playing up a storm.

Morel beamed at nothing in particular.

No, he wouldn't swap with Marco for anything.

The pastor was late for class. No matter how fast he went, he wouldn't make it back on time. Still, he kept up a steady pace along the street.

He ran.

Away from the boy. What he'd learned from the child had opened up a well of fear in the old man's heart.

It had been so pleasant, at first. They had lunched together in a bistro in Rue Daru, with its exotic array of Russian shops and restaurants. The Bistro Russe, its name spelled out in Cyrillic letters on the dark red awning, stood near the Alexander Nevsky Cathedral. Though he himself preferred to worship in more modest surroundings, the pastor took a childish pleasure in the cathedral's gilded onion domes and neo-Byzantine curves. As they walked past it on their way to lunch, he pointed out to the boy the contrast between the church and the bourgeois architecture of the neighbouring buildings. He felt happy, even in such silent company. At the bistro, the day's special was home-made *pelmeni*, and even though dumplings were the last thing he felt like eating on a hot day the pastor ordered two portions. The boy looked like he could use a hearty meal.

On the way back he suggested they visit the cathedral. He didn't know what the boy's beliefs were, but the cathedral was frequented by the Russian community and the pastor thought this might be of some comfort to him. Throughout lunch he'd been struck by the boy's lonely demeanour. The pastor had talked and talked, to fill the void. Hoping to clear the darkness in the boy's eyes.

Maybe a little excursion into the beautiful nineteenth-century building would be something nice for him, reminding him of home.

They entered the cool interior. The smell of incense wafted through the air and the church was half full of people standing as the priest officiated. On closer inspection the pastor saw that an infant was being baptized. The mother was holding the child and nearby was a large receptacle full of water.

He gestured to the boy to remain with him at the back of the room so as not to intrude on the ceremony. While the priest spoke words the pastor didn't understand, he looked around the cathedral. The golden icons, the candelabras and the liturgy overwhelmed him. So much gilt and pomp. It was nothing like the simple, unadorned rituals he was used to and had grown to love over the decades. He felt bloated and wished he hadn't eaten the *pelmeni*. It sat in his stomach like a brick.

When the priest undressed the infant, the pastor felt the boy stiffen next to him. He turned to find him staring wide-eyed at the naked baby. His hands were fists, the knuckles bled of all colour.

'What's wrong?' the pastor asked, worried that perhaps the *pelmeni* didn't sit well with the boy, either. What a stupid choice.

The boy shook his head. He didn't stop, just kept shaking it. His hand gripped the pastor's arm so hard he had to remove it gently. A moan escaped from the boy's lips, loud enough for the people nearest to them to look their way.

'Ssshh. What's wrong? Shall we go outside?' The pastor tried to lead the boy out but instead he was being tugged forward, towards the infant who had started to cry, a thin wailing that seemed to add to the boy's distress. The pastor began to panic. The child's strength, fuelled by a strange determination, was surprising.

'Stop it!' the pastor hissed. He was about to berate the boy but then something happened.

The priest faced the crying infant forward and plunged her once, twice, three times into the water, immersing her completely.

There was a tense silence, or was it the tension coming from the quivering boy at his side?

Then a wail like nothing the pastor had ever heard rose through the church and bounced off the walls. Everyone turned to look at them. Even the singing stopped.

Keeping his eyes lowered to the ground, the pastor dragged

the boy shrieking and trembling down the aisle and out into the street.

As soon as they found a place to sit, an unoccupied bench, the pastor forced the boy to sit next to him. For several minutes neither of them moved. The boy had stopped wailing but his body still shook. His eyes were restless, shifting from the pastor to the street as though expecting something to happen.

The pastor looked down at his arms. Despite the heat he had goose-bumps.

'Perhaps you should tell me what happened in there,' the pastor said.

Nothing.

Struck by inspiration, the pastor dug in his pocket and pulled out a notepad and a pen.

'Perhaps you can write it down for me,' he said. The boy looked at him then. He seemed to be hesitating.

While he waited, the pastor rubbed his chest to ease the stinging sensation there. Heartburn.

Those damned dumplings, he thought, before automatically mouthing a silent apology for his use of profanity.

Now the pastor was running, leaving behind the words scribbled on his notepad and the one who'd written them down for him. How innocent words were, until they were strung together into sentences and armed with meaning. Then they could fell you as effectively as any weapon and rob you of your power.

He ran, oblivious to the mounting tension in his body. Sweat poured down his face, blinding him. He didn't try to wipe it away.

The pastor was only a hundred metres or so from the faculty. He could see the tall gates in the distance and the whitewashed building which he called home. As he ran, the words began to fade, the fateful sentences decomposing in his mind until he forgot their meaning.

Without warning, his heart clenched. Like someone was squeezing it hard. The sensation was so acute he cried out, scaring a well-to-do young woman with a designer pram whom he'd been about to overtake.

She too let out a shriek and swerved out of his way as he fell to the ground, fighting for breath through a miasma of pain.

Dear God, he prayed.

He wasn't ready for this.

SEVENTEEN

Morel knew most of the journalists in the room. He liked very few of them. There was a hubbub of noise and activity as people greeted each other and got comfortable on their chairs. The camera crews positioned themselves along the side of the table where Perrin sat.

Morel would have preferred to stay away from the podium but that wasn't an option. Reluctantly, he took a seat next to Perrin. His boss could barely contain his excitement. At last, the audience he pined for. Morel didn't mind so much; it was a nice change from Perrin's daily haranguing about the case.

'Ladies and gentlemen, thank you for coming at such short notice. We know how busy you are but we are at a crucial stage of our investigation and hope that you will assist us in speeding things up. Time is of the essence.'

The first of many clichés to come, Morel thought. The same well-worn expressions he'd heard a hundred times from Perrin. He made a silent bet with himself to see how many the commissaire would come up with over the course of this briefing. He guessed ten, at least.

Thanks to a projector installed earlier at the back of the room, the drawing of the man and the boy who'd visited the widows' homes appeared up on the wall directly behind Perrin.

'This is a composite sketch of two people we believe may be able to help us with our enquiry. We know that the two women who were killed were visited by these people a week or so before their death.'

A murmur went around the room.

'Two women have been killed. Are we dealing with a serial killer, then?' a man asked from the second row. Morel recognized the *France-Soir* reporter. A weaselly-looking character whose stories always stank.

'We do believe there is a connection between the two murders. However, I am reluctant to use the words serial killer,' Perrin said, making 'reluctant' sound a great deal like 'eager'. 'All I can say is that at this stage we are treating them as the work of a single person.'

'Do we know why they were targeted?' a woman asked. Her name was Laure Rousset and she had been with *Le Monde* ever since Morel had known her. They had dated for a while, nothing serious, but he liked and respected her.

'We are still looking into that,' Perrin said.

'Are these the ones who killed the two pensioners?'

'How big is your crystal ball?' Perrin said while Morel cringed. 'It would be great if we could be that certain. At this stage it's too early to draw such conclusions. But we think they – the man in particular – can help us solve these murders. It's crucial that we find them.'

There were more questions. Morel had a feeling Perrin would sit here all afternoon if he could, but after a while even he saw that it was time to end the briefing. Several of the journalists were looking at their watches. He stood up and called the briefing to a close.

'Time to let us get on with our work,' he barked. 'Thank you for coming.'

As the camera crews gathered up their equipment and the room slowly emptied, Laure came up to Morel.

'Have you got a minute?'

'Sure.' He kissed her cheek. 'How are you, Laure?'

'Well. I expect you're pretty busy with this going on.'

He nodded, waiting to hear what might come next. She hadn't spoken to him in over a year. He figured her sudden interest in him had more to do with the dead widows than with any nostalgia about their brief encounter.

'Any chance we could catch up over a drink?'

Morel gave her a rueful smile. 'In other circumstances, I'd be delighted. But I don't think Perrin would be too happy to see us huddling over drinks together while this investigation is open.'

'Well, maybe when this case is closed,' Laure said, looking around the room, perhaps for someone else who might buy her a drink. 'Any idea how close you might be to catching your killer?' she asked, turning to him again. He saw her feign an interest she did not feel, hoping no doubt to sway him.

'I'd like to say we're close. But you know I can't talk to you about it.'

'Fair enough. I had to try,' she said. She touched his arm. 'Keep in touch, OK?'

'Sure,' Morel said.

No one else was there just yet when he returned to his desk. Making the most of his time alone, he dialled Solange's number and arranged to meet her after work.

An evening with beautiful, kind-hearted Solange was just what he needed.

At lunchtime Morel's team watched the midday news in the office. They were joined by Patrick Sergeant, whose team

Perrin had assigned to provide support in Morel's investigation.

As expected, the faces of the two they were looking for loomed large on the TV screen. It was the lead story. A number flashed across the bottom of the screen for people to call if they had any useful information to pass on.

'Let the madness begin,' Sergeant said. He was referring to the flood of calls they would undoubtedly be getting from every Tom, Dick and Harry who thought they might have seen the pair or who simply wanted their two minutes of fame, to be part of the story.

Sure enough, the phones started ringing shortly after. A team had been set up to deal with the incoming calls and forward those that seemed genuine and vaguely promising. Every call that wasn't put through would still be logged in detail, for Morel's people to review at the end of each day.

By 6 p.m. they had received 120 calls from people claiming they had sighted the man and the boy shown on television. Several, Morel found out when he checked the log book, were from self-dubbed mediums who had apparently managed to talk to both Elisabeth Guillou and Isabelle Dufour beyond the grave. Morel had dealt with five callers personally. One seemed promising, a man who claimed to have met the two evangelists at a Baptist convention in the US state of Louisiana. Morel felt his pulse quicken until the man declared he himself had recently been born again after wandering for years in the desert. When he finally confided that he was Jesus Christ, Morel thanked him politely and hung up.

By 7 p.m. Morel started packing up. Only Lila was still there, sitting with her feet propped up on the desk. Neither felt much like talking.

'I'm getting out of here. You should do the same,' he told Lila.

'Marie Latour,' Lila said. 'She attended the Russia exhibition.'

'Bingo,' Morel said softly.

'I'll give Guillou's children a call,' Lila said. 'They might be able to tell us whether she attended the exhibition too. You never know. She might have gone with her son or daughter, or told them about it.'

Morel nodded.

'Marco is on his way back from Versailles, by the way,' Morel said. 'They've agreed to be a little bit cooperative. One of their guys will be on night watch.'

'He'll be happy to hear it,' Lila said.

'And Marie Latour is staying with her daughter for a few days. So I won't have to rely on our colleagues in Maisons-Laffitte any more.'

'Good.'

'Are you OK?' Morel asked. He couldn't see Lila's face but he could tell by her stiff posture that something was on her mind.

'Fine. Just tired, that's all.'

'Go home.'

'OK, OK.'

Lila grabbed her jacket and headed down the stairs. She found her car and drove it towards Neuilly with her window rolled down. The sun was setting and while the traffic flowed reasonably well, the footpaths were crowded, mostly, she guessed, with people from out of town. Along the Champs-Élysées, they ambled down the side lanes converted into pedestrian zones, past luxury shop fronts and cinemas. There was a constant flow of people coming up the steps from the Métro stations and the cafes and restaurants were doing a brisk trade.

If Morel knew where she was heading, he'd have a fit, she thought.

In Neuilly, Lila found Jacques Dufour's house and parked outside. She rolled a cigarette while she waited. She was sitting outside their home for the second night in a row, waiting for him to do something. During the first interview with the Dufours, she had watched Jacques closely. He'd been twitchy. She was certain she'd recognized the signs. The way he pinched his nostrils and wiped at his nose. All his little ticks. The dilated pupils.

The twitchiness, the latent anger. It fit together.

Anne had been equally twitchy during their second interview yesterday, though clearly for different reasons, and Lila hadn't for a moment believed her when she'd said Jacques would be away for the week. The previous night, nothing unusual had happened, he had returned from work around eight and not gone out again. Not out with the mistress, then. She was fine with that. But she knew it was just a question of time before he revealed himself.

She was rolling her second cigarette when his car passed her and turned into the Dufours' driveway. The gates closed and it went dark and silent again.

An hour later the gates opened and Dufour drove his car out again. He turned in the opposite direction from the one he'd come from earlier, and turned left onto Avenue de Neuilly before heading towards the motorway.

'You're making it too easy for me, Jacques,' Lila said.

For all she knew, he could be heading out for a game of bowling with some work mates. But if he had anything to conceal, she would find out what it was and shove it in his face at the earliest opportunity.

*

Morel lay naked on his back, enjoying the feel of Solange's fingers against his chest. He had no intention of moving for the next seven hours or so.

When his phone rang, he looked to see who it was. He recognized the number as police headquarters and answered.

'I've got a woman on the phone, says she has something to share regarding the two suspects,' the duty officer said.

'Put her on, then,' Morel said, too tired to argue that the call was probably a waste of time.

'Morel speaking.'

'Hello?'

'Yes. Who is this?'

'My name is Amelia Berg. I have something to tell you regarding the man whose portrait you broadcast on television. I would have called earlier but I only saw it just now. By chance, in fact, as I don't watch the news every day.'

'What is it you want to tell me, madame?' Morel prompted, thinking that otherwise it would be a while before she got to the point.

'It's an incredible likeness. Whoever drew the picture has a real gift. Anyway, he and my son went to school together.'

'What's his name?'

'Armand Le Bellec,' she said.

'Where does he live?' Morel said, gesturing to Solange to get him something he could write with. He watched her step across the room naked and return with pen and paper.

'I'm not sure. But I can tell you he was just here, in my garden.'

Morel frowned. 'Where are you calling from?'

She named a village in Brittany Morel had never heard of.

'Listen to me carefully, Madame Berg. I need you to hang up and call the gendarmes,' Morel said.

To his amazement, he heard the woman laugh. 'For what? I've known Armand since he was a child. I have nothing to be afraid of.'

He was about to speak when she continued. 'To tell you the truth, I'm more worried about *him*.'

Morel looked at his watch. 'Would you mind leaving me your details? I'd like to be able to call you back. We're going to have some questions.'

'Certainly.' She gave him her address and phone number and told him she would be home all week.

After he hung up, Morel turned to Solange. He hugged her and tenderly kissed each of her breasts.

'I'm sorry but I have to go,' he said.

'Somehow I knew you were going to say that,' she said.

EIGHTEEN

When they said Russia, at first he baulked. He had never travelled outside France. First the village, then university in Rennes, only an hour from home. He was expected to catch the bus back every Friday afternoon and spend the weekends with his mother. There was no money to do anything else, in any case. He knew so little of life. Russia seemed like a place where he might get lost and never be found.

But he had to get away.

He packed one suitcase. He had so few belongings. His books stayed behind, with his mother. He gave his notice at the dorm where he lived during the week and on the last night took his mother out for dinner. She'd wanted to cook for him but he felt more comfortable going out somewhere where she couldn't make a fuss. When the time came to leave the restaurant, she offered to put him up for the night. They could drive back to the village together, and she would drive him back in the next day, in time for his flight. Wouldn't that be nicer than to spend the night before his departure alone in town? He could see she was hurt by his response, could feel it as he walked away from her. But he knew he couldn't face the house and his old room.

There was no one else to say goodbye to. He flew Air France days after the airline ended its strike. Normally he didn't drink but on the plane he had two small bottles of wine. It was a mistake. Afterwards he had to throw up in the toilet. He spent the rest of the flight in a stupor, staring at the picture on the screen of a toy plane drawing a line across a map of Europe.

As the plane circled Sheremetyevo airport he heard the hostess say the temperature was minus twenty on the ground. Minus twenty! He closed his eyes and tried to imagine what that was like. All he could picture was a pointless immensity, a silence you could drown in.

How dreadfully anxious he'd been, during those first, wintry months! How tempting, to take the first flight back and bury himself in a small town somewhere. But he didn't. And after a couple of weeks it became a lot easier than he'd imagined. He found that he was a good teacher and that his students liked him. They weren't a bad lot. Precocious for the most part, privileged and pampered, but also a hell of a lot more mature than kids that age back home, the ones he'd gone to school with.

At first he was afraid of them. These kids who smoked in the snowbound courtyard before the bell rang, whose life experiences surpassed his in unimaginable ways. Some days he walked into the classroom with a strong sense of paranoia, imagining that behind his back they were sniggering at him, the provincial boy, the country bumpkin. Kids were good at digging out the very thing you wanted to keep buried. Just because he was older than them didn't give him an advantage. It wasn't even much of an age difference. Many of the kids were also taller than him. At one metre sixty-five, he was hardly imposing.

But however hard he searched for evidence that they ridiculed him, he couldn't find it. After a while he relaxed and began to look forward to the classes. It gave him a kick, to see how far he had come. If his mother could see him now! Commanding respect. When he spoke, they listened. When classes ended there were always a couple of them hanging back, waiting with a question. It wasn't always about school work either. Often they just wanted to chat. For the first time in his life, he felt like someone.

Other things were less gratifying. Even he was sheltered, of course, compared with the average Russian. Unlike them he was just passing through and whatever discomforts he experienced were temporary. But still, he struggled with the place where he lived. While his students went back to their sheltered surroundings, the embassy kids and the ones whose parents worked for corporations, every day he encountered squalor. The door to his building needed fixing and the entrance always smelled of piss and cabbage. You could never be sure whether the lift would make it to your floor. Armand would have taken the stairs but he was afraid of what he might find there. Sometimes his heart sank when he walked through the door to his flat and saw the brown carpet and cheap furniture, the kitchen with its peeling brown linoleum floor that was always sticky beneath his feet, so that he took to keeping his socks on all the time. In winter the flat was overheated and stuffy. Outside his window, a factory belched smoke and a thousand empty sockets stared back at him, rows of windows in grey concrete blocks just like the one he lived in.

He became used to his new life. One of his colleagues put him in touch with a local, middle-aged woman who gave Russian lessons. He was a good student and learned quickly. In winter he found it was easy to lose all sense of perspective. Lines became blurred, then non-existent. He walked through the city like a blind man. But rather than mourn the loss of familiarity, he celebrated it, finding freedom in the absence of recognizable signposts.

He was lonely, of course. He could have done what some of his younger colleagues did, those who like him were teaching overseas as an alternative to military service. Get himself a Russian girlfriend (or two at a time, like the maths teacher Gilles, who appeared at school the next day looking smug, dying to tell his story), or he could socialize with the teenagers, invite them to his home. Armand tried the former. He came home one night with a girl who moaned and writhed under him with such intensity, his longing evaporated. They drank vodka together until she pulled a syringe from her bag and asked him to inject it into her breasts. He found himself contemplating this obscene act for a moment, before shoving her out of the apartment. He spent the night tossing and turning in self-disgust, both excited and repelled by the memory.

As for the parties with the kids he taught, Armand couldn't bring himself to take part. He remained friendly with them at school but turned down the invitations from colleagues and pupils alike. It wasn't that he cared whether it was appropriate or not. In that setting he worried that he might stand out.

He didn't go entirely unnoticed. That year, two students attached themselves to him. Like him, they were singular, quiet. The girl was taller than Armand, with lustrous black skin and long, muscled legs. Puberty had reached her long before the other girls in the class. Armand noticed that this seemed to give her a comfortable edge over them. Without trying, she summoned envy. The boys, too, were mesmerized. Because he didn't desire her, Armand did not find her intimidating. He found it easy to talk to her. They became friends, in a sense. She was a natural at philosophy, her mind embraced the concept of an open-ended world where a single question might reveal a dozen different truths. In the mornings before school they sat sometimes in his box-shaped Lada and argued about Heidegger and Kierkegaard, the heater turned up high. Their intimacy was the closest he had come to anyone since Charles.

Once he began to take Olivia out, he noticed how the Russians stared, what a novelty she was, because of her black skin but also her beauty, which was nothing like the anaemic, wilting-flower looks of the girls he saw here. Blonde and thin and forever pouting, as though surliness were somehow seductive. Olivia had a smile that was broad and unreservedly joyful, a panorama of dazzling teeth that lit up her face and made her eyes gleam.

Then there was the boy. A quick-witted Moroccan adolescent, lithe and handsome, with dark hooded eyes and a way of snubbing the world with every gesture. When he had to address this student, Armand could not look him in the eye, though he knew the boy shared no such qualm about him. He watched Armand in class through lowered lashes, as though trying to provoke some sort of response.

Armand, Amir. The words formed a sing-song in Armand's mind. Soon, the boy's name accompanied his every waking thought.

Two syllables: that was all it took to undo him.

NINETEEN

'Le Bellec. Did you know the name is derived from *beleg*, a word that means priest in Celtic?' Jean said.

'Really? How the hell do you know that?' Morel asked.

The team were assembled around Lila and Marco's desk. Jean had brought coffees for everyone. They were all feeling more cheerful, including Morel. Now they had Le Bellec's name, they had something tangible to work with.

'I knew a Le Bellec once,' Jean said. 'He was my brother-in-law for a while. My sister looked up the name and once she found out what the origin was she decided to keep her maiden name. She is, shall we say, a devout atheist.'

'Seems an appropriate name for our evangelist,' Morel said. He was feeling better than he'd felt for weeks. That morning he'd bought himself a new office chair and also invested in a heavy-duty upright fan for the office. Now it was blowing in their direction while Lila and Marco snatched at the papers on their desk before they were blown away.

Like Marie Latour, Irina Volkoff had grown tired of having a permanent police presence in her home and decided to stay with a friend for a few days. Morel was glad he no longer had to rely on colleagues outside police headquarters to provide support.

'Armand Le Bellec. Age thirty-four,' Lila read from the

folder before her. She was wearing a pair of black jeans and a tight red singlet. One of her bra straps, a bright orange, had come off her shoulder and she absent-mindedly returned it to its rightful place while Marco looked at her. Morel wondered whether he needed to talk to the young officer. Let him know he didn't stand a chance with tall, spirited Lila and that, the way he mooned over his colleague, he was probably heading for a punch on the nose. But it wasn't his business, after all.

Before Lila could proceed, there was a knock at the door. Everyone turned to see who it was. The man with the cropped black hair and honey-coloured eyes was familiar to the team.

'Akil Abdelkader, come and join us,' Morel said. He turned to the others. 'I've asked Akil to help us out. His boss has kindly agreed to spare him for a few days.' He caught the look of dismay on Marco's face. 'With Vincent away and Jean still tied up with the warehouse killing, I think we could really use an extra pair of hands. I know Patrick's team is helping out but I reckon it'll be good to have someone sit here with us who had some involvement with this early on.

'Akil has been reading up on the recent developments in the case. I value his input because he's already shown us what he's capable of. Without him we might never have had access to Dufour's flat. Not until it was too late, at any rate.'

Lila stood up and shook Akil's hand, and Marco followed suit, though he looked distinctly unhappy. Jean pulled a chair over but Akil shook his head.

'I'm happy to stand.' His voice was deep and his manner relaxed. Lila looked at him briefly so no one would notice her checking out the new guy.

'Lila was just running us through what she knows about Armand Le Bellec. He is our number-one suspect at this stage, for the murders of Isabelle Dufour and Elisabeth

Guillou. We don't have the boy's name yet but hopefully now we have Le Bellec's we'll be able to move much faster.'

'Sounds good,' Akil said.

'Carry on, Lila.'

'Le Bellec is from Brittany. Not so much the picturesque part of the region, further inland. This is a tiny village about an hour's drive from Rennes. The sort of place you can't wait to get out of, I imagine.'

'Spare us the commentary,' Morel said.

'I checked to see whether he has any priors and came up empty-handed,' she said, giving Morel a dark look. 'But I did find out quite a bit about him. Apparently he studied philosophy and theology at the University of Rennes and went on to obtain a PhD. Wrote his thesis titled "A new perspective on Kierkegaard's relation to Hegel". Whatever that means. He taught philosophy to Year 11 students at the French Lycée in Moscow. As part of his military service.'

'How old was he when he went over there?' Morel asked.

'Just twenty-four.' Lila pulled her hair back and tied it into a ponytail. She caught Akil looking at her. She stood up and went to open the window. When she returned she picked up her coffee cup and sat on the edge of her desk. Suddenly she felt self-conscious. The way she was sitting was completely unnatural.

'Then?'

'He was sacked.' Lila returned to her seat. 'He was never charged with anything,' she continued. 'But there was talk that he had got involved with a fifteen-year-old schoolgirl, the daughter of the Senegalese ambassador. The parents claimed he took advantage. It was all kept quiet, but the school told him to leave.' She took a sip from her coffee and looked at Morel. 'When he returned to France, he wasn't alone. According to his passport, he had a Russian boy with him. At some point before he left the country, he adopted this kid.'

'Do we know what Le Bellec's been up to since he got back?' Morel asked.

'He taught at a school in Rennes for a while. Then he moved up to Paris.'

'Is he teaching here?' Morel asked, startled.

'Not sure. I haven't been able to track him down yet. There is no listing for him that I can find. But I have a contact at the Ministry of Education and he's looking into it for me. Nice guy,' Lila said. 'I promised we could have dinner sometime.'

'And the Senegalese girl? Have we got a name?'

'She lives here in Paris,' Lila said. 'After her baccalaureate she moved here to take up medicine. She lives in Montmartre with her boyfriend. Also a medical student.'

'Both students? How do they manage?'

'The parents aren't exactly destitute,' Lila said.

'So the parents are supporting the young lovebirds?'

'I'd say so.'

Morel looked at Lila and shook his head slowly. 'How the hell did you find all this out?'

'I have my ways,' she said, clearly pleased with herself. 'I spoke with someone who worked at the school in Moscow. And like I said, there's my chum at the Ministry of Education.'

Morel turned to the others. 'The first thing we need to do is track down this Armand Le Bellec. The call from Amelia Berg tells us he was back in his village. It's unlikely he's still hanging around. I think, though, that we need to get down there and talk to people who knew him. It might help us find out where he is now. Lila, you and I will drive up there.'

'What? How far is it?'

'Three to four hours maybe? In the meantime we can't

wait for Lila's friend to turn something up. Akil and Marco, I need you to run Le Bellec's name past the schools. If he is still teaching, he'll be in or close to Paris. We'll start with Paris then move outwards if we don't come up with anything. Akil, why don't you take Lila's desk while she and I are away. That way you and Marco will find it easier to share the workload and communicate what you find.'

Akil nodded. His face didn't betray anything but Marco's was long-suffering.

'Make sure you don't touch my things and don't mess anything up,' Lila told Akil.

He grinned. 'I wouldn't dare.'

'We're getting close to him,' Morel said. 'I don't want him to find out we're on his trail and have him disappear.'

'In other words, let's make sure Perrin's happy and doesn't feel the need to splash the story across the papers again, just so he can get another profile shot of himself in *Le Figaro*,' Lila said.

There was laughter all around. Everyone remembered the news story. A five-year-old girl had been kidnapped and Morel and his team had tracked down her abductors within thirty-six hours. The article showed Perrin being interviewed in his office. They had taken a shot of him gazing out the window with a moody, introspective look on his face. The look of a man battling against the odds. He'd kept a copy of the article on his desk for weeks.

'Lila, why don't you give the medical student a call, the girl who had Le Bellec as a teacher,' Morel said. 'Let's talk to her. Just tell her we want a simple chat, we can do it at her place or somewhere else if she prefers. I'd like to know a bit more about our friend Armand.'

'Right.'

'I want to see her today,' Morel continued. 'The more we

know about Le Bellec before we talk to people in his village, the better.'

Morel clapped his hands.

'All right, back to work everyone. Let's see whether we can locate our guy. The sooner the better, for everyone. And Marco,' Morel said, turning to him. 'Make sure Akil feels welcome.'

'Sure,' Marco replied without a smile.

Morel and Lila recognized Olivia straight away. It was hard not to. In this predominantly white, middle-class neighbourhood you did not see many blacks. She was alone. Morel had thought she might bring the boyfriend and was glad she hadn't. It would be easier to talk to her this way. Though she was sitting, Morel could see she was tall, possibly taller than him. Her dress was short and emphasized the length and shapeliness of her legs. He noted how people walking past looked her way. It was hard not to.

'I wonder why she chose such a public place?' Lila said.

'Sometimes it's easier to talk about difficult things in an open, public space like this one. If the story is true then she can't be too happy about having to talk about it again.'

Morel noticed that Lila had taken her hair down and put lipstick on since the team meeting. She was in a good mood, and Morel wondered whether maybe she had a date later on. It wasn't the sort of question he'd think to ask her. But there was a definite glow about his young colleague.

'Olivia?' he said when they got close to the girl. She looked at them and nodded but didn't get up. 'Thanks for meeting us,' Morel offered his hand. She extended hers but didn't smile.

'I didn't want you in my house. I don't want Diallo to know about all this. It's in the past. My boyfriend is a jealous guy, the last thing I need is for him to hear about other men.' Her voice was deep and measured, her gaze direct.

'Yes, of course,' Morel said. It wasn't the opening he'd expected.

'There is no reason at all why he should know,' Lila said, sitting next to Olivia.

Olivia looked at Lila as if she hadn't seen her there, which was possible, given how intently she'd been looking at Morel. She looked uneasy and Morel wondered about this Diallo character and his jealous nature.

'We won't keep you long at all but there is something we need to ask about.'

'Armand.'

'That's right,' Morel said. 'About your relationship, I—'

'What has he done?'

Lila started to say something but Morel shot her a warning look. 'We don't know yet that he has done anything particularly bad.'

Olivia looked at him with a puzzled air. 'Then why are you bugging me with your questions?'

'Because we think he may be linked to something bad and that it might get worse. And I want to stop it if I can.'

Olivia shook her head. 'I wish I'd never met him,' she said. She looked at Lila, as though seeking another woman's understanding. Her next sentence surprised them both.

'Though it's long ago now, Armand broke my heart.' She touched her chest, below her left breast. 'It still hurts, right here.'

'Can you please explain that? You were in a relationship with Armand and he left you? Is that it?'

She surprised them by throwing her head back and laughing. They waited till she stopped. She looked at them both with eyes wet from laughter.

'You don't know the first thing about Armand, do you?' She wiped her eyes and looked at Morel intensely again. He felt she was making her mind up about him and wondering how much to say.

She stood up. Morel had been right. She was taller than him.

'If you want to understand Armand, then it's Amir you should be looking for,' she said.

'Amir?' Morel said.

TWENTY

He always thought of Amir as a boy.

Armand liked to get to school before his colleagues and often he arrived when it was still dark, to prepare for the morning classes. There'd be no one about but then he'd see the kid Amir slouching between the two sets of doors that led from the street into the school's entrance hall, smoking filtered Camels and kicking the snow from his boots. In the overheated space the snow quickly formed dirty puddles beneath his feet.

In the courtyard at recess Amir was always in motion, running or chasing one of his class mates, loud and boisterous. When it was his turn to supervise, Armand stood among them all and pretended not to see the flakes of snow melting on the boy's black hair and how bright his eyes became out in the cold, the colour in his cheeks. The long eyelashes and full lips gave him an almost feminine allure and a false air of pliancy.

The classes were usually a real mix but that year Amir was the only Arab in a predominantly white community. Where Olivia was easy-going and relaxed, Amir was proud and susceptible, quick to take offence. Maybe it had something to do with the colour of their skin and the fact that they were in a minority, both from the same continent. Maybe not. Either way, Amir and Olivia became friends. Armand never knew if they were anything more. The thought that they might be made him unhappy, was physically unendurable, and so he closed his mind to it. Instead he pretended not to care when Olivia suggested that Amir join their little outings.

The three of them went for walks along the Moskva, bought ice-cream sandwiches at Gorky Park or sat in over-heated cafes eating *pelmeni* and borscht with great dollops of cream. Armand veered from feeling anguished to thinking that he couldn't imagine being any happier than he was now. All week he waited for the weekend when they might be out together. It was always the three of them and they always met outdoors, never at his flat. Armand felt that by having them over to his place he would be crossing a line. He had probably crossed it already, by spending so much time with his two students outside school hours, but he didn't feel he was doing anything wrong.

The main thing was that he and Amir were never alone.

One Saturday afternoon Amir knocked on his door. Armand did not ask how the boy knew where he lived. Instead he let him in and offered to make coffee. The boy looked around the flat. He was flushed and sweating.

'Have you been running?' Armand asked. The boy was a stellar long-distance runner. Armand had seen him in action, leading the others out of the school and towards the athletic grounds where the sports teacher, a ruddy Corsican, took his classes.

Amir ignored the question and with a gesture of impatience pulled his shirt off. He acted as though he wanted to get this over with. Armand knew he should be sending the boy away but the sight of his hairless torso and dark nipples, the fast pace of the boy's breathing, kept him paralysed. If he could have moved, he would have made a run for it, bolted down the stairs and into the relative safety of the courtyard with its bundled-up children and hazardous play equipment, but his feet were rooted to the ground.

Now Amir was standing before him in his boxer shorts, with his arms loosely by his side. Did he smile, or was Armand imagining it?

'Can I use your shower?'

Night was falling. Mid-afternoon and already the overcast sky was fading into black. Armand stood close to the window and stared at the muddy streets below, cutting dark trails through a blanket of snow. How would Amir get back now? It was too dark and cold. He would have to drive him. A woman wearing a scarf around her head went past, pulling a shopping trolley. A couple of black-winged birds trailed each other in the sky. He could hear the lift creaking as it made its way down. The sound receded until, for a single minute, there was complete silence. Then the slushing of tyres, the sound of shrieking, a door slamming somewhere close by.

When he turned, Amir stood before him stark naked. His wet hair fell across his forehead. He still held his hands by his side. His cock stood proudly between his legs, erect and big. Much bigger than anything you'd expect on a boy, but then Amir was sixteen. Technically did that make him an adult, or close enough that the distinction didn't matter?

The silence lasted so long, the swelling in Armand's heart so quick and overwhelming, that he wondered whether he would be able to stand it and for how long.

'You'd better get dressed.' He heard his own voice, ragged and harsh.

Amir shrugged in an exaggerated gesture of indifference. He turned and walked back into the bathroom.

They drove back to Amir's place in complete silence. The boy lived in an exclusive apartment block close to the school.

'Goodnight,' Armand said.

'Thanks for the drive.'

'Sure.' *Thanks for dropping by*, he almost said, but it would have sounded flippant and it was the wrong thing to say to this boy. A *boy*, his *student*, Armand reminded himself.

When he got home, Armand poured himself a shot of vodka. He sat at the kitchen table without bothering to turn on the light. He wanted to cry but felt he didn't deserve to. He thought of France, of home, and wondered about what had driven him to come here. It seemed like the very thing he had tried to escape had found him anyway.

A series of bleak days followed. It didn't help that it was night-time before classes even ended. Armand spent Christmas alone and woke up in a stupor the next afternoon. The silence and the utter pointlessness of it all frightened him into action. He found himself knocking on his Russian neighbour's door and being invited in. Before he knew it, he was sharing the man's lunch in his equally stuffy apartment.

The man introduced himself as Volodya. Later they sat at the table amongst the remains of their shared meal, talking about Russian authors. Armand confessed he wasn't fond of Pushkin. The man's response was to scrape his chair back and stand to deliver an impassioned tirade on the poet's genius. They talked about Tolstoy's feelings towards Anna Karenina as he wrote her character, and Chekhov's humanism. For that hour, the world outside this messy, lived-in flat ceased to exist for Armand.

The man then said he had to leave shortly to pick up his girlfriend from the orphanage where she worked, an hour out of the city. The Russian was a university lecturer and his girlfriend a nurse's aide. Normally she would get a lift home with a colleague who had a car but the colleague had gone home sick at lunchtime.

'It's a long and boring drive. I could use some company,' the man said. He was tall and unshaven, with a mop of dark hair. Fingers stained with nicotine. In his mid-forties, Armand guessed. There was something strange about the way he stood, and Armand realized it was because of his left arm, which hung by his side, the fingers of the hand permanently curled.

'I'd love to come,' he told Volodya. His Russian wasn't fluent by any means but he managed. Volodya smiled and offered him another cup of tea before they left.

They took the ring road, the streets thick with salt to melt the ice, and drove through a succession of dreary suburbs that all looked the same to Armand's weary eyes. It was terribly hot in the car and the Russian played pop music at full volume, but Armand didn't protest. Once they'd left the suburbs the road became treacherous and once or twice Volodya lost control. The car slid into the opposite lane, but there was no traffic about. He turned the radio down then and drove more carefully.

Armand dozed and woke, blinking through whiteness. Naked birch trees and the sun like a ghostly halo. The pressure from the all-encompassing whiteness made him squint. There was no way to gauge the shape of the world. After a while he gave up and he let his eyes settle on nothing, exhausted.

Driving up through a tunnel of trees garlanded with snow, the orphanage loomed up unexpectedly. There was nobody around. The building was cold and grey. For a moment Armand imagined that everyone inside had frozen, icy statues on each landing waiting to be thawed. He wanted to turn and flee.

'We are here,' his neighbour said, and before he knew it, they were knocking on the door and being let in.

It all seems like such a long time ago, Armand thinks as he reaches the outskirts of Paris. It has been a long day and he's having trouble maintaining his concentration. By the time he reaches his *arrondissement*, he's starving. He stops at a supermarket and buys bread and fruit. It'll have to do; he's too tired to cook.

It's close to midnight when he reaches the faculty. There is no one about and there is no sound coming from behind the closed doors. He has never walked down the carpeted hallway so late and the thought that he might be the only person still awake in the building unsettles him.

He opens the door quietly so he doesn't wake César up. The boy is fast asleep in his bed, the covers drawn up to his chin. There is an unfamiliar smell in the room. Perfume, maybe, or air freshener. Armand tries to think what it could be. He is too tired to let it worry him.

He undresses down to his shorts and slides in next to the boy. César moans something in his sleep. Armand cradles the boy's body – half hoping he will wake up, even though he doesn't want to disturb him either. But it's too dark, too quiet here. There is an unpleasant scurrying sensation in his head, as though a swarm of insects has invaded his brain.

He thinks that he should never have made the trip to Brittany. What had he been hoping to achieve? Seeking comfort like that from a relationship that had died a long time ago.

He is exhausted but still he can't get to sleep. After a while he gives up trying and goes to the kitchen to make himself a hot drink. Two scoops of Nesquik and milk, which he heats in the microwave. There is a copy of today's *Figaro* on the table. Armand is surprised. César never reads the newspapers. He sits down with his drink and leafs through the paper, hoping to distract himself from his thoughts.

The story is on page three, headlined 'Serial killer?' A woman called Elisabeth Guillou has been found dead in her house. Police say it was foul play. Another woman was found dead a week earlier. The reporter wonders whether there might be a link, though the police will not confirm whether they see the murders as being the work of a single killer. The lack of information is a minor inconvenience which doesn't seem to have fazed the reporter. 'There is a killer on the loose and he is targeting elderly women. What are the police doing about it?' he says. The article ends with a commentary on soaring crime rates and how vulnerable the elderly are.

Armand sits still for a long time, forgetting to drink from the cup in his hands. Then he gets up and goes over to César. He shakes the boy, gently at first, then harder, until César opens his eyes. As soon as he is awake, he sits up, as though he has been trained to do so. Armand sits next to him. The boy's expression is impossible to read.

'Get dressed,' Armand says.

The boy stands up and does as he is told.

TWENTY-ONE

Marie Latour had a list of grievances as long as the Amazon. She could list them if anyone asked. Before she opened her eyes in the morning she would hear the neighbour's front door slam and wonder what sort of person makes a point of letting the world know they are off to work. The rubbish truck came rumbling down her street and once she heard the men calling to each other in the pre-dawn stillness, in a language she didn't recognize. It made her wonder why, with so many unemployed, they needed to bring foreigners all the way here to do the job. Whenever she left Maisons-Laffitte to go into Paris, which wasn't often these days, she found herself frazzled. Dog shit on the footpaths, people of all shades jostling for space in a city she now barely knew. Everything moved too fast.

Though she didn't dare tell her to her face, she thought the suburb where her daughter lived – and in which she was currently residing – particularly vile. If she hadn't been meeting Guy, she might perhaps have never ventured out.

'How dreadful Paris has become,' she told Guy. Ever since her husband's death three years ago, Marie made a point of meeting once a week the man who had been Hector's best friend for thirty-five years. Guy was alone too, and their friendship with its enduring loyalty brought them both a great deal of comfort. They agreed on most things. For instance that the country they lived in today might as well be Morocco, with all the foreigners that lived here.

'Of course they want to live here, who can blame them? Coming from those dreadful places. But enough is enough,' Guy said, and Marie could only concur.

She had not told her daughter that she was going out. But what harm could it do, after all? She was just meeting her old friend and would head straight back afterwards.

Now they stood together before a painting by Matisse, whose work Marie secretly admired; but she would wait to see what Guy said before pronouncing herself. Matisse had painted this work during his stay in Morocco and there were things that she knew Guy would disapprove of. Take, for example, the portrait of the young dark-skinned boy. She felt embarrassed looking at it, with Guy by her side. It was all too – well, *physical*.

Still, it was her admiration for Matisse that had made her suggest that she and Guy meet at the Arab World Institute, a rectangular and modern building on Rue des Fosses Saint-Bernard, in the fifth *arrondissement*. She arrived early, and as she waited for Guy she gazed for a while at the structure. The sun was high in the sky. She watched the play of light and shadow against the building's glass and metal facade and wondered what she thought about it. Sometimes it was hard to tell what one's true feelings were. Especially with something so foreign.

As usual, Guy was happy to impart some of his encyclopaedic knowledge and to help Marie form an opinion.

'The inspiration is Moorish,' Guy said when he arrived and saw Marie looking at the building. Marie wasn't going to ask what Moorish meant and she simply smiled. 'See how behind the glass wall they've installed a metallic screen with geometric motifs,' he said. 'These motifs are actually 240 photo-sensitive motor-controlled apertures – shutters, if you like. They open and close to control the amount of light and heat entering the building from the sun. It's rather clever, I think. Even if the building itself is a little terse.'

Clever but terse, Marie thought. That sounded about right.

They spent an hour viewing the Matisse exhibition. After-wards, they sat together in the cafe and sipped from tiny glasses of tea packed with mint leaves and sugar. Marie had never tasted anything like it. It was immensely invigorating. The Arabs did do some things extremely well.

'Where shall we meet next?' Guy asked.

'Perhaps next time you should come to Maisons-Laffitte,' she ventured. She didn't mention that she was living with her daughter. Hopefully that would not last much longer. Suzanne clearly found her presence trying. Why else was she always working so late?

'What on earth would we do there?'

'I could make us a nice lunch.'

'It's a long way for me to go.'

'Well, it's a long way for me as well, coming into Paris,' she said.

Not another word was spoken while she and Guy finished their tea. Marie feared that she had perhaps been a little abrupt and wondered what she might say to break the silence. She thought about the place their friendship held in their lives. Neither saw their children often. This weekly get-together was the thing she looked forward to most.

Finally, it was Guy who spoke first. 'Has that man been back? The one with the boy?'

'No, thank goodness. Although—'

'What?'

'Nothing. I've just been preoccupied by it, that's all.'

'Did you speak to the police?'

'Yes, but what can they do? He hasn't done anything, really.'

'Well, just make sure you lock your doors when you're home.'

'I always do.'

She thought about what she had not told Guy. The other night, before packing a small suitcase to take to Suzanne's, she had taken her rubbish out and thought she saw someone on the driveway, watching her. It was absurd, but she'd thought for a moment that it was the boy, the silent one who had accompanied the man with the religious pamphlets. She had hurried back inside and locked the door. When she'd looked out again, there was no one.

She must have imagined it. It had been so fleeting and so dark after all. A scaredy cat with an overactive imagination, her husband used to say. If she had told Guy he would have found her silly.

Still, she had to admit she was scared. What if someone *was* watching her, waiting for an opportunity to rob or attack her? Who would protect her? She was alone, after all. These days she didn't even know her neighbours. On both sides over the past year new families had moved in with young children. There was no one her age who might understand her isolation.

'Are you ready to go?' Guy said.

Marie looked at him and wondered what he would be doing with the rest of his afternoon.

'I think I might have another cup of this delicious tea,' she said.

He seemed to perk up at her words. 'Excellent idea, I think I might join you.'

Marie watched him walk up to the counter and place their order. On his way back he smiled at her. He looked relieved.

TWENTY-TWO

It was still early, but Maly was wide awake. Slowly, she got up. She looked over at Karl, who was still fast asleep. She pulled on a dressing-gown and left the room, closing the door behind her. Karl would usually be the first one up, making coffee so he could bring it to her in bed. But he'd come in late from the airport. Knowing him, he would probably still go into work, but he would allow himself an extra hour's sleep.

Though she hated to admit it, she was glad he was still asleep. Mornings were better spent alone, greeting the new day in silence. She liked the empty space around her and the way her thoughts drifted. Now she and Karl were living together there were fewer moments like these. She missed them.

She thought about her brother, who had left several messages on her phone. She should call him back but she knew Adèle had told him the news. For some reason she couldn't bear to hear him congratulate her, to have that inane conversation. He would say all the right things while thinking something quite different.

Her brother, the policeman. One of the rising stars of the Criminal Brigade, judging by the way his career had been progressing these past years. Maybe his career was what prevented him from having a steady relationship. Though

Maly knew better. Even if he were working regular hours at a Monoprix check-out counter he would struggle with commitment issues.

He probably thought she was making a big mistake getting married.

Tonight she and Karl would go out for dinner and celebrate a year's anniversary of being together. A long time in her book, if not in his. They'd also celebrate the fact that they were now engaged. Karl had wanted to set a date for the wedding, but she had said that could wait. One step at a time. Empty words, but he had taken them to heart. He was so sweet, and gorgeous with those deep blue eyes and that crooked smile. And successful to boot, at least the sort of success that means something in the world of academia. Most women would be green with envy.

Most of all, he worshipped her. There was nothing he wouldn't do. He was patient and kind. And there, Maly thought, was the crux of the issue.

What was wrong with her? She was always picking men who were too nice, too pliant. Men who wanted to make her happy and almost did.

At the other end of the flat she heard the alarm go off. With a sigh, she walked back to the bedroom.

Anne Dufour tiptoed back into the bedroom to turn off the alarm. Jacques would not want it to go off today. There was a good chance he would wake up in a foul temper.

She closed the door quietly and on padded feet headed down to the kitchen: her favourite room in this house, which otherwise held little attraction for her. Most of what was here had come from her mother-in-law's house. Little by little, Jacques had divested his mother of the pieces she had which he liked best. Anne didn't know where her mother-in-law had found the things she had filled her flat with, to replace the ones her son had pilfered.

There was a great deal she didn't know or at least pretended to ignore. She had lived like this for so long that she had almost convinced herself that this was normal enough, that all marriages had their share of nasty little secrets. Now her mother-in-law was dead. She'd died alone and frightened, with no one to love or comfort her.

She turned the electric kettle on and stood by the sink waiting for it to boil. It was getting light but the street was quiet still.

She watched the steam from the boiling water fog up the window. Gingerly, she touched her left hip. There'd be a bruise, but luckily no one would see it. Last time Margot had commented on the red mark on her arm and she'd had to lie. She could see Margot didn't believe her. It was strange, lying to her best friend. But the alternative was worse.

She hardly saw Margot these days. It was too difficult, pretending that all was well, having to meet her probing gaze with a casual smile. And Jacques hated Margot. The feeling was quite mutual.

Last night she and Jacques had gone out for dinner. It was a celebration, Jacques said. He was in a particularly good mood, having been promoted to a position he'd coveted for months. It meant more money and more travel. The money made little difference to Anne: ever since the beginning of their marriage, Jacques had kept her on a tight leash, handing out money at the beginning of each week and demanding to know what it was being spent on. The travel meant he would be away for longer periods. For a start, the company wanted to send him to Shanghai and Beijing, to Seoul and on to Tokyo, to meet with clients. All in all he would be away for three weeks. He was being trusted with an important task, a sign that his bosses were pleased with his work.

She had been pleased for him. But she thought about the three weeks where she would be alone in the big house with the furniture she hadn't picked and where she had never felt quite at home. She should have kept quiet, but she still hadn't learned to keep her mouth shut.

'It's a long trip,' she said. 'Maybe I could join you somewhere along the way and we could spend a weekend together,' she added, thinking that maybe it would please him that she should miss him.

The brutality of his response had shaken her.

'It isn't a fucking holiday,' he'd said. In his eyes was a look of such hatred that she flinched. If he'd slapped her it would have hurt less.

She had stopped right there, not wanting to end the evening with a fight. Over dessert and on the way home he was sullen. They'd finished a bottle of red wine. Neither of them was drunk but she found his behaviour altered, strange to understand. When she tried to touch him, at home, he shoved her away. She lost her balance and fell against the corner of the dining table.

He'd gone to bed without saying a word. She'd debated whether to sleep in their son's room but in the end she'd slid next to her husband. She hadn't slept at all.

It had been an accident. But Margot wouldn't see it that way.

The phone rang. Anne ran to pick it up, worried that it might wake Jacques. It was the policeman, Morel.

'I'm sorry to disturb you but I wondered whether we might be able to have another chat with your husband sometime this week.'

'He's asleep right now,' she said. She realized all of a sudden that she was whispering and she made an effort to speak up. 'I can get him to give you a call when he wakes up.'

'That would be great, thank you. We just have a couple of questions. We'll try to keep it short.'

'OK.' She thought of the female officer who had visited and tears sprung to her eyes, which she quickly brushed away.

As she hung up, she felt Jacques's hands around her hips. He pressed himself against her and she felt the hardness of his erection against her lower back. She tried not to show how much his hand hurt against her hip.

'Who was that?'

'The police. That man Morel. He has a few more questions to ask. He wants to know when he can come and talk to us.'

He laughed. 'They probably just want to take another look at the house. I bet they don't see many like ours in their daily rounds.'

She felt his hands move up her rib cage and find her breasts.

'I'm sorry about last night,' he said.

'So am I.'

'Come back to bed.'

She didn't feel like it. She wanted him to get ready and go to work. But he wasn't in a hurry this morning.

'Come on, baby,' Jacques said.

She closed her eyes. He was pinching her nipples a little too hard, but she didn't say anything. Instead she turned towards him and let his hand move down her stomach.

'OK,' she said.

*

180

Morel was lying against Solange, his head resting in the crook of her arm while she ran her hand through his hair. The palm of his hand brushed against her nipples, followed the curve of her breasts. He was sweaty and sleepy, happily drained from lovemaking. Mildly triumphant, the way good sex can make you feel. Morel knew he could sleep like this, with her hand in his hair and the feel of her skin beneath his fingers.

For a moment, he dozed off. But then his thoughts turned to Mathilde, and he found himself wide awake again. He moved away from Solange and got up.

'Where are you going?' she asked.

'Just to get a drink. I'll be right back.'

He pulled on his trousers and tiptoed downstairs, hoping he wouldn't run into Henri. But Solange's husband had gone to bed hours ago. In the middle of the night like this the house seemed pointlessly grand, full of unvisited spaces.

In the kitchen he poured himself a glass of orange juice and got a glass of sparkling water for Solange, knowing she would want one. He drank the juice and headed back up the stairs with Solange's drink.

When he lay down beside her she reached over and kissed his lips. She pressed her lips to his chest.

Morel closed his eyes and let out a contented sigh.

Ever since that time when he'd parked outside Mathilde's home and seen her appear so close to him, he'd thought more frequently about her. Wondered whether to give her a call, make it casual and suggest they catch up over coffee. But she would wonder how he'd found her. There'd be nothing casual about his contacting her.

He'd seen Mathilde for the first time at a bus stop. Twenty-five years ago. She wasn't waiting for a bus. She was doing her laces up. She had obviously been running. Her face was flushed and she'd loosened her hair. Thick and red and down to her waist, it was beautiful. She was small, with narrow, muscly legs. From the back she had seemed younger, so that when she turned, he found himself gaping at her profile. He wanted to see her face better and moved closer, pretending to look at the bus schedule. He stood next to her, squinting at the information above her head. When he finally looked at her he saw she wasn't fooled for an instant. Her eyes were deep, of the darkest blue, the expression more informed than anything he'd been prepared for in that snippet of a woman.

He found out soon after that she was addicted to running. That she liked having someone around who could make her laugh and that her laughter was unrestrained. That she didn't like her freckles and was self-conscious about her breasts, though the self-consciousness wore away quickly under his adoring gaze. That she could be sharp-tongued and unkind but also intensely loyal. He was slogging his way through his first year of mathematics, feeling trapped, knowing full well that he wasn't going to make it, while she worked her way through an architecture degree with the same diligence she applied to her long-distance running. It didn't take long for them to move in together. He took his cue from her, sitting down to his studies when she did, waiting for the moment when she'd be done so they could be together. Neither of them had much money, Morel had not wanted to rely on his parents and worked in a bookshop during the day and in a bar three nights a week to pay his way. In between studying and working they did a great deal of walking through the streets of Paris, stopping only when their feet grew sore for a cup of coffee in the nearest cafe.

Morel collected the things he found out about her like a person collects unusual shells and smooth pieces of green and white glass in the sand, storing these in a private box of treasures. Loving her revealed good things about himself. He found that he thrived in the burrowing closeness of their domesticity, that intimacy suited him.

And leaving that aside, the panting euphoria of first love! Wet tongues and breath and fingers, feeling and licking and groping, heading towards that delirious first fuck. The lead-up to it had made them both ache with anticipation – they were so incredibly ready, desperate for it – till finally they had given in one afternoon on his bedroom floor, his fingers bruising the flesh around her hips, her black tights hanging from one ankle as she held her legs high and wide around his body, her red hair spread across the carpet like a flood. Over the next twelve months they had lived in a state of permanent hunger, undressing each other at every opportunity, drunk with a sexual happiness they felt certain no one else could know.

Sleeping with Solange was delightful too, of course, but it was tempered by knowledge and experience. With Mathilde, Morel had known nothing except the moment. He and Mathilde had loved and lusted with blank, unwritten minds. Unselfconscious and free. After that, nothing could be taken out of context and lived as a thing apart from the rest.

He felt Solange's hand on his thigh. She reached for his cock and laughed.

'Again? My God, I don't think I've ever felt you this hard.'

Solange bent her head towards him. He felt her nipples graze his chest and then his thighs. He raised his arms around his head and closed his eyes. He found in the midst of his pleasure that he could conjure up Mathilde, just as if she were the one doing this to him. When he came he gritted his teeth so he would not say her name and shatter every-thing.

TWENTY-THREE

The wind kept coming, in sudden gusts that shook the car before abating again. The sky was a swirling mass of clouds. Raindrops rolled up the windshield, leaving a trembling trail in their wake. Cars moved towards them on the opposite lane with their headlights on. Every once in a while, one of them would raise a wave of water and Morel would slow down and stare at the blindness ahead, waiting to regain his sight.

Lila yawned.

'What crappy weather.'

Morel had picked her up from her flat early so that they could get on to the A11 before the morning commuter rush.

Now she inclined her seat and put her feet up on the dashboard. One look from Morel, though, and the feet came down. She sighed.

'What's this music we're listening to?' she said after a long pause.

'Andrés Segovia. One of the most famous classical guitar players ever.'

He glanced at her.

'You can change it if you want.'

'Nope, it's fine.'

She yawned again.

'How long till we get there?' she asked.

Morel looked at the odometer.

'Less than two hours.'

'Thanks.'

He shook his head. Lila looked at him.

'What?'

'Nothing. For a moment there I thought I was travelling with a five-year-old, that's all.'

There was another pause while she tried to come up with something smart to say, followed by a big sigh.

'So this Segovia? Is he still alive?'

'No.'

Lila snorted. 'Thought so.'

'What is that supposed to mean?'

'Nothing.'

Halfway to Rennes Lila pleaded for a change of music. It was Fun Radio for the rest of the drive. When they reached the city they spent some time looking for a place where they could have an early lunch before driving the next stretch to the village.

Once they'd decided where to eat, Morel found a place to park and turned the ignition off. The sounds of a band whose name Morel didn't know died out. It had been like listening to a pig being slaughtered, though Lila had declared it was one of her favourites. They would be touring Europe soon and she planned to go to their Paris concert.

Morel got out and stretched his legs. As he waited for Lila to get her things together and join him, he thought regretfully of the TGV train. The trip from Gare Montparnasse to Rennes was less than two hours. He could have worn headphones.

They found the house easily once they were there.

'Obviously everyone must know everyone in a place this

small,' Lila said. She wore a black sleeveless Puffa jacket, jeans and boots. Still she shivered and rubbed her hands. 'You wouldn't think it was the middle of summer, would you?'

'No.' Morel looked at the sky. 'It looks like a proper storm coming.'

'Coming? What do you mean? It's been stormy for the past three hours.'

For some reason, Charles Berg was nothing like what Morel had expected. The man who opened the door had the look of an athlete. He was strong and well built, with a chiselled jaw and piercing blue eyes.

Charles smiled at them, almost as though he'd been looking forward to their visit.

'Make yourselves at home. I'll get us some coffee.'

Inside they were led to a living and dining area that looked as though a hurricane had swept through it. There were books on the floor and clothes strewn across the room. A piece of half-eaten toast lay buttered side down in the middle of the floor. Morel stepped around it and walked to the sliding glass panels at the back of the house.

The mess inside did not take anything away from the loveliness of the view from this room into the garden. The glass-panelled walls revealed a vista of apple trees and rose bushes. A tree house and a tyre swing.

'What a wonderful spot,' Morel said. 'A children's paradise.'

'I guess that's the advantage of living in a place this small,' Charles said. 'The fact is you'd have to be a millionaire to own a house with a garden in Paris. And I think the kids are better off growing up in a place like this than in the big city.'

'Absolutely.'

'Won't you sit down?'

Morel and Lila looked for a place where they might sit and finally perched themselves on the edge of a sofa littered with crumbs.

'Coffee? With sugar?'

They both replied yes to the first question and no to the second. Charles switched the coffee maker on.

'Sorry about the mess. It isn't usually this bad,' he said.

Lila gave Morel a look which he pretended not to see.

'Please don't apologize. It's good of you to see us,' Morel said.

'Well, I'm happy to help.' Charles handed two cups of coffee to them and pulled a dining-room chair over to where they sat. 'If I can be of any help, that is. I'm not sure where I fit in.'

'We'll fill you in, then,' Lila said.

Morel pushed his knee against Lila's as a warning to behave herself.

'You probably know that your mother called us, to tell us about Armand Le Bellec. She said she saw him at her house,' Morel began.

'Yes, that's right. I was there, in fact.'

'Did you see him?'

'No. But he gave my daughter quite a fright. He was lurking in the bushes for some reason.'

'Your mother says the two of you went to school together.'

'That's right.'

'Were you close?'

Charles took a sip from his cup. 'Not particularly. I mean, when we were kids we did occasionally spend time together. But later we went our separate ways.'

'When was the last time you saw him?'

Charles made a show of thinking, and shook his head

slowly. 'I can't really remember. It was while we were still at school.'

'Did you two fall out?'

Charles smiled. His teeth were perfectly aligned. 'Like I said, we were not that close. There was no reason to fall out.'

'Did he come to your house at all?'

Charles seemed to hesitate, then he shook his head to indicate no.

'So you have no idea where we might find him?'

'None at all, I'm afraid. Sorry I can't be more helpful.'

'One last thing: would you happen to have a photo of Armand?'

'I don't think so,' Charles said.

'Are you sure? A class photo, perhaps?'

'I'm afraid not. I'm not very good at keeping that sort of thing.'

Lila looked at him. 'Do you work out, Monsieur Berg?'

'Yes I do.'

'It must be hard to find the time, what with three young kids.'

'Well, I get to travel a fair bit for my work. So I make the most of the work trips and I use the hotel gyms, I run—'

'What do you do for a living?'

'I work for Picard, the frozen-food company. As a senior representative.'

'Interesting work?'

'I suppose.'

'Do you travel to Paris much?'

'Yes, at least once or twice a month.'

'Did you know that Armand Le Bellec is probably based in Paris these days?'

'Like I said, we haven't been in touch and I have no idea where he lives or what he does for a living,' Charles said. He got up to put his cup on the kitchen bench. On his way back he picked up several plastic dinosaurs that were lying on the floor.

'If you have so little to do with Armand,' Lila said, 'and if you two were never that close, then why was he lurking in your mother's back garden? Why was he spying on your family?'

'I really don't know,' Charles said.

He held Lila's gaze for a while. Finally it was Morel who stood up and held out his hand.

'Thank you for your time, Monsieur Berg. We'll be dropping in on your mother and then heading back to Paris, no doubt.'

'I'm sorry I can't be more helpful,' Charles said.

'Where is your wife, Monsieur Berg?' Lila asked as Charles walked them to the door.

'She's visiting her sister.'

The moment they'd left, the phone began ringing. Charles watched it, wondering whether to pick it up. In the end he reached over and held the receiver to his ear. He listened to the woman's voice at the other end tell him the thing he least wanted to hear.

'Please,' he whispered, his voice breaking. 'Please don't leave me.'

Outside the house they buttoned up their jackets. It was drizzling. Morel looked at Lila. Shifting from one foot to the other, biting her lip.

'Interesting little exchange, wasn't it?' Morel said.

'Did you notice how messy the place is? Dad's home, looking

after the kids, while Mum's off visiting her sister. Doesn't that seem a bit off to you?'

'Maybe she's taking a break, having some time alone.'

'Maybe there's something he isn't telling us,' Lila said as they got into Morel's car. 'Maybe we should talk to his wife.'

'Maybe,' Morel said, starting the car. 'What I find interesting is how serene he was about this guy spying on his family like that. Neither angry nor worried. I mean, if it were you, and someone you were at school with a long time ago, whom you weren't particularly close to, turned up in your back garden out of the blue to spy on you and your family . . .'

'I'd give them a beating to remember.' Lila rubbed her hands and raised herself slightly so she could sit cross-legged on the passenger seat. Morel pretended not to mind the fact that her knee got in the way every time he had to change gear.

'It's as though he doesn't see Le Bellec as a threat,' Morel said slowly. 'He knows enough about him to realize he has nothing to worry about.'

'Either that or he's lying about not seeing Le Bellec before he turned up at his mother's house. Maybe he wasn't surprised to see him because he already knew he'd come back.'

Morel was thinking of Charles's relaxed demeanour and wondering how much of that was real.

'Let's go back and get him to be a bit more forthcoming. Give Charlie-boy a bit of a grinding,' Lila said.

'No. We'll go see Amelia Berg first. Maybe his mother will tell us something. We can always come back here later if we need to.'

Amelia Berg's house was twice the size of her son's. It was probably the most lavish one in the village. Charles must have given her a call to let her know they were coming because she stood on the doorstep, holding an umbrella.

'Come in, come in,' she said.

Morel and Lila found themselves in a room with an open fire. The flames leaped high and the heat was almost too much. A grey Siamese cat lay on a chair in a comatose state and remained unresponsive when the two visitors walked in. There was a smell of freshly baked apples.

'I hope you don't mind the fire, but I get cold very easily these days,' Amelia Berg said. 'We haven't had much of a summer around here. It must be this global warming they keep talking about.'

She invited them to sit down and left for a few seconds.

'Did you talk to Charles?' she called on her way back. She was carrying a tray. On it was a coffee pot and an apple pie. Morel shook his head to indicate he didn't want any but Lila accepted both a large slice of it and another cup of coffee.

'It gave me quite a shock, I can tell you, when I realized he'd been lurking in my bushes,' their hostess said, sitting opposite them.

Lila noticed the dirt under Amelia Berg's nails. The coffee table held a couple of books on gardening. She took a big bite of the pie and sank back into the sofa.

Morel shot her an irritated look and turned to Madame Berg with a sympathetic smile. 'I can imagine,' he said. 'When had you seen him last?'

'Gosh, it must be, what – let me think. Sixteen years ago, I believe. He and Charles went to the same school, the local one – but after that they went their separate ways. Charles did a business management degree and Armand went to Rennes to study, I think.'

'The boys weren't close?' Lila asked with her mouth full.

A look flitted across Amelia Berg's face, before she answered.

'You know how it is, at school. One minute someone's your best friend, the next they're not. Friendships are made and unmade every day.'

Lila took the last of her slice of pie in her hand and put it in her mouth. When she'd finished, she licked her fingers.

'So for a while they were best friends?' she asked.

'Yes, I suppose you could say that.'

Was it regret on the old woman's face? It was hard to tell.

'What happened?' Lila asked. There was something they weren't being told. She was determined to find out.

The old lady shrugged her shoulders. 'I don't know. I think perhaps Armand disappointed Charles in some way.'

'Disappointed? How?' Morel asked.

Lila glanced at him. He was leaning forward, smiling. Doing that thing with his dimple, which seemed to affect most women regardless of how young or old they were.

Amelia Berg wavered, her lips opened as though she were about to say something. Then she visibly retreated.

'I think Charles just felt that it was time to make new friends,' she said in a way that suggested the topic was now closed.

There had been a moment there. Lila felt that the old woman had been on the verge of revealing something important. Something she might have wanted to get off her chest. But they would get nothing more from her now.

'Tell us a little bit about Armand's mother,' Morel said.

'We had nothing to do with each other,' Amelia Berg said. 'She died some years ago.'

'Did her son return for his mother's funeral?'

'No,' Amelia Berg said. 'It was a very small, quiet affair. A number of the women she knew from church went, but otherwise—'

'Did you go?'

'No,' she said.

Lila changed tack. 'What was she like, his mother?' she asked.

'Why do you ask?'

'It would help us if we knew a little more about Armand, that's all.'

'Do you think he's actually responsible for what happened to those women?' Amelia Berg asked.

'At this stage we're not certain of anything, but that's why it's important that we find him. So we can talk to him,' Morel said.

That seemed to satisfy her. She leaned back in her chair. The cat woke up and stretched. It jumped on her lap and curled in a ball. It looked at Lila through narrowed eyes.

'Armand's mother was a difficult woman,' Amelia Berg said.

'Difficult how?' Morel asked.

'Possessive. Harsh.'

'Possessive with her son, you mean?'

Amelia Berg nodded.

'Was she unstable?'

The old woman turned to Lila. 'Unstable?'

'I mean did she have problems? Psychologically?'

Amelia Berg laughed. 'You know nowadays everyone has a psychological problem. In my day when someone acted badly it was put down to meanness of character or a lack of education. We didn't feel the need to run to a psychologist the minute it happened.'

'So would you say his mother was a mean person?'

'It was hard to warm to her. Though I hate to speak ill of the dead.'

'Do you know why Armand Le Bellec didn't bother to return for his mother's funeral?'

Amelia Berg shrugged. 'I can't say. But she was a difficult woman to love. I imagine he was not close to her.'

She said this with a touch of smugness. The cat jumped from her lap and walked past Lila with its tail up in the air, pointedly ignoring her.

'What sort of child was Armand?' Lila asked.

'Solitary, withdrawn.'

'But he was Charles's friend.' It was said as a statement.

'Yes,' the old lady replied, as though it was a relief to acknowledge the point. 'He was Charles's friend.'

'Would you have a photo of him, by any chance?' Morel said.

The old lady thought for a moment. 'You know, I probably do. Let me get it for you.'

Outside, it looked as though the rain had cleared. But the wind showed no signs of easing off.

'I might have a little look around the garden,' Morel told Lila.

'Absolutely, be my guest,' Lila said. 'You know what, I'll just sit here and have another slice of this delicious pie.'

Lila watched Morel pick his way among the plants, careful not to step over any lovingly tended flowers. His trouser legs were getting wet. She thought about how that would irritate him and tried not to smile.

'It must be nice, having your son and his children live so close to you,' Lila said when Amelia Berg returned to the room. 'By the way, would you mind terribly if I helped myself to another slice?'

'Not at all,' Amelia Berg said. She handed a photograph to Lila. 'Here. Armand and Charles. I guess this was taken when they were around fourteen years old.'

Lila looked at the two grinning faces before her. Despite the smile there was a brooding look on Armand's face. His eyes were on the person taking the picture but his thoughts seemed to be elsewhere. Charles's gaze was direct. He seemed to be laughing.

'Who took the photo?'

'I think it was me. Armand used to come and play. See the background? That's the maze I had made in the garden, for the children to play in. Not much of a maze but fun for them to run around in when they're little. Charles's children love it.' Amelia Berg smiled wistfully and gazed at her garden. 'It is nice having the little ones near,' she said.

'Your son tells us his wife is away at the moment,' Lila said.

'Yes,' the old woman said. 'The two of them have had a bit of a tiff, I think. Nothing serious, though.' Seeing Lila's face, she faltered. 'I thought he would have told you.'

'He just said she was away for a couple of days. Visiting her sister.'

'Her sister? Yes, that's right.'

Lila could see Morel heading back. 'Is there anything more you can tell us about Armand?' she ventured. 'Anything at all.' She remembered something. 'You told Commandant Morel on the phone that you were worried about Armand. Why?'

Amelia Berg was quiet for a moment. Then she spoke.

'He was a good child,' she said, almost as if she was speaking to herself. 'But his mother took him out of school for half a year. When he came back he gave the impression that he was no longer himself, somehow. It's hard to explain,' she said, looking at Lila. 'All I know is that I didn't feel comfortable around him. I'd run into him sometimes, after all it's a small place and you're always running into people you know. He was so withdrawn. He literally shrank away from me. I noticed he crossed the street a few times just so he wouldn't have to say hello. Given how different he'd become, I was glad in a way that he and Charles had stopped being friends.'

'Oh?'

'Yes. I think Armand was dragging him down, somehow.'

Lila thought it interesting that Amelia Berg had so much to say about someone her son claimed not to have known that well or for very long.

'You don't know anything about this boy he adopted in Russia?'

'No.' She looked concerned. 'I know nothing about that.'

Morel slid the door open and stepped in, rubbing his feet on the doormat before entering the room.

'You really are a remarkable gardener, Madame Berg,' he said.

The old lady beamed with pleasure. Then she looked at Morel as if she'd suddenly remembered something.

'You know, there's someone you should talk to,' she said. 'He taught Charles and Armand. It's a long time ago, but maybe he'll be able to help.'

They walked back to the car in silence. Lila scoffed.

'"You really are a remarkable gardener, Madame Berg,"' she said.

'Very funny.'

'No, I'm impressed with your seductive skills. She loved you.'

'I was trying to compensate for my colleague, sitting there pigging out on the old woman's food.'

'A different form of flattery. I was paying homage to her culinary skills.'

As they got into the car, Lila grew thoughtful. 'Why do I get the feeling no one is telling us the important stuff?'

'My little stroll in the garden was interesting,' Morel said.

'Was it?'

He pulled something from his pocket and showed it to Lila. It was a photograph of Charles and his family.

'Where did that come from?' she said, surprised.

'It was in Amelia Berg's garden, in the bushes where she said Armand was hiding.'

'But—'

'I noticed when we were at Charles's place that one of the frames on the bookshelves was missing a photograph. I didn't think anything of it at the time but now . . . Le Bellec must have dropped it when he ran out of here.'

'So Armand did visit Charles, not just Charles's mother,' Lila said.

'It seems likely.'

'I knew the bastard wasn't telling the truth.'

'How about a drink?'

'Don't you want to drop in at Charles's place first? Ask him when he noticed the photo went missing, and whether maybe he'd like to stop lying to us?'

'I'm thirsty.'

'Oh well, in that case,' Lila said.

As they walked towards the village bar, the sun emerged timidly from behind the clouds.

TWENTY-FOUR

The bar was a five-minute walk from Amelia Berg's house. In fact, it was probably a five-minute walk from most houses in the village, Lila thought as she opened the door and Morel held it back, waiting for her to enter first. She tried to picture what life would be like in a place where everyone knew each other. You wouldn't be able to walk down the street without stopping every few minutes to talk to someone who knew you. People would make up stories about you out of sheer boredom. Your life would be constantly under scrutiny: whether you went to church, whether your marriage was a happy one, whether your children did well at school, whether you cooked and cleaned and prayed as well as you should.

Hell.

While Lila went to the toilet, Morel took a look around the place. The bartender was pouring *pastis* into glasses for a pair of crusty-looking individuals who looked like they'd had a few already. They sat at the bar with raw hands clutching their drinks. Morel ordered a glass of red wine and for Lila a glass of cider, as requested. When the drinks arrived he noticed the glasses had an unwashed, oily sheen about them. He tried not to mind and sipped at the wine. It was the sort that would scour your insides as effectively as bleach, but it would do.

Over on the other side of the room a jukebox played a

lambada. Every time the tune ended one of the men shuffled over to put another coin in the box and play it again.

Unsurprisingly, perhaps, there was no one else around.

Lila returned and sat opposite Morel. Just then his phone
rang. Morel looked at it to see who the caller was.

'It's Jean,' he told Lila.

While he listened his expression darkened.

'Well, thanks for letting me know,' he said after several
minutes. He hung up and looked at Lila. 'Jean managed to
track Amir down.'

'Great,' she said.

'Yes, well, it would be, in different circumstances. Amir
died in a car crash five years ago.'

'Shit.'

They sat in silence, mulling over this latest piece of news.
After the inconclusive interviews they'd just had with Charles
and his mother, it seemed like another step backwards.

'This is cosy,' Morel finally said, looking around the room.

'Yeah, if you like a dive in the middle of nowhere popu-
lated by a bunch of losers,' she said. 'Did you notice how
they all stopped and stared when we walked in? It was like
being in a western.'

'Except no one tried to shoot us.'

'They're too drunk.'

'It reminds me of when I was younger,' Morel said.

'Really?'

'My father was from Brittany. We used to come here once
a year, over the summer.'

'You mean this kind of summer?' Lila said, pulling her
jacket closer.

'It was great. We loved it, as kids.'

They drank in silence for a while, listening to the rain.
Morel thought about one of the holidays he and his family

had spent in Roscoff. Once, his father had gone missing for a couple of hours. Looking back now, he realized his parents must have had a fight. His mother had sat behind the steering-wheel with tears running down her face while they drove at a snail's pace through the narrow streets, looking for him. For once the children did not have to be told to be quiet. They huddled together in complete silence, staring at the darkness around them.

They'd finally found Morel Senior in a bar much like this one. It was Maly, calm and collected, who had gone in and convinced him to come home with them.

The next day he had been back to his usual immaculate self. Not a trace of the tantrum he'd thrown the previous night.

While he sat and drank his wine, Morel thought of his father's recent erratic moods, the episodes where he seemed to become confused or forgetful. Perhaps some of it had been there already. The moodiness and sudden emotional outbursts. From a man who prided himself on his composure and who intellectualized everything. Maybe that was why. He was like a pressure cooker: at some point, there was a need for release.

'Will you have another?' Lila said.

'Yes.'

'Me too, I'll get this round,' she said, pushing her chair back and standing up. The lambada was finishing for the umpteenth time. 'If someone plays that tune once more I swear I'll kick them in the balls.'

She stood by the old men at the bar and ordered drinks. Morel saw her give them a dark look while she waited. He hoped for their sake that they'd run out of coins for the jukebox.

His sisters had come back from Brittany with boxes inlaid with seashells, bright, dazzling things which they forgot to fill and simply admired. Morel's most treasured possession was a tiny ship captured in a bottle. Though it was explained to him time and time again, he never quite understood how it was done and to him it remained a magic trick.

When she returned to their table with the drinks, Lila said, 'There's something fishy about Charles. For one thing, how is it his wife is away while the kids are still in the house? They're obviously around, judging by the mess.'

'Maybe the two of them had a tiff, like his mother said.'

'Then why didn't *he* say so?'

'Most people don't like to air their dirty laundry in public.'

'He was airing plenty of that when we visited.'

'You know what I mean.'

Morel started on his second glass. He was beginning to relax. The bar seemed cheerier than when they had first walked in.

'What about the lies? Why didn't he tell us that he'd seen Armand earlier, before Armand went over to his mother's house and hid in her garden?'

'That's what we're going to find out,' Morel said. 'We'll drop in on him in the morning. Before he leaves with the kids to take them to school. Then we'll visit the schoolteacher, the one Amelia Berg told us about.'

Morel reminded himself of what they knew about Le Bellec so far. He was sure they were on the right track now. But what eluded him still was the motive. If Le Bellec was their man, why had he targeted two old widows? He thought of what Amelia Berg had said. Armand hadn't come back for his mother's funeral.

'Maybe the schoolteacher can tell us something about Le Bellec's mother,' Morel said.

'OK. Then we head back to Paris, right?' Lila said.

'Yes. Hopefully Jean will have some news for us. Maybe

he'll get lucky and track Armand Le Bellec down, teaching at one of the schools.'

'Maybe. Either way it'll be good to get back.' Lila took a gulp of her cider and looked around the bar. 'What a shithole,' she said.

When they emerged from the bar an hour later, the temperature had dropped by several degrees. The light had faded to a muted grey. There was absolutely no one about.

'We're not spending the night here, right?' Lila said.

The place where Morel had booked rooms was halfway between the village and Rennes. So many places were closed in August that he'd had to make a few calls before finding a place that wasn't too expensive or out of the way. They reached it twenty minutes after leaving the bar, with Lila managing to complain several times along the way that she was starving.

The place was a former coaching inn and boasted a four-star restaurant. The woman who showed them their table told them it had seen four generations of innkeepers. The great-grandfather, a horse lover, had built it and christened it the Grey Horse Inn, in memory of a spirited horse he'd never managed to tame. It was his grandson Matthieu who now held the reins, so to speak, the woman told them with a smile, revealing a set of teeth badly in need of repair.

Lila ordered an entrecôte and Morel had the *andouille* sausage, which she wrinkled her nose at when it arrived.

'Why anyone would want to dig into a cow's intestines is beyond me,' she said when he urged her to try it.

'What a Parisian you are. You can barely cope with being somewhere not quite as urbanized for more than five minutes, admit it.'

'Not *quite* as urbanized. Must be the understatement of the century,' Lila said, biting into three *frites* at once.

'The problem with you is that you're too set in your ways. Not open-minded enough,' Morel said, shearing off a thick slice of the sausage on his plate.

'I can live with that,' she said, before spearing a big chunk of Béarnaise-coated meat and shoving it in her mouth.

After dinner they sat in Lila's room and again went over what they knew of Armand Le Bellec.

'Do you mind if I get changed while we talk?' Lila said.

'Go ahead. Will you have a small cognac? I will.'

'Sure.'

She emerged from the bathroom wearing grey cotton pyjama trousers and a faded red sweatshirt. She sat on the bed and folded her long legs beneath her.

'Here,' Morel said, handing her a glass. He turned the chair to face her and sat down. 'OK, so we know that Le Bellec and a boy he adopted in Russia, thought to be somewhere between fourteen and eighteen years old, visited Isabelle Dufour, Elisabeth Guillou, Marie Latour and Irina Volkoff. They may have visited others but these are the four women we know about.'

'If they'd visited others, you'd think we would have heard by now. After we put that composite out. We haven't received any other reports.'

'True. Or there may be others who haven't kept up with the news.' Morel finished his cognac and got up to pour another. 'Let me continue. Two of the women were drowned in their homes and then dressed up and displayed in a ritualistic way. Both with crosses in their hands. Their faces coarsely made up, in contrast to the meticulous way they were dressed and laid out. Both wearing red wigs.

'We have good reason to believe Le Bellec is responsible for the killings. He and the boy dropped in on both women some time before they died. The pamphlets are his, presumably. We know his mother was a strict Catholic. Maybe Le Bellec gets his religiosity from her. We can assume he composed the pamphlets. They don't make much sense but they're his way of advertising his beliefs.'

'This is the part I don't get,' Lila said. 'Why does he need to advertise them? And where did he meet the widows in the first place?'

'I'm leaning towards the Holy Russia exhibition. Isabelle Dufour's daughter-in-law told us the two of them attended it together. We don't know about Guillou, but we know that Marie Latour and Irina Volkoff went. It makes sense. Le Bellec has spent time in Russia and is religious. It's an exhibition he's interested in. He might also think it's a nice thing to do for the boy. So he goes there, and for some reason he marks these women.'

'Maybe it has something to do with their age,' Lila said, sipping at her drink. 'What about the boy? What's his involvement?'

'I don't know. We know he's with Le Bellec when they make that initial contact. It's hard to know whether he is there the second time around. When Le Bellec comes back to drown them.'

'God. I wonder whether they knew at the orphanage what sort of loon they were handing the boy over to,' Lila said.

She gulped the remainder of her drink and set the glass on the bedside table.

'How did he manage that adoption so easily anyway?' she said. 'I thought these things took years to process. Our guy was in Russia for less than a year.'

'That's something I'm going to try to find out,' Morel said.

He kicked his shoes off and stretched his legs on the bed too so that they ran parallel to hers. 'We know something happened to Le Bellec. There is clearly some tension with Charles, something that happened but that Charles and his mother are not telling us. We know Le Bellec ran into trouble in Russia. With the girl and with this Amir,' Morel said.

'But we know from Olivia that he never laid a hand on her. In fact that's what got him into trouble. She saw Armand fall for Amir and that upset her, because she had a crush on him,' Lila pointed out. 'Yet she also seems certain that despite Armand's feelings for Amir, nothing actually happened between them. So is Armand gay or not?'

Morel yawned and looked at his watch. 'Maybe he's gay and maybe he's straight, or maybe he doesn't swing either way.'

'It would be good to know more about his upbringing. From what Amelia Berg said, Le Bellec's mother was a piece of work.'

'There is definitely something there. Le Bellec never returned for her funeral. Then there's the religious zealotry, his own messed-up version of redemption. He's all over the place,' Morel said.

Lila snorted. 'Or maybe he's a very clever, manipulative man who knows how to identify and prey on people who are vulnerable and easily swayed. Religion is just a tool to get a foot in the door.'

'Maybe. But why? To what end?'

Lila shrugged. 'Hopefully we'll find out more tomorrow.'

He sighed. 'I should have asked Jean earlier whether he had any luck with the school search. But I'm sure he would have told me if he had any news. Let's talk to him tomorrow morning. In the meantime we should probably get some sleep.'

He looked at Lila. 'Any news from your friend at the Ministry of Education?'

Lila shook her head. 'Last time I spoke to him, he told me there was no record in their files of anyone called Armand Le Bellec.'

'OK.' Morel stood up. 'Well, I'm going to bed. Goodnight.'

'Goodnight.'

Back in his room, Morel unscrewed the flask of cognac and poured another drop. It would help him sleep, he told himself. He felt restless and mildly claustrophobic. If only he'd chosen a room that wasn't directly under the eaves.

He paced the floor for a few minutes, listening to the sounds of people climbing the stairs. There were only ten rooms in the inn, all on this level. The laughter stopped abruptly, as though they'd suddenly realized how late it was. There was complete silence after that. The smells of the kitchen below hung in the air, mingling with the odour of air freshener which the cleaning woman must have sprayed before he'd entered the room. A synthetic smell like nothing in nature, though it probably claimed to be lavender or some-thing similar.

After a while he sat down with the square sheets of paper he'd brought with him. Slowly, in between small sips of cognac, he set about folding, all the while thinking of Mathilde.

Eventually he became so caught up in the structure grad-ually taking shape before him that he stopped thinking about her.

By the time he finished it was close to 1 a.m. He lay on the bed for a long time, thinking of family holidays. Running along the beach, stumbling across wriggly, worm-like deposits of sand beneath his feet, thousands of them formed by the ebbing tide. The grey black rocks and salty taste of winkles, which you drew out from their shells with a pin before putting them in your mouth. Traditional *galettes* filled with ham, cheese and sometimes an egg, followed by chocolate crêpes for dessert. Toffee apples at the fair, which left you with stickiness in the most unaccountable places, in hair and on shins.

In Roscoff, he'd stayed with his family at the Hôtel Angleterre, listening to the seagulls squabbling for scraps in the morning while his father slept. This was shortly after the Christmas when Philippe Morel had given him an origami book. He'd sat in bed folding paper, waiting for his father to wake up while his mother and sisters walked along the beach before breakfast. Such space and quiet were the closest thing to happiness, he felt now. Gingerly he'd sat and folded, discovering the thing he would grow to love in this room with its clean white lines and simple furnishings.

The family gathered in the dining room every morning for breakfast. The children wolfed down thick slabs of bread spread with salted butter which they dipped into large bowls filled with creamy hot chocolate.

Regardless of the weather, as long as it didn't pour with rain, they had played on the beach with their sets of buckets and spades, the girls making castles decorated with shells and seaweed while Morel dug holes to see how deep he could go. His father had watched and commented that it wasn't hard to tell which kid was the least creative of the three.

On one beach outing his mother had stepped on a rusty nail. They had driven her to the hospital and waited while she received a tetanus injection. She had emerged, shaken, from the curtain-enclosed recess where the nurse applied a dressing to her wound. They had gone for ice-cream after that, to lighten everyone's mood.

Even though he was nowhere near the sea now, Morel went to sleep with the sound of waves in his ears.

TWENTY-FIVE

What Armand missed most while he was in Russia was the sea and the rugged, untamed coastline back home. Not that he'd grown up near it, and his mother had rarely let him out of her sight. But from Rennes it was an easy train trip to Quimper or Saint-Malo. Once he enrolled at university and moved out of his mother's grasp he took to solitary trips to the coast. It didn't matter what time of year it was. He could sit on a beach for hours on end, looking at the dark waves rising over the jagged outline of rock, surging from the shallow waters near shore. A savagery that kept him hypnotized until he became numb from the cold wind and had to shake himself free.

In Moscow, as the seasons changed, his nostalgia came in waves too, like the sea-sickness he had experienced on the fishing trip with the Berg family. That was the weekend they had offered to take Armand with them to Île de Ré, and Armand's mother, by some strange miracle, had agreed to let him go. That was the weekend that changed everything.

The Russian winter was spectacular, blinding and imperious. Then spring came along and the ugliness showed. People emerged pale and unsmiling from their overheated homes and left dirty footprints everywhere. The melting snow revealed the squalor beneath, the dispiriting neglect and uniformity of concrete blocks. A broken swing; a vandalized car;

a bike cannibalized for its parts, even the seat eviscerated for reasons too obscure to contemplate.

Armand got on with things. He prepared his lessons and marked essays. In class they talked about Nietzsche's *Übermensch* and Sartre's existentialism. They talked about Kant's daily routine and Wittgenstein's introverted nature as though they knew these men. They also discussed spirituality. What it meant to different people. His students were surprising, eager and attentive, absorbing knowledge like sponges.

When the head called him in he didn't think it was anything serious. But it proved to be worse than he ever could have imagined. Olivia's parents had called the school to complain that she had developed an unhealthy relationship with her teacher. They were worried about her. She was losing weight and not communicating. The head teacher laid a hand on Armand's arm. She was fond of him, she said, and appreciated the work he did. She didn't believe for a moment that he had done anything unethical. But the school could not afford to anger people like Olivia's parents. She told him he could finish the school year, since there were only three weeks left, but he would not be able to stay on.

Three days later, he received a telegram informing him that his mother had died. She'd suffered an aneurism, it said.

As the snow thawed and the first buds of spring appeared, Armand withdrew from his students. He kept away from Olivia and avoided Amir's eyes in class. Each lesson became agonizing; he returned home at the end of the day with a pounding headache.

Over the next week, he spent time with Volodya. The professor, who taught history at Moscow University, was grateful for his company, with his girlfriend Nina working at the orphanage and spending several nights a week there.

The two of them talked about Russian literature and art, and about the role of religion in Russian life.

When Nina was home one evening the two of them invited Armand over for a meal and he asked questions about where she worked. He noticed she was a lot younger than the professor. Small and frail-looking, like a mouse, with wide brown eyes set beneath a fringe. But judging by what she told him, she must have been a lot tougher than she appeared.

She told him about the children who were abandoned by their mothers at birth, urged on by the doctors who warned them of the stigma attached to a disability. Even though the disability might be nothing more than a club foot or a hare lip. Even when sometimes there was no handicap at all, but the parents were alcoholics and the doctors said there was most likely some brain damage. Maybe the infant was quiet at birth. It could be anything and nothing. The doctors prey on the mothers' fears, and every mother is scared, Nina said, rubbing her tired eyes.

She told him about the toys, donated and then locked away. And the lying-down room where the children were left in cots all day, some of them tethered and heavily sedated, all of them deprived of touch and stimulation. Not even a soft toy to cuddle up to for comfort. Until the children eventually shrivelled up. They might not have had anything wrong with them to start with, she said, but they sure as hell did after a stint in the lying-down room.

Armand looked at Nina's red-rimmed eyes and wondered how she coped.

All this talk of abandoned children, deprived of love. Armand returned to his flat and thought with horror of the lying-down room. The images it evoked merged in his head with memories of what his mother had done, though he fought to keep those at bay. At night he lay in bed with a sadness in his heart that ballooned until there was room for nothing else. Despite everything, he missed his mother, though he knew that he really shouldn't. But without her he was quite alone in the world.

Each night he mourned his own fate. What could he make of himself? There had been so many betrayals. His mother. Charles. Olivia, Amir. Their faces appeared in his dreams at night, taunting him. He also mourned the fate of those orphans Nina cared for. Neglected and betrayed by those who should have protected them. How well he understood those kids.

Gradually, an idea formed in Armand's head. At first it was nothing, a barely formed notion which he didn't take too seriously. But slowly it came to him that he could make it happen, if only he could work up the courage. It would be the thing that made sense of his time here.

One evening he invited Nina and Volodya over for dinner. He made a real effort, cooking a coq au vin and sautéed potatoes, followed by a chocolate cake he'd baked himself. He'd bought vodka and wine.

The chicken was scrawny and the potatoes still raw in the middle, but the three of them worked their way quickly through the vodka and wine. By the time they ate dessert no one noticed how dense the cake was. Armand's guests scoffed it down quite happily and complimented him on his baking skills.

When they had all finished eating and were drinking at the table, he asked Nina if she could help him. He'd given a lot of thought to how he would argue his case and he chose his words with care.

At first she seemed reluctant. She didn't want any trouble with the orphanage, she said. They wouldn't like it if they knew she'd been talking to him, a foreigner, about conditions there. But Armand assured her it would be fine. She would not be implicated in any way. The thing was to say she knew someone who was interested in adopting a child. And to help arrange an appointment with the director. They could have met by chance, he said. If she could find it in herself to help him, he might be able to make a difference in the life of an orphan. Maybe there was a particular child she thought especially deserving; a little boy, for example, whose hopes of living a better life were particularly slim.

Judging by Nina's face, he saw this was the right thing to say. Volodya sat by her side looking as if he was holding back from saying what he really thought, as if the minute Armand was gone he would open his mouth and a torrent of words would pour out. But it didn't matter because Armand saw that Nina had already made up her mind.

For several weeks he heard nothing from her. He wondered whether he had misjudged the situation. But he was patient, knowing instinctively that if he pushed any further she would not help him at all. In the meantime he'd worked out his notice at the French Lycée and found a job teaching at a local school. He would start there at the end of the long summer break. The money was pitiful but he could manage if he was careful. Now, as he saw it, he would be no different from his neighbours, who commented often and anxiously on the city's spiralling food prices.

Then the day came when she said she had arranged for him to meet with the director on a Saturday morning. It was probably a good idea to wear a suit, she said.

It was six weeks after their first conversation when he finally made the trip back to the orphanage.

He'd had to borrow a suit from a former colleague at the Lycée whom he'd kept in touch with, pretending it was for a wedding. Now that it was summer the road looked completely different. The sun was high in the sky and a dusty haze covered everything. Armand felt excited and slightly sick.

He turned into the orphanage's car park and walked towards the main entrance. In the courtyard, children were chasing chickens. They squawked and ran in panicky circles around the yard.

The woman who greeted him was the one he'd spoken to on the phone to confirm the appointment. A blonde anaemic creature with dark circles under her eyes. Scrawny and nervous, she fussed and flapped, just like one of those mad chickens sprinting past his feet a moment ago. She led him into an office with a desk the size of a single bed and told him to wait. The painting on the wall behind the desk was of a forest filled with row after row of emaciated birch trees. The background was painted black and the trees white. Armand stared at the painting and tried to breathe normally.

The woman who walked in ten minutes later introduced herself as the director. Armand had a feeling she had delayed her entrance to make herself look important. That and the smell of cheap perfume that preceded her arrival meant he took an instant dislike to her. But he was on a mission and determined to win her over. While she practised her French on him he pretended to be interested in her cleavage, and she rewarded him with a smile, lipstick stains on her front teeth.

She asked questions and jotted notes in an exercise pad before her. After a while he realized that his answers meant little to her. She was going through the motions but she had already made up her mind.

'We have a boy I think might be suitable; he is six years old and unfortunately is unable to talk. But he understands perfectly what you tell him and he is a quiet and accommodating child. You won't have any trouble with him.'

Armand had expected a long, drawn-out process. Frequent trips to the orphanage, letters and phone calls, references the director would want as proof of good character. Instead she casually named an exorbitant sum of money that she said was standard procedure and would help speed up the administrative process.

'If you like the boy, of course.'

The sum was half of his inheritance, Armand calculated. The thought of it made him dizzy.

He stood up and swayed before the director, who was picking up the phone now and talking to someone. When she hung up he grasped her hand and thanked her with tears in his eyes. It was the right thing to do. She too grew emotional and embraced him. He found himself squashed against her ample bosom, half-hanging on to her because he was sure otherwise he would faint from the smell of perfume and his own panicked state.

He was still in her grasp when he felt her stiffen.

'The child is here,' she whispered in his ear.

As the boy stepped forward, Armand felt his past slipping away from him. What had happened before, all the things he'd done, were of no consequence.

'As I mentioned before, Dima has just turned six,' the director said. She pinched the boy's cheek. There was no response. Armand tried not to show how shaken he was. The boy was exactly as he had imagined him to be, as he had hoped. A slender child with big dark eyes. His hair was cropped short. *I will let his hair grow*, Armand thought.

He wanted to say, *When can I take him?* Instead, he asked if he could take the boy for a stroll down the road, not too far. The director shrugged as if to suggest it no longer concerned her.

He followed the boy out of the room, noticing that he

walked with a limp. The boy's faded T-shirt and trousers looked as though they had been passed down several generations of other children at the orphanage. They weren't fit to be worn.

Armand stepped outside. The light was harsh and for a moment he hesitated, wondering which way to go. But the boy was right behind him, waiting to be led. Armand began walking towards the forest.

There was no one on the path. When they reached the edge of the woods, where the trees began, Armand stopped and wiped his brow. The boy was watching him coolly, as though he was looking at something up on a screen that was not part of his reality. All this time Armand hadn't said a word to him. He didn't know how to communicate with the boy.

Back at the orphanage, they insisted on putting him up for the night. The world outside seemed forbidding, harsh. He accepted.

They put him in a small, airless room with a single bed. The mattress was thin and the steel frame dug into his back. He tried to open a window but the latch refused to yield.

For a long time he tossed and turned.

Sometime in the night he felt the child climb in next to him. The two of them barely fitted in the narrow bunk. Despite the heat and the clamminess of their bodies, they held each other as though lost in the middle of a storm. Gradually, Armand forgot about the discomfort and fell asleep.

When he woke up, the boy was gone.

TWENTY-SIX

Breakfast was included. They had brioches and coffee in the dining room at 7.30 before checking out of the inn and getting into the car. They would stop at Charles's house before meeting with Armand Le Bellec's old schoolteacher.

'Shall we tell Charles we're coming?' Lila said.

'Let's surprise him instead,' Morel said.

When they got to Charles's house his car wasn't in the driveway and there was nobody about.

Lila looked at her watch. 'Do you think it's possible he's already left to take the kids to school?'

'Maybe. We'll come back after we've spoken to the teacher.'

They drove to the school, where the teacher waited for them. It was a small building with a playground. A rabbit hutch and a vegetable garden.

'Pierre Fourmond?'

'That's me.'

They shook hands.

'It's a nice school you've got here,' Morel said. 'And the kids have got rabbits, I see.'

The teacher nodded. He reminded Morel of his old physics teacher. Greying beard and khaki trousers. Tall and narrow-shouldered, with a soft paunch in an otherwise lanky body.

'We've got three rabbits. Every once in a while one of them dies and we replace it without making a fuss. The kids seem to take it in their stride,' he said. 'Come on in. I thought we could sit in the staff room; there's no one about yet.'

The room he took them to could clearly have done with some funding to replace the shabby armchairs and worn carpet.

'It's comfortable enough,' the teacher said, following Morel's gaze. 'So you want to talk to me about Armand? You know it's a long time ago.'

'I know. But we were hoping that you'd be able to help us.'

'Is he in trouble?'

Morel looked at the man's concerned face. It was funny, the way everyone's first thought seemed to be that Armand was in trouble.

'We need to find him and ask him a few questions,' Morel replied. 'I hope you don't mind if I don't tell you what it's about; right now we know very little. If we could talk to him it would help.'

Pierre Fourmond offered them tea, but Morel shook his head.

'I remember him as a shy kid,' the teacher said, turning the kettle on.

'Do you remember a child called Charles Berg?'

'Yes, of course. Charles still lives here.' Pierre Fourmond seemed to think for a while. The kettle began to whistle. 'He and Armand were friends. He was Armand's only friend, in fact. Charles was the sociable one, but somehow he picked this introverted boy. It seemed odd to me in a way, though I could also understand it.'

'Why?'

'Because Armand was a kid who didn't seem to care what anyone thought of him. He didn't care about making the right impression. I think Charles respected that in him.

Charles didn't have that kind of strength. He needed to be liked.'

'How is it you remember so much about all of this? I'm just curious. As you said yourself, it's such a long time ago,' Morel said.

The teacher shrugged. 'This is my life. I remember many of my students well.'

'Was Armand a good student?'

'Exemplary. Very bright and diligent.'

Lila leaned forward. Waited for Fourmond to finish making his tea. He sat down with his cup and a biscuit.

'What can you tell us about Armand's mother? Do you remember her at all?'

Pierre Fourmond bit into his biscuit and chewed thought-fully. 'I do.' Morel tried not to betray his impatience.

'Madame Le Bellec was a very possessive parent. This is why I remember Armand so well, in fact. Halfway through the year she pulled her son out of school. After that we didn't see him again till the following year. I'm not sure what happened.'

'Surely a parent can't just remove their child from school without the school getting involved and asking a few questions. Someone must have approached her.'

'Sure. But nothing came of it.'

'Who was it? The head teacher?'

'Yes.' Guessing their thoughts, Pierre Fourmond said, 'But you won't be able to talk to him, I'm afraid. He died of a heart attack some years ago. I can tell you in any case that whatever was said or done didn't make any difference. She didn't budge and Armand missed school for six months.'

'So what happened when Armand came back?'

'He kept to himself. Got on with his school work but that was about it.'

'He and Charles weren't friends any more?'

'No.' Pierre Fourmond looked at Morel. 'It was quite striking, the contrast. One minute they were always together, the next they were avoiding each other. Well, Armand wasn't talking to anyone. And as for Charles, his grades started slipping.'

Lila raised an eyebrow.

'I remember it well, you see, because it's not the sort of friendship you see often between boys at that age.'

'In what way?'

'So intense. Usually you see the boys playing together as a group. There isn't that exclusive behaviour which you tend to see more among girls.' He smiled at Lila. 'I know this is a simplistic way to look at it but there is a great deal of truth there and I've observed the same patterns of behaviour again and again amongst my students.'

'Tell us a bit more about Charles,' she said.

'He was an easy-going sort of kid. Open and friendly. He got on with everyone, and everyone liked him. From what I remember he was doing well across the subjects. Not in a spectacular way but well enough. He was good at sports. But there was a transformation.'

'When Armand came back, you mean?'

The teacher thought about it for a while. 'No. It was when Armand left the school.' He nodded his head. 'That's when Charles became disengaged with school.'

'Any idea what happened?' Morel said.

'No. But I'm guessing it had to do with Armand; and that Armand's mother had a hand in it.'

'What was going on between her and her son? What was the problem?'

'I'm not a psychologist, obviously, but all I can say is she was terribly possessive and she seemed to play a very active role in Armand's life.' He thought for a while. 'I got the impression that she was never far from him, no matter what he did. It was almost like she was shadowing him. I don't know how else to explain it.'

'I think I understand,' Lila said. She was thinking about Anne Dufour and the constant fear in her eyes. A woman who lived like she was always under scrutiny.

'It's like she was always in the room with him,' Fourmond was saying.

Lila's skin crawled, as though something was moving up her back. The teacher looked at her and shrugged his shoulders.

'I can't really tell you more than that. I'd be sorry to hear he was in trouble, though. Let me know if I can be of any further use.'

'You've been a great help already,' Morel said.

The teacher stood up and stretched out his hand.

They followed him outside and Fourmond watched them get into the car and waved as they drove off.

Once they were back on the road that led to Charles's house, Morel turned to Lila.

'What do you think?' he said.

'I think Charles has a lot of explaining to do.'

Charles was in his driveway, about to get into his car, when Morel and Lila drew up to the house. The man they saw was different from the one they'd interviewed the day before. He looked defeated.

'We came by earlier but you weren't here,' Lila said accusingly.

'Yes, I had to drop my boys off at school and my daughter at my mother's. She's sick. And now I have to go into work.' Suddenly realizing they were here to see him, he said, 'What do you want now?'

'This won't take long,' Morel said. 'Do you mind if we go inside for a moment?'

'What for?'

'Well, for one thing I thought you might want this back.' Morel handed the photograph over. 'I believe your friend Armand may have borrowed it from you when he dropped by.'

Morel saw Charles hang his head. What a contrast, he thought. He wondered what had happened in the short time since they'd spoken to him last.

'Come in, then,' he said.

Morel and Lila looked at each other before following him inside.

Despite the clutter the living room looked desolate. Charles perched on the end of a sofa while the two detectives sat opposite him. For twenty minutes they'd listened to Charles and not said a word. When he finished there was a silence. He looked up at them.

'It might sound sordid to you but the simple truth is we loved each other.'

'How often did you two – get together?' Morel asked.

'Fuck, you mean?' Charles gave a bitter smile. 'We call ourselves liberal and progressive but funny how difficult we find it to spell it out, when two men sleep together.'

'Two boys,' Lila said.

'We were young, but we were not children,' Charles said, looking her in the eye. 'What happened, happened naturally. We were more than ready.'

'So. How often did you have sex, and when did it stop?' Morel asked.

'A dozen times, maybe. Then one day Armand's mother caught us.'

Lila glanced at Morel. 'How?'

'It was stupid, really. We should have known better. I was over at his house, I'd walked him home. Normally I didn't linger, she made me uncomfortable. But she was out.' Charles bit his lip, remembering the scene. 'We were just fooling around. I think it excited Armand, to be doing it right there in his mother's living room. He pulled my shirt off and kissed me. One thing led to another and eventually we both had our pants down. He was on top of me when she walked in.' His face turned red, as though he was reliving the moment. 'It was horrible. She didn't yell or even say anything. She just looked at us. We were both terrified, fumbling with our clothes and rushing to get them back on. All the time she was quiet. But the way she looked at us . . .'

He didn't finish his sentence. He was far away, experiencing the same terror and humiliation all over again.

'And then?' Lila prodded.

'And then nothing. I left in a hurry. The next day Armand didn't return to school. He didn't come back all week. I realized shortly afterwards that his mother was keeping him out of school. I didn't hear from him again. Not till he came back.'

'Did you try to contact him?'

Charles hung his head. 'No.'

'Why not?'

Charles's head shot back up. 'What was I supposed to do? I was frightened of her and what would happen if it got out. What Armand and I had been up to.'

'But you loved him. Didn't it occur to you that he might need you?' Lila said, a sharp edge to her voice.

'I was sixteen,' Charles said.

'Did your parents find out?'

'No.' A slight hesitation in Charles's voice.

'But your mother suspected, didn't she?' Lila said.

Charles nodded. 'I think she knew all along. I don't know why she chose to keep quiet about it. Maybe she didn't want to face it. Or she hoped it would go away.'

'What happened when Armand returned to school?' Morel asked.

'It was like we had never been friends. Armand never once spoke to me. He barely looked my way. I tried to approach him a couple of times but he would walk away from me every time. So after a while I gave up.'

'What happened to him, Charles?' Morel asked.

Charles shook his head slowly. 'I don't know,' he said. 'All I know is that when he came back to school, he was a different person.' He looked at them in turn. 'Whatever happened while he was away, it changed him radically. The way I saw it, the Armand I knew no longer existed.'

They watched Charles drive off, late for work. Then they both got into Morel's cherry-red car. It occurred to Morel that the whole village must be aware of their presence. The Volvo wasn't the sort of car that went unnoticed.

'What now?' Lila said. She looked thoughtful.

They sat in silence for a while thinking of the things they had just heard. All of a sudden Morel felt drained.

He started the car and drove out of the village.

After several minutes Lila looked at him. 'Weren't you supposed to turn off back there?' she asked.

'We're taking a little detour,' Morel said.

'Where are we going?'

'Have you ever been to Saint-Malo?'

'What?'

'I thought we might stop there before we go back. Never mind if we're running a bit late.'

'You're kidding, right? Perrin's expecting us to brief him this afternoon. He'll be furious.'

'Then what are we waiting for?' Morel said.

They reached Saint-Malo in less than an hour. The town was overrun by tourists. They were everywhere, filling the cafes and restaurants and walking in groups through the cobblestoned streets, talking and laughing loudly. What a contrast to the Saint-Malo he remembered, Morel thought. Quiet and self-contained.

After a twenty-minute wait they were shown to a table at a restaurant where they ate mussels in a white-wine sauce and grilled sardines, with a carafe of Muscadet. All around them people were speaking English, Italian, Russian – everything but French.

'I haven't been here in years,' Morel said. The tension in his shoulders made his back ache and he stretched, willing his muscles to relax.

'It looks like all of Europe is here,' Lila said. She had finished her drink and poured another. For a while neither of them spoke.

Morel gulped the last of his Muscadet. He looked at Lila. The sun emerged briefly to light up her face, and her eyes were sparkling from the wine. She gave him a questioning look and he shook his head.

'Let's go for a walk,' he said.

They left the jammed town centre and headed towards the walled jetty, curving into the harbour like some giant prehistoric tail. A man and a boy were fishing from it, a bucket at their feet. In a state of quiet watchfulness, oblivious to everything but each other and any sign of life at the end of their fishing rods. Morel thought of his father, cooped up in his bedroom in the same dressing-gown he'd been wearing for at least the past decade.

I must bring him here, he thought. Maybe when this case was over he could take a few days off and he and his father could rent a place up here. Bring plenty of books and good wine. Take walks along the beach and read. Eat well. His parents had always loved to eat out.

Morel breathed in and out, letting the events of the past weeks ebb from him like the water below. Slowly the tide was going out, leaving clumps of seaweed in its wake. The air smelled of fish and sea and the rain-soaked clouds that were threatening to spill even as they stood there with their faces looking out to the distant horizon.

'I'm so glad we did this,' Lila said after a while.

He had almost forgotten her presence but now he looked over at her and found himself glad she was there with him.

They stayed for a while longer, watching the boats. A pair of red and yellow canoes out on the horizon. A giant white cruise ship. A yacht was coming into the harbour, its sail tugging at the mast in cheerful surrender. The clouds that had threatened to open up went on their way and the sun came out quietly again. The sky was a cool and watery shade of blue, the wind frisky, ruffling their clothes.

'This is almost like being on holiday, isn't it?' Lila said.

Morel looked at her again. She was wearing her Puffa jacket and jeans again but she appeared like a softer version of herself, standing there with her elbows up on the parapet, her hair blowing about her head. Her cheeks and the tips of her ears were pink and her eyes clear when she met his gaze.

'Being almost on holiday seems to suit you,' he said. 'You look different.'

Lila looked carefully at him, as though she were trying to figure him out, then she laughed.

'What?'

She moved closer and with her hand brushed some dirt from his suit. It would have come from the wall which they had been leaning against. He fished in his pocket for a handkerchief. For a minute he remained absorbed, rubbing at a stain that wasn't there.

She grinned at him.

'What?' he said again, annoyed now.

'You. You still look exactly like you.'

Charles looked at his watch. He would probably still make it to his meeting. Either way, it didn't matter.

The kids had been clingy that morning. There had been whining and tantrums and in the end he'd had to shout. At his mother's house, and at school, they had insisted on multiple hugs before he left.

Maybe it wasn't just that their mother had been gone for a week. Maybe they were worried about him. Chloé, the eldest, had always acted as though she was the parent. Ever since she was four or five. It made him sad at times to think that she felt she needed to look out for her parents. It should be the other way round. It should be him making *her* feel safe, guarding her against anything harmful that might come her way.

He didn't want to think about Armand, but driving to Rennes in slow traffic he found the conversation with the police had brought everything back. It was like an avalanche. A road sign warned him to slow down to forty kilometres an hour. He passed orange traffic cones and workers in sleeveless shirts and Day-Glo vests.

It is a story he knows by heart. He has played it in his head over and over again, as though somehow he might discover a way to change the outcome. If not that, then at least he might learn to live with it better. There is still that hope.

Armand is fifteen, Charles is a year older. Fourteen months and two days older, Armand likes to say. He says it half jokingly but the truth is that he is always this literal. Charles knows it and accepts this is part of who Armand is. This is the strange thing. He can accept most things about Armand. Why is that? Is it because Armand is everything Charles isn't? Armand seems oblivious to what people think. He doesn't seem to need anyone's backing. This is probably what draws Charles to him. Later, there is something else too: Armand's neediness, which Charles finds both repellent and attractive.

When Charles asks, 'How long is it we've been best friends?' Armand is prepared with an answer. Three years, eight months, six days. He could add the hours, minutes and seconds but Charles places a finger on his lips and that shuts him up.

At school they are always together. When the bell rings they catch the bus back to the village. The last two kids to get dropped home. The ones who live furthest from the school. Armand doesn't get invited to other children's houses and, besides, his mother wouldn't allow him to go. As for Charles, he is more popular. But he turns down invitations and doesn't tell Armand about them. They spend long afternoons at Charles's house, listening to music and making up games that most of the other boys in their class would probably find childish if they knew. Hiding deep in Charles's closet, they are on their way. The closet, like the one in the Narnia tales, is a doorway into other worlds. In the dark, Armand's face is grave and composed. With his arm around Charles's shoulder he gives life to a cast of characters that make Charles forget everything else but this cramped corner in the cupboard with its jumble of old toys and discarded clothes.

They never play at Armand's house. Armand's mother

doesn't let her boy out of her sight, except when he is with Charles. It isn't clear why that is but Charles suspects it is snobbery on her part. It's because Charles's parents own the nicest house in the village.

Armand's fear is something other people will never understand. Armand's mother possesses a presence that will live beyond the grave. She has a way of knowing things she can't possibly know. Things that are never spoken out loud. She burrows into Armand's head and sniffs around in there for anything she might be able to use against him.

Charles's father has a boat moored in Saint-Malo. One weekend they offer to take Armand sailing with them. To everyone's surprise, Armand's mother agrees to the trip.

The weather is unbelievable. They sail out of the harbour with just the right amount of wind to carry them through. There are no clouds in the sky and it is warm enough to sit out on deck and enjoy the sunshine. Charles is wearing the sailor shirt that Armand gave him for his birthday. Armand is wearing a frayed shirt and jeans that he has outgrown. The cuffs stop above his ankles and the sole is coming off one of his shoes. Charles's mother has suggested she hand over his old clothes to Armand as he is now bigger and taller than his friend, but Charles has pleaded with her not to. He knows Armand is too proud to accept any cast-offs from them.

They arrive at Île de Ré in the early part of the evening, sailing into a spectacular sunset that feels as if it's been put on just for them, though other boats are heading in. For a moment Charles feels as if he and Armand are one person, experiencing the same mystical moment.

'Look at you two!' Charles's mother says. Charles turns to Armand. He is tanned and his eyes are burning bright like the luminous sea and the sun-tinted clouds. Everything is suffused with evening light. Charles's pretty mother in her green two-piece bathing suit that matches the colour of her eyes, and his father in red, white and blue bathing shorts hold each other tight and kiss with their lips open. The boys look away and at each other. Charles winks at Armand and they both laugh.

'What – you've never seen anyone kiss before?' Charles's dad says, cuffing them lightly. He places a hand on his wife's bottom and grins.

Charles's father pulls the boat up alongside a yacht so large that theirs seems puny in comparison. Charles's mother is wearing a long T-shirt over her bikini now. She cooks lamb chops and mashed potatoes and Charles helps her without being asked, by washing and preparing the salad. The four of them eat together below deck. It is cramped and after an afternoon of sailing and being exposed to the wind and the sun, they are all too tired to speak.

Afterwards Charles and Armand pile the dirty dishes into a bucket and carry it ashore to a sink near the toilets, where they set about washing them as best they can. The owner of the big boat comes along. He is German and he is smoking a cigar. He stands close, puffing away and watching them rinse the bucket, rinse the dishes and pile them back inside. His grey shorts ride so high up his legs you can see his balls. His chest is hairy and his stomach sags over the shorts.

'Want a puff?' he asks in heavily accented French. They say no and return to the boat, their feet thudding across the wooden planks of the pontoon. There is a rotting smell in the air, and the lingering odour of the German's cigar, acrid and mildly addictive. Though neither will admit it, the encounter has unsettled them. There is something in the man's manner that they can't identify but which causes a stir. Both unpleasant and titillating, in a strange kind of way.

'What a creep,' Charles says, and Armand agrees.

When they climb back on board, they sit for a short while with Charles's parents who are leaning back on deck chairs, drinking wine. But they soon grow bored and decide to go below deck. The parents wave them away, content. They murmur goodnight to the boys.

Charles and Armand don't bother brushing their teeth. They strip down to their T-shirts and shorts and climb into adjoining bunks. Their conversation is a whisper among the waves. Charles has rarely felt as happy as he does now. He feels deeply connected to Armand. Feels that somehow he has found his soul mate. How lucky he is. How many people ever have that experience? They lie still, listening to the murmur of voices up on deck.

'What's the story with the German millionaire?' Armand whispers.

'He's a bit of a pervert, I reckon. Did you see the way he looked at you?' Charles says.

'Hardly. It was you he was lusting after.'

'Errgh, gross. Stop it.'

'Really. He was staring at you. He was practically dribbling.'

'I mean it. Stop it.'

'Who can blame him, though?' Armand says lightly.

Charles doesn't know what to say to that. Instead he turns to look at Armand, who is lying on his back. He has taken his shirt off and closed his eyes. He is all skin and bones. Wrists and ankles as narrow as a girl's. Whereas Charles is strong and muscular. In the dark Charles can just make out the outline of Armand's chest and the shape of his arms crossed behind his head. He likes Armand in profile, with his broad forehead and long lashes. There is something noble about him. This isn't something he's ever likely to say to Armand, though he often thinks it.

They talk and doze off, and talk some more. At some point, their hands meet. It isn't clear who makes the first move, and anyway does it really matter? What is clear is that it's Armand who untangles his fingers from Charles's and rests his hand on his stomach. Moves his fingers lower, so casually it's like it is happening without him guiding them. Moves his hand under the elastic waistline and wraps his hand around Charles's penis, which twitches and comes to life. It is Armand who raises himself on an elbow and lowers his face until they can feel each other's breath.

It is Charles, breathing heavily, who raises his head so that their lips can touch, and who parts his just enough to encourage Armand to do the same. Their tongues come together, charging the air with electricity.

Charles can still remember every beat of that moment. The feel of Armand's lips, the salty taste of his skin. The hot, musky smell of his own body. He's tried hard to forget it, but no matter how hard he tries, his life is forever split in two. There is his life before Armand, and then there is his life after.

Everything after is a lie.

Charles stared at the truck bearing down the opposite lane. Just a quick turn of the steering-wheel and it would all be over. He probably wouldn't even have time to feel pain. Screeching of tyres, impact of metal on metal, followed by silence.

He must have been driving too close. As the truck passed him, the driver tooted his horn and gave him the finger.

He pulled over. Waited ten, twenty minutes till the shaking stopped.

TWENTY-SEVEN

It was late and most people had left the building. The light was still on in the fourth-floor office where Morel's team sat. A warm summer breeze floated through the open windows. Outside, lights had come on along the quays and bridges.

Morel had just checked his phone messages and he returned to the others, triumphant.

'We've got him,' he said. 'I just got a call, from the head at a school in Denfert-Rochereau. One of his staff members recognized Armand from the composite sketch in an article in *Libération*. He's been working under the name Antoine Leroy.'

'That explains why my friend at the ministry couldn't find him,' Lila said.

Morel nodded.

'Apparently he hasn't been in for a couple of weeks. The listed address he gave the school is a two-bedroom flat in Clichy. It's actually under his real name but he doesn't live there. It's being rented out to a couple of teachers who haven't heard from him in months.'

After Saint-Malo, Morel would have gladly driven home and poured himself a solitary and well-deserved drink in the privacy of his study. But he and Lila still needed to brief the others about their trip.

At least Perrin wasn't in. According to Jean, he'd waited

all afternoon for Morel, striding in every half-hour to
see whether he and Lila had returned from Brittany yet.
But then he'd been called to a murder scene by one of the
other team leaders, one that had nothing to do with Morel's
investigation. Morel couldn't help feeling just a little bit
grateful.

He was bone-tired and unsteady from the long drive – the
lunchtime Muscadet hadn't helped – but to alleviate everyone's
mood he opened a bottle of red: the best one from his father's
cellar, which he kept in his bottom desk drawer.

'Just because we have to work doesn't mean we have to
forgo the *apéritif*,' he said, handing glasses out. Only Akil
declined.

'I know we all want to go home but I want to make sure
we've covered every angle and that everyone's up to speed.
This is what we know. Armand Le Bellec was last seen in
his home town in Brittany three days ago. We have good
reason to believe he is back in Paris. We know he had a relationship with Charles Berg – a strong friendship that developed into something more. They fell in love. They carried
on in secret until they were found out by Le Bellec's mother.
A deeply religious and conservative woman, by all accounts.
A woman people found it difficult to get on with. After she
found out what the boys were up to, she took Armand out
of school for six months. We don't know what happened
during those six months but we do know that when Armand
came back to school he was a different person. He avoided
Charles and withdrew into himself.'

'What was Le Bellec doing back in the village?' Lila asked.

'We don't know. Maybe he's feeling the pressure and he's
scared. Maybe he was reaching out to his old friend.' Morel
looked at his team. 'Anyone want to say anything at this
stage?'

'Why the false name?' Lila said. 'And if he is guilty, which the false identity implies, I still don't get what the motive was. What has this Le Bellec got against old women?'

'I've thought about that,' Morel said. 'When I spoke to my old friend Paul Chesnay last week, he mentioned that the American Baptist preacher Billy Graham had made quite a splash when he visited Moscow in the nineties.' He shook his head. 'I was a fool not to work it out earlier. Baptism in the Baptist Church is traditionally by complete immersion.'

Everyone stared at Morel. Akil was the first to speak.

'You're saying that the drownings are a kind of cleansing. By performing the Baptist ritual of immersion, the killer, this Le Bellec, is allowing the victims to be born again.'

'Exactly.' Morel looked at Akil approvingly. 'I think our friend Armand Le Bellec drowned Isabelle Dufour and Elisabeth Guillou as part of some misguided perception in his head that he is opening a door to a better life for them – a new beginning.'

'Seriously?' Lila said.

'There are other churches that perform baptism by immersion,' Morel said. 'Traditionally the Russian Orthodox Church, for example, practises baptism by immersion. Particularly with infants. But given the language used in Le Bellec's pamphlet, there is good reason to believe that he is a Baptist.'

There was silence.

'So when Le Bellec drowned Dufour and Guillou, he was actually baptizing them?' Lila said.

Morel nodded. 'It explains the way the two widows were dressed and the way they were laid in their beds.'

'What about the make-up? Is that a Baptist tradition too?'

'It does seem to be in complete contradiction to the rest,'

Akil said. 'The purity of the act, followed by the desecration of the face.'

Morel turned to Akil. 'You know, there's something in that,' he said slowly.

'What?' Lila asked.

'What Akil said. First the ritual, the immersion of the victim, a baptism of sorts. Then the make-up. The make-up comes after. It's almost as though Le Bellec himself is undergoing a change as he performs this act.'

'Almost as though he is two people,' Jean said.

Morel gave him a sharp look. 'Exactly.'

'So what does the make-up symbolize?' Lila asked. 'Is it a reminder of the victim's sinful past?'

They all laughed. But there was confusion on everyone's faces.

'What about the boy?' Lila asked.

'We have to do our best to track him down too,' Morel said. 'It's hard to imagine what his part is in all this. But I'm concerned about his welfare.'

'Should we be talking to the child-protection squad?' Lila asked.

'We may have to at some stage. But at the moment I don't see how they can help us.'

Morel stood up.

'We need to find every Baptist organization there is in Paris and its outskirts and run our photo of Armand past them. If he calls himself a Baptist then at some point he must have had some contact with one of these organizations.'

'We've been through all that,' Lila said.

'Then we go through it again. This time we focus on the Baptists. Meanwhile, I've asked the school where Armand worked to let us know if he shows up again.'

'Seems unlikely. The story's been in the papers; there's no way he's going to waltz into the classroom as if nothing's happened,' Lila said.

'I would have thought by now we'd have had a sighting. Given, as you say, that the picture's been in the papers. Yet no one's seen him apart from Charles and Amelia Berg. We've had dozens of calls, but none of them have given us anything useful,' Jean said.

'We can only hope that changes,' Morel said. 'Maybe we'll get lucky. I'm also making contact with Moscow,' he continued. 'Until now we've focused all our efforts on finding Le Bellec. But we need to find out more about the boy. How and where Le Bellec found him, whether the adoption process was legal. And also when and where Le Bellec converted. My feeling is that the more we know about the boy, the closer we are to understanding Le Bellec.' Morel looked around the room. 'Any questions?'

No one spoke.

'Good. Then I suggest we all head home and catch up on some sleep. I'll see you all here tomorrow morning, bright and early.'

Morel watched Jean and Marco leave the room while Lila gathered her things. He was completely exhausted. But they were close. For the first time he allowed himself to relax, just a little.

Maybe tonight he would spare some time for his plans. He was almost at the point where he could begin with the folding. Give shape to the owl.

Tomorrow, he would track Le Bellec down.

Lila headed for the stairs and was surprised to encounter Akil, whom she thought had already left. She realized now that she hadn't once been alone with him. She was annoyed to find herself blushing.

'I'm starving,' he said, with a smile that made her blush even more. 'Want to join me for a quick bite?'

Before he left the office Morel called a number in Moscow. He was surprised when the man answered. He had expected to get the answering machine.

'Good evening, comrade,' he said.

The man at the other end of the line laughed. 'Monsieur Morel, very pleased to hear from you. By the way, you know that word is out of fashion these days.' His accent was thick but his French was good.

Morel had met Ivan Golyubov during a three-day international symposium in Paris on policing and security. Morel had warmed to his gruff Russian counterpart and even spent an evening with him, trawling the streets around the Porte Maillot conference centre for a quiet place to drink. They'd ended up in the Russian's room, drinking into the early hours of the morning. Maybe it was the vodka, which Morel wasn't used to, but he had ended up talking more openly with the man than he'd done with anyone in years.

'I have a favour to ask of you,' Morel said now.

'Of course. Happy to help if it is within my capacity.'

'It's just that I'd like to avoid the paperwork and the bureaucracy.'

'What is it you need?'

Morel explained the case to Golyubov, who listened carefully and didn't speak until Morel had finished.

'So, what can I do?'

'I need to know more about the child and the adoption process. Someone must have helped with the adoption. Maybe they can tell me more about Le Bellec and about the boy.'

'I'll see what I can do.'

'Thank you.'

It was past 10 p.m. by the time Morel turned the lights off and headed to his car. He checked his phone messages and saw he had missed a call from Solange. This was the second call from her in two days and he hadn't even returned the first.

I'll call her as soon as I get home, he thought.

When Morel arrived at his house he was surprised to find Adèle sleeping soundly on the living-room sofa. For some reason she was wearing a pair of his pyjamas. The lights were still on and there was a half-empty bottle of wine on the table beside her.

He debated whether to wake her up but she was sleeping so soundly that he decided not to. Instead he carried the bottle of wine to the kitchen and poured himself a glass. In the fridge was some leftover shepherd's pie. He dished some onto a plate and heated it up in the microwave.

He returned to the living room with his drink and supper and sat across from his sister. She opened her eyes.

'You're back,' she said. She sat up and looked at her watch.

'What are you doing here?' Morel asked.

'Something happened with Dad,' she said.

'What? What happened?'

'He's all right now,' Adèle said. She came over and touched his arm. 'You look worn out, Serge. Dad just had a funny turn. Augustine found him wandering down the street in his pyjamas this afternoon.'

'In his *pyjamas*?' Morel said.

'She brought him back and now he's asleep. It was lucky she found him. That it was her rather than a complete stranger, I mean.'

Yes, because appearances matter above all else, Morel thought.

'How come no one called me?'

'Augustine called me instead. She was worried about disturbing you at work.'

'Right.'

'Does it matter?'

'No,' Morel lied.

'He needs to see a doctor,' Adèle said.

Morel looked at his shepherd's pie. All of a sudden he didn't feel so hungry any more. He set the plate on the table and poured more wine into his glass.

'Serge.'

'Yes.'

'Did you hear what I said? I can take care of it if you like. I can see you've got a lot on your mind at the moment. This case you're working on—'

'It's fine. I'll take care of it. I'll call Dr Roland in the morning and make an appointment.'

'Dad hasn't been to see him in years. He always reckons he's the only healthy one in the family. You know he's going to be difficult about it, don't you?' Adèle said, smiling for the first time since he'd walked in.

'Nothing new there,' Morel said, before emptying his glass as if all it contained was water.

TWENTY-EIGHT

Once he left the Moscow Lycée and started teaching at the local school, Armand lost contact with most of his former French colleagues in the city. It was just as well. Better to make a fresh start, after all, untainted by the rumours that he knew must be circulating about him. Neither Olivia nor Amir ever attempted to contact him.

At times, he missed their company, particularly Olivia's. Even though she had betrayed him, there had been a real connection there. He tried not to dwell on it and kept himself busy, waiting for the moment when he would be able to take the boy back to France with him. There were a few more formalities to process, and he would be on his way.

He saw more of Nina and Volodya. Nina told him she had recently converted to the Baptist faith and asked whether he might like to come to a service with her on Christmas Day.

It wasn't that he was lonely. Soon, he would have the boy. But weekends were empty and long. On Christmas morning he accompanied Nina for lack of anything better to do.

She drove him through deserted streets to a draughty assembly hall in a school building. The hall was filled with elderly people bundled up against the unseasonably cold weather. As they came in they took off their coats and scarves and hung them on hooks along the walls. Conversations were subdued and the floor was slick with melted snow.

'Meet Mike,' Nina said, and Armand found himself shaking hands with a man whose long blond hair and beard gave him the look of a prophet. Pale blue eyes, pale skin. Bloodless lips. He must have been in his early thirties. A modern-day Jesus in jeans and a check shirt.

'Welcome,' was all he said. Armand watched him move away, shaking hands with people as they came in, holding back all the while as though he didn't want to occupy the centre of the room, when in fact he was the focus. Everyone's eyes were on him.

Later, Armand would find out that Mike was from Louisiana and that he'd been born again in a state prison halfway through a seven-year sentence for aggravated assault. God had helped him overcome a drug and alcohol problem, Nina said.

Meanwhile the dreamy-eyed American shook hands and smiled at everyone he made contact with. He might have given up drugs but he still looked spaced out, Armand thought. He watched Mike get on stage and pick up his guitar. A fat woman in a red hat and a red dress two sizes too small for her shook a tambourine, swaying from side to side. The people standing before them swayed too, as if mesmerized. Up on stage there was a makeshift altar with a candle burning, the words 'The Lord Is Thy Light' inscribed on it. A tacky souvenir, that's all it is, Armand thought. He felt ashamed for these people and their readiness to join in. Were they so lonely and afraid that they needed an ex-convict from Louisiana to give them hope?

Mike stopped strumming and the woman placed her tambourine on the stage. You could have heard a pin drop. Then Mike looked around him and spoke up.

'The question is this: if you are a believer, where is your faith? If you are a Christian,' the man said, raising his voice, 'then where are you serving Christ?' The 'where' resonated with meaning. A ripple of words ran through the listeners. 'Today, we come together to serve Christ in this assembly hall, our church, humble as it may be.' He spread his arms and the woman in the hat did the same.

The words rose to a torrent of noise. Mike came down from the stage and moved among the people. Armand took a step back, but the man's gaze rested on him. Armand's thoughts were all over the place, jumping from fascination to repulsion, and back again. He could not see or feel what these people saw and felt, yet he envied them their easy acceptance. How convenient it was to simply believe!

Mike obviously had no clue what Armand was thinking. He came up to him and placed a hand on his shoulder.

'You know, we don't just open our doors to anyone who wants to join,' Mike told Armand. 'But I can tell by your eyes that you're one of us. You belong right here.'

Armand could have told him he wasn't the joining type. But Nina was standing by his side and he didn't want to disappoint her. Not after what she'd done for him.

So he smiled and nodded. It was easier than starting an argument about faith. He could tell this Mike a few things about what religion did to a person. His own mother, for example. But looking at the man before him, caught up in his comforting little daydream, he knew there was no point.

When Nina finally suggested they go he was relieved. He thought he would never go back there again.

Until the following Sunday, when she knocked on his door and asked whether he would like to join her. He thought for a while before agreeing. This time, he told himself, he would explain a thing or two to Mike about faith and forgiveness.

Gradually, in his own time, Armand became a convert. Not in the mindless, gaping sense that he attributed to others.

He would not sway and weep, nor would he nod at every word the American preacher uttered or sang, as though pearls of wisdom fell from his lips.

There was nothing Mike could tell him that he couldn't work out for himself. He would follow his own way.

Armand and the boy left Russia and arrived in Paris in early summer, a day before the boy's seventh birthday. They booked into a hotel room in Montmartre for a week. On Dima's birthday, Armand took him out for breakfast, at a cafe on Rue des Abbesses. Armand watched as Dima gobbled up his croissant and emptied his cup of hot chocolate in one gulp. With his pale face and wide eyes and his cropped black hair, he drew stares. There were shadows under his eyes and he was too thin. He looked like he'd been in hospital and was convalescing.

After breakfast Armand took Dima for a walk along the river. He bought clothes for the boy. Two pairs of jeans and five long-sleeved shirts, to cover the boy's arms. Sneakers and a baseball cap. The boy was completely taken by the cap. He looked at his reflection in the mirror for a long time while Armand paid for the things he'd bought.

Wherever they went after that, the boy wore the cap.

It rained often but that didn't stop Armand from taking Dima out each day to introduce him to his new surroundings. He bought a toy sailboat and they watched it float across the fountain at the Jardin du Luxembourg. At the Jardin d'Acclimatation amusement park they rode a boat along the magic river, through a landscape of reeds and weeping willows. They ate candy-floss and Armand won a blue teddy for Dima by knocking down three milk bottles in a row. The boy's face never changed but he wanted more. Insisted on going on the merry-go-round six times, changing his ride each time from a rocket to a car to something else, before Armand was able to drag him away. Dima rode a pony with his back ramrod-straight, both hands on the animal's neck. Not like he felt the need to hold on but like he was discovering the feel and shape of its hide and bones. When Armand urged him once to choose a toy in a shop and Dima chose a fluffy white dog, he ran his hands over it again and again with the same thoughtful gesture.

From the beginning, Armand spoke to the child in French. He wanted to make sure the boy would be ready for his new life. Classified as an idiot by the orphanage because of his muteness – despite the fact that he was in no way mentally retarded – the boy had not received any education.

Beneath the expressionless gaze Armand could see Dima's mind at work. Intensely processing every new thing that came his way. At times the light seemed to hurt his eyes. He ate every meal as though it were his last and Armand had to hold him back, beg him to slow down.

Armand had never walked so much. It was the boy who insisted, his skinny little legs infused with unexpected strength. The left leg determined to keep up with the right. The boy walked as though he was making up for a lifetime of immobility.

Armand was the one with blisters on the soles of his feet at the end of the day. The boy did wear himself out, though. He fell asleep within seconds each night, his face and arms pressed tight against the fluffy dog.

Every day after they had been walking Armand ran a bath for the boy. There were sores on his arms and legs, particularly over his elbows, knees and ankles. With clumsy hand gestures, he quizzed the boy about his past. The boy's awkward response, traced in the air with delicate fingers, coupled with what Nina had told him about the lying-down room at the orphanage, told Armand all he needed to know. Dima had been bedridden for so long that he had become covered with bed sores.

They took to hanging out for hours in the museums because they were free. Armand loved to walk through the galleries with their displays and share what he knew with the boy. Teaching Dima was like teaching a child half his age. He was a blank page to fill.

Armand had been surprised by the amount of money his mother left him. Even after paying for Dima's adoption, he had enough for a down payment on a two-bedroom flat in Clichy. He took the boy to Ikea near Charles de Gaulle airport and let him pick a few things for his room. A lamp, a toy train set and a couple of duvet covers, one with robots on it and the other with cars. After lengthy discussions with the head teacher, he enrolled the boy in a school close to where they lived. He would be older than the other children in his class but still, Armand had scored a small victory by managing to get him in. The boy couldn't speak but his hearing was fine, as was his intelligence, he'd told the head. Would she prefer that he receive no education at all? He knew how to speak to her. This had always been his strength, after all, the ability to convince people.

Once he'd sorted the boy out, he got a job at a school in Denfert-Rochereau, a long way from Dima's school but it didn't matter. At least he could start earning money again, rather than keep digging into his dwindling funds.

Over the course of the first term, he spent many hours with Dima going over the alphabet, performing basic maths.

Dima's adoption had to be fate, Armand thought. How could it be otherwise when, as he saw it, the boy's experience so closely mirrored his own?

Though Armand tried hard to keep it at a safe distance, the memory of his own confinement returned vividly night after night. The loss of Charles and the price his mother made him pay for his sins. Even animals knew better, she said. She could not let him out of the house, not until he became pure again. Shapes and smells he'd managed to forget returned, precise and real. The outline of his own bed and the tenderness around his wrists where the knots dug into his skin; the indifferent expanse of the ceiling overhead; the sour smell of unwashed sheets and fear; the extent of his disgrace and of his longing for escape, from her and from himself.

Armand took Dima to the doctor's but didn't tell him anything about the boy's past, fearing that he would court scrutiny. Instead he listened in silence while the man told him that the boy's limp was probably due to muscle atrophy. The doctor recommended physiotherapy, though it probably wouldn't make the limp go away entirely.

Armand soaped Dima and repaired his skin with oils and creams which a dermatologist prescribed. At night he kept a close watch on him, waited till he stopped staring at the ceiling with his eyes wide open and went to sleep, before going to sleep himself. Huddled close, the boy retreating as far as he could into Armand's waiting arms until they formed a single unit.

It was when he first read a comic to Dima that it happened. The book was *Asterix and the Laurel Wreath*. The words held little meaning for the child but he drank them in. When Julius Caesar appeared on the page, the boy pressed his finger against him.

'That's César, emperor of the Romans,' Armand said.

*

In the picture, Caesar wore armour and a wreath of leaves in his hair. The boy was thinking that where he came from, the man could never have got away with it. Not if he wanted to survive. Where he came from, laughter was never kind. As far as he was concerned, Caesar was a joke and it was no wonder he always got thrashed by the Gauls, the short one and the fat one in the blue and white striped trousers.

But then Armand opened other books, with maps that showed the colours of the Roman Empire bleeding across a continent, till the rest seemed puny and insignificant.

When they reached the end of the comic for the third time, the boy turned back to the page where he had first seen the image of Caesar. He pointed to the Roman and to himself. He did this several times, bracing himself for laughter, but it never came. Armand looked up from the picture and into his eyes. He nodded, in a way that showed he understood.

When Armand had gone, the boy lay with his eyes wide open for a long time. The moon's outline was clearly visible through the blinds. Somewhere a dog barked, until a man shouted for it to stop.

During the day there was so much to absorb that he never stopped to think. At night, he tried to give a name to his feelings, but found there was nothing inside him except a black hole. The day's events were noise, subsiding as soon as he found himself alone in the dark.

There was nothing about his previous life he wanted to hold on to, except maybe for the soft touch and gaze of the woman who had cared for him at the orphanage.

But thinking about her made his heart ache intolerably. It was calmer in the black hole, where he could float without pain.

How would he climb out of the hole and make a new life for himself? Was it even possible?

Maybe the answer was in a name. Something that would enable him to shape a new identity for himself.

A new name, a new life.

César. My name is César.

TWENTY-NINE

The storm rode through the city in the middle of the night, causing minor havoc wherever it passed. When Morel opened his window in the morning he found the wind blowing in gusts and the courtyard awash with debris from the trees planted along the footpath on the other side of the gate. The rain fell steadily and water gushed onto the cobblestones from the downpipe outside his bedroom wall.

The cool air was a welcome reprieve and he turned his face to it. His body ached and he felt like he'd barely slept. For a moment, he stood still, letting the slanting rain drench him.

He had called Solange around midnight, thinking that she wouldn't answer but feeling an urge to hear her voice. To his surprise, she had picked up the phone. Henri was asleep, she said. He had nothing much to say, and thankfully she didn't feel compelled to fill the silence with chatter. She seemed to guess that he simply wanted company. He was dozing off when she finally hung up. Now he couldn't even remember what they had talked about.

He was starting to shiver. He shut the window and went into the bathroom to get ready for work. Once he was dressed, he headed towards the living room.

It was deserted. Adèle was gone. Morel made coffee and

waited a while for his father to show up for breakfast. But there was no sign of life from upstairs.

The phone rang and he went to answer it, coffee cup in hand.

'Good morning, it's Augustine.'

'Good morning,' Morel said. 'I'm glad you called. I wanted to thank you for taking care of my father yesterday. It must have been a shock for you to see him like that.'

'It certainly was,' she said. 'I'm glad I was there, I can't imagine what would have happened otherwise. He wouldn't have wanted a stranger to approach him, not in the state he was in.'

'I'm truly grateful,' Morel said. 'Adèle is too.'

'Never mind that,' she continued briskly. 'I'm calling because I'm not supposed to be in today, but I thought that perhaps after what happened yesterday you might feel better if I came this morning. You know, just in case.'

Morel hesitated.

'I don't want to impose on you, Augustine.'

'You're not imposing at all. That's settled, then. I'll come in this morning.'

'I think he's still asleep, and I have to leave for work. But I'll do my best to get home early.'

'Don't worry,' she said. 'You do what you have to do.'

'Thank you.'

He finished his coffee, hoping to catch a glimpse of Philippe before he left. In the end he climbed the stairs and quietly opened the door to his father's room. The old man lay in the dark, buried beneath the duvet. Only his head stuck out. He was snoring lightly. Morel listened for a while before closing the door.

He decided to leave the car and walked the hundred metres or so to the nearest Métro station. The rain was easing but the wind kept up. Morel stepped around an overturned bin, its contents strewn across the footpath. A black spaniel stopped to sniff at the rubbish, wagging its tail, but its owner tugged at the lead and dragged the mutt away.

On the train, he was so caught up in his thoughts about the investigation that he nearly missed his stop. He headed up the stairs towards the exit with the other commuters. When he reached the top, he stopped for a moment, trying to make sense of the confusion in his head.

Over the past couple of days, Morel had pulled together enough information about Le Bellec to form a picture of the man. It was enough for him to feel that if he had him across the table, he would know where to begin a conversation.

Yet something wasn't right. Morel couldn't work out what it was, but the fact that he didn't quite understand what he was looking at made him uneasy. Part of the picture was out of focus.

As he entered the police building, he thought about his Russian counterpart and wondered how soon he might hear from him. He needed Golyubov to come through fast.

'Everyone's in nice and early,' Morel commented as he walked into the office. 'I know it's Saturday. Thanks for being here.'

Jean was hanging his leather jacket on the back of his chair. Lila, Akil and Marco were standing up, getting ready to go.

'We're off to see if, by some divine miracle, someone's seen our man,' Lila said gloomily, waving Le Bellec's photograph at Morel.

'Speaking of which, I've been thinking,' Morel said. 'I know I said we should take a closer look at the Baptists. But I think we need to cast our net a little wider.'

'How much wider?' Lila asked, with a look that said she was not enthralled by his suggestion.

'I'm thinking about where they're staying. We know Le Bellec and the boy aren't at the Clichy flat. So where are they? I'm thinking somewhere cheap, and relatively discreet, where no one's going to pay too much attention to them. A youth hostel, maybe? We need to look further afield.'

'Let me handle that,' Jean said, glancing at Lila. 'These guys have enough on their plate. I'll draw up a list.'

'Thanks, Jean.'

Lila, Akil and Marco left and Morel sat at his desk and checked his email. There was one from his friend Paul Chesnay. It was a continuation of the conversation they'd had in Chesnay's office at Nanterre University.

I thought I'd send you this – an article written around the time of Billy Graham's trip to Moscow, Chesnay wrote.

The article described the 1992 Baptist mission to Russia in great detail. The size of Graham's operation was astonishing: 1,500 billboards across the city, ads on buses and subway cars, in the newspapers and on television, as well as three million leaflets sent through the mail. Graham had chartered a dozen trains to bring thousands of people in from outlying cities in Russia, the Ukraine and Belarus. Tens of thousands of people had gathered at the Olympic Stadium to hear him speak.

One could say he started a revolution, Chesnay went on. *Introducing God as a friend to people for whom God was more like a stern and distant father figure. The sort of parent who tends to think of their offspring as something of a disappointment.*

There was a PS: *Any chance of interviewing your suspect when you catch him? The more I think about it, the more*

I believe he could form the basis of an interesting paper. Or a lively discussion with my students, at the very least.

Morel wrote to his friend thanking him. Rather than address the possibility of handing Le Bellec over to Chesnay to liven up his lectures, he promised instead to let him know how things developed.

Then he sat and thought about Le Bellec, with his absent father and bigoted mother. What had happened to this man since leaving his village? And where was he now?

For the next couple of hours, he prepared his report for Perrin, knowing it wouldn't be long before his boss appeared and demanded an explanation for the past forty-eight hours. Sometime after lunch, Morel heard Lila and Marco come back, well before they entered the room. Lila's voice carried all the way from the ground floor and Morel knew before she entered the room that she was in an argumentative mood.

He left his lair, grateful for a reprieve from the paperwork, and stopped before Lila's desk while she dumped her bag on the floor.

'If I have to talk to another religious nut, I'm handing in my resignation,' she told Morel.

'Nothing new, then?'

'No.'

'Where's Akil?'

'Getting coffee.'

'A Baptist pastor in the thirteenth tried to convert Lila,' Marco said, grinning.

'I would have loved to see that,' Morel said. 'He must have seen that you were suffering.'

'I was suffering. Suffering from all the pointless traipsing around.'

Jean stood up and came over to them. 'I've pulled together a list of places where our guys might be staying,' he said.

'Anyone care to do the rounds with me this afternoon? Some of these are quite close.'

There was a loud groan from Lila, and a limp protest from Marco who had taken his shoes off and was massaging his feet.

'New shoes,' he said, when Jean raised his eyebrows.

Akil entered the room, bearing a tray of coffees.

'At last,' Lila said. 'Someone who cares.'

Just then Perrin, who had come in to work at lunchtime, popped his head into the office and glared at Morel. 'In my office, now.'

'Certainly.'

When Morel returned from his meeting with Perrin, he found only Marco and Akil. Akil was sitting in Lila's chair and Marco was doing his best to pretend the other man wasn't there.

'Perrin is in good spirits,' Morel reported, noting the relief on Marco's face at no longer being alone with his colleague.

'How come?' Marco said.

'That other murder, the one he was called to yesterday. It looks like they're going to close the case, in less than twenty-four hours. He's over the moon.'

'Press conference?'

'Of course.'

Perrin had asked Morel whether there was any sign of progress in his investigation.

'It's all in here,' Morel said, handing his report over. He gave his boss a brief summary of the trip to Brittany.

'What a pity this case isn't going quite so smoothly as the other one,' he told Morel.

There was no point in responding. At least he seemed to have forgotten Morel's late entrance the day before.

In the afternoon, Morel tried to call Golyubov but the Russian wasn't answering his phone. Using the mobile number she'd given his team, he called the deputy head at the school where Le Bellec taught, even though it was Saturday and there was unlikely to be any news.

'We did tell your colleague that we'll be in touch if he shows up,' the deputy head said.

'I know. Thank you.'

All this waiting around. It was maddening.

He left the office at half past four. On his way home, he called Augustine to tell her not to wait for him. Stepping out of the Métro in Neuilly, he heard the frantic siren of an ambulance drawing nearer and his heartbeat quickened, until it faded out. It had rained earlier and the sky was the colour of chalk.

When he got home, he found his younger sister sitting in the kitchen, leafing through a copy of *Voici* magazine.

'Guess what? Britney's in love,' she announced without looking up.

'What are you doing here?' he asked her.

Adèle shrugged her shoulders. 'I thought I'd drop by to see how everyone is,' she said. 'I had a chat with Augustine before she left. I was just leaving myself.'

'You don't have to go. Why don't you stay and have dinner with me?'

'I can't, I've got to go. Dinner date.'

She picked up a pair of red sandals lying by the door and slid them on. Then she kissed her brother's cheek.

'He's taking a nap, but according to Augustine he was OK today,' she told Morel.

'Thanks for coming,' he said.

Part of him would have liked to ask her to cancel

her dinner, to stay to take his mind off things, but he let her go.

Once he was alone, he spent a couple of hours in his room, folding a succession of birds. They were quick and basic, and he threw them out one after the other.

Hunger finally drove him out to the kitchen, where he found his father sitting at the counter in his dressing-gown, eating quiche. Morel joined him and they ate in silence. It was clear to Morel that his father didn't want to talk about what had happened to him, and besides, Morel wouldn't have known what to say. He thought about his mother and wished she were here.

Later, in his study, Morel laid out the plans for his owl and tried to work on them, but his heart wasn't in it. He tried Golyubov's number again, and again he got the answering machine.

It was getting late, and there was nothing more he could do.

He opened the window to let in some air. Then he poured himself a cognac and sat at his desk for a while, nursing his drink and watching shadows flit across the wall as the wind came and went with a mind of its own.

THIRTY

It was dark when Marie Latour finally got home. She had called her daughter to say that she would be going back to her own place tonight. Her daughter had been out and she'd ended up leaving a message on the answering machine.

She was nervous at the prospect of being back home, especially since the tall police officer, the good-looking one, had made it clear she should not be alone. But she was relieved too. Her daughter was finding her presence a strain, Marie could tell. The fact that she wasn't even home yet, that she had chosen once again to work late, made it even clearer.

Then there was also the fact that Guy would be coming over for lunch the next day.

They had spent the afternoon together. Marie was never out this late but in the end Guy had suggested she come over to his house after their excursion to the Museum of Primitive Arts (no one called the Quai Branly museum that, but in essence that's what it was, Guy said). The museum's artefacts had provided plenty of opportunity for commentary. They were both still shaking their heads as they came out into the bright sunshine.

Then they had caught a taxi and ended up at his apartment. Together they watched an old François Truffaut film which happened to be on television. Guy offered coffee and biscuits. Marie limited herself to one. She couldn't really hear what was being said on screen but she wasn't going to point out just how much she needed the earphones nowadays. Instead she smiled and laughed when Guy did.

She'd turned down his offer of dinner and said she'd better be going. It wasn't dark yet but by the time she got on the train the light was beginning to fade. Guy stood on the platform and waved as the train pulled out.

Luckily it wasn't crowded and she was able to pick her seat. Watching through the window as the landscape changed from rows of warehouses to residential homes and gardens, she felt happy and thought about the next day when Guy would come over. For the first time since Hector's death, he would travel to Maisons-Laffitte. Maybe she would splash out and make a *confit de canard* with diced potatoes fried in duck fat, something Hector had loved too. A fleeting sense of sadness washed over her but she brushed it away.

By the time she got home, it was dark. She turned all the lights on and took off her coat and shoes. Then she made herself a two-egg omelette and had a yoghurt with a spoonful of sugar in it. After dinner, she changed into her nightgown and brushed her teeth. She put on her earphones, sat down to watch the late news and resisted the urge to get a bar of chocolate from the pantry. Somehow she could never stop at one piece.

When she heard the knock on the door, she wondered fleetingly how long the person had been knocking. With the earphones on it was impossible to hear unless someone was banging the knocker hard. The doorbell had stopped working several months ago and she hadn't bothered getting it fixed.

For a moment she wondered whether it might be Guy at the door and she panicked, wondering just how untidy her house was and what she looked like. Then it occurred to her that it would be strange for him to have followed her back after they'd just spent the day together.

She looked through the spy hole and saw a familiar face, though she couldn't immediately place it. It must be one of the new neighbours, she thought. Nowadays her memory failed her when it came to new names and faces.

But when she opened the door and saw the person more clearly it gave her a shock.

'You!' she started, aware suddenly that she was standing there in her nightie and slippers, her pale shins exposed.

The person at the door stepped in and quickly closed it so that suddenly they were standing too close together in the hallway. Instinctively, she took a step back. He raised his arms and she flinched, thinking he would strike her. Instead he stepped closer and hugged her tight. The intimacy of this gesture horrified her so that she simply froze with her arms by her side, unable to move or make a sound. He held her for a long time, and when he pulled away she saw he was crying.

He led her down the hallway and into her room. She waited, trembling, trying to summon up the strength to run or pick up something she could fight him with. But instead she just stood there, listening to the splash of water coming from the taps in the bathroom.

When he returned she saw that he had dried his tears. There was a new resolve on his face, like he had steeled himself for whatever came next. When he started unbuttoning her shirt, she made a weak attempt at stopping him. He removed her hand gently. After that she just closed her eyes.

She felt his hand on her shoulder, leading her into the bathroom. The air was cool against her skin. The bath warmer than she liked it. She knelt in the bath like a supplicant, not daring to look at him, ashamed of her nakedness.

After what seemed like an eternity, she felt his hands on her. Moving in slow circles across her chest and back. Soaping her like a newborn child.

THIRTY-ONE

Nina Dimitrova unlocked the door of her apartment on the twenty-sixth floor and let herself in. The smell of damp clothes in the cramped, overheated flat filled her nostrils. She could smell dinner too, reminding her of how hungry she was. She hadn't eaten since breakfast. She could hear her mother say she was too thin and should eat more. But she had always been small, finding her clothes in the same places where adolescent girls shopped.

The memory of the large, old-fashioned department stores where her mother took her as a child, with their stout, unsmiling saleswomen and drab offerings, belonged to a different era. Nowadays, the women who could afford it flocked to Benetton and French Connection and the Gap and the salesgirls were young and glamorous, thinking they'd somehow made it, that selling foreign goods meant they had gained access to a better world. Nina knew that things were probably a great deal better now than they had been for many Russians, but in some ways she regretted the old days. She wasn't deluded like those women who stood at street corners waving Stalin's portrait. But some things she had valued were lost forever.

Not all of these were tangible or easily identifiable. Which was why she never talked about the way she felt.

'I'm home!' she called out.

She could smell fried onions and chicken, making her stomach rumble. The trip home always exhausted her. Going to the hospital wasn't so bad because she started after lunch and she wasn't stuck with the other commuters. But coming home so late on the tram she struggled to keep awake. And there was always an element of anxiety. Moscow really wasn't safe any more. Several of Nina's friends had told her how unhappy they were to see her taking public transport so late. She would generally respond to say she preferred to be sitting in a crowded tram than alone in a stranger's car. There was another thing that had changed. She remembered how, in the old days, she and her mother could get in a car with someone they didn't know without thinking twice about it. It was an easy way for people to make some extra money and sometimes it led to an interesting exchange along the way. Nowadays she wouldn't risk it.

In the dark hallway she took her shoes and socks off. The socks were soaked through. She needed new shoes, but not this month. The money was running out faster than she'd expected, and the shoes would have to wait.

'You look tired.' Her husband Volodya stood before her in the hallway. He touched her face with his right hand, leaving the useless, left one hanging by his side.

'I wish you would tell them you want to work a different shift. How long are they going to keep you on this one? It's not right,' he said.

'Soon, soon.' She was too tired to have this conversation. Instead she reached up and kissed his cheek. There was comfort in his height, the way he towered over her. At the university she had fallen in love with this man who was twenty-two years older than her before they'd ever exchanged a word. Lately he'd decided to grow a beard. It grew unchecked and made him look even more like the earnest and distracted academic he was.

He sat next to her and watched her while she ate, his legs touching hers under the table. Only when she had finished eating and thanked him with her eyes, too tired to speak, he said, 'There's a letter for you.'

She noticed the envelope then, her name and address in bold capitals across the front. There was nothing on the back.

'Open it.'

She could see he was anxious too. No one ever wrote to either of them. There was something ominous about the envelope with her name written in black ink.

She opened the envelope with a knife. Inside it was a single sheet of paper, with a few lines of writing. She looked at the signature to see who it was from. She was so startled she let out a cry.

'What is it?'

'It's from Dima.'

'Dima? Which Dima?'

'You know. The boy.'

Volodya gaped at her. 'My God.'

All of a sudden she felt dizzy with exhaustion. She thought of the boy with the big dark eyes that never blinked; the quiet and stillness that always accompanied him. A boy so defenceless she had thought he would soon be swept away, like a scrap of paper in the wind.

'Where is it from?' Volodya held the envelope up and peered at the stamp.

Nina rested her head on her hands. Despite the shock of receiving the letter, she was falling asleep, her stomach filled with chicken and rice, her feet tingling with warmth. She heard Volodya laugh, a short, sharp sound that made her look up, sleepy-eyed, at her husband.

'Your little orphan has come a long way. See, he's in France!' He showed her the stamp on the envelope. Nina stared at its serrated edges. She was too tired to read.

Nina forced herself to laugh too. As though it were a surprise for her as well, though of course she had known all along. After all it was thanks to her that Dima had left. The Frenchman had taken him to France, to start a new life. But she had never told Volodya. All he knew was that the man had visited the orphanage once. He would not want to know about the money that had changed hands. The risks she had taken. For his sake, she had kept quiet about it.

Now Dima had written. It meant that he hadn't left her completely behind. She thought of the scrap of paper she had slipped into his pocket all those years ago, the day before his departure.

'This is where I live,' she'd said, forcing a smile so he would not guess how she felt. 'If you ever need to get in touch.' Thinking that she would never hear from him again.

In bed, Nina looked at the letter. Dima's handwriting was tidy. He'd written in French. That must be his first language now. Nina wondered whether he still spoke Russian. She felt a surge of pride at how far he'd come. In the morning she would have to find a way to translate the words.

Later, in bed, she had time to wonder why Dima had written. Was he in some kind of trouble? She thought of the child she'd known, who had never asked for anything. Now he'd written to her. The thought disturbed her, but she was too tired to think it through. She fell into a deep sleep, full of incoherent dreams in which she drove home from the orphanage and each time got lost, moving further and further away from Moscow. In the car beside her there was always someone. Her husband, Dima, or her mother, who was dead now. There were voices in the back seat but she could not see who else was with her.

It was still dark when Nina got up. She felt worn out, like she'd been up all night doing housework – which would probably be a good thing, she reflected, looking at the mess around her. Her arms and legs ached.

She pulled a top over her head and went to the kitchen. She made a cup of tea and took it with her to the living room, where she curled up on the sofa in her T-shirt and underwear. Outside the window the sky looked menacing. It was going to be another dusty, muggy day, but maybe it would rain, Nina thought. Rain would be good, to wash away the dirt.

'What are you doing up so early?' Volodya asked. She'd closed her eyes and hadn't noticed him come in. He sat next to her and she moved into his arms.

'I couldn't sleep.'

'Come back to bed. I'll rub your back while you close your eyes and try to.'

She knew she wouldn't sleep but she followed him anyway and lay on her side while Volodya moved behind her and started running his hand along her spine. He knew she loved this and that it comforted her.

No one had ever worked out why Dima wouldn't speak. There was nothing wrong with his vocal cords, according to the doctor who had come once, stopping at each bed to examine the listless children. A brusque man with a self-important manner, who kept looking at his watch and was clearly in a hurry. Examining the children as if they were chickens, or sheep, except that chicken and sheep would probably be treated with more care. Prodding and pinching and opening their mouths. He had never visited again, which was just as well.

When Dima arrived at the *internat* Nina had been working there for ten months. There was so little of him you'd hardly notice he was there. Except for his eyes. You couldn't get past those.

She had never figured out why he was assigned to the lying-down room. As far as she could tell there was nothing wrong with him. He didn't talk but he understood everything. She could tell. When she brought him his food she spoke about anything that came through her mind, keeping her voice light and carefree, and she saw that he listened intently, his eyes never leaving her face. For some reason the fact that he didn't say anything, just stared at her, made her blabber on. The words just kept pouring out of her. You would have thought she had no one to talk to the rest of the time.

'Why him?' Volodya had asked back then. 'What's so special about him?' If she hadn't known him as well as she did she might have guessed he was jealous of the child who occupied so many of her waking thoughts.

I don't know, she told Volodya. Even though she guessed. Something about the boy's intense loneliness and her own faith. Maybe she had finally found a way to translate that faith into something real. Something that would confirm that she had been right all along to believe in something more than the ordinary, gruelling existence she knew.

The way Dima looked at her. Like she was the child and he was the adult. All that unwanted knowledge in his eyes. She wanted to rub it out.

She was careful not to show the other nursing aides. Instead she went about her work just as they did, treating the children the same, pretending not to see the neglect all around her.

At night she cried herself to sleep in Volodya's arms until after a while she ran out of tears. Then she just kept quiet. What was the point of crying or talking about things, when nothing changed?

Until the Frenchman came along and something in his eyes told her that he was the one. That was when it changed. The hope that had been extinguished, the faith she was beginning to question, it all came back.

Now Dima had written to her. A wave of emotion swept over her. How long had it been? Seven years, at least.

'Are you thinking about him?' she heard Volodya ask. 'The boy?'

She didn't answer directly. Just followed her train of thoughts, hardly aware of her husband's presence.

'I was never sure what Dima was feeling or thinking,' she said out loud. Volodya was still stroking her back, lying behind her. She was glad he couldn't see her face.

'He was always observing. He never communicated. I tried at first to bring him out of his shell. He was so – ' She turned partly towards Volodya and made a gesture, as though she were enclosing a fragile insect in her hands – 'so small, and delicate. I used to think he wouldn't survive. I tried not to care too much, because that is what you must do, but with Dima I found I couldn't. I lifted him in my arms, I cradled him. He was so small he fitted in my arms like a doll.'

'It was for you as much as for him,' Volodya said, turning her away from him again so he could keep caressing her. With his right hand, he kneaded her shoulders, digging his thumb into the places where she was all knotted up. He heard her sigh.

'The other carers didn't like it. The only way we could carry on was to keep our distance. I was making it hard for the others.'

Nina kept very still. After a while a shudder ran through her body. She pressed her back against him and he wrapped his one good arm around her waist.

'It was so cold, that building,' she said after a while.

He stroked her back for a long time until he heard her breathing change and knew she was asleep. Never mind if she was late for work. He would not wake her up. She needed a rest.

He lay on his back and thought about the boy. The first time Nina had mentioned him, Volodya had seen a side of her he hadn't known. A dark place full of restless shadows that called out to her at times when she was tired or vulnerable. Dragging her down, away from the light. Over the past couple of years, he had managed to shut that door firmly on Nina's past. She was sleeping and gaining weight. At times she allowed herself to be happy.

But now the past was rearing its ugly head again.

He is back in our life, he thought. As he thought this, there was no feeling attached to it. He thought only of Nina. When she had been speaking of Dima, of his fragility and her own burgeoning tenderness, he had seen only Nina and his own fierce desire to watch over her. Sometimes it kept him awake to think how feeble he was. An academic with only one fully functioning hand, whose instincts always called for caution. He was the guy who took a step back so that he would not be picked or noticed.

He hugged Nina and moved his legs closer, so that he could feel the back of her thighs against his skin. She stirred and murmured something in her sleep. His ribs ached from the swelling in his heart.

Nina looked at her watch and shuffled her feet to prevent them from going completely numb. Katya had said one o'clock and it was already twenty past. She wished they had agreed to meet at a cafe or somewhere where at least she could keep warm.

She hadn't expected to go back to sleep. When she woke up again she saw that Volodya had already left for university. It made it easier for her to do what she'd planned.

She got dressed and grabbed a piece of toast before heading out the door.

It had been at least two years since she had seen Katya last. She felt bad about it but it wasn't just her fault, after all. Katya could have called or written too.

She spotted her, walking towards her with a grin on her face. And suddenly it was as though the years in between had slipped away and never happened. They kissed and hugged. When they drew apart, Nina was surprised to see Katya wipe a tear from her face.

'It's been so long. Thank you for meeting me at such short notice,' Nina said. 'Where shall we go?' She too felt like crying, but she managed to contain herself. She hadn't cried in so long she worried that once she got started again she might never stop.

They chose a new cafe, two steps away from the apartment where Nina's favourite writer Mikhail Bulgakov once lived. Katya ordered soup but Nina, ever conscious of the money, stuck to a coffee.

'You look wonderful,' Nina told her old friend. And it was true. Katya had always been pretty but she was particularly radiant.

'So do you,' Katya responded. But Nina knew she was being kind. She knew she had aged a great deal over the past few years.

While they waited for their order to arrive, they chatted

about their respective lives. Like Nina, Katya had gone on
to qualify as a nurse and she was working in a hospital now.
But where Nina worked five days a week, Katya worked
two. She was married to a man who had an import–export
business, she said, without giving any further details. And
she was pregnant.

'That's wonderful! I'm happy for you,' Nina said.

'And you? No baby plans?'

Nina shook her head. 'God, no.' Seeing Katya's face, she
regretted the way she'd said it. 'I mean, I don't think I am
cut out to have children. It is such a big responsibility. Volodya
would like to, I think, but as for me—'

The coffee and the soup arrived. The two of them sat in
silence for a while.

'You know,' Katya said, 'you shouldn't be so hard on yourself.'

'What do you mean?' Nina asked. The coffee was strong
and sweet. She took small sips, savouring it.

Katya seemed to hesitate. 'I feel as though you are still
dwelling on the time we spent, back at the orphanage. The
conditions we saw . . . but we did our best for those kids.'

'Maybe.' All of a sudden the coffee tasted bitter. She put
her cup down. 'I had a letter from Dima,' she said, and saw
Katya's eyes widen.

'How did he find you?'

Nina shrugged her shoulders. She knew better than to tell
Katya that the boy had always known where to find her.

'I don't know. Does it matter? I knew, somehow, that I
would hear from him again.'

She looked at the table and at Katya's hand, carrying the
spoon from the bowl to her lips. The ring on her slender
finger was studded with diamonds.

'I think he may be in some sort of trouble,' she said,

lowering her voice though they were quite alone in their corner of the room.

'Why are you whispering?' Katya asked.

'I'm not sure.' Nina smiled. She looked at her friend, whose figure gave no indication yet of the new life she was carrying. At this stage the baby was probably little more than a tiny beating heart. Yet so much tenderness and hope had already been invested in this unborn child.

Nina pulled out the letter she'd received and handed it over to Katya.

'I thought maybe you could help me translate it. He's written in French.'

'In French! You always said he was clever. I hope my French is good enough. You know I only studied it for a couple of years.'

'Katya, did you ever – you know – tell anyone about what happened?'

Katya looked at her. 'Never.' Katya's eyes clouded over. 'You know I had mixed feelings about what you did. Interfering like that in the boy's fate. What you did could have landed you in jail. But I never told a soul.'

'Thank you.'

Nina waited in silence while Katya read the letter. When she'd finished she looked up at her friend with troubled eyes.

'You're right. He does seem to be in trouble.' She slid the letter across the table to Nina. 'He is asking for your help.' She pointed to the words and read them out loud. '*Aides-moi*, it says. 'Help me.'

THIRTY-TWO

It wasn't seven yet and there was nowhere to park. Morel circled the block a couple of times. By the fourth time he entered the street, a car was pulling out. Morel took the empty parking space and waited.

Over the next twenty minutes, several men exited the building. There was no sign of Mathilde. Morel sat and thought about Marie Latour with a heavy heart. He rubbed his eyes. The case was threatening to overwhelm him.

If only Mathilde would appear. He had really tried to stay away since driving here last, by telling himself there was nothing to be gained by following her. But here he was again, watching her building. He could barely recognize himself.

Morel tried to guess which of the men exiting the building was Mathilde's husband. Was it the bald one with the pin-striped suit? The good-looking one in jeans and a loose white cotton shirt which he wore untucked, whose hair was too long and definitely needed a trim? He hoped it wasn't that one. Or the one with the violin case who finished his cigarette as he stepped onto the street and stubbed it out with his shoe.

It was 7.22 when Mathilde appeared with her son. He was wearing his school bag on his back and Mathilde was wearing a navy blue dress and the same sandals she'd been wearing the last time he'd seen her. They walked quickly, as though they were running late. He knew the school wasn't far and that she would walk back this way once she had dropped the boy off.

Morel looked at his watch. There wasn't any time to linger. He couldn't be late for Marie Latour's friend. With one last look at the building and the floor he knew Mathilde lived on, he drove away.

'How did she look? Did she look – did she seem . . .'

'She looked peaceful. But we're certain that she didn't die of natural causes,' Morel said.

There seemed little point in telling Guy Charon that his old friend's wife whom he had been so fond of had been stripped naked and drowned in a bath, before being dressed and made to look like a geriatric hooker, with excessive make-up and a cheap red wig.

Charon had called the police after turning up at Marie Latour's house for lunch on Sunday. She hadn't come to the door.

It had been a long day for Morel's team.

Thankfully, the details about the killings hadn't made it into the papers. It was only a matter of time, though.

The man sitting before him looked so helpless that Morel almost felt like leaning over and giving him a hug.

'I'm very sorry, Monsieur Charon,' Morel said again. And he was. Angry and upset that another woman had been killed. He'd never felt as powerless as he did now.

'I was Marie's closest friend, you see,' the man said. 'Since her husband died. I knew Hector would want me to look out for her. She wasn't used to doing anything on her own.' The memory of the dead woman stopped him for a moment. He shook his head. 'But the fact is, it wasn't just me looking out for her. The fact is, we looked out for each other. I never thought . . .' He paused and lowered his head.

'No one ever thinks about these things until they happen. Why should you?' Morel said.

'But she was worried,' the man said, looking up at him. 'I should have listened.'

Morel leaned forward. 'Worried about what?' he said, though he suspected he knew.

'That man and the boy. They'd made her uneasy.'

'What did she say about them?'

'She said the boy was strange.'

'And the man?'

'He was a con artist.'

'Is that what Madame Latour said?'

'No, that's what I told her. That these sorts of people prey on people they think are gullible enough to believe them.'

'But what did she say?'

'That he seemed nice enough. But then she is a good woman. I've never heard her say an unkind thing about anyone.' He seemed to realize that he was using the present tense and he swallowed, visibly shaken. 'She was a good woman.'

For a moment it looked like he might cry and Morel felt a moment of panic. But then he seemed to pull himself together.

Morel picked up the picture of Armand that Amelia Berg had given him.

'Take a look at this. Did you ever see this man, in any of your outings with Madame Latour? The one on the right?'

Guy looked carefully at the photograph. He shook his head. 'No. Who is he? Is this the man who distributes those pamphlets? Is he the one who killed Marie?'

Morel took the photo from Guy's hands.

'We think he might be,' he said carefully.

'What are you doing to catch him?' Guy asked.

'Everything in our power.' *And yet we can't seem to track him down*, Morel thought.

'Well I hope you find him in a hurry. Marie didn't deserve to die,' Guy said, his voice breaking.

Morel nodded.

As he walked the old man to the top of the stairs he felt the full weight of the investigation on his shoulders. Don't blame yourself, a voice inside his head said. His old boss, who knew Morel better than anyone else he'd worked with, had told him you had to shoulder the blame as a team. It wasn't healthy for a single person to carry the entire load. It was how some policemen ended up leaving the force, or leaving this world altogether. One day they just gave up. Their wives or children walked in on them hanging from a rope or sitting in their cars with the windows fogged up.

Morel told himself that he had tried to keep Marie Latour out of harm's way. It wasn't his fault that she had chosen to return to her house without alerting the police. By the time her daughter had checked her answering machine and heard her mother's message, it had already been too late.

They had dozens of bodies out on the streets looking for Le Bellec. He wasn't alone in this. He reminded himself that there were others who shared the burden of responsibility.

But it was a waste of time. As he headed back up the stairs he could not deny the tide of despair rising inside him. Isabelle Dufour. Elisabeth Guillou. Marie Latour. Their deaths were on his conscience.

The call from Ivan Golyubov came in the next day just after 2 p.m. Morel had been about to walk up to Perrin's office. He was bracing himself for another bollocking. The papers had begun questioning the competence of the police force. Perrin took this sort of negative media personally.

Lila caught him just as he was heading out the door.

'Morel. It's for you.'

She looked worn out, like the rest of them. Yet she had a smile on her face. Despite the strain they were all under. Morel wondered whether it had anything to do with the Moroccan-born man who sat in Marco's spot now with his head down, going through the case notes. Marco was back on duty at Irina Volkoff's place. At least during the day. She had lasted one night with her friend before deciding she'd had enough and wanted to sleep in her own bed.

'Monsieur Morel,' came the Russian policeman's drawling voice. 'I believe I have some new and interesting information for you.'

'Really? I could do with some of that,' Morel said. He stood by Lila's desk, where he'd picked up the phone, and rubbed his eyes.

'I have been speaking to a woman who worked as a nursing aide at the orphanage where the boy was staying just before he was adopted. Dima was five when they moved him from the baby home to the *internat*, the older children's ward. He was adopted a year later.'

'Who adopted him?'

'This was difficult to find out, believe me. I sense a great deal of reluctance on the part of the orphanage director. It was a French man. His name is Armand Le Bellec.'

So far, so good, Morel thought.

'Was the adoption legal?'

'The paperwork looks OK. But that doesn't mean much. We've had a few issues with some of these adoptions. The government is trying to deal with this now. It's a slow process but I think we're getting there.'

'Where did the boy come from? Can I talk to the woman? The nursing aide?' Morel asked. Out of the corner of his eye he saw Akil lean towards Lila from his side of the desk to tell her something. She leaned back towards him with a smile. She seemed strangely pliant. Nothing like the standoffish Lila Morel knew.

'I wouldn't object to it but she says she doesn't want to speak to any foreign police. She wasn't that happy speaking to me either, believe me.'

'OK.'

'I can ask her, if there is anything else you want to know?'

At 4 p.m. Nina closed the door to the nursery and headed into the nurses' station to make herself a cup of tea. As she put the kettle on, she ran through the conversation she had had earlier with the burly police officer. He'd shown up at her work. Luckily she had been due for a lunch break. They had sat in a coffee shop across the road, away from inquisitive eyes.

He had been nice enough. He'd asked lots of questions but he'd been polite and patient, waiting for her to finish her sentences before he moved on to the next one.

He had wanted so many details about Dima. She had tried her best to answer but really she knew so little about Dima's past. Where he had come from and why he'd been delivered to the orphanage. And the stories were always the same, one way or another.

As she poured boiling water into a teapot, she thought how strange it was that the things that mattered most when it came to Dima were the things the police officer hadn't asked. In any case she would have found it hard to be truthful. He was a total stranger. How could he possibly understand?

Still, part of her would have liked to unburden herself and to speak of her loss. To try to describe the intimacy she and Dima had shared.

She sat in the kitchen taking small sips of her tea. She imagined the questions she would have asked in his place and the answers he would have received:

HIM: Could you describe your relationship with the boy?

HER: He was like a son to me. Or maybe like a brother. A son, a brother, a friend. I know that seems vague but what I got from him was so intense and so complete. It was more than one thing.

HIM: Did you and Dima spend much time together?

HER: As much as was possible without attracting attention. Everyone did their job in such a businesslike way. There was no room for sentimentality.

HIM: Describe the time you spent together.

HER: I talked to him about anything and everything. I took him in my arms and rocked him gently at night. He had trouble sleeping. I didn't dare walk with him down the hallways or take him outside, though I could see he pined for movement and for the sensations he was being deprived of. The feel of the wind against his cheek, the sound of his steps on the frosty ground, the night's chill against his back. The smells of the forest. But I feared we would be caught and then we would not be allowed to spend that time together any more.

HIM: So what did you do instead?

HER: I did my best to keep him engaged. Even though I could see he was withdrawing further and further into himself. I read to him sometimes. I even let him listen to music, with the headphones on so no one would hear. But this happened rarely. It was too risky, for both of us.

HIM: You loved him, didn't you?

HER: Yes. Yes, I did. I still do.

HIM: What about him? How do you think he feels about you?

HER: Now? (A lengthy pause, while she feels her heart break all over again.) Now I'm not sure.

She hesitates, but not for long. She knows the answer. Her heart tells her she's right.

'Yes. He loves me too,' she whispers.

When Morel got home, he went upstairs to see his father but the old man was asleep. He seemed to sleep a great deal more these days. Maybe it was the pills he was taking.

In the kitchen, Morel found a note in Augustine's hand, next to a bowl of pasta.

'Don't forget to eat.'

Morel set the bowl in the microwave and turned to the fridge to see whether it contained an open bottle of wine. The knock on the door startled him. Before opening it to see who it was, he looked at the time. 9.30 p.m.

Mathilde was standing there, looking at him angrily.

'Jesus Christ,' was all he could think to say. 'What are you doing here?'

'I thought since you seem to enjoy stalking me I should return the favour.'

He couldn't think of anything smart to say in return and instead just looked at her in silence.

'So now I'm here, Serge,' she said, stepping past him into the house. It had been raining and her hair was dripping wet. 'I'd like to know why you've been sitting outside my house watching me.'

Morel followed her into the kitchen and poured himself a glass of wine while she looked around, opening the cupboards and the fridge.

'Do you find this problematic, when I walk into your life like this and examine your things?'

'No,' he said, watching her.

'Well, I do,' she said, turning to him. 'I do mind having someone stalking me.'

'I'm sorry. I know it was wrong and it was intrusive. I just wanted to see you.'

'In that case, why not pick up the phone and call? Wouldn't that be the normal thing to do?'

'Perhaps.' He shrugged his shoulders. All of a sudden he couldn't be bothered explaining.

He watched her pour herself a glass of wine and take a long sip from it. She held the glass and stared at him.

'Do you remember why we split up?'

'Yes. No. I—'

'You told me that you needed to experience other things, that it would be a mistake for us to stay together as we were so young. You wanted to meet other women and explore what life had to offer.'

'I—'

'It was perfectly natural, of course. I'm not blaming you. You were probably right. We were so young. I wasn't too happy about it at the time but eventually I got over you. I imagine you've had plenty of women. I know you've done well professionally. So what I don't get is why you're following me around now. What is it you want from me?'

Morel kept silent. What was he supposed to say when he hardly knew himself what he wanted from her? He felt her eyes on him still. She took a step closer and touched his arm. In the ensuing silence he heard the *ping* of the microwave, reminding him that he had warmed something up and that the food was ready.

'I need you to leave me alone, Serge. I have enough on my plate without you following me around like this. Either you stay away from me or I'll have to report you to your bosses.'

He was surprised at the bitterness in her voice. And by how much her words stung.

'I know how it looks and I'm truly sorry. I'll leave you alone, I promise.'

She looked at him carefully. 'You look like you haven't slept in weeks,' she said.

'I've been busy with work.'

'Are you OK?'

'Yes, yes, I'm fine.'

She looked at her watch and sighed. 'I'd better go,' she said. She put her glass down.

'Goodbye, Serge,' she said.

Morel waited a while, as though she might come back.

After five minutes, he took the bowl from the microwave and emptied the contents into the rubbish bin. Then he went to his room, taking the open bottle of wine and a glass with him.

THIRTY-THREE

When it happens he is two weeks short of his fourth birthday. One minute he is living with his grandmother in the village, playing in the street, chasing the chickens and dogs with the other children. The next he is whisked away to a place where he is deprived of everything he knows.

He likes his life. At mealtimes he sits by the stove with his *babulya*. She rarely speaks but the silence between them is comfortable. There is no need for words. The house is very small with only one bedroom and Dima has to sleep in the kitchen by the stove at night. He doesn't mind it because this is the warmest room in the house. He likes the house, even though he's heard his *babulya* say that it could do with some renovation because it sinks into the ground a bit further each spring. What they need is a pair of strong arms to take on some of the manual work. But there is no one to ask. The men in the village are useless, his grandmother says, in a rare fit of anger. When she speaks like this it's like she is addressing an invisible presence in the room.

He has no idea where his mother and father are, or whether they are alive. And his grandmother has never spoken about them. If he had lived with her longer, if she hadn't died, then maybe he would have asked. But he is three and a half years old. This is all he knows and he is not fully conscious yet that it might be less than what other children have.

One day in the middle of summer his *babulya* dies. He doesn't remember when he realizes that she is gone. And when he does he doesn't tell anyone straight away. Not until the smell drives him out of the house.

He doesn't remember how he got to the *dom rebyonka*, the baby house. This is where they put the children who have no one to look after them. He is one of the lucky ones in a way, because his grandmother is dead. There are those whose parents and grandparents are still alive but who've given them up anyway. He doesn't know this yet but he learns a great deal as the years go by.

For example, he doesn't understand yet that because of his muteness, he is classified as an idiot. Medically this transcribes as someone with the most profound degree of mental retardation. Someone who is helpless and requires supervision. Again this is something he will understand later. That's when he will realize the extent to which the label has branded him.

There is no reason for him to be bedridden but despite this they assign him to the lying-down room, with the other bedridden children. What else are they to do with this child who never says a word and instead stares at them with great unblinking eyes? He never smiles. Later, he understands that he makes the adults uncomfortable.

Many of the other children in the baby house are younger. Most of them in fact are infants. It is always noisy and always smelly. There is nowhere to escape from the incessant presence of others.

Here at the *dom rebyonka*, he learns to soundproof his mind.

It takes a long time. Many weeks go by during which he lives in a state of fear and incomprehension. Sometimes, when he is lying in the dark on his filthy cot, his terror builds to a point where he thinks he might not be able to draw another breath. He is convinced he will die.

Later he will come to experience the same terror when he is baptized.

He is desperately lonely. But then gradually he adjusts. He does this by chipping away at himself, the way a sculptor might chisel a block of limestone, until all feeling is carved out and only a grey stillness remains.

He builds a wall of silence around himself. The only trouble with that is that the more he isolates himself, the harder it is to re-enter the real world. Soon the world of his thoughts, this silent, sterile world, is the one he is most familiar with. The one he would call *real*, if anyone were to ask and if he knew how to respond.

Shortly after his fourth birthday they move him to the *internat*. It is full of bigger and older kids. Some of them make a habit of taunting and abusing the young arrivals. But Dima is left to himself. In the lying-down room here it is mostly quiet.

Most of the time he has no idea what time it is. He dozes through the day and sometimes when he wakes he is only partially aware of where he is. Sometimes they come and feed him. Usually with a bottle, even though he is too big for it. Sometimes they come and change his cloth nappy. Every once in a while they have to lift him to turn the rubber-covered mattress underneath. He does not notice how bad the smell is, though sometimes his eyes sting from the disinfectant they use.

There is one person who lifts him more gently than the others. Who talks to him even though he can't talk back. When it is dark and the others are asleep she leans over him and strokes his forehead. Her fingers are cool and gentle. There are times when she leans in further and takes him in her arms. He is not a baby any more but she lifts him without effort. Sits by his cot and cradles him in her arms. He feels her warm breath against his cheek.

After she goes he feels a sadness that wasn't there before. He doesn't know which is worse, the state of numbness he is used to or the emotions she stirs within him. The tenderness she gives comes at a price.

THIRTY-FOUR

The school bell sounded and still there were kids arriving. Pimply, self-conscious boys with long and straggly hair; painfully thin girls decked out like Christmas trees. All piercings and beady scarves, bracelets and black-painted nails.

'If this is human evolution, we're screwed as a species,' Jean said. He was sitting in the front of the car with Morel, while Lila and Akil sat in the back. They were waiting outside the school for the deputy head to give them the go-ahead. 'Somewhere down the track, not far from here, we will face complete degeneration and the world will self-implode.'

'What the hell have you been smoking?' Lila asked.

A few latecomers appeared, looking pretty relaxed about whether they would make it to their classrooms on time.

'I was incredibly punctual as a schoolkid,' Lila said.

'Miss Goody Two-Shoes, were you?' Jean said.

'Yes, I was. A straight-A student and the teacher's pet.'

'Why am I not surprised?'

They laughed at that while Lila cuffed Jean on the head.

'The other kids must have loved you,' Morel said, shaking his head.

They waited in the car opposite the school for several minutes more. Akil sat without saying anything. Lila sighed loudly and started rolling a cigarette.

'How long is she going to be?' Lila said.

The deputy head had called at eight that morning to say that Antoine Leroy, aka Armand Le Bellec, was back. He hadn't given any further explanation for his long absence, which he'd initially taken for health reasons, and had simply said that he was ready to go back to work.

'What's he playing at? Turning up like that,' Lila had said when the four of them had turned up at the school half an hour ago. They'd taken pains to park discreetly, some distance away but near enough to be able to observe the school grounds. 'Surely he knows we're on to him. His face has been plastered all over the news.'

'I agree. It's not what I expected,' Morel said. 'We'll need to move carefully.'

Now a woman came across the grounds to where they were parked.

'You can come in now,' she said. 'The children are in their classrooms.'

'Right. Well, where can we find him?' Jean asked.

'How are you going to do this?' the woman said. She seemed agitated. 'I would rather the students weren't upset.'

'Maybe you could call him to the head teacher's office. Tell him it's an administrative matter. Make something up. We'll take it from there,' Morel said soothingly. 'The students won't be bothered. Is there someone who can take over the class?'

'Well, it'll have to be me at this stage. I haven't had time to call in a replacement teacher. I'll take care of that, though. As long as you can manage your end.'

Morel and Jean waited in the head's office. Outside, Lila and Akil watched the school's entrance, on the off-chance that Le Bellec decided to make a run for it. The head was away and only the secretary was there. She kept on working, pretending to be oblivious to the presence of two police officers in her work space.

When the deputy head returned with Le Bellec, Morel and Jean stood up. Morel moved towards the man, who was a good deal shorter than him. He looked at Morel with questioning eyes. Morel had a feeling, though, that he wasn't surprised.

'Armand Le Bellec, I am arresting you on suspicion of the murders of Isabelle Dufour, Elisabeth Guillou and Marie Latour.'

While the secretary gaped, Morel read Le Bellec his rights.

'Hey, you.' Fingers snap before his eyes and Armand is reminded of where he is.

The air in this room is stale. With every breath he wonders whether he will be able to take another. The young female officer, the one wearing a man's shirt and black lace-up Doc Martens, is looking at him with distaste. He finds it offensive, to be judged in this way. *You know nothing about me*, he wants to tell her. But he is not a brave man. He can see by the expression on her face that she knows this.

'Do you understand what we're saying? Why you're here?'

'I understand.'

'And that you have the right to a lawyer? Do you want a lawyer?' Lila says.

Armand shakes his head.

'Right, then.'

At that moment the door opens and the man, the tall one who arrested him, walks in. He gestures to the woman to move away and takes her place across from Armand. The woman remains in the room but sits further back. Armand can't see her face but he knows she is watching him closely.

'I'm Commandant Serge Morel and this is my colleague Lila Markov. We've been looking for you for a while,' the man says. He has a quiet, gentle manner. Unlike the woman. 'I'm glad to finally meet you.'

Armand doesn't say anything. Just looks at the door through which the man entered. For some reason he wonders whether it's locked. Whether anyone else is watching them. He raises his eyes and searches for a camera. There is one in the corner of the room. He lowers his eyes and tries not to think about it.

'You've been away from work for, what, three weeks?'

'I wasn't feeling well.'

'For three weeks?' Morel asks.

Armand nods. What does it matter whether they believe him or not?

'How long have you been a teacher there?'

'Quite a long time actually. Seven or eight years.'

'That is a long time. Can you explain to me why you were teaching under a different name? You do realize that taking on a false identity is a serious offence?'

'I wanted a fresh start.' Amir's face looms before him. He can hear the head teacher at the Lycée in Moscow carefully telling him that, regretfully, she has to let him go. He clears his throat and rests his eyes on Morel. 'My life hasn't always been easy.'

Morel crosses his legs and then folds his arms. Armand notices his shoes. Everything about the man is expensive. He looks perfectly relaxed. He could be at a dinner party, waiting for coffee to be served.

'Do you know why you're here?'

Armand shakes his head.

'Three women have died,' Morel says. 'I was hoping that maybe you could help me figure out how, and why.' He pauses. 'Isabelle Dufour. Elisabeth Guillou. Marie Latour. Do you know these names?'

'I don't know them.'

Morel takes three photographs from a folder and places them before Armand.

'Maybe it will help if you see their faces.'

He has been waiting for this moment. Now that it's here, he is prepared.

Armand takes his time looking at them and finally nods. 'Yes. I have delivered pamphlets to them.'

'Tell us about these pamphlets.'

'They are what I believe.'

'What do you believe?'

'That it is possible to be born again.'

He hears the woman snort. Morel's expression is cool and measured. He looks like he's thinking about what Armand has just said. He nods slowly, like he gets it.

'To be given a second chance, you mean.'

'Something like that, yes.'

Morel's questions meander. At times he is direct, asking Armand about the murders. Other times he seems to veer off track. He wants to know what Armand thought of Moscow. Whether he thinks times have truly changed in the former Soviet Union. In a different context, Armand would enjoy talking to this man.

He loses track of time. Morel is still talking. He looks like he could sit there forever on the metal chair, conversing.

'What made you convert to the Baptist faith, Armand? I mean, why not something else? I understand your mother was a Catholic.'

'How do you explain these things?'

'I'd like you to try.'

'Faith is a matter between God and the individual.'

'I agree,' the detective says. 'I have always thought too that it was a personal matter. Which is why I've always struggled with the idea of institutionalized religion.'

Armand nods. 'The Baptist faith rejects human authority over spiritual matters,' he says. 'It allows a direct link with God. If a Church's hierarchy is too entrenched then that connection with God is lost. There are too many intermediaries, you see. The words we send up to God become garbled. The message is completely misinterpreted.'

'Like Chinese whispers,' Morel says.

Armand smiles. 'Exactly like Chinese whispers.'

'Do you feel that you have a direct link to God?'

'I believe I don't need anyone to help me have a conversation with him.'

'What does it mean to you, to believe in God?'

'God helps me make sense of the world.'

'Because the world doesn't make any sense?'

Armand doesn't answer.

'Tell me about your mother, Armand.'

'She died a long time ago.'

'What was she like?'

'What sort of question is that?'

'Did you two get on?'

'I don't know. Does it matter?'

'We had a long chat with Charles, your old childhood friend. Remember him?'

Armand nods. He's been prepared for this question for some time, too. 'We were friends at school. We went our own ways eventually, and lost touch.'

Morel's voice is gentle. 'Charles spoke a great deal about you. He told us how much he loved you then. Were you in love with Charles, Armand?'

For the first time Armand wavers. If it weren't for the woman sitting in the corner of the room he doesn't know whether he could maintain his composure.

Halfway through the day Morel steps out of the room with Lila, leaving Le Bellec alone.

'Let's get some food in. And coffees. Can I let you take care of that?'

'Sure.' Lila's eyes are blazing. 'He knows a lot more than what he's telling us,' she says. 'When are you going to ask him about the deaths? I mean, the philosophical debate is interesting and all that but—'

Morel cuts her off. 'In my own time.'

As she turns to leave, he stops her.

'This afternoon I want you to focus on trying to find the boy.'

'But I thought I was sitting in—'

'I want Akil to sit in this time.'

Lila stares at him blankly.

'It'll be a good experience for him.'

He sees her face close up while she struggles to rein in her feelings.

'Fine.'

How many hours is it since he was brought into this room? At some point food is delivered. Sandwiches and coffee. There is a jug of water before him. Morel is eating. Armand can't even remember whether he accepted any food or not. But he does have a coffee before him.

There is another cop in the room. This time it's not the woman. It's a man who looks a great deal like Amir. He smells of cigarettes and a zesty fragrance, just like Amir used to. It is disorienting and Armand struggles to keep his mind sharp and clear. He can't afford to make any mistakes.

He wonders whether they know about Amir, that he died in a car crash some years ago. He is glad in a way. At least he can't be ridiculed.

It is late in the afternoon, he thinks. Surely they will let him go now. He feels an intense urge to lie down and close his eyes. Where will he go after this? He doesn't much care, as long as there is a mattress to lie on. As long as he is here, he thinks, the boy will be left alone.

'Tell us again about your stay in Russia,' Morel says. The other police officer isn't looking at Armand. He is sipping at his coffee and looking at the floor. It means Armand can observe him. He isn't tall but he is broad-shouldered, with closely cropped hair.

'Does my colleague remind you of someone, Armand?' Morel's voice cuts across his thoughts like a razor blade. Sharp and painful. Armand blinks. He is acutely aware of the other man's eyes on him.

'No.'

He looks straight at Morel, keeping his gaze steady. He has always been good at concealing his feelings.

'What can you tell us about the boy?' Morel asks.

He hates to hear the boy mentioned, the way they speak about him even though they don't know him in the slightest. At the same time, he is grateful. They don't know either of César's names. His anonymity is a shield, it protects the boy and it protects Armand.

It's evening. Armand has lost track of time. Morel teeters on the edge of his chair. For the first time he looks like his energy is flagging. The other man has been leaning back in his chair with his arms folded and legs stretched out before him. He's kept quiet all this time but now he draws his chair up so that he is sitting in the light just inches from Armand's face. His eyes are pure gold. Under the table, Armand clenches his fists.

'What is your relationship with the boy? Are you lovers?'

Armand is so surprised by the question that he sputters and laughs. 'You must be joking.'

'So you picked the boy up in Russia? Tell us about that.'

'I adopted the boy, yes. It was perfectly legal.'

'So where is he?' Morel interjects. 'Where is the boy?'

Armand's heart soars. For the first time since they led him down the school hallway and drove him here in handcuffs he feels in control.

'I have no idea,' he says.

He realizes now that he did the right thing, by allowing himself to be caught.

Whatever happens in this room doesn't matter. The main thing, the only thing that matters, is that they must not get to the boy.

THIRTY-FIVE

At 10 p.m. Morel called a ten-minute break and left Akil with Le Bellec while he stepped out for a cigarette. Never mind that he had managed to stay off the weed for an entire month. He needed one now like never before.

He stood in the courtyard puffing away. Since she'd turned up at his house, Morel had tried his best to forget Mathilde, but now he felt the full impact of her words all over again.

You need to let it go, Morel told himself. Surely, the person he still loved no longer existed. How could he possibly claim to know the woman who had walked into his kitchen the night before, demanding to be left alone? They had each gone their own way and lived separate lives over two decades. He knew nothing about her except in the most superficial terms.

Morel finished his cigarette and dropped the stub on the ground. He looked up. There were still lights on in the building. There was always someone working late.

He checked the time on his watch. Ten hours before they had to let Le Bellec go. Unless there was enough evidence to convince the prosecutor that he needed to be detained longer. Morel wasn't sure there was. No fingerprints, no witnesses at the crime scenes who might be able to tie Le Bellec to the murders. All they had was the fact that Le Bellec had visited the three widows at some stage before they were killed.

Morel took another deep drag of his cigarette and felt his chest constrict. He needed something more if he was going to detain Le Bellec longer. And time was running out.

While he watched the smoke drift upwards, he thought about the man they had locked up. The main thing you could say about Armand Le Bellec was that he was unimpressive. Morel had expected something more. A slick salesman, a con artist with the sort of oily charm that might make him popular with the ladies and help him gain their trust. A man with a degree of charisma. He was none of these things. Not bad-looking, but overall pretty ordinary. Le Bellec was a man who seemed, if anything, lost. Throughout the interview Morel had observed him. At times, Le Bellec's moist eyes had met his and held his gaze. It was the sort of look you'd expect from a spaniel waiting to be reprimanded.

Lila had found him repellent. Morel did not find Le Bellec repellent. He found him incomplete, the sort of person you met and erased from your memory without difficulty.

As Morel plodded back up the stairs he found Akil running down to meet him.

'Irina Volkoff,' was all he managed to say.

'They're on their way to the hospital now, Volkoff and Marco. Looks like someone came in and attacked them. The neighbours heard her screaming and called it in. Versailles police turned up and found Volkoff and Marco unconscious. They called an ambulance.'

'Shit. What the hell was Marco doing there still?'

'Someone from the Versailles station was supposed to relieve him at eight. They never turned up.'

'Fuck.'

He would pursue this, Morel thought. Those bastards had been uncooperative from the start.

'Did they say where they were taking them? Which hospital?'

'André Mignot,' Akil said, naming the hospital in Versailles.

'Right, I'm heading there now,' Morel said. 'I want you to stay here with Le Bellec, Akil. Until I come back.'

'Sure. Shall I give Lila a call?'

'No. She's probably just got home. Let her catch up on some sleep before we get her back here. I'll call her myself once I know what the hell is going on.'

Morel drove over the speed limit all the way to Versailles and parked outside the hospital. He was trying to concentrate but his mind was in a whirl. Once he got inside he headed straight to the reception. He held up his police card.

'I'm looking for a woman called Irina Volkoff, and for a colleague. They would have been brought in half an hour ago or so.'

'She's being looked after. She's going to be OK, I think,' he heard a voice behind him say. When he turned round he saw Marco standing before him. His face was a mess. One eye was completely closed up and blood was oozing from a head wound above his left ear. There was a deep gash in his upper lip and he looked like he might have a broken nose. He swayed as he faced his boss. Morel gripped his arm to prevent him from falling.

'Bloody hell, Marco. What do you think you're doing here?' he said, before calling out to the woman at reception. 'I need some help for my colleague here. Now.'

The woman at the desk picked up the phone and Morel turned back to Marco.

'I wanted to catch you first,' the young detective said. 'I'm sorry I screwed up.'

'Never mind that. What happened?'

'I don't know. One minute I was watching TV. The old woman had gone to bed. The next I was whacked in the face with something. I didn't even have time to see who it was.'

Without warning, Marco turned pale and lost his footing. Morel caught the weight of his body as the boy collapsed against him.

'Someone give me a hand here,' he bellowed. A couple of nurses came running towards him. One of them was pulling a trolley bed. Morel helped them stretch Marco out on it and watched as they wheeled him into a room.

A wave of regret washed over Morel. Perhaps he'd been too tough on the lad.

'Make sure he's looked after,' Morel said. But by then he was standing alone in the corridor and there was no one to hear him.

By 2 a.m. he'd been told that Marco would be OK and that Irina Volkoff was out of danger. She'd been knocked on the head with a blunt instrument but luckily was suffering from nothing more than concussion.

'At her age, though, this sort of thing needs watching. I'd like to keep her here for a day or two,' the doctor said. He looked about twenty-five years old. Morel suddenly felt his age.

'Can I talk to her?'

'Five minutes,' the doctor said.

When Morel entered the room Irina Volkoff was lying with her eyes closed. He waited by her side until she opened them. He had a suspicion that she had been awake all along.

'I'm glad you are all right,' he said.

'I am glad too,' she said. 'How is the young man?'

'He'll be fine. They had to stitch up his head. He's going to be sore for a while but he's OK.'

'Good.'

'Did you see who it was that attacked you?'

Irina Volkoff shook her head. 'No. It happened very fast.'

Morel's heart sank.

'But I know,' she said.

Morel waited to hear what she would say next.

'I saw it in his eyes from the start,' she said.

'What did you see?' Morel asked. He could hear his heart thumping hard against his chest, as though straining to get out.

'I have seen that kind of suffering before. The kind that can't be repaired.' Irina Volkoff closed her eyes. 'When it's like that, there is nothing you can do. The damage is too great.'

Morel nodded. He watched her for a while before turning back down the corridor and moving out into the darkness.

He sat in the car for a while without turning the engine on. A thought formed in his mind. He needed the answer now.

'Ivan, sorry to bother you at this ungodly hour but I need something from you now. It's urgent.'

He heard the Russian groan at the other end of the line. 'You French never sleep, is that it?'

'Sorry. I wouldn't do this if it wasn't important. You mentioned that this Nina, she spent time with the boy. Can you ask her what she did with him? Did she ever play music for him, for example?'

'That's your question?'

'Yes. And Ivan?'

'What now?'

'If she did, can you ask her what? What music she played for him?'

'Sure.'

'It's important. I need you to wake her up and ask her now. I'm sitting in my car waiting for you to call back, OK? Please call me as soon as you find out.'

'OK. I will call her now.'

It took Ivan five minutes to call back. It felt like an hour.

'Yes?' Morel could feel his heart beating erratically again. This time he pressed his hand against his chest and willed himself to keep calm.

'Her man was not too happy to be woken up. I got the feeling he never knew I'd been talking to her. I really had to insist for him to wake her.'

'What did she say?' Morel asked, resisting the urge to hurry Ivan along.

'She played music to him sometimes. On her CD player.'

'What CD?' Morel asked, knowing the answer now but needing to hear it.

'*Requiem* by Gabriel Fauré. A French composer! Why not a Russian composer, I asked her. We have plenty of those.' There was a pause while the Russian waited for a response from Morel. 'Is that it?' he said finally.

'No. There's one more thing,' Morel said. 'What does she look like, this Nina?'

'Why, you want to meet her? She is quite good-looking. Big eyes and a nice smile. But I have never been much into redheads.'

'What did you say?'

'Her hair. It is bright red, like a traffic light. Not my style. I much prefer blondes.'

Morel wasn't listening any more. He dropped the phone on the seat next to him and got out of the car.

He needed to breathe.

THIRTY-SIX

Nine-thirty a.m. Morel looked at his watch for the tenth time and out at the building where he'd dropped his father off an hour earlier for a doctor's appointment.

He was so tired he was beginning to see double. He considered seriously whether to leave the car here and get a taxi back to work. But then the thought of abandoning his precious Volvo was too daunting. He would surely get back to find a scratch or a dent in it.

Morel looked at his watch again. The prosecutor had granted a twenty-four-hour extension, which meant they didn't need to let Le Bellec go. Morel had argued that without Le Bellec they would never find the boy.

The boy was the key to everything.

In the past twenty-four hours Le Bellec hadn't given them a thing. But Morel felt that he might just get through to him now. He saw quite clearly where his weakness lay.

The technicians were going over Irina Volkoff's place taking blood samples and lifting prints. Meanwhile the woman in Russia, Nina, still refused to speak to him. And Ivan was being stubborn about respecting her wishes. It was infuriating but there was nothing Morel could do.

He needed to find the boy. And the only way to do that was through Armand. He had failed so far to get him to talk. Even though there had been a connection there, at one point. The man had definitely responded to him. He'd looked like he might want to unburden himself. But once the boy was mentioned things had changed.

He is protecting him, Morel thought.

Halfway through the night, he had returned to the Quai des Orfèvres and told Le Bellec about Irina Volkoff.

'Your boy is alone and scared. He is losing it. With you in here, there is no one there to keep him together,' Morel had said.

He'd watched the other man's face for any change in expression. For the first time, Le Bellec had looked unsettled.

'How long do you think you can protect him for?' he'd asked Le Bellec. 'What's your plan? Do you think you can walk out of here and hide him away somehow? What happens when someone else dies?'

Nothing. It was like banging his head against a brick wall.

He looked up at the building where his father was seeing the doctor. Adèle was right, he should have left it to her to sort this out. He had too much on his plate at the moment. But he felt he owed it to Morel Senior to do this.

On the phone Morel had told the doctor about his father's more frequent bouts of forgetfulness. The way he seemed to lose his words, to mix things up. In order to get his father to see the doctor, he had told him Roland insisted on giving him a general check-up and making sure everything was in order. Philippe had been surprisingly docile about it all.

The appointment was taking a great deal longer than Morel had expected. Jean had called twice already and Lila once, to ask when he would be in. Akil had gone home for a couple of hours, to sleep.

Morel rubbed his eyes and yawned loudly. Just then he saw his father emerge from the building. He was about to open his car door and get out but something in his father's manner made him pause. He had stopped on the footpath and seemed to be examining his feet, as though checking whether his shoelaces were untied. He took a few slow steps, pausing and looking at the ground before him, like a man who's lost something. Morel took a sharp breath. His father looked like a stranger to him.

After what seemed like an eternity, his father came towards him, dragging his feet.

Morel got out of the car and opened the door on the passenger side.

'There you are,' his father said.

Morel waited till he was seated and closed the door. Then he got in on his side.

Maybe it was the extreme tiredness. He felt like he was about to cry.

The pastor couldn't sleep. It was a nuisance, the way these days he couldn't just doze off as he used to. Often he found himself lying awake, thinking about the events that had led to his collapse.

The woman with the pram had called an ambulance. When he'd woken up in hospital they'd told him he'd had a mild heart attack. It hadn't felt mild. It had felt like he was dying.

Either way he took it as a warning that he should take it easy.

The boy and his father had left the faculty. The pastor wondered now whether the child had been telling lies. The more he thought about it, the more he felt he had been led up the garden path. But the things he'd read on that piece of paper, the horrors the boy had written down, continued to bug him. Which was why he found himself brooding in the middle of the night. Nowadays he lay in bed with his Bible, taking comfort from a number of well-loved passages

– Isaiah was his absolute favourite – until exhaustion took over.

Earlier tonight, he'd found the lines which he knew would help alleviate his sense of foreboding: *Your sun will never set; your moon will not go down. For the Lord will be your everlasting light. Your days of mourning will come to an end.*

He had finally gone to sleep with this mantra in his head. Now it was 3 a.m. and he was wide awake again. With a heavy sigh, he got up and made himself a cup of peppermint tea.

It was so warm in the room. Suddenly he decided he needed to get out and breathe some fresh air. He put on his dressing-gown and slippers and walked down into the courtyard. There he sat on a bench with his drink.

It was a beautiful night. The sky was clearer than he had seen it in a while. He counted dozens of stars.

He started thinking about the boy. His reaction troubled him. The child had clearly needed to get things off his chest and, instead of comforting him, he had run away. Like a coward.

Impulsively, he entered La Maison and walked down the hallway towards the rooms that Le Bellec and the boy had occupied. They were empty now. Since the new university year hadn't yet begun, it would take a while to work out who would take over. The pastor had in mind an Estonian boy whose thesis he was helping him research.

As he stepped past the room he thought he saw a light underneath the door.

My eyes must be deceiving me, he thought. He stopped and listened. Nothing except the sound of his breathing.

As he turned to leave he heard a sound. It was a noise like a wounded animal makes. A low, keening groan.

Without waiting, he hurried away. Back to his room where he stood panting against the door.

Then he pulled himself together and called the police.

THIRTY-SEVEN

It's evening again. Armand has lost track of time but he can see that the light has faded and knows this is his second night here. The female cop is back in the room and the one who looks like Amir is gone. Morel seems to have aged in the past day and Armand wonders whether he too looks this spent.

'I have some news for you, Armand,' Morel says. He seems to be weighing his words before he speaks. He is still wearing a suit but it's looking pretty shabby now. He obviously hasn't changed since he brought Armand in.

'There is a man in the next room who says he knows you. He's a pastor. Even though we've broadcast your face on television, and the boy's, this man had no idea we were looking for you. He says he hardly ever watches television. Luckily for us, one of the faculty students did catch the news. He doesn't speak much English so he had no idea what it was about. But he told the pastor he had seen you on TV. And Dima.'

At the mention of the boy's name, Armand flinches.

'Yes. We know Dima is the boy's real name. Does that trouble you? You look concerned. The pastor says you called him César. Why was that? Did Dima tell you that he and the pastor had lunch together while you were busy looking up your old friend Charles last week? Apparently Dima told him a few things about himself. And about you.'

'What things?'

'That you killed those women. But I don't know whether I can believe that. Because of the make-up and the wigs, you see.'

Armand sits very still. Waiting to hear what Morel will say next.

'I was confused about that for a long time, I must admit,' Morel says slowly. 'On the one hand, the ritualistic aspect of the killings. The way the widows were dressed and displayed in their beds. So tidy and methodical. On the other hand, the make-up and the wigs. This looked to me like a joke at the women's expense.' He gives Armand a sharp look. 'But it wasn't like that, was it?'

Armand shrugs and doesn't bother replying.

'I had a chat with a colleague in Moscow,' Morel continues. 'And he's been talking to Nina Dimitrova. You know who I'm talking about, right?'

'Yes. She worked at the orphanage.'

'Dima's had a harsh life, hasn't he?' Morel says. 'Much harsher than any of us can possibly imagine. It's a wonder he's come out of it intact. In fact, it's highly likely that he isn't the same boy he was before he was brought to the orphanage. To be abandoned, then neglected like that . . . surely that would cause irreparable harm to anyone. Don't you agree?'

'He was such a sweet boy,' Armand whispers, before realizing he used the past tense.

'Yes.' Morel nods. 'Nina too realized he was something special and she took him under her wing, didn't she? She was the only one who provided any kind of solace for Dima in his new situation. She has told my colleague in Moscow that she loved the boy. She cared about him so much, in fact, that she was willing to bend the rules so he could be adopted and escape the fate that awaited him. The prospects in a Russian orphanage for a child diagnosed as being disabled are pretty dire.'

'And Dima loved her too.'

Morel gives Armand a searching glance. Then he stands up and walks to the other side of the narrow room and back in just a few paces, as though he needs to stretch his limbs. All the while, the woman hasn't said a word. She sits with her legs crossed, watching Armand. In the room's dim glow, he can't read her expression.

'Yes, Dima loved Nina too,' Morel says as he starts pacing the room again. 'One might even say that he still does. But to have such feelings can also be a source of great torment, don't you agree?'

Armand doesn't answer. He doesn't trust himself to speak.

'Particularly,' Morel continues, walking back across the room to stand straight across from where Armand is sitting, 'when that love is betrayed.' Without waiting for a response, he sits down and leans across the table towards Armand. 'When Nina helped organize the adoption, she saw it as a way to save the boy. To get him away from the orphanage and give him a new start in life. She liked you, didn't she? You made sure of that.'

'There was nothing devious about it.' Armand says. 'I liked her, too. She is a good person, genuinely interested in Dima's welfare.'

'Yes, she is. But look at it from Dima's perspective. As far as he was concerned, the woman he loved and whom he believed loved him was giving him up and sending him away. Further away than he could possibly have imagined. How could she? So to Dima,' Morel continues, looking at the wall behind Armand as though he is just talking to himself, 'the wigs and the music serve as references. Reminders of the woman who provided comfort to him, when he needed it most—'

'And then broke his heart,' came the female officer's voice. She leans in and searches Armand's face. He turns away from her and looks across the table at Morel.

'Dima has done nothing wrong,' Armand says. His voice is cracked and sounds as though it's coming from a long way away.

'What happened, Armand?' Morel asks. He seems to be pleading, almost. He is at the end of his rope too, Armand thinks. 'What happened to Isabelle Dufour, Elisabeth Guillou and Marie Latour?'

Maybe it's all the hours he's spent in this room and the desperate longing for sleep. He's so exhausted he can barely keep his eyes open. Maybe it's the lighting and four grey walls that give no indication of what time of day it is, or the intense looks he is getting from Morel's colleague, making him feel like a lab experiment, some kind of specimen being dissected. He can feel clearly that he has reached the end of a road and has nowhere to turn.

This doesn't trouble him that much. He's left so much of himself behind. What's left is hardly worth preserving.

'Dima and I visited seven women in total,' Armand says, slowly and clearly, as though they might misunderstand otherwise. He sees Morel and the woman exchange a look. 'We returned first to those three you mentioned. The way they reacted to our first visits, I was afraid they would report us. They were so frightened, and angry. We planned to revisit the homes of the others later.' He takes a breath. 'I killed those three women. Dima was there but he didn't do anything. It was me, the whole time. Even the wigs and the make-up.

I did that to reassure him. I played the music he loved. I made it so he could be in a safe place with her, with Nina. He was away in his mind then, reliving that memory of something good, while it was going on.'

'While what was going on?'

'The drownings.'

Morel's eyes are full of disbelief. Armand is almost relieved to see that the man is angry. For the first time, he looks ruffled.

'Why did you do it to them?' Morel asks.

'They are better off where they are now.'

'Where is that?'

Armand shrugs. 'If you have faith, then you know this life is not all there is. I can't possibly explain this to you.'

'What was your motive, Armand?' the woman asks. 'Unhappy childhood, unloving mother, is that it?'

Armand gives her a look of pure hatred. He sees Morel gesture to her. After a moment's hesitation, she leaves the room.

Armand is still seething with anger. Then he hears Morel's voice.

'What did she do to you, Armand?'

He says it like he really cares.

This is where it pours out of him, like he knew it would some day, only who could have predicted it would be here, with the policeman's thoughtful eyes trained on him with a look of – what – pity? Compassion?

He and Charles on his mother's ugly sofa. He is straddling Charles, looking down at him while every inch of his body trembles and strains towards the half-naked body beneath his. He moves back a bit so that his hand can reach Charles's lower belly, where the pubic hair begins, soft and curled. Charles's blue eyes are watching him while his hand grabs Armand's, sliding it further down.

When Armand's mother walks in, his hand is on Charles's cock and their tongues are in each other's mouths.

His mother doesn't raise her voice. Instead, she politely asks Charles to get dressed and leave. Then she sends Armand to his room. He spends a terrorized afternoon there, waiting, not daring to come out even when he desperately needs to use the toilet.

It is evening when she finally comes to him. Without a word she takes his clothes off. He is too petrified to move. Once he is naked, without looking at him she guides him into the shower and turns the cold tap on. He is made to stand there for a good ten minutes, while she stands and stares at him with cold eyes.

Afterwards she hands him his pyjamas. Once he's dressed she points to the bed and speaks for the first time since she caught him with Charles.

'Get in.'

That's when the unbelievable happens. Quickly and without warning, she grabs one of his wrists and ties it to the bedpost behind him with a rope she had in her hand. She does the same thing with the other hand. Once he's tied with both arms raised by his head, she steps back and takes a good long look at him. He is too shocked and scared to say anything.

'This way you'll keep your hands to yourself, I expect,' she says. Then she walks out of the room.

For the next three weeks, he remains strapped to his bed for eight hours a day. After that, he is free to move about the house, but for six months he isn't allowed out and he remains indoors under her watchful gaze.

She never looks at him with anything but contempt again.

Once Armand stops talking, there is a heavy silence. Several minutes go by before Morel speaks.

'You didn't kill those women, did you, Armand? But I can see it all more clearly now. Who better to understand Dima than you? Now there is a sacrifice worth making. A soul worth saving. You want to save him, don't you?'

Armand shakes his head. 'I killed those three women. I hated their empty, useless lives. They are better off now.'

He sees the first signs of defeat in the detective's eyes.

It was somewhere between three and four in the morning. Morel, reeling with exhaustion, fetched coffees for Lila, himself and Armand from the dispenser in the hallway. For once, Lila took hers without complaining. Armand looked at his as though they might be trying to poison him.

'Have it,' Lila said. 'It's crap but it'll keep you going.' Her voice was rough but Morel noticed she was looking at Armand differently, like she wasn't so sure what to think any more.

'Tell us where you first saw the widows,' Morel said.

'It was at the Holy Russia exhibition at the Louvre, in May,' Armand said. He took a sip of the coffee and winced. 'I wanted César to see it. It was so emotional for both of us. I was excited by what the exhibition represented. Finally, a religious revival in Russia. Twenty years earlier an exhibition like that one would have been unthinkable.' He shook his head. 'We visited the exhibition every day over the two weeks it lasted.'

'Every day?' Morel asked.

'There were hundreds of exhibits. We wanted to see everything.'

'And the widows?' Lila said impatiently.

'Isabelle Dufour was the first one I noticed. She was wandering around on her own. Looking at the icons without seeing them. Pretending to be interested, but it was obvious she was just killing time. She didn't understand what she was looking at. She seemed more interested in the cafeteria and the cakes on offer there.'

'What the hell was she supposed to understand?' Lila asked.

Armand seemed to get annoyed. 'It was a stunning exhibition. It was supposed to make people think, to amaze them. Instead I watched these women walk around like chickens. Just like stupid chickens.'

Lila looked like she was about to say something but Morel placed a hand on her arm.

'And then?'

'Then I followed them. That first time I followed Isabelle Dufour to her home. I returned to the exhibition the next day and the same thing happened with Elisabeth Guillou. She too was just killing time at the exhibition. She looked bored. Then Marie Latour, then the Russian woman, and the others too. Each time I noted where they lived, so I could return. I thought maybe I would teach them a thing or two about faith. Inject some meaning into their lives.'

'That's generous of you,' Lila said.

'So you noted where they lived and sometime later you returned with the pamphlets,' Morel said. 'Were the pamphlets just a ploy to gain their trust? So you could check out their homes and plan your next visit, the one where you would kill them?'

Morel saw Armand hesitate then. It was a moment so brief he wasn't sure, in his sleep-deprived state, whether he'd imagined it.

'I gave them a chance to improve themselves. But they rejected it.'

'So you killed them.'

'I gave them a way out.'

'Out of?'

'Out of their empty lives. And the possibility of a new beginning.'

'Do you seriously expect us to believe that crap?' Lila said.

'You can believe what you want,' Armand said.

'What makes you think you are big enough to make these sorts of decisions?' Lila said. Morel turned to her, surprised. 'Do you think you are God, that you can decide a person's fate?'

'Listen, Armand,' Morel said without waiting for an answer. 'The pastor told us that Dima was in your old rooms last night. He must have gone back there after what he did to Irina Volkoff and to our colleague. We checked and there was no one there. But we think he'll come back. And we'll be waiting for him when he does.'

Armand looked at Morel. 'You do what you have to do. Now just tell me what you need from me to make my confession official, then let me sleep.'

When they finally leave him alone Armand drops his head onto the table and closes his eyes. He wonders what possessed the boy to return to the faculty instead of staying put. Granted, the place at the back of the church where he'd settled César was more of a cupboard than a room, but it was safe. Armand knew the church community there and he knew they would look after the boy when they found him. He'd left César with a letter to make sure of that. The letter absolved him of all blame.

A sob escapes his throat and he digs his fist into his mouth so that no one will hear him.

César! he thinks, sorrow washing over him like rain.

César, what have you done?

THIRTY-EIGHT

Everyone except Akil was in the office when Morel arrived.

'The kid's confirmed everything that Le Bellec told us,' Lila said. 'He also confirmed he'd beaten both Marco and Volkoff. He said he was terrified and he panicked. Because he couldn't find Le Bellec.'

'How did he tell you all this?' Morel said.

'In writing.'

They hadn't had to wait long for the boy to return to the faculty. He'd returned the night after Le Bellec's confession.

'He had a letter that Le Bellec had given him,' Morel now told the team.

'What letter?' Marco said.

'It's essentially a signed confession. Le Bellec admits to killing Isabelle Dufour, Elisabeth Guillou and Marie Latour. He says the boy was not involved in any way and that he's sorry for exposing him to this violence, that the boy is as much a victim as the others.'

'Well, not quite,' Lila said. 'He's not dead, for one.'

Morel had asked colleagues from the child-protection unit to sit in today while the boy was being charged with assaulting Marco and Irina Volkoff. He would need to undergo a psychiatric evaluation before anything else happened.

If what Le Bellec said was right, and the boy had been

present during the killings, then he would be needing some serious therapy.

Morel thought about Dima. He looked to be about fourteen or fifteen. With his baseball cap and oversized clothes, he looked like an ordinary teenager.

But his eyes had made Morel pause. There was no light in them.

Morel thought about Le Bellec's detailed confession. Something didn't sit well with him. For one, he couldn't see Le Bellec messing about with the make-up and wigs, just to comfort Dima. It was clear Le Bellec cared about the orphan. In which case, why would he expose him to such horrors?

It made little sense. But they had Armand's confession, and the boy had corroborated his statement. Perrin was ecstatic, planning his next media briefing with all the enthusiasm of a fame-seeking starlet.

'Is the kid going to prison?' Marco asked Morel. Marco had returned, looking pale but determined to get back to work despite the bandage he still wore around his head. Morel didn't have the heart to send him home. He felt partly responsible for the boy's injuries.

'I don't know,' Morel said. 'He did after all attack you and Irina Volkoff. But I think it's unlikely. Given the boy's age and history, and the trauma he's undergone, I suspect he's more likely to spend some time in psychiatric care.'

'Is that a good thing?'

Morel looked into Marco's youthful face. He was waiting for something, for his boss to tell him that everything would turn out OK.

'I don't know, Marco,' Morel said. 'It probably isn't the worst outcome for the boy. But I seriously doubt whether it's a *good* thing.'

At that moment the phone began to ring. Morel went to

answer it. He listened for a while and spoke quietly into the receiver. When he got off the phone, he stared into the distance for a moment before summoning the other three.

'That was Vincent,' he said. 'Calling to say his wife died in hospital this morning.'

Lila followed Jacques Dufour's car even though there was no need. She knew exactly where he was heading.

Once she'd arrived, she parked the car and walked the rest of the way. She could hear voices, the same ones she'd heard on two previous occasions when she'd followed Dufour. Now she could match names to the two voices that weren't his.

Taking care not to be seen, she took photos while the men carried out their exchange.

'That's a big bag, Jacques,' she muttered to herself. 'Surely that's not all for you?'

When she was satisfied she had everything she needed, she walked back to the car and drove off.

It was time to tell Morel. He might be pissed off with her for having tailed Dufour without telling him what she was up to. But once he found out just what the man was doing, he would see things differently.

I've got you, you son of a bitch, she thought.

With that amount, he must be selling. He might actually have to serve time.

Anne Dufour might finally have a life.

Charles's life was falling apart. There was no other way to look at it, he thought, standing in the reception area waiting for the orderly to take him through.

His wife had left him for good. The kids stayed with him for now because it was easier that way. But he knew that as soon as Geraldine had found a place of her own she would fight him for custody. It was just a matter of time.

He had lost his job. Too many missed opportunities, too many days off when he felt incapable of dragging himself to work. He was getting by on the dole, but what with the divorce he would have to find a job soon.

'Sometimes things need to fall apart completely in order for a person to sort themselves out properly,' his mother had said only yesterday. He couldn't quite see it that way, but hey. At least it was hard to picture how things could get much worse.

'It's this way,' the orderly said, interrupting his thoughts. Just as well, they weren't particularly uplifting. He followed the man down the hallway. The orderly stopped outside a door.

'He has his own room?' Charles asked.

'Yes.'

'Will you be staying?'

The orderly examined him. 'If you want me to. But I am sure it will be fine.'

'OK.'

He entered the room and heard the door close softly behind him. The boy sat at a desk with his back to him. He looked like he was drawing something. He turned briefly to look at Charles, then returned to what he was doing.

It was a pleasant room, with white walls and a wide window overlooking the grounds. There were posters of rock bands on the walls, typical teenage stuff, and Charles wondered whether the boy had put them up himself.

'Do you mind if I sit down?' he asked. His voice sounded shaky and unnatural. When there was no answer he sat on the edge of the bed. 'It's a nice room you have. The staff seem nice too.'

He realized how inane he sounded. Better to shut up than come out with such platitudes, he thought.

'Do you mind if I just sit here for a while?'

César didn't respond but Charles thought he saw him relax his posture a little.

Light streamed in from the window. Outside, the trees were beginning to look quite bare. Someone was raking up the leaves, making a pile of them in the middle of the lawn.

Charles thought of Armand and wondered what he could see from where he was sitting.

He could easily have wept, but he reminded himself that he wasn't alone.

See where I am, Armand. Making amends.

The minutes ticked past. The boy never turned around but somehow that was OK. With a shaky sigh, Charles unfolded the newspaper he'd brought along and began to read.

Everything was still. Charles felt the warmth of the sun against his face. He sat further back on the bed and leaned against the wall. He stretched his legs. After a while, he dozed off.

He didn't see the boy turn to look at him. His eyes as wide and distant as two moons.

EPILOGUE

They were looking at a mass of dark clouds. The wind had risen and it was so cold Morel's ears had gone completely numb. As for Philippe, he looked like he'd turned to stone some time ago.

'Maybe we should call it a day.'

'What? Already?'

Morel didn't bother pointing out to his father that they had been fishing on the jetty for two hours now. During that time they hadn't caught a single fish, though they had pulled up plenty of seaweed from the choppy waters below. Morel's fingers were raw from the cold and the effort of untangling his hook from each slimy catch.

'Fine, let's go,' his father said. Very slowly, he reeled his line in. Even dressed up in a grey coat and a woollen hat pulled over his ears it was obvious he was cold. He was taking great pains not to show it.

'Let's get a drink,' Morel said. 'And then we can decide where to go for dinner tonight.'

'If we're going out we'd better tell Augustine,' his father said.

Morel didn't say anything. Instead he looked at the wind-swept outline of Saint-Malo ahead of them, a subdued version of the town he'd come through with Lila four months earlier. It was hard to believe this was the same place. The beach was deserted aside from a couple walking their dog and a group of teenage boys desultorily tossing a ball around.

He had finally finished his owl, according to the plans. It was better than he'd hoped. So lifelike that sometimes when he worked at his desk or lay in bed reading, Morel had the feeling he was being watched. He half expected the owl to swoop down from its perch on the bookshelf with a papery rustle of wings.

In the New Year his sister Maly would be getting married. At her request Morel had agreed to be Karl's best man. Maly had seemed happy. He was pleased that she had decided to do this. Whatever the future held, at least she was moving forward.

Morel felt the tiredness settle in his limbs. It was a different kind of tiredness, brought on by the great gusts of wind and salty air. He would sleep well tonight, aided by a few glasses of wine. Tomorrow morning he would decide how they might spend the day. There was no point asking his father.

'Come on,' he said.

He passed the bucket to his father and picked up the fishing rods. Together, they made their way into the town centre under a shifting and unpredictable sky.

Acknowledgements

I drew inspiration for *The Lying-Down Room* from many sources, including a 1998 Human Rights Watch report on the state of Russia's orphanages entitled 'Abandoned to the State – Cruelty and Neglect in Russian Orphanages'. I have taken liberties with certain event dates, such as the Paris strikes, where it suited the narrative. Any factual errors in this book, intentional or otherwise, are entirely my own.

I am deeply indebted to many people who made this book possible. Thank you to my agent, Peter Robinson, and to Alex Goodwin, for believing in this book. Thank you to my wonderful publisher, Maria Rejt at Mantle, and to my warm and talented editor Sophie Orme. A big thank you to Ali Blackburn, Stacey Hamilton, Praveen Naidoo and all the other lovely people at Pan Macmillan UK and Australia.

I also want to thank:

My parents Renji and Christine Sathiah, who taught me the value of storytelling, and took me around the world; Amanda Holmes Duffy, Louise O'Leary and Carol Pollaro Ross, for their enduring friendship, loyalty and support; the author Michael Pye, for his unfailing kindness and encouragement; Hervé Jourdain, for his invaluable insight into the world of the brigade criminelle; Malcolm Dodd, for sharing his experiences as a forensic pathologist; and Robert J. Lang, for unveiling the art of origami.

And finally, to the three men in my life, big and small – Selwyn, Alex and Max: who would have thought so much love and laughter was possible?

If you enjoyed The Lying-Down Room, *you'll love*

Death in the Rainy Season

– the second Commandant Morel novel.

Far from home, secrets can be deadly . . .

When a French man is found brutally murdered in the Cambodian city of Phnom Penh, Commandant Serge Morel finds his holiday drawn to an abrupt halt. The victim – Hugo Quercy – was the dynamic head of a humanitarian organization which looked after the area's troubled local teenagers. But what was Quercy doing in a hotel room under a false name? What is the significance of his recent investigations into land grabs in the area? And who broke into his house the night of the murder, leaving behind a trail of bloody footprints?

A deeply atmospheric crime novel that bristles with truth and deception, secrets and lies, *Death in the Rainy Season* is a compelling mystery that unravels an exquisitely wrought human tragedy.

Out now

An extract follows here . . .

ONE

The moment he turned down the alley, the dog started barking. He hurried towards the gate and crouched down, where the mutt could see him. Immediately, the barking stopped. The dog came up, wagging its tail, and sniffed his outstretched hand.

'Good boy,' the man said, scratching the dog's head.

He wasn't familiar with this part of Phnom Penh, though he'd been invited to the house often enough. Each time, he'd lost his way coming here, riding his motorcycle through a maze of narrow streets. This time was no different. It was pitch-dark and all these alleyways looked the same. There was no one about.

Most of the families living around here were local. He left his motorcycle at the end of the street and walked past the sleeping houses. Each had an outdoor Buddhist shrine, with its miniature wooden temple or house mounted on a pillar. So did the place he was looking at now. Through the gate, he could see the spirit house mounted on its pedestal in an auspicious corner of the concrete yard. It would contain the remains of the morning's offerings. Rice, lychees and dragon fruit. A couple of burnt-out incense sticks. Such meagre gifts to appease the spirits. He knew, better than anyone tonight, what little difference these rituals made. Life had a way of choosing for you, regardless of what you threw at it.

The gate was shoulder-high, white and metallic, one of those that slid open electronically. Everyone else he knew lived behind higher walls, with a security guard posted outside their front door seven nights a week. These two had never worried about their safety. It seemed to him now that this was arrogance. They had thought they were immune to the threats others faced. Well, it had turned out they were wrong.

Normally he'd ring the bell and someone would buzz the gate open from the inside. He wouldn't be doing that now, of course. Slinging his backpack over his shoulder, he climbed carefully and within seconds was on the other side. No big deal. He was careful not to step on the dog. Through the darkness, he could make out the whites of its eyes.

He knew where the spare key was hidden and he let himself in, remembering to drop it back where he had found it. Inside, the house was dark but for some reason this didn't frighten him. From the moment he'd stepped away from the scene in the hotel room on Sisowath Quay in the early part of the evening, he'd been guided by a fierce desire to salvage something, to compensate for his calamitous loss. *My brother, my friend*. These words went round and round in his mind. A refrain of mourning.

Several hours had gone by since then and he'd lost track of time. But he knew it was late. He crept across the living room with his hands reaching before him, like a blind man. Slowly, his eyes adjusted to the darkness and the room became familiar. The rattan two-seater and armchair with the square off-white cushions, where he'd spilled a glass of wine the first time he'd been invited for dinner. A Balinese print of women picking rice, like a child's work with its exuberant use of blues to convey the terraced paddies; a pair of lean Masai warriors, crafted in ebony. Along the hallway leading to the kitchen, an emerald-green silk Laotian print, hanging from a bamboo pole. There were many ornaments, collected by the couple over the years. A favourite of theirs, he knew, was the handcrafted bullock cart sitting on the bookshelf in the living room. Lovingly made by a Cambodian refugee staying in a camp across the border in Thailand. Over several glasses of wine they'd told him how they had befriended the man and kept in touch throughout the years he and his family lived in the camp, waiting for a new life to begin. Wood, bamboo, copper wire and string had gone into its making.

He'd heard all the stories, sitting here drinking their booze and enjoying their warmth and hospitality. He'd begun to feel more at home here than at his place, among the few knick-knacks he had accumulated during his own overseas missions.

His gaze wandered over to the bullock cart and picked out several other ornaments he had admired before. It did occur to him, just then, that only a lunatic would do this. Wander at night through the home of a dead man. He should take his pick now, and leave. But he didn't. Instead, he moved quietly up the stairs, listening for signs of life. He was vaguely aware of the dirty footprints he was leaving behind. He should have thought about that. It would be upsetting for her to find them. That wasn't his intention.

Still, it occurred to him now that maybe this was what he had really come for, this voyeurism. There was no one to witness the extent of his obsession.

Outside the master bedroom he paused, and then opened the door quietly, holding his breath. First he saw the empty side of the bed, and then the shape of the woman lying on the other side with her back turned to him. Gently, he closed the door and turned to the next room.

What was he looking for, exactly? A memento? A trophy? The American Indians liked to scalp their victims. A scalp was a trophy of war. Some Indians even sewed them onto their war shirts, or used them as decoration for their lodgings. He liked that. The warrior-like aspect of it. But this was different. What he wanted was something private, that only he would know about. And he wouldn't leave without it.

The second bedroom had been converted into a study. Even she had not been allowed in here. It had been *his* sanctuary. Outside this room, he hesitated. Behind this door lay the core of the man he'd admired and envied all at once.

When he stepped into the room, it was as though that part of himself, which he had silenced until then, broke loose. He realized for the first time that he was sweating heavily. He was intensely aware of his own smell. For a moment, he panicked. He must remain in control and not give in to fear or any of the other emotions running wild inside him. He must not think of the hotel room he'd come from, and what it contained. Above all else, he was afraid of going mad. What if he were to lose his mind and forget where he was or what he was doing?

Just at that moment, from the next room he heard her stir and call out something. The dead man's name, spoken in a half-dream. He froze. Then he heard her say it again, this time louder. To hear it spoken out loud like that, in that clear, hopeful tone, made the hairs on his arms stand up. He heard the rustle of sheets as she moved in the bed. Followed by silence. He waited for a while but there was nothing more. She must have gone back to sleep.

With an effort, he turned back to the desk and looked carefully at the things spread out there. He took an object and ran his fingers over it. It was a large stone, smooth and black, which *he* must have used as a paperweight. He had probably enjoyed the sleek, cool texture of it, and you could see why. Few things in life came like this, unmarred.

Something else on the desk caught his eye. A green folder. He opened it. As he skimmed its contents, a look of puzzlement crossed his face. He closed it again and took it.

And then he shut the door and walked quietly back down the hallway, towards the front door.

Outside, the night was warm, bristling with noise. The whirring of cicadas. A rustling in the leaves. The dog whimpered in its sleep. Overhead, a large bat detached itself from a branch and flapped past. It settled on a different tree, its winged form like an omen, blacker than the night sky.

He began walking towards the lights along Sisowath Quay, away from the darkness.

TWO

From where he stood near the bedroom door, Police Chief
Chey Sarit could see that the dead man was Caucasian and
young – in his early thirties possibly, though it was hard to
be sure from what was left of his face. He had bare feet and
was dressed in a short-sleeved T-shirt and long trousers. It
was impossible to tell the colour of his shirt from this angle.
It was soaked through with blood. His eyes were open and
he lay slumped against the wall, his arms bent at the elbows
and held against his body as though he had tried to shield
himself from his attacker.

A futile attempt, Sarit thought. Whatever was left of the
dead man didn't add up to much.

It wasn't as though Sarit hadn't been exposed to violence
before. He'd seen plenty. But the savagery of this attack
seemed to be of a very personal nature and that made him
uncomfortable.

Sarit turned to the older man who had entered the room
with him. Having Sok Pran here was a lucky break. To con-
ceive of a fully functional forensic pathology service in Phnom
Penh was like trying to imagine a future where spaceships
zipped across the skies. But in the meantime there was Pran:
not a pathologist but a doctor, one with real credentials,
which he'd obtained in France. He was perhaps a hard man

to like, moody and unpredictable, but there were few in Phnom Penh as qualified as he was.

A dedicated, hard-working man. Those were esteemable qualities, but Sarit knew that the hospital staff who had to deal with Pran on a daily basis used different, less flattering words to describe him.

'The manager says the room was booked by a man called Jean Dupont. Presumably this is him,' Sarit told Pran, gesturing towards the body. 'Take your time but make sure you get as much information as you can.'

'This dead Frenchman is your problem?'

'For now.'

There was a grunt from Pran, who was pulling a pair of rubber gloves onto his hands. He was looking at the murder scene through a set of black-framed glasses and shaking his head, like a professor assessing a particularly mediocre student assignment.

'Let me know when you're finished and also whether there is anything you need to do your job,' Sarit said.

'What I need, you cannot provide,' Pran said. His tone was gruff but his manner gentle as he eased the dead man's shirt collar open. 'A modern mortuary, for a start. A qualified forensic pathologist would be helpful, too.'

It wasn't the sort of statement that required a reply, and so Sarit didn't respond. Instead, he directed his gaze to the view outside the window.

It had rained heavily during the night. Now there was a pause in the downpour, but it was just that – a brief respite. The sky was still heaving with rain; any moment now the clouds would burst open again to relieve the pressure building up inside them. The second-floor hotel room had a generous view of the Tonle Sap. On the other side of the river, the low-lying shrubs and reeds had taken a battering and stood drenched and exhausted. In the provinces, the floods had claimed dozens of lives over the past few weeks. Sarit looked at the river and wondered how much more it could take before it overflowed. So far in Phnom Penh they'd been spared, but the water was inches from the top of the embankment. He couldn't remember a monsoon like this one.

Sarit turned to his colleague, crouching over the dead man.

'I should go talk to the girl, the one who found the body.'

'Where is she now?'

'In the manager's office. I'm sure she wants to leave as soon as she can so she can run to the temple and rid herself of any contamination from the murder scene.'

Pran had no time for superstition. He gave a dismissive snort.

'You'd better go then.'

Sarit nodded, but made no move to leave the room. He knew he should, but he didn't feel much like questioning an impressionable young employee who was probably too terrified to provide a sober account of what she'd seen. Someone – presumably the victim or the murderer – had hung a sign on the door asking for the room to be cleaned and she'd walked in, found the dead man and started screaming.

What irritated him was the certainty that she would be spinning stories in her head and to others about the victim's departing soul. He knew from experience that his people could be matter of fact about flesh and blood, but spirits were another matter.

Sarit resisted the urge to rub at his leg, just below the knee. Though it was five years since he'd lost the lower half of his leg to a traffic accident, an ancient pain took hold of him, as though that part of him still lived as more than a distant memory.

It must be the rain, he thought, looking out the window.

Sarit looked at the corpse one more time. It would take hours to clean up the mess. Days for the hotel staff to get over this and get on with their work. Beyond these considerations, he didn't waste any time thinking about the dead man – who he was and why this had happened to him. He didn't think this case would occupy him for much longer. Antoine Nizet, the French police attaché from the embassy, was already on his way. Nizet, an energetic sort of man, would likely want to immerse himself in the investigation. Officially just as an observer, but who knew, maybe more? The thought that this could end up being someone else's problem cheered Sarit up somewhat.

'Well, well, well,' Pran said, and Sarit turned his gaze to the pathologist, who was holding up the dead man's driving licence. He'd pulled the victim's wallet from his pocket and he read now from the ID card in his hand.

'The victim's name is Hugo Quercy. The room's booked under Jean Dupont. Which means that, unless he was just visiting someone who was staying here last night, there's a possibility Quercy checked in under a false name. And another interesting fact: he lives just five minutes from here. So what was he doing in a hotel room?'

The two men exchanged a look. Pran snorted.

'He was probably caught with his pants down, what do you think?'

Moments later Pran's face changed. He had pulled a folded piece of paper from the man's wallet and opened it up to see what it contained. Now he handed it to the police chief, whose smile froze as he scanned the document.

'Looks like this could be more complicated than you and

I thought,' Pran said, turning his eyes away to look at the dead man.

Outside, thunder erupted like a prolonged drum roll. Rain pelted the half-open window as though someone were hurling handfuls of stones at it. The wooden shutters banged against the window frame. Pran swore and stepped widely to reach the shutters with one hand without leaving more bloody footprints on the carpet than he needed to. With the window shut, Sarit became aware of how stale the air was.

He frowned. As far as he was concerned, this was a straight-forward business. It was personal, a settling of accounts between *barang*. Westerners. Still. The contents of that piece of paper Pran had found gave the affair a new, unwelcome slant.

Sarit thought again about the imminent arrival of the French police attaché and looked at the paper in his hand. After a moment's hesitation, he folded it and slid it into his pocket.

Pran looked at him. 'Are you sure you know what you're doing?'

'It is not relevant information and will only complicate things,' Sarit said. He held Pran's gaze until the older man looked away, shaking his head.

The police chief turned his head to stare out the window, waiting for Pran to finish the job. Pran had come at Sarit's request. Without him, the body would never have been examined. Thankfully, he was a practical man. He did not speculate about the soul's journey after death.

Through the rain, lightning flashed and thunder boomed. The river was a deep brown. Water would be filling the drains, Sarit thought. It would be running, swift and deep, beneath the city's footpaths. The thought of all that water made him unsteady, like the ground was brittle beneath his feet.

Gradually, as the rain intensified, everything blurred, until the world outside the window lost its familiarity and only the stark, gruesome scene inside the room remained.

extracts reading groups
competitions books new
discounts extracts extracts
competitions discounts events
books new extracts reading groups
extracts discounts
new books events
events extracts reading groups
books new titles reading groups
interviews events
events extracts extracts
discounts books
new books events interviews new books extracts
events new events
discounts extracts discounts
www.panmacmillan.com
extracts events reading groups
competitions books extracts new books